SEVEN

Ghazi Algosaibi

S E V E N

Translated from the Arabic by
Basil Hatim & Gavin Watterson

Saqi Books

British Library Cataloguing-in-Publication Data
A catalogue record for this book is available from the
British Library

First published as
Sab'a, by Dar al Saqi, Beirut 1998
© Dar al Saqi, 1998

This edition first published 1999
© Ghazi Algosaibi, 1999

*The right of Ghazi Algosaibi to be identified as the author of this work has been
asserted by him in accordance with the Copyright, Designs and Patents Act of 1988*

ISBN 0 86356 088 1 (hb)

Saqi Books
26 Westbourne Grove
London W2 5RH

To Humanity
Which has been able to live
With the wild fancies of the poet
The nightmares of the novelist
And the ignominy of the bureaucrat

Contents

Two Clarifications

First: Arabistan X is every Arab country, yet no one Arab country.

Second: Any similarity between the characters in the novel and real persons
            might be coincidental . . . then again, it might not.

Prologue: The Island

Whoever understands the world and people as I
Will plunge in the knife and no mercy show
Al-Mutanabbi

My seven men and I. 'On Medusa'. The small beautiful island. With the stars of my TV programme: *The Eyes of the World Are Upon You*. With the élite of the Arabistani nation. With my men who frantically lust after me and who have only agreed to come to the island out of desire for my body. I told them, in all candour, that I couldn't be a woman who is public property – I have to choose one of them, just one. He has to be the most exciting. And for me to choose that man each of them will have to tell me about the most exciting week in his life. I will listen and on the last night I will make my decision. The poet would have to begin.[1]

---

1. From Galnar's diary.

The Poet

Not a single poet of the Jahiliyya could hold a candle to me
And poetry as magical as mine the People of Babel did never hear
Al-Mutanabbi

Identity Card
Full Name: Shahta Ken'an Abu Al-Qasayim Filfil
Known as: Ken'an Filfil
Occupation: Poet and Editor-in-Chief
Age: 41
Wealth: None to speak of
Place of Birth: Arabistan X
Place of Work: Arabistan X
Academic Qualifications: BA English Literature (University of Nottingham)
Marital Status: Married
Children: None

Saturday, the Capital, Arabistan X
The Cow! The fat, non-lactiferous cow. How can a poet live with a cow? A poet as sensitive and delicate as I. My growing anger at my wife/the cow has crystallized into a poem. I wrote it this morning in the kitchen while she was there prattling on as usual. It never entered her head that I was writing a poem about her. And if it had entered her head to come over and look, she wouldn't have understood a thing. Since when did cows understand poetry? Some mummified poet, I can't remember his name, said something about cows and poetry. He must have been married to a cow as well. Like T. S. Eliot who had no sooner married a cow than she went mad. Mad cows! Are there any cows which aren't mad?

I put the final touches to it at the office. Naturally, I didn't call the poem 'The Cow'. Had I done so, there was the chance, albeit one in a million, that my wife/the cow would realize that the poem was about her. I refuse to allow anyone to know the experiences which my poems are about. I refuse on principle. I totally and utterly refuse. This is my business and my business alone. I despise those poets who explain their poetry and I have nothing but contempt for poets who write books about the experiences which led them to write such and such a poem. They make up for the ugliness of their poetry by even uglier prose. The text alone, that is what is important, as Chateaubriand said. Did Chateaubriand really say that?! I don't think so. But the cows who read me don't know anything. They don't know that most of the references in my critical essays are made up, as are most of the quotes. There is not a single article which does not have a reference to some imaginary writer, or an imaginary citation. So far the cows haven't discovered this, and I doubt they ever will. So am I calling them cows for no reason? I do the same thing in my poems – making things up. I make up words which don't exist. I refer to myths which no one can ever have heard of. I write things that don't make sense. This rare talent for invention is what has made me the editor of *The New Poetic Prowess*. This has brought me an army of admirers and acolytes. The little cows! When 'The Cow' comes out in the next issue it will look like this:

Mazarine
In Hawaii there is an ancient myth about Mazarine, the goddess of infertility, who destroys the harvests whenever she passes over them in the form of a black butterfly.

> The eyes of Mazarine are cobholed wells
> Leading to the nether/higher world
> Peopled by phantoms deflowered by a consumptive lust
> To fester as a black blood
> Exuding from the eyes of Mazarine
>
> The fluttering of wings!
> The fluttering of wings!
> Glishines the black butterfly
> So let the makers of salt have their day wherever they are
> And let the lamps ring out
> And let the bells burn
> And let the peasants kiss their scythes
>
> This butterfly
> Has not eaten for centuries
> Bring its holy food
> The umbilicus of the feotus
> The hymren of the virgin
> And the crown of the crimson parrot
> And let the makers of salt have their day wherever they are

The eyes of Mazarine contemplate the banquet
The bells light up
And the lamps chimmer
And the scythes stab the guts of their bearers
Black magic!
Black magic!
So let the makers of salt have their day wherever they are
Wherever they are!

There is no myth about Mazarine in Hawaii, or anywhere else. And nobody, before me, has ever heard the words 'glishines' or 'hymren' or 'chimmer'. But this is of no import. What is important is that the poem is pregnant with possibilities, pregnant to the point of bursting. Some acolyte will come along and say that the poem epitomizes the human tragedy, another will see in it the end of an agrarian society and a third will swear that it symbolizes the backwardness of the Third World. As for me, I won't say a word. I'll just watch the makers of salt have their day all over the place.

My secretary/the cow came in to tell me that Hammad Sihlaoui, the cultural-page editor for *Good News* had arrived. Hammad is one of the most gifted admirers of my poetry and makes sure that he interviews me every month. He came in with his pens and papers and that look in his eye which I adore: the look a small dog gives its master. The interview began with a question about the last collection of poetry I had read. '*The Illusions of Chimneys* by the ex-Soviet, now Russian, poet, Nikolai Ishmatshov,' I said. 'The poet speaks in a symbolo-impressionistic mode about the collapse of the Marxist dream. Unfortunately, the collection has not been translated yet.' The gleam of piercing wonder in the eyes of the small dog. 'And which critical works have you been reading recently?' I clear my throat and say: 'The most recent book of critical essays I have read was *The Death of the Monologue* by Professor Arnold Ishbakhtik who teaches linguistics at the University of Darmstadt. Ishbakhtik talks about the coming literary phenomenon: the 'encapsulated text'. Unfortunately, the book hasn't been translated yet.' Another look of wonder in the eyes of the small dog. 'And what about recent work in this country?' I sigh, look up to the ceiling and reply slowly: 'There is hope. There is hope. There is hope, my friend. Poetry, in its material essence, is mephiterism. The mephiterism of things. Their decremunence. Their franescence. An emanatory battle against bovinification and mummification. An ennaturivical bomb which explodes in the face of all that is logical, and everyone who is logical. Real poetry is a revolt against real poetry. A revolt which gives birth to itself and devours itself. It gives birth with itself the things which are against it. Promising things burn up as soon as they breathe. There is hope my friend. There is hope. I see a rising generation of mephiteristical poets rebelling against real poetry.' A third look of wonder gleams, perhaps a fourth, before the mephiterized cultural editor collects his papers and leaves the office.

I asked my secretary/the cow for the tenth time if there was any news from the ministry about the Alhambra Poetry Symposium. And for the tenth time my secretary/the cow told me there wasn't. Cows, offspring of cows!

Sunday
I had no idea why the under-secretary of state wanted a meeting with me this morning. To talk to me about the Alhambra symposium? Or was there another attempt to remove me as editor from *The New Poetic Prowess*? The slanderers and back-biters will never stop trying. The bastards. They want a mummified poet. A poet who writes words people can understand. A poet who pisses, along with his camel, among the remains of an abandoned encampment. And as he weeps he asks everyone to stop and weep with him and piss if they can to moisten the ground. They want a poet who talks about gazelles, sheep and jackals. These bastards don't understand anything about poetry. And the under-secretary of state doesn't understand anything about poetry either. But he has known me since secondary school and fully appreciates my talent.

'Good morning, Professor Sabir,' I said.

Professor Sabir Hayir's response was a broad smile followed by a flood of words:

'Ahlan! Ahlan! Ahlan! I've missed you man. You've no idea how I've missed you my friend. Where have you been man? It's been so long. Where have you been? Where have you been hiding? All this wretched travelling. We sure have missed you.'

Those of you who know the under-secretary of state as well as I do will understand that this warm welcome was not for nothing, nor was it for poetry or for old times' sake. There was going to be a catch somewhere, without a shadow of doubt.

'You've got a lot on, Professor Sabir. Your responsibilities are many,' I said cautiously.

'True. True. But I always have time for you, you know that. It seems the muses don't leave you any time for your old friends.'

'The muses. The muses.'

'And I need the services of one of your muses.'

So. Here it comes. Sooner than I'd expected.

'I'm sorry?!'

'I wish to hire the services of one of your muses.'

'Hire?!'

'I wish to hire her services for a short while. At a very tempting rate.'

'But Professor Sabir, you know me well and you know I'm a poet with principles.'

'Of course! Of course! And I value these principles. The truth is, I have chosen you for this mission out of respect for your principles.'

'Mission? You want me to write poems for some other person to call their own in exchange for money?'

'No! No! I'm not talking about the kind of person you think. I'm talking about a child. A gifted child.'

'You want me to write poems for a child?'

'Yes. By way of encouraging a budding talent.'

'And why should you want to encourage this budding talent?'

'Frankly, to be perfectly honest, because his father is a dear friend of mine. We studied together in the States.'

'And how old is this child prodigy?'

'Almost ten.'

'And what's his name?'

'Muharib Harbi Al-Hurayabibi.'

Noting the etymology of his name, I said:

'A military, somewhat aggressive name.'

'Ha, Ha, Ha.'

'Why can't he write his own poems if he's so talented?'

'He's just a budding poet. Just starting out. He needs someone to nurture him. He needs a push forward from a giant poet. A giant like you. A push would help him on his way.'

'But I only write modern poetry.'

'The child only writes modern poetry.'

'Professor Sabir, with the greatest respect . . .'

'Don't be too hasty, Ken'an. Think of the reward.'

'Yes?'

'There is a token remuneration.'

'Do you think principles can be bought?'

'Ten thousand dollars.'

This was no token compensation. This was a small fortune. But I went on vociferously:

'I asked you: Do you think principles can be bought?'

'God forbid! God forbid! I realize that the treasure of Solomon couldn't buy even one of your principles. But I also know that you can't turn me down. I've been your friend since childhood.'

'How many poems do you want?'

His Excellency, Professor Sabir Hayir, took a piece of paper out of his drawer and began to read:

'Wanted: A poem entitled "The Homework Exercise Book"; a poem entitled "The Teacher and I"; a poem entitled "Longitude and Latitude"; a poem entitled "The Lavatory"; a poem entitled . . .'

'That's enough. I'm only writing four poems.'

'I don't know how to thank you.'

'When do you want the poems?'

'I want them published under the name of our young poet in the next issue of *The New Poetic Prowess* with a short introduction by you as the one who discovered his talent.'

'I'll try. I can't promise anything. But I'll try.'

'I'm sure you'll have no difficulties. You were a child once and you know how children think.'

'I'll do my best.'

'We might need some more.'

'I'm not doing any more.'

'This gifted child will be giving a poetry evening. What he has already might not be enough . . .'

'A poetry evening?!'

'Yes.'

'Where?!'

'Here.'

'And when is this momentous event to take place?'

'The minister is looking into it now with the prime minister.'

'The prime minister?! What has the prime minister got to do with a poetry evening by a child prodigy.'

'Professor Ken'an! You know that the prime minister has spent most of his life in education. You will find no one more keen to encourage budding talent than the prime minister.'

'What do you mean?'

'I mean that the poetry evening will be held under the auspices of the prime minister.'

'You mean he'll be there in person.'

'Yes.'

'You're joking, aren't you?'

'I am not joking. You should be pleased by the news. By honouring the occasion, he is raising the status of poetry and poets.'

'And budding children.'

'And budding children. We might need some more poems for the poetry evening to pass off in an appropriate manner.'

'I can't do any more.'

'Ok! For the time being, I'll just take the four.'

His Excellency, Professor Sabir Hayir, put his hand into the drawer of his desk and pulled out an envelope which he handed to me saying:

'A token remuneration.'

Immediately, I said:

'I'm not taking it.'

His Excellency, Professor Sabir Hayir, raised his astonished eyebrows and said:

'Take it for my sake, Ken'an. For friendship.'

'I'll take it on one condition.'

'Which is?'

'I want to take part in the Alhambra Poetry Symposium.'

'Nothing would give me greater pleasure. But the delegation has already been named.'

'Put my name on the list.'

'But the delegation is leaving the day after tomorrow. There's not enough . . .'

'I know that. That's why you have to make your mind up straight away. Now!'

The under-secretary of state sighed and said:

'Ken'an! Ken'an! You know I can't say 'No' to you. You'll be in the delegation. Consider it done. Who knows, maybe the symposium will stimulate the muses to write some poems for our budding poet. Don't forget your envelope, Ken'an!'

When I returned to my office at the magazine, I found a beautiful young girl sitting in the secretary's/the cow's office. A beautiful woman at the offices of *The New Poetic Prowess*?! It must be the end of the world. Here, as a rule, there were only cows. Poets/cows, women critics/cows, women readers/cows and the mother of all cows was my secretary/the cow. I went into my office and called in the secretary/the cow and asked her about the female visitor. She said she was a final-year student at the faculty of letters and she wanted to do an interview with me to help her with her dissertation. Why not? Why shouldn't I give this beautiful creature a short tour of the worlds of my genius? I asked my secretary/the cow to send her in five minutes. I took out the envelope and placed it inside an old tattered book and placed the old tattered book in a draw and locked it. If only my wife/the cow could see the money, she would devour it in a flash, like her clover.

The beautiful student came in and sat in front of me. She showed none of the signs of intense confusion which admirers, both men and women, are normally afflicted with in my presence. She was composed. Cold. Icy. She smiled at me and said:

'Professor Ken'an! Thank you for your time.'

A western expression! A western concept! Thanking people for their time is a western custom. In the east, time has no value and so no one ever thanks you if you give them half your time or all of it. Where did this eastern beauty with this western concept come from? I should have been alert to the coming threat, but, unfortunately, I was not. I said:

'Don't mention it, Miss . . .'

'Waves. Waves 'Isa.'

'Waves?'

'Waves'

'Is that your real name?'

'The only one.'

'Is your father a poet?'

'My father is a businessman.'

'So where did this poetic name come from?'

'Can't you guess?'

'Were you born on a ship?'

'Yes.'

'Really?'

'Really.'

Wow! A beautiful sea creature. The ebb and flow. Shores and sand. Tempests and hurricanes. Shipwrecks. Ships at anchor. Scenes of farewell. Scenes of greeting. Sea shanties. Sailors sobbing. Pirates. Sharks. Buried treasure. Mermaids. Sea shells. Sand. Coral. Distant isles. Waves!

I was apparently somewhat lost in thought. Her cold voice came like a breeze:

'Professor Ken'an! Professor Ken'an!'

'Yes! Yes! I'm sorry. I'm at your service. Please go on.'

'Do you mind if I record the interview?'

'Please do.'

The beautiful sea creature pulled out a microcassette recorder and placed it between us. Then came the voice of ice:

'Professor Ken'an! Some people say that your poem "Phantoms of the Port" is taken from a poem by the Mexican poet, José Tequila, entitled "Field of Phantoms". What is your opinion?'

This dastardly question caught me unawares. Completely unawares. How did this beautiful sea creature hear of a Mexican poet who has been dead for more than a century? Is there a conspiracy to character-assassinate me? Who is leading this conspiracy?

'Professor Ken'an!'

'Yes! Yes! Intertextuality, Miss Waves, intertextuality. Have you heard of intertextuality?'

'I have heard of intertextuality. But don't you think in this case that what is at issue goes beyond mere intertextuality?'

'There is restricted intertextuality and open intertextuality.'
'Here we are dealing with something more than open intertextuality.'
'One cannot confine intertextuality because . . .'
The ice-cold voice interrupted me:
'Listen Professor Ken'an. Please listen. Tequila says:

I stand beneath a burning sun
I dig the ground
Searching for the seeds I planted with my hands
At the harvest passed
I dig up the earth
But I do not see the seeds
I see human skulls
They stare at me . . . and smile

'And you say:

At dawn
I stenbed beneath the cold rays

'By the way Professor Ken'an, what does "stenbed" mean?'
'I don't explain my poetry.'
'I've looked for it in all the dictionaries but can't find it.'
'This word, before me, had not been born. You won't find it in the dictionaries of today. You will find it in the dictionaries of tomorrow.'
'But what does it mean?'
'I told you, I don't explain my poetry.'
'Fine. Let's get back to the poem. It says:

'At dawn
I stenbed beneath the cold rays
Searching for the boats I launched with my hands
At the fishing season passed
But I don't see the boats
I see human skulls
They look at me . . . and guffaw

'Don't you see, Professor Ken'an, that this has gone beyond intertextuality.'
'Miss Waves. My dear Miss Waves You have to understand one of the major truths of literature. You're still a student and the road before you on the way to the veiled secrets of literature is still long. Human experience is not the personal

property of Tequila or mine or yours or that of your great professors at the university. Human experience is the common heritage of all humanity. No one can stop me talking about an experience just because someone else has talked about the same experience. This is literary fascism. An odious dictatorship Miss Waves. I am talking about a well-known human experience. As old as humanity itself. The dialectic of good versus evil.'

'But Tequila preceded you. By a whole century.'

'True! True! And in a hundred years time someone will come writing a poem which intertextualizes my poem.'

'Do you mean we're dealing here with a phenomenon which the classical Arab literary critics called: "Following in the Footsteps of the Forefathers"?'

The beautiful sea creature had begun to get on my nerves. Really get on my nerves. With an irritation I made no attempt to conceal, I said:

'Arab critics! Hah! Did the Arabs have any critics? Did the mummified poetasters who wrote pallid books of rhymed prose understand the alphabet of poetry? They just puffed out words. Soap bubbles of words. If you had talked to them about a poetic experience, they wouldn't have understood the meaning of "experience".'

'Excuse me, Professor Ken'an! The classical Arab critics had specific terms for the "experience" and the "structure" of a poem. They believed . . .'

This creature had begun to lacerate my nerves with her ice-cold voice. If only she had drowned in the ship she was born on. If only she had drowned and all that remained was a silent human skull. The ice-cold voice continued to outline the absurdities of the mummified rhymers. I broke in resolutely:

'Structure? With how many floors? Experience? What experience? Miss Waves! There is no such thing as literary criticism in the heritage of the stuffed rhymers. All there is are ad hoc principles: "Obfuscate and you'll be the greatest poet among the Arabs". "Run girl and you'll be the greatest poet among those with two breasts". . . .'

Without realizing what I was doing I found my eyes stealing their way towards the creature's proud breasts under her blouse.

The evil bitch noticed. She smiled. Immediately, I said:

'I'm sorry! I'm sorry! I intended . . .'

'You intended to refer to what Al-Nabigha said to Al-Khansa' when she was reciting her poems in the market in 'Ukaz.'

'Of course! What is important is that your friends were using vague principles which don't mean anything. Give it some thought. How can someone who hasn't studied structuralism make critical comments about a literary text. Robert Lassé said . . .'

'I'm sorry, you mean Joseph Lassé?'

This beautiful cow was beginning to infuriate me. Really infuriate me. In a voice which I hoped conveyed the maximum degree of sarcasm, I said:

'Joseph Lassé. Don't ask me to repeat what he said because you know everything he said because you, apparently, know everything.'

She seemed not to notice the sarcasm. She said calmly:

'Joseph Lassé's *Death of the Poet* is out of date. It was out of date when it was published in the fifties. As for "the pallid books" of the classical Arab critics, they're still pulsating with life. One only has to mention Al-Jurjani who was way ahead of . . .'

I interrupted in fury:

'Miss Waves! Forgive me. Save this talk about Al-Jurjani and Al-Ajzakhani for the university. My time is somewhat crowded. Do you have any further questions?'

'I have a lot of questions.'

'I only have time for one more question.'

'Fine! In your poem "The Shadow of the Mirror", I see many shades of the poem "Questions of a Mirror" by the Irish poet, Scott MacGregor . . .'

The straw that broke my back. Without being fully aware of what I was doing, I stood up and shouted in the face of that beautiful cow:

'And I see that you have exceeded the bounds of decorum which a student should observe when talking to a teacher who could teach her own teachers at university. And I see . . .'

The ice-cold voice interrupted me:

'I would like to thank you once again. I'll be sending you a copy of the dissertation when it's finished.'

She calmly picked up the microcassette recorder and calmly stood up. At the door, she turned to me and smiled. I was hit by a cold gust of air mixed with a strange perfume. Damn her! And damn intertextuality! In an outburst of anger I began to write:

On the Lavatory

I am sitting on the lavatory
I write on the wall
The names of all the critics
The names of all the professors
The names of all the readers
Then I wipe the wall
With a white piece of paper
It lubeioates
I flush the paper down the bowl
And watch it change name by name

Into small waves
To float for a while
Then swallowed down the bowl

The bitch, born on a boat! Boat/brothel! I wish she could read the poem. I wish she could see how I've transformed her into the ripples floating on the surface of the water in a drain. I wish she would come across some Hungarian poem which intertextualizes with 'On the Lavatory'. The bitch! I hope she never reads the poem. I hope she never discovers it was not written by a child prodigy. I wish she could read it. I wish she would die and leave me in peace. Ripples in a fetid drain!

Monday
I spent most of the morning getting ready for the trip. An endless routine. A strange, complicated world. Even poets are subjected to routine procedures. They share the lot of butchers, donkey-drivers, pimps and corrupt building contractors. Poets are delicate creatures. They weren't created for passports and visas. They were created for women and poetry. The world of the Arabistans is wretched. You can't leave an Arabistan without an exit visa. God exit their souls! And you can't visit a 'sisterly' Arabistan without an entry visa. God enter them in hell! A single Arabistani nation with thousands of visas. If I were going to the Alhambra in Spain, I would see the point of a visa. But to visit an Alhambra in Arabistan a visa is obscene. Adulterous. And for a poetry symposium! Didn't Nizar Qabanni say that the birds don't need an entry visa? Aren't poets, I mean some poets, the most beautiful birds in the world. Luckily, my secretary/the cow handled most of the arrangements. Cows have some uses, unlike my wife/the cow who is utterly useless.

I phoned the head of the delegation, the deputy under-secretary of state, to make sure my name was on the list. The deputy under-secretary assured me I was a part of the delegation then added:

'When do you want to present your poems?'

'I haven't got any new poems,' I said.

'You can give some of your old ones.'

In an anger I tried to suppress:

'You know my theories. Everyone knows my theories. Reading poems aloud is a thing of the past. Now poems are to be read in silence. It's what Dr Mandur calls "whispered" poetry. It's time to put an end to this mildewed tradition which . . .'

'Am I to understand that you no longer wish to attend,' interrupted the deputy under-secretary.

'Not at all. Not at all I,' I said in a flash.

'Every poet attending the symposium has to read out a poem. I don't want our delegation to be the only one which is out of tune.'

Out of tune! Out of tune! What does a deputy under-secretary/cow know about music and discordant notes. These are vile times when a fat bureaucrat is turned into the head of a delegation and an innovative poet becomes a discordant note.

'I will give a selection of my published work,' I said.

'Give what you want. But try and choose something comprehensible.'

I was on the point of protesting when I heard the phone put down at the other end. This worthless, mildewed bureaucrat! He wants poetry which can be understood! A grandiloquent pompous poem. The cow!

My secretary/the cow came in to remind me that today was the deadline for my two weekly articles for the cultural supplement *Impressions*. I glared at her and when she had gone I began to write:

The Psychology of the Modern Poem

Ever since Freud established that an individual's psychological balance depends on an osmotic relationship between the ego and the super ego, there has been intensive research investigating the effect of the poet's osmotic balance on the structure of his poetry. At the University of Nottingham recently, it has been shown that upsetting this balance leads, with ritualistic monotony, to a qualitative levelling out in the articulation of the created poem. In an interview published in The *Sunday Times* two weeks ago, Professor William Havilland says that a research team, which he heads at the above university and whose activities are funded by a generous grant from the Shockberg Foundation, after five years of continuous experiments, has produced astounding results explaining the poet–poem dialectic. Professor Havilland said that the team used, for the first time, a technique to analyse the poetic visions that entice the poet while in a state of introspection. The technique consists in giving the poets under test small electric shocks in their toe nails while they are writing their poems. These electric shocks create brain waves (Damn that word! Cross it out!) brain oscillations which can be measured and which give a clear indication of the psychological state of the poet . . .

The article would fill a full two-page spread in the supplement. The cows would believe all the strange and wondrous things in the article. They would believe that poets are being experimented on using electricity at the University of Nottingham. They would believe that the experiments had produced amazing

results which overturned many common assumptions. They would all believe
except that marine bitch, Waves.

I looked at the list of poets participating in the Alhambra symposium: Bahij
Al-'Awwad – a mummified poet; Ra'fat Jaridi – a dinosaur gnawing at a weak
style; Na'na' Fasada – a charlatan who thinks he's a modern poet. (What do you
expect from someone whose name means 'bloodletting'?) Mazan Al-Hanbaki –
a stuffed mummy, literally – he's over ninety. (What's this specimen of the
living-dead doing here?) Oh! I almost forgot! The deputy under secretary of state
– my friend and champion of child prodigies, married to Al-Hanbaki's daughter.
And to make up the numbers – that woman Mayy Al-Baslawi. The human tank.
The talking lump of lard. A cow that writes poetry. Modern poetry! There should
be a law against anyone over 70 kilos spouting poetry. This lump of lard is over
100 kilos at the latest estimate. (Who would be brave enough to ask her? To
weigh her?) She writes love poetry. And what kind of love? Erotic. What does this
flabby cow know about the love of the erotic or the eroticism of love? I think the
only love this woman has ever known is the love of beans and lentils. A
delegation of cow poets. What am I doing with this lot? A flash of genius among
a herd of cows. What am I doing? Keeping an eye on the cows. Having some fun.
Having a laugh. Being given the souvenir gifts which are handed out at every
symposium in Arabistan.

Tuesday, Alhambra, Arabistan X
We arrived late in the morning. They had put us in the Sea View Hotel. The filthy
pigs! – the symposium organizers. The deputy under-secretary gets a whole
wing. Well, he is the head of the delegation. But why is Mazan Al-Hanbaki
entitled to a wing to himself? What gives him the right? The wretches of the
bureaucracy! And why have I, a real poet, been left in this cramped room? In this
cell which doesn't have a view of anything? Me, the one who makes language
explode, revolutionizes it, puts bombs under it, mephiterizes it.

There was a light knock at the door. I opened it to find an unbelievable
surprise. A beautiful woman. A very beautiful woman. And in these vile, ugly
days of cowdom. She asked to be allowed in. I let her in. She sat on a chair in the
cramped room and began to sing like a bird:

'In the name of the Ministry of Culture and Reconstruction, I would like to
welcome you to your second home. My name is Basima Souakin. I am an official
in the poetry section at the Ministry and a member of the organizing committee
for the symposium, I hope everything is to your satisfaction.'

No it isn't! No it isn't! Everything is asphalt, mud, dust and depravity.
However, in appreciation of your beauty, I will not explode. I will express my
displeasure in a civilized manner:

'I was hoping my room would look out over the sea. It is distressing for a poet to be in Alhambra, the bride of the coasts, and not see the waves, (Damn the waves!) I mean, the sea.'

The beauty smiled and began to sing:

'Professor Ken'an. You carry the sea with you wherever you go. You are the sea. Remember what you said in your poem "Alga":

'Filled are you with me
As far as burning desire
Filled are you with me
There is no escape
There is no escape
You are the alga of my algae.'

This very beautiful woman had memorized my poem. The critics/the cows say that modern poetry cannot be memorized. If only they could be here to hear her sing – yes, sing – a modern poem. Before I could get over the delicious shock, Basima began to sing again:

'And remember, my dearest Professor, what you said in your poem "The Oyster Kills No One":

'A pearl you are
A grain of sand you are
Sleeplessness made her tired
The oyster clasps it in her arms
I am below you, above you, between you
The oyster am I
The ocean am I.'

I forgot the cramped room so far from the sea. I forgot the swine. And I said to this singing beauty:

'Basima. How many of my poems have you memorized?'

Immediately she said:

'All of them.'

In genuine wonder I said:

'All of them?! Even I haven't memorized all of them.'

'At least those poems published in the collections I have read: *The Cactus is a Heart, the Rose is Claws*; *Dracula: a Pallid Pleasure*; *The Unpotency of Lust*. Are there any others?'

'There's one coming out shortly.'

'What's it called?'

'*The Basima of Seasons to Come.*'

The beauty sang as she laughed. Or laughed as she sang:

'My dearest Professor! You're just saying that! What's it really called?'

That was the second time she had said it. 'My dearest Professor.' Dearest? Does she know what she's saying I have been called 'Professor' a thousand times. But until today I had never been called 'My dearest Professor.' I don't think this educated beauty uses her adjectives haphazardly.

'*The Season of Stagnant Dreams.*'

She smiled as she chanted:

'It's a brilliant title. As usual. Should I have hopes of receiving a signed copy?'

'You'll have one as soon as it's out.'

'As soon as it's out? Are you going to send it over the Internet?'

'Internet'! What is the 'Internet'?! I didn't like to ask the educated beauty in case she thought I was a stuffed mummy.

'Yes,' I said.

'Really? Do you mean it? Have you sent collections of your poems over the 'Internet' before?'

God help us! To me – and all a poet needs is his intuition – she seemed to be talking about a new express postal service. I decided to end this 'Internet' discussion at once:

'You'll get it and that's that!'

The beauty smiled and said:

'You were saying that the room was too small and too far . . .'

I interrupted:

'It doesn't matter, Basima. I mean, my dear Basima. As you said, I carry my sea with me.'

.The beauty fell silent, then whispered:

'You shall have an opportunity to see the sea. By moonlight.'

With my breathing getting shorter, I asked:

'What do you mean?'

She began to sing the words:

'I would like to invite you to my apartment. After the evening session. We can sit on the balcony overlooking the sea. You'll be able to watch the sea as it embraces the moon. You'll be able to read aloud your poem "When they stabbed the moon, it was I the dagger". Oh! that poem is so beautiful. I always cry when I read the part which goes:

'In me I am
They stabbed the moon
Which looked at me with a look full of feeblicity
And whispered
'You too?!'

But they stabbed me in the heart
And the moon stopped speaking
In mid-sentence.'

There were indeed tears glistening in her eyes. The critics/cows say that modern poetry cannot stir one's feelings. The swine! This very beautiful woman is crying – crying would you believe it – while reciting my poetry.

'We'll leave at ten. I'll wait for you in front of the hotel,' said the beauty.

I stammered:

'That would be a great honour! A big honour!'

When the beauty had left, I realized why my poetic instincts had led me to Alhambra. I realized with the inner eye of the poet which can tear away the veil that fate had hidden this enchanting woman for me. My dearest pupil! How I hope all those stuffed rhymers will be at the hotel entrance to see us leave together. Love–Beauty–Poetry. The Eternal Triad. The Sempiternal Triad.

The afternoon session began at four o'clock. Poets everywhere. Drifting and creeping about. Poets without poems. Bubbles of words exploding with drivel out of the corners of mouths. The bovine hordes would only applaud the contemptible, that which flattered their bovine sentiments. Bahij Al-'Awwad was delivering a poem saying:

'Alhambra! Why do they call you red?! How names deceive. The sea is green. The shores blue.'

Oh crap! A paint box! Red, green and blue! What about brown, navy blue or violet?

His voice began to bray like an ass:

'Love is a battle. Closeness the spoils. Separation is a debt. Longing is open-handed.'

The room shook with applause. Damn this bovine horde! I was taken over by a strong desire to stand up and shout at the top of my voice:

'Form is disorder. Poetry is scrawl. The atmosphere imbecilious. The name a chameleon.'

The only thing that stopped me rising to my feet was the vow I had made one rainy evening in Nottingham at The White Fox with my blonde-haired girlfriend, Jean Gingerbread. I swore to her that I would never write a line of poetry which balanced and rhymed. And I have stood by that oath. Those who want things weighed should go to the butchers. Those who love their metres can go and choke on them.

Bahij began to cry out like a severely constipated camel:

'I carried my heart in my palm and it lay there, heavy
Is there relief from the burden of carrying a beautiful woman?'

Feeble-mindedness chewed over for a thousand years. The bovine horde applauded warmly. This is beyond belief! In the afternoon session there was no poetry apart from a poem recited by a slim blonde-haired woman poet. I said 'blonde', not 'beautiful'. She said:

'As you sleep, like a virus I penetrate
The furthest, furthest, furthest of your atoms
Where I declare war against
The remnance of regret. I purify you with my agonies
Of all your good, good, good intentions. And of all
Sense of virtue. I steal your disgorged innocence
I burn it burning, burning, burning so that
You don't grumble about the smell of my vicious teeth.'

'Disgorged innocence'! This is poetry! The bovine horde listens in silence. They don't applaud. They don't understand. I'll ask the slim blonde for a copy of the poem to publish in *The New Poetic Prowess*.

In the early evening session there were tons of God-forsaken poems imitating those of the past and tons of applause. One poet, just one, caught my attention. A bald, one-eyed poet said in a beautiful poem:

'And I, mistress of secrets, have not drunk
Of the kohl but its first gasp.
And I have not danced with the poison
Which the spidron squeezes
Into my veins when your kohl
Overcomes the poison. And the poison envies your kohl
I know not whether it is my poison or yours
Or we were both the victims, and the body
Haunted by secrets was the gallows.'

Dancing with poison. A radiant symbol. A symbol that went over the heads of the herd which listened in its sleep. It was only when Ra'fat Jaridi began to bark that the herd stirred from its slumber. The bovine horde applauded warmly when the stuffed rhymer said:

> 'Alhambra! If love were not my homeland
> I would abandon it and make you my homeland.'

'Such a pile of bullshit deserves such poems' as my friend, the pioneering René Abu Gharab says whenever he encounters any of the herds that go to poetry evenings.

The evening session had begun. My heart was palpitating. Basima was walking round the auditorium. I had almost forgotten she was a member of the organizing committee. The sexual member! Ha! Ha! A silly poetic joke. She walked around, smiling, glancing furtively at the big clock in the front of the auditorium. It reminded me of the rendezvous which I could never forget. Around me the bubbles of words continued to explode. Explosions that would terrify the bravest of the brave. And the stuffed rhymers spat out the filth that they had been chewing from the vomit of the ancient style. There was only one poet, just one, who caught my attention and quenched my thirst for revenge against the herd. He said:

> 'I told you I told you I told you
> From this your putrid podium. I told you
> You offspring of monkeys! I hate you
> Monkey by monkey.
> I told you this torn shoe of mine
> Is cleaner than the cleanest among you.
> I told you my syphilitic underwear
> Is more honourable than the most honourable among you. I told you
> I hate you as much as I hate diarrhoea
> As much as I hate farts . . . As much as I hate America.'

The horde received the poem with resounding laughter. A horde abusive and laughing at the same time, monkey by monkey!

After the session, I found myself overjoyed to be sitting with Basima in her small car. As she drove, the breeze played with her hair. We discussed the sessions and her opinion was the same as mine. How sweet for a poet to find a beautiful woman able to distinguish between a poetry pulsating with the exuberance of life and a versification spawned from a shabby death. After a few minutes I found myself with her on her balcony. We looked out over the sea which flirted with the moon beams. She began to recite excerpts from my poems. After the third poem, we were suddenly intruded upon by a huge man who went

straight up to Basima and kissed her. He turned to me and shook my hand.
Basima said:

'Professor Ken'an! This is my husband, Sabih. He is also one of your
admirers.'

Sabih began to prattle away. He said the moment he saw me was the happiest
moment in his life. He went on and on while I boiled with repressed anger. After
twenty minutes, I begged to take my leave of the happy couple. The huge
husband offered to take me back to the hotel. The whole way back he was
reciting my poems. A miracle! A huge husband had memorized my poems. A
miracle! How great was the difference between my poems being sung by a
beautiful woman and being bellowed by this bull!

In the hotel lift I met Mayy Al-Baslawi, weighed down by her burden of fat.
And maybe poetry. We exchanged greetings and got out of the lift together. I
said to Mayy:

'They've put me in a room where you can't smell the sea air.'

Immediately, Mayy said:

'Come with me. My room looks out straight on to the sea.'

I would not have responded to this open invitation from this quivering lump
of lard if it hadn't been for the suppressed anger welling up inside me and the
desire for revenge against Basima Souakin. The beautiful married cow! And how
is one to exact revenge against beauty if not by seeking the companionship of
ugliness?

I sat on the balcony in silence with the lump until she said:

'Why don't we become the guests of Bacchus?'

The lump of lard knows Bacchus! I smiled and agreed to the idea. The lump
of lard spoke on the phone and the waiter arrived with two bottles of white wine.
And we began to enjoy the hospitality of Bacchus. We began to recite poetry to
each other. She went first. I followed. She began again. I began again. Two more
bottles of wine came. Then something very strange began to happen. The fat
began to disappear and disperse. The weight began to diminish and vanish. The
bulk slimmed down, decreased in size. I heard myself telling her:

'My enchanted forest is you
My forest the old enchantress
The young enchantress
The embryonic enchantress
The forest of the devourishing cave
And I am the terror-struck hunter
I towerabovestand
And I search . . . I search
For your devourishing cave'

Mayy Al-Baslawi began to come closer. She began to kiss me. I began to kiss her. I don't know how we flew, like two butterflies, from the balcony and alighted on the bed. I heard her alluring voice coming from the forests and caves:

'My forest is a many-coloured asp
Entwining around you,
Breaking your ribs . . . rib by rib
And planting where each rib had been
A mouth with red fangs
Sucking on the asp'

I heard strange noises. Cats miaowing. Asps hissing. A bed creaking. Then I hear nothing.

Wednesday, Alhambra, Arabistan X
The ringing of the phone woke me up. I lifted the receiver and said in a voice in which I tried to convey the anger of all the volcanoes in the world exploding:
    'Hello!'
    At the other end was the voice of the deputy under-secretary of state:
    'Who's that?'
    'Ken'an.'
    'What are you doing in Mayy's room?'
    'I'm in my own room.'
    'Fine! I must have misdialled. I was going to talk to you after Mayy, anyway.'
    'Good?!'
    'Why are you late in coming down?'
    'Diarrhoea. Terrible diarrhoea.'
    'What about your poems? You're on this morning.'
    'This morning? Impossible. Terrible diarrhoea.'
    'So what are we going to do?'
    'Please ask them to put me off until the afternoon session.'
    The receiver on the other end was put down. The deputy under-secretary apparently knew no other way of ending a phone conversation. I turned to find a greasy degenerate cow sleeping beside me. Mooing. A naked cow! Stark naked! Layers upon layers of fat. Flaccid breasts. A dented stomach. A liquefied face. Red marks all over the body. Teeth marks. Teeth?! Who had been biting this fat cow? The answer came in a flash. It was me who had bitten this fat cow. It was me who had spent the night in her arms. I mean in her lard. What had happened? What had happened? God curse Bacchus! I dressed and left at once. The mooing of the naked cow filled the universe.
    In the bathroom I stood for a long time under a cold shower. A terrible

headache. The stuffed rhymers had an expression for it. Thomas Dylan had
called it a 'hang over'. He often suffered from them and had prescribed a cure:
'A hair of the dog that bit you.' Or as the stuffed rhymers had it: 'treat me with
what caused the disease.' But it was still early. Only alcoholics drank at this time
of day. Eleven in the morning. How long had I been asleep? When did I go to
sleep? How did I sleep? Bacchus! The biggest pimp in history! The cow! She'd
raped me. I hadn't been fully conscious. Not even half conscious. The raping,
nymphomaniac cow! I'll have to get my own back. A new poem for the child
prodigy:

The Homework Exercise Book

On the first page I draw my teacher
On the second page I draw her as a dragon
On the third a succubus
On the fourth an ogress
On the fifth a crocodile
On the last page
A cancrix
On the last page
Nothing.

Thus had I transformed the lecherous cow into a dragon, succubus, ogress,
crocodile and a cancrix. And what's a 'cancrix'? Mayy Al-Baslawi. Thus did I
exorcise her. Thus do poets exorcise evil spirits.

I went down into the auditorium with the morning session drawing to a
close. I heard that Mazan Al-Hanbaki had passed out after reciting two verses.
The poem was entitled 'The Revival of Nations through the Nobility of Character
of the Individuals' and had 299 verses. The bovine horde had got lucky. Fate had
spared them Al-Hanbaki's epic. My attention was drawn to the last of the
morning's poets screaming form the podium:

'Kill me!
Kill me!
It was me who ravaged your wives
It was me who humiliated your women
It was me who roamed in your orchards . . . burning . . .
As lightning . . . raping
Kill me!
Kill me!
Throw my flesh to the crows . . . beginning with my eyes.'

I was really tempted to kill him there and then. Damned hangover! With great difficulty I managed to overcome the temptation. But I couldn't fight the definite feeling that this suicidal poet would have his wish granted in the near future.

In the afternoon session I recited a selection of my famous poems. This brilliant poetry was received with a painful silence. Even the poem that had bewitched acolytes and admirers throughout the Arab world, from the Atlantic to the Gulf, 'With the Haemorrhage of Lust I Dye Your Spine'. Even this historic poem failed to move anyone. When I began to recite 'You are my Enchanted Forest' an uproar interrupted me. For a fleeting moment, I thought that the assembled cows had begun, suddenly, to appreciate poetry. Then I discovered the source of the uproar: Mayy Al-Baslawi in the third row. She was clapping. The noise here hands were making was not greatly dissimilar to the sound of thunder. The ignorant horde maintained its ignorant silence. Monkey by monkey!

On returning to my room, I found a gift-wrapped package with my name on and the calling card of the minister of culture and reconstruction. My heart raced. This must be the Rolex which those who spend their lives going to conferences had been talking about. With trembling hands, I opened the box. Damn! Damn! Damn! The monkey! His Excellency the minister, the son of a monkey! Pamphlets about the industrial and agricultural renaissance of Arabistan X! Damn the industrial renaissance! Damn the agricultural renaissance! Damn Arabistan X! Damn the Alhambra poetry symposium! Damn the members of the organizing committee! A non-oil state, we understand. No Rolexes, we understand. But isn't there some sort of halfway house between Rolexes and pamphlets? A crate of peaches, for example. Wouldn't peaches be evidence of an agricultural renaissance? What about a case of wine? Isn't wine a national industry? An ugly world! A world of cows! Pamphlets, statistics and figures given as a gift to a poet!

In protest at the perverse gift, I decided to boycott the closing session. I went to the hotel bar. There I found Na'na' Fasada who, apparently, had also decided to boycott the session. He greeted me using the name which he knows full well I hate:

'Greetings, Abu Falafel!'

I returned his greeting using the name I knew full well he hated:

'Greetings, Abu Fasada!'

I sat down beside him. We began to pour scorn on the symposium: the participants, the organizers, the Ministry of Culture and Reconstruction. We were the guests of Bacchus slurping down the wine. We were laughing away when, like a nuclear bomb in a hurry, that stuffed rhymer, Ra'fat Jaridi, descended on us, sat down at our table without so much as a by your leave and began the familiar lecture:

'What a fiasco! These modernists should be banned. Are we Arabs or foreigners? What a fiasco! It was supposed to be a symposium for poetry not for all this rubbish. Why all these disgusting turns of phrase? All these repugnant expressions? Why all these conspiracies against our nation and its heritage? (While so saying, he gulped down a glass of red wine.) Why this insolence towards all that we hold sacred? (While so saying, he gulped down another glass of red wine.)'

In a voice which reminded me of a gurgling tap, Na'na' Fasada said:

'Calm down, Jaridi. Calm down. The world's changed. Poetry has got to change. We can't go back to the age of the camel. Now we're in the age of the Internet.'

There goes that wretched word again! In heaven's name what is this 'Internet'? Why won't anybody tell me? Why do I have to ask a stupid question? Apparently the mummified poetaster didn't understand either. He screamed at Na'na':

'Stuff the Internet! Stuff prose poems! Sod the Internet! Sod prose poems! Immortal poetry never changes. Their exalted meaning remains for ever. All that is sacred (filling his glass with red wine) does not change.'

I don't know why I suddenly lost control:

'Listen you mummified rhymer! You dinosaur! You and your lot are extinct. You're extinct and you don't even realize it. Finito! All that's left to do is to bury you on the Internet. All that's left . . .'

Ra'fat Jaridi stood up, picked up a bottle of red wine and poured it over my white suit. My suit which had cost me 300 dollars of the money I had got for the child prodigy. The beautiful new suit which I had been going to save for poetry gatherings. My very best suit for special occasions. My sharkskin suit. Before my eyes it had become an empierced cadaver washed with blood. I tried to stand up to kick this mummified poetaster. But I felt an overwhelming desire to cry and remained seated weeping in agony. Na'na' looked at Ra'fat. The damned pair laughed and sneaked out of the bar leaving me to reverberate alone.

I got back to my room in a black melancholic mood. From start to finish, a disaster of a day. From first to last, a disaster of a symposium. I tore up the pamphlets about the industrial and agricultural renaissance and threw them in the wastebasket then spat on them. I asked room service for a lemon and squeezed the juice out over the red stains. I finished packing my case. I resolved to treat the malady with another. I heard a faint knock at the door. I went over apprehensively, expecting the worst. The door was opened and a beautiful perfumed apparition entered the room. Basima! She was wearing a dress with a low neckline which plunged down almost to her breasts. You could almost see the Mound of Jasmine. I turned my gaze away with difficulty and said rudely:

'Yes, Mrs Souakin. How can I help you?!'

She laughed but said nothing.

'Have you got any more surprises? Perhaps your mother-in-law this time?'

She laughed then said gently:

'I'm sorry, I really am sorry for what happened.'

'Did you really have to put me in such an embarrassing situation?'

Her cheeks reddened. And she began to sing:

'Believe me what happened was just as much a surprise to me. He was supposed to be out of town the whole night. He had some work to do but finished it and came back early. He suddenly came in, as you saw. Luckily, he's a great admirer of yours. Otherwise I'd have had some explaining to do. He might have thought ill of me.'

'Nothing gives me greater pleasure than an unsuspicious husband surprising me with his wife.'

She laughed again and began to sing:

'My dear Professor Ken'an! Forget yesterday. I beg you. Forget yesterday. I came tonight to make it up to you. And to make it up to myself.'

My resistance began to weaken. My eyes began to turn to the Mound of Jasmine. I asked cautiously:

'What about that husband of yours?'

'Out of town. He won't be back tonight. This time I'm sure. I swear to you.'

'Swear all you like, but I'm not going back to your apartment with you.'

She sang the sweetest melody I had ever heard:

'My dear Professor! I don't expect you to go to my apartment. And don't expect me to leave your room. This is the chance of a lifetime. Destiny. I'm not going to let myself miss it. Who knows if we'll ever meet again.'

Dumbstruck, I said:

'What do you mean?'

The beautiful woman did not say much. She came closer and closer. Then her mouth closed over mine. All the kegs of gunpowder exploded in my body. All of them! I never knew that a kiss could turn into a nuclear explosion. Another kiss followed. She began to moan. And with the moans came whispers:

'At last! After all these years of waiting, I hold you to my breast. My Ken'an. My very own Ken'an. My beloved Ken'an! My poet! Finally I kiss you as I used to kiss your books of poetry. I drink from you as I used to drink from your poems. Ahh! How I have dreamed of this moment. And the reality is better than the dream. Tell me you love me. My love! My poet! My one and only poet! My one and only true love! Do you know what I feel now? I feel I am kissing every man in history. I am aflame as Layla was aflame . . .'

And in between kisses, I was panting:

'Basima! "The Basima of Seasons to Come". Where did you come from? How did you find me in this world of cows? You are an incredible woman. You are the epitome of womanhood. Where have you been all these years? Why did you let me waste my life without you? Why didn't you come to talk to me? In this age of the 'Internet'. Basima! Basima! Basima! I love you! Basima! Basima! Basima!'

We found ourselves on the bed. I stretched out my hand to the Mound of Jasmine and began to tremble. Basima began to tremble. Our trembling was interrupted by a knocking at the door which began softly then grew much louder. I cautiously opened the door. I found myself retreating before a quivering lump of lard. Mayy Al-Baslawi looked at Basima then looked at me and said:

'What's this creature doing here?'

For reasons I cannot explain, Basima began to laugh.

I said firmly:

'Miss Mayy! What are *you* doing here? Can't you see I'm busy? Can't you see I have a guest?'

Mayy Al-Baslawi hissed like a dragon with haemorrhoids:

'A guest. This half-naked tart is a guest? What is this woman doing here? And on the bed?'

I summoned up the courage to say:

'Mayy! Mind your own business. Be gone now! Please! Go!'

The hissing returned:

'It's not my business? Am I intruding? Did I come off the streets? Did I come uninvited? Didn't we agree yesterday to meet here? Now?'

With my throat rattling, I said:

'Yesterday? I didn't know what I was doing yesterday. I did things I didn't mean to. I said things I didn't mean.'

Basima's laughter had become a guffaw. The quivering lump of lard came closer to me. A ton of steel suddenly settled below my right eye. The cow apparently kicked me, punched me or butted me. I don't know exactly what happened. All I know is that I fell to the ground. The quivering lump of lard headed towards Basima who leapt to the door in a flash leaving with her laughter filling the corridor. The lump followed making a noise which was no different to that of a steam train. I think I went to sleep straight away. I dreamt, the whole night, about a steam train running over me and breaking my ribs one by one.

Thursday, The Capital, Arabistan X
I returned to Arabistan X in a bad mood which was exacerbated merely by entering my house. My wife/the cow noticed the black blotch which perched like a crow under my right eye.

'Drunk again?' she asked.

'I was not drunk, woman.'

'What happened to your eye?'

'Nothing.'

'Did some husband hit you for making a pass at his wife?'

'Be sensible woman! Since when have I been making passes at other men's wives?'

'Ever since I've known you.'

'Are you looking for trouble?'

'What happened to your eye?'

'I trod on the bar of soap in the bathroom. I slipped! I slipped! Are you listening?'

'You fell on your eye?'

'I fell, and that's all there is to it. Something must have hit my eye.'

'Do you expect me to believe your lies?'

'I expect you to shut up.'

She reluctantly did so. The barren non-lactiferous prattling cow!

At the office, my secretary/the cow looked at me and, with genuine sympathy, said:

'Professor Ken'an! What happened to your eye?'

'The soap! The bathroom!'

Luckily she was satisfied with this abridged explanation. I was just about to begin to write the third poem for the child prodigy, 'The Teacher and I', when my secretary/the cow came in with the latest issue of *The Awakening* and said:

'Have you read Waves 'Isa's article about you?'

In some trepidation I said:

'No. What does she say?'

She handed me the paper saying:

'A disaster! Read it for yourself!'

So what's this whore going to say? I began to read:

'The Shack'
between Robert Hanson and Ken'an Filfil
Plagiarism or Intertextuality?

While reading 'The Shack' by the well-known poet Ken'an Filfil in *The Awakening*'s literary supplement a few weeks ago, I had the feeling that I had read the poem before, but I could not remember where or when. I did some research in the library but could not find what I was looking for. I asked an English lecturer at the Faculty, Dr 'Arfan Mashuhur, and his photographic memory was most helpful. He told me there was a poem entitled 'The Shack' by a virtually unknown black American poet who died in the 1930s. He had quoted from the poem in one of his lectures on American literature. I compared the two poems and found that there was a high degree of similarity between the newly composed Arab poem and the American one. I knew that if I confronted Ken'an with this similarity he would attribute it to the phenomenon of intertextuality. I decided to leave the verdict to the reader. After reading the two poems, the readers should ask themselves the question: is this a case of plagiarism or intertextuality?

The Shack
by Robert Hanson

From my whole childhood
I don't remember anything
I don't remember a face, name or ghost
Except that shack
In which my eyes opened to life

They told me my mother was crying
And that my father was laughing
And that my grandmother was dancing
The day I was born
But I don't remember anything about that
I only remember the shack
The shack was white

The day my mother died
They told me I was crying
And that my father was crying
And that my grandmother was silent
But I don't remember anything about that
I only remember the shack
The shack was black

And now my body is weary
On the old chair
My father used to sit on
I try to remember the setting years
But I don't remember anything
I stare at the shack
And I see it is grey

The Shack
by Ken'an Filfil

I was born in the shack
I spent my whole childhood in the shack
I spent my whole adolescence in the shack
I locorooted my life
In the shack

My mother was crying the day I was born
She wept copiously
My father laughed . . . and guffawed
My grandmother was ululating
Incantating
The shack was coloured white

I cried the day my mother died
I cried a lot
My father cried in despair
The shack cried with us
I turned my face
I found that the colour of the shack had changed to black

In my forties
I enter the old shack
I sit on the old chair
I try to assemble my memories
Of the years which had passed
But I don't see anything
I only see the shack
And its colour has changed to grey.

The bloody bitch! I asked my secretary/the cow to get my lawyer friend, 'Adil
Kashshar, on the phone.
    "Adil! I need your services.'
    'Adil called me by the name he knew full well I hated:
    'What's up, Abu Falafel?'
    'I want to sue someone for libel.'
    'Who?'
    'Waves 'Isa.'
    'And who is this Mr Waves 'Isa?'

'It's a woman, 'Adil, a woman!'

'Ok! Who is she then?'

'She's a literature student.'

'So why do want to bring a libel case against a university student?'

'Because she has written an extremely impudent article.'

'There's no law against that.'

'She's accusing me of plagiarizing.'

'Plagiarizing?'

'Yes.'

'Plagiarizing what?'

'Plagiarizing a poem.'

At the other end of the line I could hear a shrill laugh. The man of the law said:

'I wouldn't put it past you! Did you do it?'

Damn these lawyers! The cows!

'What sort of question is that? When have I ever plagiarized a poem from anyone?'

'I don't understand poetry Abu Falafel. I understand the law.'

'But I want you to prepare a case. What do you think?'

'I think you should send me the article right away. I'll study it carefully and consult expert opinion and I'll tell you what I think in a day or so.'

I asked my secretary/the cow to send the article to 'Adil Kashshar straight away. Before she left the office, I told her:

'If you like, you can send it over the Internet.'

My secretary/the cow looked at the black blotch as if to say that she thought it was the cause of a sudden fit of madness. She said:

'Send it over what?'

I retreated immediately:

'In some countries of Arabistan people call express delivery "the Internet". A somewhat strange folk.'

'Do you want me to sent it by post?'

'No! No! Send it by courier. Now!'

Expert opinion! Does a perfectly clear broad-daylight libel case need an expert's opinion? I returned to the poem for the child prodigy:

The Teacher and I

This isn't a wolf
Despite its long canines
And sharp claws
And the saliva which drips from its mouth

It looks at me
And flares with rage
This isn't a wolf
This is a good man
This is my teacher!

And Waves 'Isa will be a good girl. When she learns her manners in the courtroom. The sea bitch!

Friday
This is the most miserable day of the week. I can't get away from my wife/the cow without some really compelling reasons. And the bitch knows, despite her congenital and acquired stupidity, the difference between fabricated excuses and genuine emergencies. Inside this mentally retarded cow is enough villainy for all the women in the world. And more. This morning I wanted to finish the fourth poem for the child prodigy but the cow wouldn't stop rabbitting on. Shots from a gun whose ammunition never runs out.

'Why didn't you bring me a dress back from Alhambra? People say that there are lots of pretty things over there.'

I didn't say anything though I wanted to say: 'Which dress could you get into, you cow? Which ten dresses?'

'The gas canister's empty. When are you going to fetch a new one?'

I kept quiet but I wanted to say:

'As soon as you're ready to burn yourself alive.'

'Our neighbour's bought his wife a car. When are you going to buy me a car?'

With difficulty, I stopped myself saying:

'As soon as I've found a car big enough for you to fit in.'

The gas. The dress. The car. The neighbours. This is the cow's universe. Clover. Water. Milk. Slaughter. The telephone that has been cut off. The fridge that doesn't work. Bulls. Artificial insemination. False pregnancies. Butchers. Clover. Water. Dresses. Cars. Food. Money. Real estate. Films. Clover. Slaughter! Slaughter! Slaughter!

Just before midday, as usual, my wife's/the cow's mother and father came round. They didn't leave until they had devoured the food, as usual. How I would love to surprise them one day with a huge banquet, a whole fat cow for the two of them to eat, with delight and relish, without them knowing that they were eating their daughter.

The revulsion which always comes over me whenever I see my mother-in-law/the cow and her husband helped me write the poem:

Lines of Longitude and Latitude
This line suddenly descends on your head
And penetrates your lung
And this line alights on your shoulder
And penetrates your liver
And in each line there is a glistening dagger
These are the lines of longitude

And this line rushes to your foot
And this line aims for your heart
And this line proceeds to your waist
And in each line there is a glistening knife
These are the lines of latitude

In the evening I was trying to watch an old film but my wife/the cow kept going on about what was happening and giving me her philosophical commentaries:
'She's the heroine. 'Ajfa' Mamsusa. I don't know what people see in her.'
'He's the baddie. Wahash Al-Shasha. He reminds me of your late father.'
'That's a Cadillac. Did I tell you that our neighbour is buying his wife a car?'
'That's the beach at Al-Ma'mura. Did I tell you that the neighbours are going to Europe this summer?'
'That's . . .'
I was really trying to focus on the film and ignore the incessant comments when the telephone rang. My wife/the cow said:
'You get it. At this time of night, it'll only be one of your drunken friends.'
In fact, it was a friend but he wasn't drunk. 'Adil Kashshar said:
'Greetings, Abu Falafel! I didn't want to keep you in limbo. I've been studying the matter carefully.'
'And the result?'
'Forget the libel suit.'
'What do you mean?'
'I mean, you wouldn't win it.'
'Why not? I've been accused of plagiarism.'
'From the strictly legal point of view, she hasn't accused you of anything. A question was raised, but not answered.'
'Yes, but what she's getting at is perfectly clear.'
'On that, I agree with you.'
'So, why won't you take the case?'
'Because we would lose.'
'Why would we lose?'

'Abu Falafel! Why can't you just leave it at that? We would lose. That's all there is to it.'

'We couldn't lose.'

'Remember I told you I don't know anything about poetry?'

'Yes, I remember.'

'Well, neither does the court.'

'Yes, but it knows what libel is.'

'True. But libel only exists where the allegation is proved to be false.'

'The allegation is false.'

'A court couldn't give a ruling on that.'

'I thought a court could give a ruling on anything.'

'True. But on questions of art, the court can only give a ruling after consulting expert opinion.'

'Critics?!'

'And lecturers in literature at the university.'

'Donkey's of poetry! They know less than anybody about poetry.'

'Maybe. But they are the experts the court would rely on. The poem would be submitted to a panel of experts made up of university lecturers and . . .'

'Can't we choose our own experts?' I interrupted angrily.

'No, but we could object to one of them if we could prove to the court that he was biased.'

'So you think that this panel . . .'

'I think they would say you plagiarized the poem,' the man of the law interrupted.

'So how did you arrive at this ludicrous conclusion?'

'Abu Falafel! I asked the experts. Three university professors said you had plagiarized . . .'

I interrupted, calling him the name I knew full well he hated:

'Kushshari, I can't begin to thank you for all you've done! Goodbye!'

I put the phone down and returned. I was hoping my wife/the cow would give me sufficient cause to kill her, a sufficient cause which the experts would not object to. The cows! I had barely sat down when the door bell rang. My wife said:

'You get it. At this time of night it'll only be your drunken friends.'

I opened the door and there was Mayy Al-Baslawi, clearly gagging for it and drunk. She was all over me and put her arms around me saying over and over:

'Ken'an! Ken'an! I'm sorry my love! I didn't know what I was doing. I was mad with jealousy. I wanted to kill the bitch but she got away. Please forgive me.'

I was trying, without much success, to escape the clutches of the quivering lump of lard, when my wife/the cow came and said to the night caller:

'Was it you who hit him? You, you immoral bitch?'

The lump replied:

'This is between your employer and me. It's got nothing to do with a maid.'

My wife/the cow exploded:

'My employer? A maid? Am I the maid? Me, you sack of rotten meat?! Me, you bag of putrid fat?! I'll cut your vile tongue out and throw it to the dogs.'

My wife/the cow went off into the kitchen looking for something sharp to cut her tongue out with. The lump went after her. The two cows clashed at the kitchen door. Mayy Al-Baslawi began the fight with a blow which felled my wife/the cow. I started to laugh. The one on the ground got up and cautiously retreated to a second line of defence, retreating until she had picked up a medium-sized saucepan. With incredible speed, my wife/the cow rushed at the quivering lump of lard and the saucepan crashed into the head which was immersed in the fatty folds of her neck. The lump fell to the ground, a motionless corpse.

'I think you killed her,' I said.

My wife/the cow looked at me.

'Go to hell! Now it's your turn, you excuse for a man.'

That was the last thing I heard before the saucepan exploded on my head, before I lost consciousness with the smell of okra filling my nose.

TWO

The Philosopher

Arabic his language
Philosophical his beliefs
Persian his festivities
Al-Mutanabbi

Identity Card
Full Name: Jamal Al-Din Marsi Shafi'i
Known as: Philosopher Pasha
Occupation: Dean of the faculty of Literature and incumbent of
                        the Chair of Philosophy, the University of Al-
                        Shuruq
Age: 57
Wealth: $3.5million
Place of Birth: Arabistan X
Place of Work: Arabistan X
Academic Qualifications: BA Philosophy (University of Al-Shuruq); MA
                        Philosophy (University of Al-Shuruq); PhD.
                        Philosophy (The Sorbonne)
Marital Status: Widower
Children: Three Daughters

Saturday
Today is the monthly faculty committee meeting. How I hate these meetings.
And how I hate this committee. How I hate Dr Buqrat 'the Epicure' Sanqar, head
of English, and his stupid remarks. How I hate Dr Nasif Mullàqat, head of
history, who belongs, both in the way he looks and the way he thinks, to some
prehistoric age. How I hate Dr Samahri Al-'Arna'ut, head of Arabic, who thinks
he's living in the epoch of Sibawayh. How I hate Dr Qundil Wahabi, head of
journalism, and his disgusting buffoonery. How I hate Dr Muhriz Bahzad, head
of geography, and his unexpected comments. The only member of the
committee I don't hate is Dr Nasri Haftan, vice-rector, who never says a word.
The only member I like is Dr Tuffaha Qut Al-Qulub, head of archaeology.

As usual, the meeting was bad. It had begun worse than usual. The secretary
was asked to read the minutes of the last meeting, but before he had barely

opened his mouth Dr Samahri had butted in with some pompous, pedantic and pointless comment about the wording of the minutes.

I politely interrupted him:

'The secretary will make the necessary amendment.'

Dr Samahri, however, was not satisfied, and launched into a tirade, quoting ancient poetry, against the stylistic infelicities he claimed were always in the minutes saying:

'On this one cannot remain silent. The minutes are always full of a thousand and one errors. I've said it a thousand times. It's as if they were written by barbarians. It's as if . . .'

Again I interrupted him politely:

'Doctor Samahri! Should there be any further stylistic errors, I would be grateful if you would point them out so they may be rectified.'

Dr Samahri continued his discourse on stylistic deviation and was joined in the uproar in turn by Drs Qundil Wahabi, Buqrat Sanqar and Muhriz making equally pointless remarks. I tapped the table lightly with my pencil and said:

'Colleagues! There's no need for all this excitement. Any errors will be rectified. Doctor Samahri is correct when he says that . . .'

But there was no stopping Dr Samahri and his tirade this time was fuelled by interventions from Drs Nasif Mullaqat, Muhriz Bahzad and Buqrat Sanqar. The noise of lines of ancient poetry being heatedly exchanged was interrupted by the sweet voice of Tuffaha Qut Al-Qulub pleading:

'Gentlemen! Gentlemen! There's no need to fall out over grammatical and stylistic issues. I propose that Doctor Samahri be called upon to prepare the minutes in the way he deems appropriate.'

Murmurs of approval were heard. I was just about to declare Dr Tuffaha's proposal as unanimously accepted when an enraged Dr Samahri screamed:

'Am I now the committee's moral law? Am I now a mere writer of opuscula? No, by God! I would rather be cut into a thousand pieces . . .'

'Just a thousand?' broke in Dr Buqrat.

Dr Samahri turned to him and said:

'Are you mocking me you little foreign man.'

Dr Buqrat immediately said:

'Am I a little foreign man you lump of camel dung?!'

Dr Samahri attacked Dr Buqrat and slapped him in the face at the very moment that Dr Muhriz said:

'True!'

Dr Samahri turned to Dr Muhriz and slapped him in the face saying:

'And you like what he said?'

Dr Tuffaha began to laugh. Dr Samahri headed for her with the palm of his hand raised in the air. I found myself forced to stand and block his path. All he did was bellow in my face:

'Are you going to defend her, Philosopher Pasha?! Defend your companion in fornication and your partner in adultery?'

Dr Tuffaha stopped laughing. She launched herself at Dr Samahri with her high-heeled shoe in her hand and brought it down on his head causing a wound which began to bleed copiously.

Dr Samahri sat down receiving the blood that flowed down his face in his handkerchief mumbling:

'What should I say? "We pay for our freedom with blood".'

In the evening, Dr Tuffaha visited me at home – the beautiful villa I inherited from my late wife. It had become entirely my property once my daughters, in gratitude, had ceded their share to me. Tuffaha sat beside me sipping her beer and said:

'What do you think, Jamal? Will Samahri take me to a disciplinary hearing?'

'How could he do that? He was the one who slandered you. You were legitimately defending yourself.'

'But I think he was badly injured.'

'No. Just a scratch. He went to the university hospital. They put a bandage on. He departed as right as rain.'

'Don't you think I should apologize?'

'I think you should help me get rid of him once and for all. This man's crazy. We'll have to get rid of him.'

'And how are you going to do that?'

'Machiavelli said: "when the interests of one noble require the annihilation of another noble then that annihilation becomes an example of the ideal."'

'I think that's one of Philosopher Pasha's sayings.'

'You're right. But we have to get rid of him.'

'But how?'

'Where there's a will . . .'

Dr Tuffaha came closer, pressed against me and said:

'There's a way.'

'And who was it who said that?'

Tuffaha whispered in my ear as she squeezed me tightly:

'Your companion in fornication and your partner in adultery.'

Sunday

The day began with a somewhat strange phone call from a friend of mine, Dr Za'il Bahran:

'How are things, Philosopher Pasha?'

'Very well Abu Al-Za'al!'

'How would you like to become a member of a committee?'
'A philosophy committee?'
'A poetry committee.'
'Poetry? Why don't you talk to Doctor Samahri Al-'Arna'ut?'
'The man's an ass!'
'You're right there!'
'I don't want him. I want you.'
'And why not? The first methodical treatise on poetics was by Aristotle in
which he explains aesthetic values . . .'
Dr Za'il Bahran interrupted me:
'And you know as much about poetry as Aristotle. Are you on?'
'What does the committee do?'
'Selecting the best anthology of poetry published by a poet under twenty.'
'In other words, child's play?'
'You could say that.'
'So why do you want me to join this committee?'
'Because I like you. I want you to get the honorarium.'
'Honorarium?'
'Twenty-five thousand dollars.'
'How many times will the committee sit?'
'Once. At the most.'
'Then count me in.'
'I'll send you part of the money right away.'
'Thank you Abu Za'il!'
'Don't mention it, Philosopher Pasha!'

Today was apparently going to be the day for dollars, the numbers of which
were beginning to increase at an astonishing rate. My secretary, Nirmeen,
ushered Hajj Boushman Al-Shouiba' into the office. He had asked to see me
weeks before. It was evident that Hajj Boushman was a man of dignity. He was
in his mid-forties with a cheerful face and a bit of a belly. He spoke most
respectfully:

'Dean! I am grateful to you for seeing me. I am grateful to you for having
arranged this appointment for me. I do not have sufficient words to express my
feelings at being in your presence.'
'Please don't mention it Hajj Boushman.'
'Please call me Bou Jawisem.'
'Don't mention it, Hajj Bou Jawisem.'
'I thank you from the depths of my heart. I would like you to know, Dean,
that I am a mere beginner. Despite my relatively advanced age in years and
despite the extent of my commercial interests, I consider myself but your pupil.
As God is my witness, I consider myself as your slave.'

'Don't mention it, Hajj Bou Shouiba'.'

'Bu Jawisem!'

'Forgive me. I meant, Hajj Bu Jawisem, that we're brothers.'

'God forbid! God forbid! You, the Dean of Philosophy in the Arabistani nation and I a mere student seeking knowledge. A mere businessman whom God has blessed with wealth and who wishes to increase his blessings from God by seeking more knowledge. It is 25 years since I graduated from this blessed college.'

'I don't recall ever seeing you, Hajj.'

'I was an affiliated student, Dean. My circumstances did not permit me to attend regularly. I would come from Arabistan X twice a year, once to take the course programme and once to take the exam. Despite being occupied by commercial matters, God facilitated things for me, and I gained a bachelor's degree. Naturally, the class of degree I was awarded was not as high as I'd hoped.'

'This is terrific, Hajj. Really terrific. The important thing was that you obtained the degree.'

'And afterwards, worldly affairs occupied my time, Dean. Business. And God has granted me such success that I became the biggest importer of vegetable oils in Arabistan X.'

'Vegetable oils? This is a strange coincidence.'

'What is, Dean?'

'Doctor Maher Ihsan, the husband of my eldest daughter, Tamader, owns the largest vegetable-oil bottling-plant in the country.'

'Glory be to God! Glory be to God! Whatever He wills will be! All our good fortune is from God. I tell you everything is written on the heavenly tablet. Would it be possible for me to become acquainted with Doctor Maher? Who knows, perhaps we could work together. The vegetable oil business, Dean, is a blessed one and its bounties many.'

'I would be more than happy to arrange a meeting between you and Maher.'

'However, this is not why I'm here, Dean. I'm not here on business. I come in search of knowledge. I have come in quest of learning.'

'Such are commendable sentiments, Hajj. The search for knowledge from the cradle to the grave. This is truly splendid.'

'I wish, Dean, to register for a doctorate in this blessed college.'

I attempted to conceal the signs of astonishment on my face and said calmly:

'Masha'allah! A doctorate? A tremendous eagerness for knowledge. But you should realize, Hajj, that after a first degree two further diplomas are required. Having obtained the diplomas, then one can register for a doctorate.'

'My dear Dean! I'm willing to take seventy diplomas! As God is my witness if certificates were for sale, I'd pay a million dollars for a doctorate.'

'Certificates, Hajj, are sold to those who are industrious and diligent, and their price is hard work. If you are serious, then you will attain your desire. And you will have every encouragement from me.'

'When should I register for the first diploma?'

'Whenever you wish.'

'Firstly, I should like to meet Doctor Maher.'

I went with Hajj into Nirmeen's room and asked her to arrange a meeting for that evening for the Hajj and Dr Maher.

I had decided to devote my lecture for the diploma students that day to an explanation of the theory on which my renown is based and by which I had entered the world of philosophy. Someone once said in derision: 'I see a lot of philosophy professors around me, but I don't see any philosophy.' After my two *magna opera* on 'Eclecticism' were published I ceased to be among the ranks of mere professors of philosophy and joined the immortals themselves. My philosophy reached the west and is taught in the universities of America and Europe under the name 'Eclectics'. I can say, without mock humility, that I am the only true philosopher in the whole Arabistani nation. So, let grudging friends call me 'Philosopher Pasha'. Whether they like it or not, I am a philosopher and a half. I began the lecture in the following manner:

'The satirist, H. L. Mencken said: "The history of philosophy, in simple terms, is one philosopher trying to convince people that all the other philosophers are asses and succeeding in convincing them." (Laughter from the students.) "The truth is, all that the philosopher has convinced us of is that he himself is an ass." (Laughter from the students.) I do not hold the writer in opprobrium for this scathing comment. Were you to review the history of philosophy, you would find that it consists of one school building on the rubble of another, one philosopher killing another philosopher – I mean killing him on the level of ideas – in order to establish his theory in the place of the theory which has been "killed". This is the history of philosophy from its birth to this very moment. With regard to knowledge, one theory says that it is possible to attain knowledge either by means of a priori reasoning or by empirical means. Yet Scepticism contends that it is impossible to know anything, anything at all. Therefore, the philosopher who believes that knowledge is possible must be an ass (laughter) or his colleague, who denies the possibility of knowing anything, must be an ass (laughter) or they must both be asses (laughter). Plato believed that it was only ideas which could be known and that we should devote all our energies to thinking about ideas (laughter), with "the Idea of the Good" at the forefront. Aristotle believed that practically everything could be realized and absorbed by understanding the natural qualities of things. Which of them is the ass, Plato or Aristotle? (Laughter). Then came the Stoics who held that everything is preordained. If what you want is not to be, then settle for what you have. This is great stuff! The problem is that then the Epicureans came along and said that we have to seek happiness. How can we seek happiness when everything is inevitable and preordained? Which of them are the asses? The Stoics or the Epicureans? In modern times nothing has changed in philosophical thought. The pendulum still swings back and forth. For the philosophers of scientism, the only knowledge is that which comes via experimentation. For the rationalists reason precedes experimentation. Spinoza said that knowledge required fundamental, self-evident truths. For Locke there were no fundamental, self-evident truths. For Locke, science is the foundation. With Kant, science is an intellectual activity, but with the intellect being unable to penetrate appearances. In all the sciences, each scientist builds on what his predecessors have discovered and the sciences develop gradually and cumulatively, with the exception of philosophy. In philosophy, development is only possible by means of destruction. This is what led me, after reflection and study, to come up with my own theory which is known and renowned under the name of "Eclecticism". The theory can be summarized in very simple terms: every philosophy is right and every philosophy is wrong (laughter). The basis of the theory is that knowledge is an extremely complex phenomenon which cannot yield to a single theory. From this starting point, I tried to select from each philosopher a part of his theory and leave the rest. In other words, my theory came along to put an end to all the talk about philosophers being asses (Laughter). Each philosopher is right to a very limited extent and wrong to an unlimited extent. Scientific methodology requires taking the bit which is correct and leaving aside the rest, provided this is done in a methodical manner . . .'

The students listened with great attention that was broken only by laughter. At the end of the lecture, there was the customary response whenever I expound my theory – loud applause!

In the evening, my daughter's husband, Dr Maher, came to see me with a big smile on his face. He gave me a hug and said:

'Thank you, pops! Thank you! Thank you!'

'What for son?'

'Hajj Boushman . . .'

'Abu Shouiba'?'

'Abu Jawisem'

'You've met him?'

'And the meeting was fruitful. Very fruitful. Believe it or not, he's taking half of next year's production. Next week we start exporting to Arabistan X.'

'Fantastic. Fantastic.'

'However, there is just a small matter.'

'Which is?'

'The Hajj, as you are aware, pops, gave up formal education many years ago.

He's a bit rusty. He's more than willing to apply himself now but he needs help . . .'

'Private lessons and things like that?'

'Exactly, pops.'

'Get in touch with Tal'at Bahjur. Do you know him? A lecturer in the history department. I think he'd be willing to provide the assistance required. Don't mention my name. I can't get involved in things like that.'

'Naturally, pops. Naturally.'

When Maher left, the telephone rang. I picked up the phone in anticipation, expecting a call from Tuffaha. However, the delicate feminine voice that came on the line was not hers:

'Doctor Jamal?'

'Yes.'

'I'm sorry to bother you.'

'Not at all.'

'Your lecture today was brilliant. It was the most brilliant lecture I've ever heard in my life.'

'You're a diploma student?'

'Yes.'

'But I . . .'

'You don't know my name and you don't remember me? There are no more than eleven female students in the class.'

'I'm sorry! My memory . . .'

The delicate female voice interrupted me:

'The famous absent-mindedness of philosophers, Doctor.'

'I'm sorry!'

'My name is Dalila Wasef.'

'How can I help you?'

'There is something which is worrying me a little bit.'

'What's that?'

'God willing, I intend to do a doctorate after getting the diploma.'

'Fantastic.'

'I'll be writing about Al-Farabi.'

'A fabulous topic.'

'However, there's something which is bothering me.'

'Every problem has a solution. What's your problem.'

'The Second Mind, the Third Mind and the Fourth Mind. I don't understand what he's talking about.'

'This requires a lengthy explanation.'

'Please, Doctor, could you explain it to me.'

'You know that my time table at the college is . . .'

'Who can talk to you at the college? I was hoping that you could see me away from the college.'

A somewhat awkward situation. There were no precedents. What could I say? I began to mutter:

'Um . . . Um . . . The problem is . . . Um . . .'

She interrupted me decisively:

'I'll come to your house. Tomorrow afternoon. Is that a good time?'

Without thinking I found myself saying:

'Tomorrow afternoon I've an engagement.'

The delicate determined voice came back:

'Fine! The day after tomorrow then. Five o'clock.'

'My address is . . .'

'I know the address.'

'How do you know?'

'I'm your student, Doctor. The Philosophy of Eclecticism.'

I went to bed immersed in thoughts. It had been a day full of wonders. But I found myself unable to concentrate on the events of the day. I found all my thoughts focused on what would happen tomorrow. Galnar! Tomorrow was my meeting with her. On the famous programme *The Eyes of the World Are Upon You*. She would begin the interview with a vicious, violent attack, then she would leave the field open for an even more vicious and violent attack from the viewers. It was this adversarial spirit which had made the programme the most successful in the Arabistani nation. Everyone she invited onto the programme could consider themselves as having made it. And those who weren't famous beforehand were famous afterwards. According to the viewing figures, more than 20 million Arabistanis watched the programme. But my problem wasn't with the viciousness, the violence or the fame. My problem was with her beauty. I think, without the slightest doubt, that Galnar is the most beautiful woman I've met in my whole life. This was my opinion when I used to see her as a young journalism student. And I still feel this way now she's a mature woman in her mid-thirties. I have no idea how an Arabistani woman can be so fair-skinned, have such green eyes and be so graceful. Galnar was the only thing in my life that was incompatible with my philosophy of eclecticism. There is no room for selection when it comes to Galnar. You have to take Galnar as a whole, warts and all. (I'll have to ask Dr Samahri Al-'Arna'ut about the etymology behind that!)

Monday

This was to be Galnar's day, I mean my day and her day. She was more radiant than ever before, as was I. From the outset, the major challenge was trying to keep my thoughts off that beautiful body whose charms she was keen to display more than ever before. But the intellectual discipline that had become second nature to me ever since my philosophical ideas were in their early stages enabled me to talk to her without looking at the breasts which her tight-fitting dress emphasized in such a way as to arouse the passions of the most incurable Stoic.

Galnar began:

'My dear Professor! This is the first time we've had a philosopher on the programme. We've had people from every profession you can imagine and from some you can't. We've had poets, businessmen, actors and actresses, snake charmers, magicians and writers right on the heels of lion tamers and hypnotists – every profession! – but tonight, for the first time we have a philosopher, Doctor Jamal Al-Din Al-Shafi'i. Doctor Jamal! I'd like to welcome you on behalf of our viewers to *The Eyes of the World Are Upon You*.'

'I'm very happy to be on such a successful show. And I'm honoured to be the first student of philosophy to be made, thanks to your show, a star.'

'Thank you. Let me start by asking a question which you will no doubt think an obvious one. But for our non-specialist viewers it isn't so obvious. What is philosophy? I mean is there a clear, understandable definition of what philosophy is?'

'Sure there is. And the definition is found in the word itself. In Greek, philosophy means "the love of wisdom".'

'Professor! You're just leading me from one word to another. What does "love of wisdom" mean?'

'Ok then! Let me give you and the viewers the definition given by that famous Muslim philosopher, Al-Khwarizmi: "Philosophy is knowledge of the reality of things and acting in the best way". Is that clear?'

'I'm sorry, Professor, but it's still a bit vague.'

'The key is the word "reality". Studying "things", in itself, is not philosophy. Searching for their underlying truths is. To explain further, we have to touch on the traditional branches of philosophy. First of all, there is metaphysics. This is the branch which is concerned with looking into the reality of existence, the reality of the self and the reality of life. Secondly, we have epistemology. This branch is concerned with the nature of knowledge, what it is, what it's based on and what its true essence is. Thirdly, we have logic. This branch deals with analysing the ways and means the mind uses to arrive at the truth. After that there comes ethics. This is the branch which deals with the nature of good and the nature of evil, and consequently the nature of what is right and wrong. Finally, we have aesthetics. This analyses creativity and how our senses are affected by beauty, whether in a painting, a sculpture or in music. In this sense, I don't think there's any difficulty in differentiating between philosophy and linguistics, history, literature, geography and . . .'

'Forgive me, Doctor. When I said it was difficult to define philosophy in a clear and precise manner, I wasn't giving my own personal point of view. Lots of researchers have touched on this difficulty.'

'That's true! That's true! And the reason is that philosophy, for a long time, was the source of all branches of knowledge. Practically every subject came under philosophy: mathematics, natural history and theology. This is why in the West a doctorate is called a "doctorate in philosophy". The old name has remained even though the justifications for calling it that are long gone.'

'But your own PhD is in Philosophy.'

'That is correct.'

'Good! To be frank, in all honesty, do you consider yourself a philosopher?'

'To be frank, I think I can claim that honour. When a person has a philosophical theory which is studied in universities throughout the world, when dozens of university theses have been written about this theory, and when the theory is in dictionaries of philosophy, I think that such a person can consider himself a philosopher, though a minor one in comparison with the Greats.'

'You mean the theory of Eclecticism?'

'Yes'

'Would you permit me to speak frankly about this theory?'

'Please do.'

'Some people say – forgive me Professor! – that the theory is just a kind of *talfiq*. What do you say to that?'

'*Talfiq* is a term from jurisprudence meaning that someone takes something from this or that school of law in a manner in keeping with his inclinations but without paying attention to the methodological principles on which each school of law is based. It is customary, by way of simplification, to divide the schools of law into two main schools: the school of legally argued opinion and the school based on the traditions of the Prophet. Imam Abu Hanifa, the pioneer of the school based on legally argued opinion, drew up extremely stringent conditions for accepting a tradition of the Prophet. These included that the tradition be very widely known to an extent almost impossible to fulfil. In the absence of acceptable traditions, he was forced to use his own juridical opinion, by legal argument based on analogous cases, to be precise. For example, Abu Hanifa did not accept the tradition of the Prophet that a guardian's consent was necessary for a marriage to be valid. Fine! So when a Hanafi comes along and says that the guardian's consent is not required for a marriage to be legal we tell him, "Ok! If that's the way you want it, that's fine." But when a follower of the Hanbali school of law, whose founder accepted the tradition about the guardian's consent being required, comes along and says he wants to follow the Hanafi school of law on this point he has committed *talfiq*. Similarly, Imam Abu Hanifa did not accept those traditions of the Prophet which permitted incorporating conditions into the marriage contract and so, to a great extent, he restricted the addition of such conditions. But Imam Ahmad Ibn Hanbal accepted these traditions of the Prophet and allowed the marriage contract to contain any conditions the two parties agreed on. So when a Hanafi comes along and says that he believes in the validity of a marriage without the consent of the guardian, i.e. following the school of Abu Hanifa, and then says that he can put any condition he wants in a marriage contract, i.e. following the school of Ibn Hanbal, he has committed *talfiq*. Abu Hanifa himself said: 'No one may reproduce our standpoint on an issue unless he first understands how we arrived at that standpoint'. *Talfiq* has absolutely nothing to do with Eclecticism.'

'So would you agree, then, that Eclecticism is just a means of reaching a compromise between opposites?'

'No, I wouldn't agree to that either, Galnar! Compromise is the meeting midway of two parties. Compromise is something we do the whole time in our daily life, in our social life and in our political life. We do it almost without thinking, involuntarily. A child asks his father for ten pounds and the father refuses. The child cries. He goes to his mother and she persuades the father to give him five pounds. Some members of parliament want to annul this or that but others refuse. The result is that it stays but is amended in some way. And on it goes. The theory of eclecticism has nothing to do with this form of reaching a compromise.'

'It would seem, Doctor Jamal, that it's difficult to push you into a corner. What about Relativism? Don't you think that there is no difference, no difference at all, between your theory and that philosophical theory which has been around a long time and goes by the name of Relativism?'

'Galnar! I must congratulate you on the breadth of your philosophical knowledge.'

'Thank you, Professor.'

'Nevertheless, I must point out that Relativism, as a philosophical concept, emerged from the discussion about good and evil, not about knowledge. For Relativism, it is the prevailing cultural and social conditions of the society which determine whether an act is moral or immoral, evil or not evil. This is what we now call cultural specificity. For a man to marry four women in a Muslim society is not considered immoral. The same act in Western society is punishable by law. None of this has anything at all to do with Eclecticism.'

'Doctor! I think the time has come for you to explain to us what Eclecticism is.'

'Fine! From the epistemological point of view . . .'

'I'm sorry, Professor! I have to interrupt you. I would remind you that this programme is watched by more than 20 million people, practically all of whom are not specialists in this field. With the greatest respect, I would remind you that you're not in the lecture hall with students in higher education. The more successful you are in simplifying things the more successful you will be in becoming, as you said a short while ago, a star of the people.'

'I will try. It is the nature of every science to claim absolute truth for itself. No mathematician would say: "I think two plus two equals four, but I'm not sure." No physicist would say: "There is a possibility that a law of gravity exists." No theologian would say: "There is as much truth in other religions as there is in mine." The trouble with philosophers, on account of their inflated intellectual gifts, is that they tend to go overboard in this direction. Knowledge is either based on conjecture or experimentation. Happiness is either rational or sensual. Eclecticism starts from the simple logic that all philosophers are right and all philosophers are wrong.'

'If this is simple logic, Doctor, so where is the complicated logic?'

'You'll see that the logic is simple by way of a few examples. Plato said many great things about the importance of beneficence and the necessity for philosophers to go out to people and tell them how important it was for human life. He was right. But Plato himself believed that the human mind could only find out abstract forms, ideas and models. That's why his theory is called "Idealism". Here he was wrong. With our senses we can understand many tangible, material things. Eclecticism neither accepts nor rejects Plato. Eclecticism says that Plato was wrong in this opinion but correct in others.'

'But this takes us back to Relativism through . . .'

'I'm sorry! I'm sorry! Galnar! Let's take another example from modern philosophy. Let's take Hume. Hume said that we should know the origin of the thought which occurs to us so that we can evaluate it. An understandable and acceptable statement. Here Hume was correct. Ideas whose origin we don't know won't lead us to certain knowledge. But Hume didn't stop here. He said that ultimately everything, everything, is just an idea in the mind, just an impression. Fine! Here, Hume was wrong. Eclecticism tries to introduce some intellectual humility into a science which, inherently, shuns such humility.'

'And we, Professor, are some of the intellectually humble. Do you mind if we start taking some calls? As usual, I'd ask my guest and the callers to be as brief as possible so we can get in as many calls as possible. We have Doctor Salah from Alexandria. Go ahead, Doctor.'

'*I would like to ask Doctor Jamal for his opinion about what the famous poet, Keats, said: 'In the dull catalogue of common things – Poetry will clip an angel's wings'.*'

Galnar laughed. Doctor Salah!! It was that vile man, Buqrat. I laughed in turn and said:

'Keats was a poet and poets are liable to flights of fancy on occasion. I would remind Doctor Salah that many poets were also philosophers. Al-Ma'arri is called the Poet–Philosopher. And Ibn Sina wrote beautiful philosophical poetry about the soul. Doctor Salah will no doubt be familiar with them: "I descended from heaven upon you . . ."'

Galnar broke in:

'Forgive me! We have a call from a Miss Sundus from Abu Dhabi. Go ahead.'

'What is your opinion about those who say that philosophy leads to atheism?'

Galnar looked at me, smiled and said:

'A difficult question.'

I laughed and said:

'No! Not at all! It's a very old question. And Francis Bacon answered the question when he said: "A little philosophy inclineth man's mind to atheism; but depth in philosophy bringeth men's minds about to religion." A little knowledge is a dangerous thing, in philosophy and in other subjects. One has to . . .'

Galnar broke in:

'We have Professor Musa from Al-Manama on the line. Please go ahead, Musa.'

'Would the Doctor be so kind as to explain to us how the philosophy "Cynicism", which in Arabic is called "The Canine Philosophy", got its name?'

Galnar laughed as she asked me:

'Did philosophers bite people in those days?'

'I don't think so. but I wouldn't rule it out. But the question is a good one. It's a problem of literal translation. The word "Cyno" is derived form the Greek for "dog", "kyon". When the name of the philosophical school was first translated into Arabic, it was translated literally and became "Canine". Some say that the school gets its name from the building in which its followers used to meet, "the Cynosarges". Others say they got the name because the followers were so contemptuous when they spoke it sounded like a dog snarling. It was a very pessimistic philosophy and held that Man was incapable of understanding goodness. I . . .'

Galnar broke in:

'Professor Musa can now handle the Cynics without fear of being bitten. With us now we have Doctor Baha' Al-Din from Cairo. Go ahead, Doctor.'

'Does not your distinguished guest believe that our noble jurists of Islam were correct when they said: "Those who dabble in logic become infidels." Does he not believe that the Shaykh al-Islam, Ibn Taymiyya was right when he said that an intelligent man did not need the logic of Aristotle and it was no use to the fool. Does he not believe that those who publish deviant, atheistical thought . . .'

Galnar stepped in at once:

'I'm sorry Doctor Baha' Al-Din! I had to interrupt. You can ask whatever you like, but you're not entitled to level accusations at people. What exactly is your question?'

'My question is, to be precise: How can Doctor Jamal prove that Philosophy is not opposed to Religion?'

Dr Baha' Al-Din was that vile criminal, Dr Samahri Al-'Arna'ut. I'd have to teach him a lesson on the air. I smiled and said:

'I am grateful to the questioner for his religious zeal and draw his attention to the fact that philosophy has lived alongside religion for thousands of years without either one of them doing away with the other. I would then say that all the Muslim philosophers aimed to provide rational evidence for the existence of God, may He be glorified – evidence to supplement that handed down from the Qur'an and the traditions of the Prophet, not to contradict it. In this regard, Al-Kindi says that philosophy is "Knowledge of the First Truth which is the cause of all truth". And the entire philosophy of Ibn Rushd is based on the existence of "the Eternal Mover". In Christianity, religion almost merged once and for all with philosophy through Saint Thomas Aquinas and the Scholastics. Lest I drag on, I would advise the questioner to read my book, *Philosophy for Beginners*.'

Galnar smiled and said:

'You're getting free publicity for your book, Doctor Jamal. We now have Doctor Layla from Beirut. Go ahead, Doctor.'

'Doesn't your guest, the philosopher, think that philosophy is out of date and that we should now be interested in things which are practical, useful and beneficial such as computers, business management, aviation and the like?'

Before I could answer, Galnar intervened:

'I have to thank Layla for that question. Since the start of the programme I've been meaning to ask my guest the same question, but didn't dare because he used to be my teacher, I mean my professor at the college where I studied. What do you say, Doctor Jamal?'

I smiled and said:

'In fact, the view that Doctor Layla has expressed is in itself a one hundred per cent philosophical view. It's a view based on the philosophy of Pragmatism which was developed by the American philosopher William James, and which repudiates any theory which has no application in reality. However, if we go beyond that, we can say that, had it not been for the philosophers of the European Renaissance who believed that the world was governed by knowable laws, the scientific discoveries which led, subsequently to all the inventions we have around us, would not have happened. I would like to say to Doctor Layla that had it not been for philosophy, there would be no computers, there would be no aeroplanes and there would . . .'

Galnar broke in:

'I think you've given the question its due, Doctor. We move on now to another question. We have Professor Muhammad from Jeddah. Go ahead, Muhammad.'

'I would like to go along with Doctor Baha' Al-Din and say that, like him, I think that philosophy is atheism and that no true Muslim can believe in . . .'

Galnar interrupted him:

'Muhammad! That's your personal opinion and we're not going to discuss it here. What is your question?'

'In fact I don't want to ask any questions I just want to explain this point and expose the . . .'

I smiled and broke in:

'Muhammad! However much you explain your point you'll never match what Imam Al-Ghazali said in *The Incoherence of the Philosophers*, and however much I explain my point I'll never be able to match what Ibn Rushd said in *The Incoherence of the Incoherence*. I suggest you read both books.'

Galnar smiled at me and said:

'We now have Munsif from Tunis on the line. Go ahead Munsif.'

'Does philosophy have any influence on our daily lives? I mean, as an ordinary human being I can go to the office, come home to the wife and kids, go to the café, live and die without being aware of philosophy having any role to play in my life.'

Galnar laughed and said:

'Thank you so much, Munsif! That was one of the questions I never dared ask.'

I smiled and said:

'I welcome all the questions. I would say to Munsif that the effect of philosophy on your life is no less than the effect of the air. Just as you're not aware of the air, you're not aware of philosophy. I'll just use the examples you gave me yourself. You say you go to the office. Fine! Instead of that, why don't you go and steal from people? Because you have a moral philosophy which permits going to work but prohibits theft. You say you come home to your wife and children. Why do you go home instead of going to see a lover? Because you have a philosophy which transcends the Epicurean concept of happiness. What about your death and your life? Don't you think they are governed by a specific philosophy derived from religion? What about . . .'

Galnar laughed and said:

'Enough, Doctor! If you carry on you'll have Munsif thinking he's a philosopher without even knowing it. We now have Miss Kawkab from Muscat. Go ahead, Kawkab.'

'I would like to ask Doctor Jamal's advice on an important matter. It's about my son. He's finishing secondary school this year and he's dead set on studying philosophy. What would you advise him, bearing in mind that our financial situation, by the grace of God, puts us in the position of being able to let him specialize in any subject he chooses.'

Galnar said laughing:

'A little philosopher! What does the big philosopher have to say?'

Pleasantly, I said:

'Kawkab! Studying philosophy is not suited to everyone. I'll give you some pointers which might help your son and you find out what is the right decision. The philosophical mind is always asking questions. Your son, for example, what does he see when he looks at a car? Does he ask how it works? What makes it move? When he's sitting in front of the television, does he ask how it can receive the image of someone a long way away? When he's asked to do something, does he ask why he has to do it? If he has such intellectual curiosity, I'd advise you to let him study philosophy.'

Galnar:

'We now have a pleasant surprise. The well-known poet, Ken'an Filfil, who was a guest on the show a few weeks ago. Hi there! How's our great poet?'

'Hi there! And how's the beautiful Galnar? I've missed you.'

Flirtatiously, Galnar said:

'Thank you, my dear friend.'

'I have two questions for your distinguished guest. Firstly, Doctor Jamal, what do you think about the expression "Philosophy is the garbage of the schools?"'

Galnar tried to stop herself laughing as she said:

'That's a very heartless question, Ken'an.'

I said smiling:

'On the contrary! On the contrary! It's an expression which is frequently used, particularly among philosophy students in Europe. My comment on it is the same as that of the British philosopher, Oakshott, who said: "Anyone who has had but a single insight into the breadth and depth of the thought of Plato or Hegel will give up all hope of becoming a philosopher." I think, Ken'an that the person who coined the expression did so only after losing all hope of becoming a philosopher.'

'My other question for your distinguished guest is: is there a relationship between philosophy and madness?'

Galnar began to laugh again sweetly. I too laughed before saying:

'With the exception of Nietzsche, history has no record of a single philosopher who went mad. As for the relationship between poetry and madness, Ken'an will know more about that than I.'

Galnar said:

'One all! We now have Firdaws on the line form Algiers. Go ahead, Firdaws.'

'Could your guest give his views on the philosophy of the great Arab dramatist, Tawfiq Al-Hakim?'

I said:

'The late Tawfiq Al-Hakim, as the caller said, was in fact a pioneer of Arabic drama. However, I don't think that he studied philosophy in any depth and I think it would be false to say that he had a philosophical theory.'

'We now have Sami on the line from Germany. Go ahead Sami.'

'I would like to ask the professor: are there any philosophers in the Arabistani world? And how many?'

Galnar smiled and said:

'I think our guest will say there's only one but he's not going to mention his name.'

I gave Galnar a look of rebuke and said:

'Well, there are many first-rate figures in the Arabistani world. They exist in all fields. In all intellectual fields there are outstanding people, and philosophy is no exception.'

'We now have on the line Doctor Intisar from London. Go ahead, Doctor.'

'Would the Doctor be so kind as to share with us the philosophical principle to which he is committed in his life and which he would encourage others to follow.'

Immediately, I said:

'Plato's moderation. Plato believed that virtue lay midway between two vices. Generosity is a virtue and lies midway between avarice and profligacy. Courage lies midway between cowardice and recklessness. In short, the philosophical principle I seek to follow is the principle which everyone knows: moderation in all things.'

'We now have Huda on the line from Damascus. Go ahead.'

'Would your guest be so kind as to explain to us the difference between Spinoza's understanding of "the Unity of Being" and Ibn Al-Arabi's understanding of "the Unity of Being".'

I reflected for a while before replying:

'Miss Huda is apparently studying philosophy. There are similarities between the two. Both believed that the Creator is manifest in His Creation and not separate from it. Each, in his own way, believed in God, but was attacked on many occasions by the godly. But there are many differences. Spinoza was a product of Judaeo-Christian culture. Ibn Al-Arabi was a product of Islamic culture. Spinoza arrived at his theory by means of mathematical and geometrical questions while Ibn Al-Arabi arrived at his by means of what he termed a "Divine Unveiling". More accurately, Ibn Al-Arabi was a mystic and it's difficult to regard him as a true philosopher.'

'We now have on the line Khalifa from Dubai. Go ahead, Khalifa.'

'I would like to know Doctor Jamal's view of Sartre and Existentialism.'

I bowed my head for a short time and said:

'Sartre, by any standard, was a great philosopher. From the standpoint of my own theory of Eclecticism, I believe that Sartre was right when he said that every person had to determine their own values, ideals and convictions and do so in total freedom. But he was wrong when he said that all the values, ideals and convictions which a person encounters in a given society are, of necessity, chains and shackles which one has to escape from if one wants to be free.'

'Doctor Jamal, I'd love to carry on this most enjoyable intellectual journey but the time is up. Judging by the number of calls which keep coming in, we can be optimistic about the future of philosophy in Arabistan. I'd like to say "Thank you" to our guest and all our viewers. So, till the next time when we'll have another stimulating guest.'

The phone calls didn't stop from the time I got home until I went to bed. Everyone congratulated me on how well the interview had gone. Another stimulating guest?! So, I was a stimulating guest hosted by the most stimulating of beautiful women? This idea alone was sufficient to make me walk on air.

Tuesday

The morning began with a visit from Hajj Boushman Al-Shouiba', who embraced me warmly as if he'd known me for years. He told me how happy he was to have met my son-in-law and I told him the feeling was mutual. I asked him to go and see the registrar the following day to have his name put down on the list of students for the diploma course. Before leaving, the Hajj sidled up to me, his face turning shades of yellow and red. Then he said:

'Dean! Swear you'll accept this simple gift. As God is my witness I'll divorce my three wives if you refuse.'

'There's no need for all that, Hajj. The gift is accepted. Thank you!'

I opened the box to find a gold Rolex encrusted with diamonds. What was I going to do with that? The watch that my late wife gave me as a present a quarter of a century ago was still going strong. I called the registrar in and said:

'Tomorrow a student who is somewhat advanced in years will be coming to see you. He's very keen. I'd like you to enrol him on the diploma course. We'll enrol him and keep him on.'

'As you say, Dean. Anything else?'

'There's a minor problem regarding the date and class of the degree.'

'That's no problem. I'll see to everything.'

The registrar got up to leave but before he'd got to the door I called to him:

'Hassoun Bey! One moment, if I may!'

The registrar returned and stood before me. I took the watch and gave it to him saying:

'A small gift. From our student friend.'

The registrar looked at the gold, diamond-encrusted watch in astonishment and muttered:

'For me? Is this for me?'

'He gave it to me. But I wouldn't wear such a watch. I'm too old for things like that. But you, you're still a young man. I'm happy to give it to you.'

Before I realized what was going on, the registrar had bowed down in a flash and was kissing my hand. One day I would become a Cynic and follow the example of Diogenes eating only stale bread and sleeping only by the side of the road. One day!

Nirmeen told me that Husni Al-Sayed, the husband of my middle daughter, Nahed, was in her office and wanted to see me. I asked her to send him in. He came in with that permanent smile of his:

'Good morning, pops.'

'Good morning Husni. Why this surprise visit?'

'An important client of mine from Arabistan X is here at the moment.'

Husni worked in the frozen meats business and exported all kinds of meat throughout Arabistan. I looked at Husni with circumspection and said:

'He's more than welcome!'

'He wants to meet you.'

'Bachelor of Arts, Diploma or Doctorate?'

Husni laughed saying:

'Have you become a mind-reader, pops?'

'I've been reading minds for a long time. Since the first time I saw you when I read in your thoughts that you wanted to marry Nahed.'

'Should I send him along to meet you?'

'Send him along. I hope he's got a secondary school certificate.'

Husni looked at me in wonder:

'Sure he has, pops.'

'Fine. Ask Nirmeen to arrange an appointment for him for tomorrow.'

As soon as he'd left, Dr Samahri Al-'Arna'ut invaded the office. He said:

'I hear you were on *The Eyes of the World Are Upon You* yesterday. Unfortunately I didn't know and didn't watch it. How did it go?'

This stupid fool who thinks he's so clever! I said:

'Very well, apart from some silly questions from stupid viewers.'

Dr Samahri blushed and quickly changed the subject:

'What do you intend to do with regard to the brutal attack on my person, my honour and my dignity in full view of you and the faculty council members?'

'I don't intend to do anything. It was merely a quarrel. It's over. It's not in our interests to get things out of proportion.'

'Out of the question! Out of the question! Over my dead body! I'm sticking by my rights – all of them, not truncated.'

'Doctor Samahri! If you make a written complaint I will raise it with the university's Central Disciplinary Committee. Then there'll be a wide ranging investigation and, who knows, maybe the committee will apportion most of the blame to you.'

'To me?'

'You physically attacked two colleagues. You impugned the reputation of an upstanding woman colleague in front of witnesses. Were she to go to court, she'd win. The truth of the matter is that I'm doing my best at the moment to persuade her to drop the case.'

'This is totally beyond belief. "The victim smiles, the criminal weeps."'

'The decision is yours. In your place, I'd forget the whole thing.'

'You're right. One shouldn't be over hasty. I'll think about it.'

'Think as much as you like. Then tell me.'

Nirmeen came in with a file containing the agenda for the Senate meeting (God help us! Just look at the number of addenda?!) to be held the following day. This meeting was going to be extremely important as the Senate was to discuss the final plans for the new university buildings. I asked Nirmeen to hold all calls and not to allow anyone in. I spent the rest of the working day studying the file.

At precisely five o'clock, Dalila Wasif was ringing the door bell at my villa. I almost gasped when I saw her. Why hadn't I noticed her before? Aahh! The clothes. Her college clothes were completely different to the ones she was wearing now. A pair of jeans which described everything. A blouse open from the top down which was not content merely to describe but also indicated and signalled. Her black hair surrounding her brown-skinned face like the diamonds surrounding the gold Rolex. I offered her an orange juice. I said:

'You must excuse me. I've been living alone since my wife died. The house is a bit disorganized.'

She smiled and said:

'The house is as wonderful as its owner, Doctor. But there is no house which would not benefit from a woman's touch.'

I cleared my throat and said:

'You were asking me about Al-Farabi and his thought. At the outset, I must make it clear that Al-Farabi took his ideas from Greek philosophy. He took them from Plotinus – Plotinus, not Plato – and he made no changes at all except to give them an Islamic gloss. He believed that the First Intellect was the Necessary Being from which emanated the Second Intellect which necessitates . . .'

I interrupted the lecture when I discovered she was looking at me in a somewhat strange manner. I said:

'Miss Dalal! I don't think you came here to talk to me about Al-Farabi and his thought.'

She laughed and said:

'The truth is, Doctor, I came here to play you a tape.'

In astonishment I said:

'A tape? A tape of a lecture?'

She laughed again – how beautifully this young woman laughed! She said:

'A tape of love poetry. Listen.'

She took a small cassette recorder out of her bag and pressed Play. And then a familiar voice hissed: 'Dalila stop dallying with me. My face and pride have I lost. Look at you! All you do is sneer at me. But now is the time for you with your graceful . . .'

In astonishment I said:

'Samahri?! Doctor Samahri?!'

She laughed and said:

'For weeks he's been calling me every night reciting love poetry like that. Some of it's a lot worse than that.'

Resolutely, I said:

'Thank you for bringing it to me. We can settle this problem in a manner that will preserve your dignity and reputation and which won't cause a scandal or affect the college's reputation. Could I keep the recorder for a while?'

'With pleasure.'

She said she had to go. I went with her to see her out. Before leaving, she turned to me and gave me a deep penetrating look. She whispered:

'Aahh! If only the person on the tape had been some other professor.'

She departed leaving the scent of her perfume behind her and leaving me hanging on to the threads of an impossible desire.

Wednesday

The first visitor was Husni's client, Shuwitr Al-Shater. I listened to the usual lecture about how much he wanted to resume his university studies, which he had been forced to interrupt as a result of the difficult circumstances that had forced him to go into business such that he was now, thanks be to God, comfortably off (i.e. a millionaire). I asked him to go and see the registrar the following day. He left the office after warmly entreating me, though without threatening a divorce, to accept a simple gift, this time a Piaget. I called the registrar in, asked him to do the necessary and gave him the watch. This time I was ready and the registrar didn't manage to kiss my hand. Instead, genuine tears intermingled with his heartfelt invocation to God for Him to bestow His blessings upon me.

'May God protect you, Dean! Now I can get treatment for my daughter. May God protect you in this world and the next!'

Treating a sick daughter was, according to all the schools of philosophy, better than keeping valuable watches one wouldn't wear, which one would, indeed, disdain to wear.

When the registrar had left I called Dr Samahri and asked him to come to my office. He came in all puffed-up unaware of the unpleasant surprise awaiting him. Contrary to custom, I didn't send for a coffee for him. As soon as he sat down I began:

'There's been a request from Al-Mu'tasamiyya University in Arabistan X. They want a professor of Arabic Literature. I don't think they'll find anyone better than you.'

Dr Samahri groaned and said:

'What a paltry offer from a paltry university! This is too good to refuse! I can do nothing but put the offer under my armpit.'

In astonishment, I said:

'Under what?'

'My armpit. Said the poet: "I've seen these petty poets pass daily beneath my armpit."'

I interrupted him:

'If I were in your position, Doctor, I wouldn't put the offer under my armpit.'

'And pray tell me why I should not?'

'I'd like you to listen to this tape.'

Dr Samahri's purple words burst forth from the recorder and his face grew paler and paler. After a few minutes, I stopped the tape and looked at him. He groaned and said:

'What can I say? I say: "The good are ever tested by evil bastards." And this vicious calumny shall I place beneath my foot and I shall take that vile student to court.'

'With regard to the hearing, Doctor Tuffaha has informed me that she is adamant about going to court.'

'That little tart!'

'In my opinion, you should accept the offer. I'll persuade Dalal to forget the harassment. And I'll persuade Dr Tuffaha to close the file.'

In a faint voice, he said:

'What can I say? I say: "More speed, less haste."'

I said smiling:

'Take all the time you want. However, I will now write to the university's chancellor putting your name forward for the post.'

Dr Samahri shrieked:

'What can I say? I say: "Go West young man! You have but yourself to think of!"'

I said:

'Exactly. I'm confident you'll enjoy your stay there. And we'll see you in the near future. A couple of years or so.'

After Dr Samahri left, Nirmeen told me over the telephone:

'There's a student who wants to see you.'

In irritation I said:

'Since when have I been receiving students, Nirmeen?'

'She says she's been recommended by Al-Farabi Bey.'

I smiled and asked Nirmeen to send her in. I couldn't believe that the Dalal standing before me at that moment was the same Dalal I'd seen the night before. The female student before me looked as if she could be the mother of another Dalal. A dress as baggy as a jallaba which revealed nothing. A white shawl wrapped around her neck. A white hijab covering her face. And glasses with thick prescription lenses. In amazement, I asked:

'Is that you?!'

She laughed and said:

'Study clothes!'

I said:

'What's up my child?'

Flirtatiously, she said:

'Please don't use that word, ever.'

'Fine! What's up Dalal?'

'I felt remorse after going home last night. I don't want anything to happen to Doctor Samahri on my account.'

'All he'll get is what he deserves.'

'Nevertheless, I think I was in the wrong when I . . .'

Nirmeen suddenly came in and said:

'Dean! The Senate meeting in half an hour.'

I turned to Dalal and said:

'I'm sorry. I have to go now.'

'When shall I see you again?'

Without thinking, I said:

'Tomorrow. Same time.'

The Senate meeting lasted five hours. At the end, the Senate passed the plans. Before the meeting closed, the Chancellor said:

'I propose a tender adjudication commission be formed made up of the dean of engineering, the dean of law and the dean of the humanities. The dean of engineering to confirm the accuracy of the specifications, the dean of law to supervise the legal aspects and the dean of the humanities to oversee the moral aspects.'

The members laughed and unanimously approved the proposal. The truth was that the chancellor hadn't put me forward for any moral reasons. He had proposed me because I'd been his friend since the first year at college and we had, aside from friendship, many mutual interests.

Before going to sleep, I asked Wahid 'Akaf, the husband of my youngest daughter, Warda, and owner of the Unity Company for Construction Contracts to come the next day, alone, to have lunch with me.

Thursday

I spent the morning at the Hayy Ibn Yaqzan Social Studies Centre. The board of the Centre had formed a committee under the chairmanship of the Centre's director, Dr Najm Al-Nahhar Rushdi, which included academics who were on the board and others who weren't. I was one of them. This was the committee's first meeting. Dr Najm Al-Nahhar began the proceedings:

'Naturally, we cannot do the work ourselves. The subject needs a wide ranging field-study and the input of a number of researchers. But, for the present, we have to work out the broad outlines of the research. I propose that the research be based on the socio-economic and political conditions in Arabistan which have given rise to the phenomenon of fundamentalism without touching on . . .'

I interrupted him and asked:

'Did you say the conditions in Arabistan?'

'Yes.'

'But we have been asked by the board to study fundamentalism and fundamentalism is a world-wide phenomenon. Why are we restricting ourselves to the Arabistani world?'

'Because at present this urgent problem is practically confined to the Arabistani nation.'

'With the greatest respect, Doctor, what you're saying is inaccurate. There's a fundamentalist government in power in India. There's a fundamentalist government in power in Israel. There are fifty million Americans who could be classified as fundamentalist. There are . . .'

Dr Najm Al-Nahhar interrupted me:

'Forgive me Doctor Jamal! If we were to study the fundamentalist phenomenon throughout the whole world we would need decades. We have to have clear priorities. Let us begin with Arabistan and when that research is complete we can begin another, broader study.'

I stuck to my guns. And Dr Jamal stuck to his. The issue was put to a vote and the majority voted with Najm Al-Nahhar. On leaving, I was just about to get into my car when Professor Wajdi Al-Najjar, editor-in-chief of *Tomorrow* came up to me and said:

'Philosopher Pasha. Are you a fool or just trying to act like one?'

In astonishment, I said:

'Yes?!'

He laughed saying:

'Do you expect the CIA, which set up and financed this Centre and which pays its running costs, including our generous emoluments, to finance a study into fundamentalism in America?'

Again I said:

'Yes?!'

Professor Wajdi laughed and went on his way. Why, until that moment, had it never occurred to me to ask myself where the limitless funds the Centre was spending came from?! I am a philosopher and it is illogical for a philosopher to be a fool. I must, therefore, be acting like a fool!

After dining with Wahid, I ushered him into my study and handed him a fat envelope and said:

'Wahid! These are the final specifications for the new building. Invitations to tender will be published in the press in precisely two months. You have a two-month window of opportunity to, if you're intelligent, beat the competition.'

Wahid said:

'I don't know how to . . .'

I interrupted him:

'The chancellor's brother works in the field of electrical contracting . . .'

Wahid interrupted me:

'Understood, pops. Understood.'

Before leaving, Wahid bowed and kissed my hand. What can I say? I say: 'This is hand-kissing week!'

At exactly five o'clock, Dalal arrived – I mean the evening version, not the university version, of Dalal. She wasn't wearing jeans this time. Instead, she was wearing a very short, and very alluring, miniskirt. Her hair she'd imprisoned in a single plait. What had happened to the glasses with the thick lenses? Were they fake? Or did she wear contact lenses in the evening? She was definitely a most unusual young woman. She sat down and looked around her. She said:

'I still think this place needs a woman's touch.'

In embarrassment, I said:

'I'm sorry!'

She said:

'About the tape . . .'

I interrupted:

'I told you not to concern yourself with the tape. What you did was perfectly natural. The man was annoying you, you behaved correctly.'

She laughed and said:

'That's true. But I didn't have to make a tape to stop him in his tracks. I could have done that, very easily, without making a tape. The truth is, Doctor, I had another objective in mind.'

'Another objective?'

'Can I speak frankly?'

'You can speak in complete frankness.'

'Frankly, I was hoping, by means of the tape, to arouse the passions of another. No! No! That wasn't my objective. I was trying to get the attention of another professor.'

'Miss Dalal I don't . . .'

She interrupted me

'Call me Dalal!'

'Dalal! I don't understand what you mean.'

'I wanted to make another professor aware of my existence, a professor who didn't know I existed.'

Parrot-like, I said:

'Another professor?'

'I'd chosen him by the eclectic method, I mean by following the philosophy of eclecticism.'

'Dalal! Please explain!'

'Wasn't it you, Doctor, who taught us that eclecticism is based on methodological principles. In other words, when a philosophical perspective is rejected it is rejected because it is not in accord with the methodology on which that perspective is based. And when a philosophical perspective is accepted then it is accepted because it is in accord with the method which led to that perspective?'

'That is correct.'

'And drawing inferences is a recognized philosophical method?'

'Naturally.'

'I still remember the first example of drawing an inference, and I learnt it from you.'

'From me?'

'Yes. At the time I was a second-year student. The example was: All human beings speak. The Greeks speak. Therefore, the Greeks are human beings.'

'Well done! That is the classic example. You have a good memory.'

'Now, I would like to present you with some of the conclusions I have reached. I hope you will correct any methodological errors if there are any errors in the methodology.'

What dangerous game was this dangerous young woman playing? Cautiously, I said:

'Please go on.'

'I love everyone who is intelligent, witty and who has a strong personality. There is someone intelligent, witty and with a strong personality. Therefore I love that person.'

'Is the method disciplined?'

'Very disciplined.'

'Good! I would like now to take it a step further: I only love people who are intelligent, witty and who have a strong personality. I only see one person who is intelligent, witty and with a strong personality. Therefore, I only love that person.'

'Is the method still disciplined?'

'Still.'

'And that person is you.'

My heart palpitated violently. Since the death of my wife more than ten years before my relationships with women had been confined to Dr Tuffaha, a widow finding solace in a widower, and passing encounters I'm too embarrassed to recall. And now before me was a young woman of breathtaking beauty who had fallen in love with me, fallen in love through my eclectic philosophy. I do not know what happened after her statement: 'There is no longer such a thing as a disciplined methodology.' I found myself kissing her in a way I hadn't kissed for thirty years and embracing her in a way I hadn't embraced anyone for forty years. And I found her reciprocating the kisses and embraces. I heard the sound of the villa door opening then I heard it closing. It did not occur to me as I embraced the appetites of my bygone youth to ask myself why the villa door had opened and why it had closed.

After a period of time I could not measure, Dalal said:

'Jamal! I must be going. It's nearly midnight.'

Without my realizing the words fell from my mouth:

'Dalal! Will you marry me?'

Her reaction was far more violent than anything that had gone before.

Friday

Today was the annual outing for the College's faculty members. We had decided, at the invitation of Dr Tuffaha, to go to that region of the desert where her latest dig was going on. Tuffaha began to take us round from one site to another as she explained:

'This is a child's grave. And this is an old house. And these remains indicate that the surrounding area was a place of worship. And that statue . . .'

I was listening but my thoughts were far, far away. After a while, I found myself walking with Tuffaha who was carrying in her right hand an axe which she was using on the dig. Suddenly, I realized that the door that had been opened and closed the night before could only have been opened and closed by Tuffaha, who was the only other person to have a key to the villa. As the thought came to me, the shudder down my spine was interrupted by Tuffaha saying:

'On the occasion of the new love in your life, I deem it my duty to present you with an appropriate gift.'

With difficulty I said:

'What new love? I mean what gift? I mean what occasion? I mean . . .'

Tuffaha laughed and said:

'Please accept my humble gift. This axe.'

With astonishing speed the axe rose and crashed down onto my head. I fell to the ground watching the blood oozing out onto my shirt.

Behind me I could hear Dr Samahri:

'What do I say? I say: "Look at what has become of our haughty rat; flat on his face, finished."'

And I heard Dr Muhriz saying:

'Precisely!'

And I heard Tuffaha laughing again. Then I heard nothing.

THREE

The Journalist

With iniquity so prevalent in the minds of men
Should an honest man you find
His own undoing shall his virtue be
Al-Mutanabbi

Identity Card	
Full Name:	Mass'oud Sa'ada Nur As'ad
Known as:	Mass'oud As'ad
Occupation:	Journalist. Proprietor and Editor-in-Chief of the *Voice of Truth*
Age:	51
Wealth:	$21 million (at least)
Place of Birth:	Arabistan X
Place of Work:	London
Academic Qualifications:	Secondary School Diploma
Marital Status:	Divorced
Children:	None

Monday

At ten o'clock, as I did every morning, I entered my office at the *Voice of Truth* and, as I did every morning, opened the window overlooking the Edgware Road and watched the Arabistani microcosm oscillating below. I picked up the phone and Kathy answered:

'Good morning.'

'Good morning Kathy. What's on the agenda today?'

'A bit more crowded than usual.'

'The migration season. When's "the officer" due?'

'In half an hour.'

'Fine. Send him in as soon as he gets here.'

I picked up the phone, and as I did before every meeting, asked Johnny to come in. Johnny entered and I said:

'Johnny! You're sure everything's working?'

'Everything' meant the recording equipment and cameras hidden, carefully, all over the spacious office. After a quick check Johnny said on leaving the office:

'Everything's fine.'

Kathy came in with a pile of British newspapers and a pile of Arabistani newspapers. I gave the British papers a quick glance and the Arabistani papers a quick glance. I stopped when I came to one of them: *Liberty* – my most serious competitor in London. And how many there are! When I founded the *Voice of Truth* sixteen years ago, it was the first publication in what subsequently became known as the expatriate press. Now, there was a new paper appearing every day. Every government had its newspaper. Every opposition had its newspaper. Every businessman had his newspaper. But the real competition came from only one source: *Liberty*. Among all the expatriate journalists, I had only one competitor, the proprietor of *Liberty*, 'Adnan Shahwan. That man copied everything I did. He copied my style, my headlines and the way my paper was produced. All that was left was for him to copy the way I walked. He claimed that *Liberty* outsold the *Voice of Truth*. The filthy liar! His usual lies filled his yellow rag, as usual. I smiled as I looked for the story which he would have made up about me and hidden away somewhere in the paper. We had been playing this game for six months. Every issue of the *Voice of Truth* had a story made up about him. And every issue of *Liberty* had a story made up about me. I don't think anybody apart from him and me knew what was going on. Here was today's story, among the adverts for shawarma restaurants. I laughed as I read: 'Another Wealthy Arabistani robbed. According to our legal correspondent (legal correspondent! What a joke!) St John's Wood police are looking for a con man who snatched a wealthy Arabistani's attaché case containing £50,000. Police sources say the thief is of Middle Eastern appearance, in his late forties, bald and with a scar on his forehead . . .' I couldn't stop myself laughing as I read such an accurate description of myself. An appropriate response would have to be published in tomorrow's the *Voice of Truth*. What would I turn him into this time. A drug smuggler? Paedophile? The telephone interrupted my thoughts:

'Mr As'ad .The officer has arrived.'

I smiled. When I first began sleeping with Kathy she had started calling me Mass'oud, even in front of other people. It took some time before she understood that a relationship based on the pillow had nothing to do with relationships based on the office. At the office I was Mr As'ad. In bed, I could become Mass'oud. I said:

'Send him in Kathy.'

I embraced the young officer as I repeated:

'Hello! How nice to see you! I've been expecting you for some time.'

'Thank you! Thank you! The honour is mine!. I've heard so much about you. You have no idea how proud we are of you and the *Voice of Truth*.'

In dealing with such people we shouldn't expect too much. With mock humility I said:

'We, my brother, are at the service of the cause, from the Atlantic to the Gulf.

Arabism is our language, Arabism is our path, Arabism is our destiny. All our efforts are part of our pan-Arab obligation. Our mutual friend tells me you have some interesting documents.'

'Very important. I think the *Voice of Truth* is the ideal place to publish them.'

'We never hesitate to publish anything which serves the cause. Even if we have to die for it.'

In fact it had almost killed us on more than one occasion. I felt the scar on my forehead. The young officer said:

'We expect nothing less from you.'

'Can you tell me something about the documents. What are they exactly?'

'Documents which show that the chief of staff of Arabistan X has purchased armaments which don't work.'

All my journalistic instincts were aroused. This could be the scoop of a lifetime. But one had to proceed cautiously. I said:

'Weapons which don't work?! You're joking? There haven't been any weapons which don't work since the days of King Farouq. And, to be historically accurate, even then there weren't any weapons which didn't work.'

'But the armaments I'm talking about are completely useless, Mr Mass'oud.'

'What do you mean?'

'Three hundred completely wrecked tanks. Left behind after the war in Afghanistan. The chief of staff has paid a billion dollars for this heap of scrap iron.'

I whistled as I said:

'A billion dollars?! A billion?! Are you sure?'

The officer opened his attaché case and pulled out a collection of documents. He handed them to me saying:

'Here you are! These are pictures of the tanks. See for yourself! Can these tanks even move let alone fight. Look! This is the contract signed by the chief of staff with the Fayet company. Look! This document proves that Fayet is just a company on paper registered in Panama and owned by Mrs Mafatin. You know who Mrs Mafatin is?'

'The wife of the new chief of staff.'

'Exactly.'

The officer handed me more papers saying:

'This document proves . . .'

I interrupted:

'I don't need any more. That's enough.'

'Enough to scupper the deal?'

'Definitely.'

'And to bring down the chief of staff?'

'Without a shadow of doubt.'

I didn't know what this zealous officer was after. Life has taught me that nobody does anything for nothing. There are no exceptions. It doesn't have to be money, though in the vast majority of cases it is. I said cautiously:

'What about expenses?'

I had given him the bait. Would he take it? The officer's face reddened and said:

'Expenses? What expenses? What are you getting at?'

Ok! Ok! Our young friend doesn't want money. I might find out what he really wants one day. Then again, I might not. Revenge against the chief of staff? Revenge against Mafatin? Nobody does anything for nothing. If the officer didn't want money, that was his business.

I said:

'I mean the expenses which you have incurred in obtaining these documents. Photocopying. Lawyers' fees. Travel expenses.'

He immediately replied:

'There are no expenses. The incidentals will be looked after by the brothers.'

The brothers? Who are these brothers? It would not be prudent to ask; and I don't need to know. The brothers will have their goals which I will know about in the future, or then again I might not. I stood up to shake hands with the officer and said:

'I don't know how to thank you.'

'The only gratitude I expect is the publication of the documents. When will you publish them?'

'As soon as possible! As soon as possible!'

The officer left and I asked Kathy:

'Who's next?'

'Barbara.'

'When's she coming?'

'Any minute now.'

I began to develop the story that would appear in tomorrow's the *Voice of Truth* about my arch-friend: 'Serious attack on Arabistani national: According to our police correspondent (police coresspondent, that's a joke!), an Arabistani national suffered grievous bodily harm after leaving a Soho bar in an extremely drunken state. According to our correspondent, the victim was fair-skinned with a small pointed beard. On his cheek . . .' The telephone rang and Kathy said that Barbara had arrived. I asked her to send her straight in.

I stood up to kiss the beautiful visitor who had once been my lover. How times change! I loved her once. And she loved me. Everything in this life comes to an end. Everything! She was now our gossip 'correspondent' demanding payment for every story that could be used. She sat in front of me and smiled. I said:

'Barbie! What have you got!'
'Last week was disappointing.'
'What do you mean?'
'The usual stuff. Rubbish!'
'Isn't there just one well-known name?'
'No.'
'Not even one millionaire?'
'No.'
'So, you won't be expecting anything from me today?'
'On the contrary. I'm expecting a lot.'
'What do you mean?'
'Tonight I've got a date with someone you're really interested in.'
'Who's that?'
'General Jacobi.'

As soon as she uttered the name I realized another scoop was there waiting for me. Jacobi was in fact no general, though that's what he liked to be called. Jacobi was a rich Jew who held a number of nationalities, including Israeli. Among his many services for Israel the most important was making unofficial contacts with Arabistani governments who want to make contact with Israel but want such contacts to remain secret.

Immediately I said:
'A thousand pounds.'
'Not enough.'
'Ok! Five thousand pounds.'
'What do you want to know?'
'The most recent contacts between the Arabistanis and Israel.'
'I'll do my best.'
'Pass by accounts and take the money.'
'In cash.'
'Naturally.'

She had only just left when I told Kathy:
'I don't want to see anybody now.'
'But there's . . .'
I interrupted her:
'Didn't you hear what I said? I said I don't want to see anybody now.'
'Ok! Ok! Ok!'
'Ask the editor to see me straight away.'

Nasif Ghawazi, the editor, came into the office preceded by clouds of smoke emanating from his luxury Cuban cigar. Every Arabistani embassy in London, almost, showers Nasif with boxes of luxury cigars. He sat in front of me, muttering:

'Morning, boss.'

'Hello Nasif. I've got an assignment for you which needs a little bit of diplomacy.'

'Shoot!'

'I want you to write three articles about Afghanistan's exports.'

'Afghanistan? You must be joking! Afghanistan doesn't export anything except Afghan Arabistanis.'

'Things are changing, Nasif. Afghanistan has become an exporting country.'

'Exporting what?'

'Almost everything.'

'What for example?'

'For the moment, you don't need to know the kind of exports. What is important is that you write three articles about Afghanistan's exports. I want the first one to be headlined "Afghanistan in the Exporters' Club".'

'But what am I going to say?'

'Nasif! Just say that Afghanistan has become a member of the exporters' club and that the rest will be in the next part.'

'And what am I going to say in the next part?'

'I'll tell you tomorrow.'

I felt suddenly cheerful after he'd gone. Today should be celebrated. I asked Kathy:

'What's the time?'

'One o'clock.'

'What about lunch?'

'Great idea.'

'Why don't you and I take the rest of the day off?'

'Even better idea. My place or yours.'

'A hotel.'

'Why a hotel?'

'Variety is the spice of life. Wait for me in the car.'

When I left the office I found Kathy at the wheel of the Rolls Royce. Kathy's numerous duties included acting as chauffeur.

'Where are we going to eat,' she asked.

'At the Star of India.'

'Are you in an Indian mood today?'

'I'm in an Afghan mood.'

'What do you mean.'

'Shush! Drive to the restaurant.'

Tuesday

I entered my office, as usual, at ten o'clock. As usual, I opened the window. As usual I began to skim through the papers. *Liberty*! Where was the fake story? I found it among the obituaries. I smiled as I read: 'Mysterious Disappearance: Arabistani media circles in London are perplexed about the fate of a journalist – notorious for his suspicious contacts – who disappeared suddenly last week. There are rumours that the journalist died during . . .' I threw the paper aside muttering 'You won't get me!' I turned to the *Voice of Truth*. There, dominating the front page, was the wonderful headline: 'Afghanistan in the Exporters' Club'. I laughed as I followed what had been penned by the quill of Nasif Ghawazi: 'Perhaps no one would believe that Afghanistan, that ill-fated country which has been so wounded and torn apart, is now an effective player on the world stage. Slow down, dear reader! One step at a time! Afghanistan hasn't got the Islamic bomb. Nor does Afghanistan have the clout to strike terror in its neighbours. You are perplexed, dear reader. And you have every right to be. How has Afghanistan managed to enter the world's battlefield so effectively and influentially. The answer is simple – exports. Exports! So what is Afghanistan exporting? That's the question! Carpets? That's old hat. Hashish! That's old hat. I am giving you the opportunity to enjoy your guesswork but I promise I'll give you the answer in the next part.'

I picked up the phone and said to Nasif:

'Brilliant! Brilliant! You've excelled yourself.'

'Thank you, teacher.'

'A first-rate instalment.'

'Thanks! And what about tomorrow's?'

'Let's have more about "thanks" and words which rhyme with it.'

'I'm not with you.'

'Things which rhyme with 'thanks'. But drop your aitches!'

'You mean "Tanks"?'

'Got it! Well done! I want an article about Afghan "thanks" with their aitches dropped.'

I put the phone down and asked Kathy:

'Who's our first visitor today?'

'The blind man.'

'Aahh! The blind man! Is he here?'

'He's with me now.'

'Send him in in ten minutes.'

The blind man was a man of acute vision and insight and one of the best correspondents to work with me. His insight had led him many years ago to go blind as an effective way of earning a living in a London teeming with rich Arabistanis who take pity on the disabled. He would put on a very thick pair of dark glasses and, as a precaution, lest his dark glasses fell off, would put drops in his eyes which turned them a dreadful blue. He had begun by copying everything blind people did until he'd got it down to a fine art. He had become better at being blind than the blind themselves. Kind-hearted souls felt sorry for him. Many doors were open to him. Aside from his blindness, the blind man had numerous talents: he could sing, play several musical instruments, tell jokes, write poetry and, when necessary, dance. Some people would do everything in front of him certain in the knowledge of his blindness and his reputation for discretion. He had only one failing – an insatiable greed.

The blind man entered, his white stick before him. He teetered from side to side. Sometimes I thought he had forgotten he could actually see, as I did when I got up to help him find his way. I sat him down on the seat in front of me and said:

'So, lets have it then!'

'No, you give me first!'

'You know the rules, my insightful friend. Cash on delivery.'

'The consul of Arabistan X'

'What about him?'

'He was at Madame Najma's party.'

'What did he do?'

'The usual.'

'Did he hit anyone?'

'He hit the singer.'

'He didn't do anything else?'

'Isn't hitting the singer enough?'

'No, it isn't. This consul hits a singer everyday. And a singer hits him every night. This story's not worth printing. We've mentioned the consul's battles more than fifty times. Haven't you got any other gossip?'

'The ambassador.'

'Which one?'

'Arabistan X'

'What about him?'

'He was at a riotous party thrown by Madam Inas.'

'What did he do?'

'He suddenly disappeared.'

'Where to?'

'Do you really need to ask?'

'Who with?'

'The sister of the Janissaries' ambassador.'

'Are you certain?'

'How can I be certain when I'm blind?'

'True! Did the disappearance last long?'

'Over an hour.'

'And they came back together?'

'They came back together.'

'What about her brother?'

'He was busy chatting up Madame Inas.'

'Thank you. Pass by accounts ...'

'A thousand?'

'Two hundred!'

'Five hundred?'

'Four hundred!'

'Ok! Ok! You have no compassion in your heart for the disabled.'

The blind man stood up and teetered towards the door. He tapped every piece of furniture he encountered on his way with his stick as if to test its quality. I began to write a paragraph for the 'Society News' column. The title was 'The Glass and the Goblet: The Diplomacy of Intimacy'. I went on: 'Our society correspondent (there's a joke!) informs us that relations between Arabistan X and the Janissaries are seeing a tangible improvement after the tensions of recent years. Our correspondent adds that observers attribute this surprise mellowing (And how sweet that mellowing was!) to the active and flexible diplomacy pursued by Arabistan X. Such a diplomacy realizes there's no point in wasting valuable time on useless correspondence, and conferences that are a complete waste of time, and has decided to take the initiative in adopting a new approach, which could be called 'Open Arms Diplomacy'. This diplomacy rests on a new principle, namely that the best way to turn an enemy into a friend is to start by embracing him. Our correspondent has promised further details on this issue'.

As soon as I'd finished the story about the ambassador, I began to develop the story about my arch enemy: 'Body found in Thames. According to our police correspondent (police correspondent! What a joke!), a bloated body surfaced yesterday in the Thames. The correspondent added that Westminster police said that the drowned man had Middle Eastern features and was in his late forties. The drowning was the result of an as yet unsolved crime.' The telephone rang and Kathy said:

'Barbara's on the line.'

'Put her on.'

Barbara's slightly inebriated voice came on the line.

'Good morning, my love.'

'Get to the point.'

'Ok! Ok! Don't bite my head off! I'm still in his apartment. He's still asleep.'

'When will I see you?'

'He's asked me to spend the rest of the day with him. I'll try and see you tomorrow.'

I ended the call and asked Kathy:

'Who am I having lunch with today?'

'Mike Pynchon. A journalist on the *Monitor*.'

'I'm perfectly aware about which paper Mike works on.'

'Ok! Ok! Don't bite my head off.'

What's all this about 'biting' today? I asked her:

'Where?'

'At Harry's Bar.'

'When?'

'Now!'

Harry's Bar! This gluttonous dipsomaniac journalist. Every week lunch and two bottles of wine. He chose only the most expensive restaurants and the best wines. Most of the time any story I got out of him wasn't even worth a penny. But on rare occasions he would come up with a story which justified these huge weekly investments. I found him at the table beginning to slurp the expensive wine which I was going to pay for.

'Hi! Mike.'

'Hi! Mass'oud.'

The waiter came over. I knew what he would order: caviar! Every meal began with caviar, to be followed by lasagne! The bastard! Caviar and lasagne! The bill would be three hundred pounds at least.

'What's the news, Mike?'

Mike began to drink, eat and prattle on. The usual scandals. Next Saturday his paper was publishing the scandal about an MP sleeping with his driver. Where was the news in that? Everyone in this town was sleeping with everyone else. Men with women. Men with men. Women with women. Now, if it had been one of our rich Arabistani brethren, it would have been a different story. There was also the whisper of a scandal which hadn't yet been verified about a minister who had two illegitimate daughters. Where was the news in that? A third of all births here are illegitimate. No one gets embarrassed. But, if it had been one of our rich Arabistani brethren, that would have been something. It was my turn. I gave him the usual snippets of information. He got to his feet, drunk and well fed. And I stayed to pay the bill.

I decided to spend the rest of the working day in the Operations Room. The Operations Room occupied the whole fourth floor of my house which was hidden behind a dense thicket of trees in Hampstead. The Operations Room was the code name for where all the phone tapping was carried out. In the room there was a scanner for monitoring mobile phones. I bought this equipment in broad daylight from a shop in London. I bought it on the condition I wouldn't use it. These Brits are crazy! Buying bugging equipment is legal, but using it is against the law. I am British by naturalization, but I still can't understand these people. Is there any other country in the world which lets you buy a piece of equipment but won't let you use it? Equipment for bugging ordinary phones is a different matter. I had to smuggle it in from Japan and Taiwan. Using this equipment is an imprisonable offence, if you're caught. The equipment only works with a small transmitter planted within range of the signals given out by the telephone itself. Planting such a device is also a crime. And the amount the person planting the device demands, a telephone company employee, is also a crime. But the results justified the dangers. And the money. Long hours of pleasure and entertainment. The news comes without preliminaries, particularly these days with London jam-packed with Arabistani visitors.

I began to monitor the mobiles. After a minute I came across a conversation between a young Arabistani man and a young Arabistani girl. The privations bottled up over the year explode in the London summer.

The young man said:

'When did you get to sleep last night?'

The young girl replied:

'After three.'

'Were you thinking of me?'

'Of course.'

'Swear!'

'I swear!'

'Who were you with?'

'With Sana and Rasha.'

'Where?'

'At Raja's'

'Did you dance?'

'Sure.'

'What about today? Where shall I see you?'

'At the usual place. In Hyde Park.'

'No! No! I can't go there today.'

'Why not?'

'My mother said she's going for a walk there.'

'Your mother?! Since when has your mother been going to Hyde Park?'

'The doctor told her to take a walk there.'

'So, the Café Rouge then?'

'Ok!'

I shook my head at life's contradictions. In his home country, this young man would be the very model of moral rectitude and in the city she came from the girl would be the perfect example of virtue. But in London? The mind boggles. Hasn't life taught me over these long years that it is a complex of contradictions? Is there any man who is not in conflict with himself? I've never seen such a man.

Can anything exist which is not in conflict with itself. I've never seen such a thing. But what's philosophy got to do with it?.

I moved over to the equipment for bugging ordinary phones. I turned the indicator to the phone of that well-known wealthy Arabistani, Khayr Barakat. The British press puts his wealth at a billion pounds. I know it's a lot more than that. God bless this equipment! His usual voice came on the line as did the usual voice of his lover. The same old conversation. A strange thing is love. Strange too are lovers. A teenage girl and a middle-aged millionaire are equal in the face of love. The same expressions, practically to the letter: When did you get to sleep? When did you get up? What did you have to eat? Have you been thinking about me? Do you remember our last meeting? I love you! I'm head over heels about you! I'm dying for you! When shall I see you? My wife has begun to suspect. Life's hell. My husband has started to notice. I wish he'd go blind. At the usual place? No! No! I can't today. It's the time of the month. Those terrible pains which you know so well. I just want to see you. We don't have to do anything. And who'll be able to control themselves? Thanks for the roses. They'll remind you of the blood in my heart, or the time of the month. Sorry! A very stupid joke! What about when the summer's over? Don't talk about being apart now! My life has no meaning without you. How can I forget you? Everyone forgets.

The same words for young and old, the conquerors and the conquered, the owners and the owned, the car owner and the chauffeur. Love transforms them into a stereotype. Cloning began long before that famous sheep.

You were the only beautiful one there. All the girls were flirting with you. I got jealous. I tried to hide my feelings. I had to go. The singer was smiling at you. He was smiling at everybody. He was only smiling at you. I didn't notice. And you smiled at him. Don't be silly! You're jealous of a singer! I'm jealous of everybody. 'I'm Jealous of the South Wind.' Who's this south wind? A young Nabati poetess. The chairman of the board asked me about you. I saw the lust in his eyes. I don't believe you're mine alone. I'm jealous of myself for having you so isn't it any wonder others are jealous of me?! Your manhood has wrapped me in chains. You are the embodiment of tenderness. You are softer than ostrich feathers. I mean a pillow made of ostrich feathers. I bet you've never even seen an ostrich? Sure I have. I used to tend ostriches when I was a child. And I used to tend lions. Money? Who's interested in money? One day I'll be free just for you alone. When you divorce your wife? Don't talk about my wife. Your conscience hurting you? Don't talk about her. And that's that! And tonight? Pizza Hut. No! No! A silly film. Aren't you bored with pizzas? And afterwards? After that we'll see what happens. What about the Gavroche? And afterwards Annabelle's. I saw Princess Diana there. In Annabelle's? Several times. Swear it! I swear! Who with? With me. Ha! Ha! Ha! She was dancing. Who with? With a man, naturally. Who was he? I don't know. The same man each time? No! Each time a different man. Let's stop talking about Diana for now. We're dining on the terrace. Do you prefer The Ritz? Ok! I think about you all the time. The dress was fantastic. Wasn't it more low-cut than it should have been? You know how jealous I get. Have you heard Amr Diyab's new CD? It's fantastic. Are you going to the party?

The usual repetitive conversations. I went into the bedroom worn out by the burden of all these enflamed feelings. I lay on the bed, picked up the phone and dialled. On the line came the voice that owns me:

'Hello!'

'When did you get to sleep yesterday?'

'After three.'

'Did you think about me?'

Wednesday

I entered my office on time, as usual, opened the window, as usual, and Kathy came in, as usual, with the papers. I began to read the *Voice of Truth*. I smiled as I read the headline: 'Afghan Exports: Thanks' My smile turned to laughter as I read on: 'No sooner had we published our story yesterday about Afghanistan's entry into the exporters club than words of thanks have been heard all over the place particularly in political, media and commercial circles. The thanks have been deafening. Especially those thanks expressed in Ireland. The reason 'why'? You'll have to wait for tomorrow's edition when the whole story will be revealed'.

I picked up the phone and told the editor:

'Well done! Well done!'

'At your service, boss! What about tomorrow's instalment?'

'There's not going to be one.'

'What do you mean?'

'Two instalments are enough. We've got what we wanted.'

'Which was?'

'Well, everybody's "thankful".'

'I'm sorry, I'm not with you.'

I put the phone down laughing. I picked up *Liberty* and began to look for the usual story. I found it on the economics page under the title: 'Arabistani Media Group in London on Verge of Bankruptcy'. I smiled as I read on: 'According to our economics editor (their economics editor! What a joke!), a London-based Arabistani media group is about to go into liquidation. Economic analysts attribute this to the total chaos and . . .'. The bastard! 'Total chaos'?! The telephone rang and Kathy's voice came on the line:

'There's someone who wants to talk to you.'

'Who is it?'

'He won't give his name.'

So, the reaction had come sooner than I had expected. I said to Kathy:
'Fine! Put him on.'

There was a thick Arabistani accent.

'Mr Mass'oud?'

'Your word is my command. Who am I speaking to.'

'I want to see you alone.'

'Your name?'

'I'll tell you when we meet.'

'Why do you want to meet me?'

'I've got an important message.'

'Who from?'

'I'll tell you when I see you.'

'What's it about?'

'Life or death.'

'God help us! Why don't you do me the honour of coming to my office?'

'No. I want us to meet away from your office.'

So, he's definitely an intelligence officer. He knows about everything in the office. Now he'll choose a pub a long way away frequented by old Brits.

'And where do you want us to meet?'

He did not disappoint me. The thick accent said:

'There's a small pub. In Wimbledon. The Red Lion. It's on . . .'

'I know where it is,' I interrupted.

An hour later I was in The Red Lion which was full of old Brits. I didn't have to look for long among the faces to recognize my unknown interlocutor. You can spot Arabistani intelligence officers a mile away. I went straight up to him and sat down beside him. He was drinking a Guinness. Without a preamble he asked:

'What are you drinking?'

'I'll have the same.'

He went over to a once beautiful, well-upholstered woman standing behind the crowded bar and returned with two glasses. He put one in front of me and the other in front of his still half-empty glass. Then he said:

'Your obedient servant, Ramzi Muhsin.'

'Your obedient servant, Rameses the Second! Pleased to meet you!'

'I have a short message for you.'

'Brevity is the soul of wit.'

'It's about Afghan exports.'

'Are you buying or selling?'

'I'm neither buying nor selling. I want to give you a message.'

'Go ahead!'

'Have a drink first!'
'See, I'm drinking. Who's the message from?'
'It doesn't matter where it comes from.'
'Fine. What does it say?'
'Don't publish a single word about the subject as of today.'
'What subject?'
'Afghan exports.'
'Why not?'
'The message doesn't give reasons.'
'And if I refuse?'
'The person who sent me doesn't expect you to refuse his request.'
'And on what grounds does he base this expectation?'
'I don't know. Perhaps he knows you.'
'You haven't told me yet who he is.'
'And I'm not going to.'
'Is that the end of the message?'
'Yes.'
'Can I go now?'
'When you've finished your glass.'
'I've had enough.'
'Take this with you before you go.'

I didn't need to open the small envelope. The usual bullet! The usual code. If you write about the subject again, we'll kill you. I felt my scar. Nothing changes in this world. Still the same old messages. The same threats. All that has changed is the size of the bullet. I returned to the office. I put the bullet in a small drawer with the others.

On my desk I found a gift-wrapped package. I opened it and found two boxes inside. In the one, a man's watch; in the other a lady's. Each was encrusted with diamonds. When will these people learn that sending me cash would save me and them a lot of time and money? Now I'll have to sell the watches, at half price, to that damned Jew.

I picked up the phone and dialled:
'Mr Ambassador?! I don't know how to thank you.'
'Don't mention it, Mr Mass'oud. Don't mention it.'
'What a lovely surprise. My wife and I are flabbergasted. We don't know how to express our appreciation to you.'
'It's nothing! It's nothing! You are aware that all of us, us Arabs, feel pride because of you, your efforts and your struggle for the cause.'
'Arabism is our language, Arabism is our path, Arabism is our destiny.'
'May God bless you!'
'Thank you again, Mr Ambassador.'

I looked at the two watches. Roughly £50,000 as against the £400 for the blind man. Not a bad deal.

Kathy's voice came on the phone:

'Barbara's here.'

'Send her straight in.'

Barbara entered. The usual kiss. I said:

'What have you got, Barbie?'

'Loads! Loads!'

'I'm all ears.'

'What about my bonus?'

'Don't worry. You won't go short. What have you got?'

'The man said a lot. After getting completely drunk.'

'I'm not interested in him being drunk or his drunken ramblings. The contacts?'

'The bonus?'

'I told you not to worry.'

'There was a very important contact yesterday. And I was there.'

'You?!'

'Me!'

'How?'

'He must've forgotten I was in the bedroom.'

'Tell me!'

'A special representative came from Arabistan X and talked with Jacobi for a long time.'

'How do you know where he came from.'

'They were talking loudly.'

'What's the representative's name?'

'Najib or Mujib.'

"Ajib?'

'Yes! Yes! That's it! 'Ajib!'

"Ajib Barkas?'

'I didn't hear his last name.'

'Barbie! I don't know how to thank you.'

'I think you know very well.'

Without thinking I took out the lady's diamond watch and handed it to Barbara who gasped:

'Is that for me?'

'Yes, for you.'

'But . . .'

'I'm having an attack of generosity. Take the watch before it wears off.'

'But this is an expensive watch. It can't be worth less than . . .'

'Less than £30,000. Take it before I change my mind.'

Barbara gave me a warmer kiss than usual and put the watch in her handbag as she cautiously backed out of the room as if she thought I would suddenly get up and take it back.

The telephone rang. Kathy said:

'Sami's here.'

'Send him in.'

Sami Nasri, the owner of The Gaiety restaurant, or more accurately, my partner in The Gaiety, or more accurately the manager, on my behalf, of *The Gaiety*, came in. It was me who had given Sami the money he needed to open the restaurant. It was me who made Sami a full partner in his property without him having to pay a thing. Over the years *The Gaiety* had become the most famous Arabistani restaurant in London. The cellar had been converted into a night club which opened its doors at midnight. It was a gold mine. Sami kept all the takings while giving me only the news. It was an investment which benefited both parties. But Sami did not know the real value of the stories he brought me because he never saw them printed in the *Voice of Truth*. Sami, like everyone else, did not realize that the most important news is the news which isn't published.

'Spill the beans, Sami!'

'The editor of *Arabism*.'

'What about him?'

'He came two nights ago with the press attaché from the embassy of Arabistan X.'

'Are you sure?'

'You bet I am.'

'But he attacks Arabistan X everyday.'

'He won't be attacking it as of next week.'

'What's the deal?'

'Mass'oud, how am I supposed to know that. I just caught a word here and there.'

'But from these couple of words you've worked out that *Arabism* won't be attacking Arabistan X from now on?'

'As of next week.'

'Well done! Have you got any other news?'

'The military attaché.'

'Our friend?'

'Our friend!'

'What's he been doing?'

'He hit his girlfriend. A famous singer.'

'Nahawand?'

'The very same.'

'Why?'

'Because she got drunk and got on the table and danced.'

'In the night club?'

'In the restaurant.'

'Any other news?'

'Shukri Yasser. The billionaire.'

'What about him?'

'He came with a new woman.'

'Do you know who she is?'

'Sure.'

'Who is she?'

'Lola. The wife of Raf'i Rif'at.'

'Are you certain?'

'Sure I am! He was kissing her.'

'In front of everyone?'

'In front of me. The restaurant was half-empty.'

'Have you got any more?'

'Isn't that enough?'

'It'll do for the time being. I'll see you next week.'

I picked up the phone and asked for the deputy editor, Younus Abu Shakhtoura, to come to my office. He came in a few moments later preceded by clouds of smoke from a luxury Cuban cigar. Every Arabistani press attaché in London showers Younus with boxes of Havana cigars. I said:

'Sit down, Younus. You've got three assignments to do. Assignments which are somewhat delicate.'

'I'm your pupil, boss.'

'I want you to meet the press attaché from the embassy of Arabistan X. Meet him away from the embassy.'

'Understood.'

'Away from the embassy.'

'Understood.'

'Tell him that the editor of *Arabism* has contacted me and offered me £200,000 to attack Arabistan X. Tell him I've turned down the offer. Don't say anything else.'

'And the second assignment?'

'Nahawand'

'The singer?'

'Yes. Talk to her and invite her to dinner at your place next week. Tell her I'll be there.'

'And if she refuses?'

'If she refuses, ask her if she'd rather meet me at The Gaiety restaurant.'
'Understood. And the third?'
'This one's the hardest.'
'I'm your man.'
'You're a man for all seasons. You know Raf'i Rif'at?'
'The billionaire? Sure! Who doesn't?'
'I want you to arrange for me to meet him.'
'But not at his home?'
'Naturally.'
'Where?'
'At The Red Lion.'
'I'm sorry?'
'It's a small pub in Wimbledon.'
'When?'
'Get him to choose a time.'
Younus went off on his difficult assignments. Kathy came in in a fluster yelling:
'Mister As'ad !Mister As'ad!'
'Calm down! What's happened?'
'This creature is getting on my nerves.'
'Which creature?'
'The officer you met on Monday.'
'How's he getting on your nerves?'
'He's phoned ten times.'
'What does he want?'
'He wants to have a meeting with you.'
'Tell him I'm very busy.'
'I've told him, but he won't take no for an answer. He says he'll be forced to barge his way in if . . .'
'There'll be no need for that. If he calls again . . .'
'You can bet on that.'
'Fine! If he calls again, tell him to come tomorrow.'
'What time?'
'Eleven. I'll be off now. It's been quite an exhausting day. I'll see you tomorrow.'

Thursday
As usual, I entered my office at the usual time. As usual, I opened the window and began to read, as usual, the papers. *Liberty*! Where's that story? There it was, on the international news page: 'Interpol Seek International Fraudster'. I began to read: 'According to our police correspondent (what a joke!), Interpol are on

a state of full alert after an international fraudster managed to cheat more than £200 million from his innocent victims. Our correspondent says that the fraudster, who goes by a number of aliases and travels on a variety of passports, has a scar on his forehead . . .' Two hundred million pounds! If only it were true! I would be writing a counter-story later. For the moment I had more important things to do.

I began to write. With every line my smile grew wider as I wrote: 'The Wonders of Diplomacy. Diplomacy is a strange and wondrous thing. I repeat: a strange and wondrous thing. Particularly the diplomacy of that hypocritical country which curses the Hebrew state by day, yet sleeps with it by night. I repeat, sleeps with it by night. A country which vilifies it in public, yet lies down beside it in secret. In public, an embargo; in private, an embrace. Are we not entitled to call such a diplomacy: 'a Diplomacy of Wonders'? Can we not . . .?' I wrote a whole page which was full of astonishment and amazement; wonders and marvels. I then began to develop the story about my arch-friend: I had him caught red-handed stealing a pair of shoes from London's Central Mosque. The dirty bastard! Stealing shoes from mosques!

Kathy's voice came on the phone:

'Younus is here. He wants to see you right away.'

'Send him in.'

'Younus entered, preceded by his customary Cuban clouds.'

I said:

'Tell us the good news, Younus!'

'Where should I begin?'

'The press attaché.'

'He said he would like to see you at the earliest opportunity.'

'What did you say?'

'I told him I'd get back to you and let him know.'

'Fine! Tell him I'd like to meet him for lunch.'

'When?'

'Today.'

'Where?'

'There's a restaurant by the river a few miles out of London called The Net and Fish. One o'clock.'

'Done.'

'What about Nahawand?'

'She was pleased to accept the invitation. Tuesday evening, my place. Should I invite anyone else?'

'No! Just me and her.'

'You'll know when to disappear.'

'You bet!'

'The third assignment?'

'Really the hardest.'

'What happened. Raf'i listened to me carefully then asked me to tell you to go to hell.'

'That's all he said?'

'That's all he said.'

'The bastard! It doesn't matter. You've done very well.'

'I'm your pupil, my teacher.'

The officer came in. I stood up and welcomed him warmly. He ignored the words of welcome and immediately said:

'Why haven't you published the report? I want to know.'

I said calmly:

'Perhaps you noticed that I printed a pre-publication story.'

'I noticed. I took it as a good sign. But the story never appeared.'

'The report was ready, but legal difficulties have prevented publication.'

'Legal difficulties?!'

'You know, my friend, we're living in England and the law here protects people from libel. If we publish a story about someone and they take us to court, we have to prove the truth of the report, we have to substantiate it conclusively. If we lose we have to pay enormous damages. We could lose our homes and, more importantly, the paper would be closed down.'

'But you can prove everything. I gave you the documents.'

'That was not the opinion of the paper's lawyer.'

'What was his opinion?'

'He was of the opinion that the chief of staff could easily win any case he brought against us. I don't think you want the paper to close down.'

'But the documents are irrefutable.'

'That was not the opinion of the lawyer.'

'What did the lawyer say?'

'Let's take the documents one by one. First, the pictures. True, the pictures are pictures of broken-down tanks which are no use for anything. However, there is no proof that these are the tanks which the contract relates to. Anyone can photograph broken-down tanks.'

'But the brothers saw the tanks for themselves.'

'I'm not doubting it. Are the brothers prepared to give evidence in court?'

'Evidence in court? This would mean their identities . . .'

'Fine! Let's take the second document relating to the Fayet company. We have found no evidence to prove that Mrs Mafatin owns the company.'

'But everyone knows that.'

'Except the court. How could we convince the court?'

'By going back to the company's articles of association.'

'We've done that. And it's clear that the Fayet company is owned by another company registered in Liechtenstein.'

'So who owns the parent company?'

'A group of Swiss lawyers.'

'But that's a cover. It's just the standard legal trick.'

'I know that. You know that. But how are we going to persuade the jury?'

'What about the contract?'

'The lawyer says the contract is our main problem.'

'What do you mean?'

The contract stipulates the purchase of 'equipment'. No more, no less.'

'But what they mean is broken-down tanks.'

'The contract says nothing about tanks, whether in working order or broken-down. Even ploughs could be considered equipment.'

'Ploughs?!! I told you it means broken-down tanks.'

'I know that. But how are we going to prove it?'

'I take it you do not wish to publish the documents?'

'On the contrary! I have a burning desire to publish them. But publishing them won't stop the deal or finish off the chief of staff. All it would do would bankrupt the *Voice of Truth* and ruin me.'

'Can you give me back the documents?'

I handed him the papers and said:

'Here you are. What are you going to do with them?'

'I'm going to get them published in another paper.'

'Can I give you a bit of free advice which will save you a lot of trouble? Don't try to get them published.'

'Why not?'

'Because you won't find a paper which will publish them.'

'On what grounds?'

'On the legal grounds I've just explained to you. Every paper here has got lawyers.'

'What about *Liberty*?'

'I would advise against going to *Liberty*.'

'Why?'

'Fear for your life.'

'Fear for my life?'

'Yes. The relations between the chief of staff and *Liberty* are very close. He could be considered the paper's main backer.'

'The chief of staff?'

'A few minutes after your meeting with the editor, the chief of staff will know everything. Your name. Rank. Everything. This will not help the cause.'

'So what should I do?'

'Get more documents. When you come across some decisive proof come and see me again.'

The officer left angrily, scowling, without bothering to shake hands. Another simple-minded fanatic! The world was full of them. Luckily for me! Kathy's voice came on the phone:

'There's a call from a woman.'

'Who is she?'

'I don't know.'

'What's her name?'

'She didn't give her name. She insists on talking to you.'

'Tell her I'm busy at the moment.'

'I told her that. She said you would speak to her when you knew she had a message from a mutual Afghan friend. I don't know what she's getting at.'

'Neither do I.'

'What should I say if she phones again.'

'Call me, I'll talk to her.'

I had barely put the phone down when Kathy came back:

'The woman's on the line.'

'Ok!'

A feminine Arabistani voice, which was smoother than silk, came on the line:

'Mr Mass'oud? My name's Lana.'

'Hello! I am honoured you've phoned.'

'Mr Mass'oud! What a charming voice you have!'

'Thank you Mrs . . .'

'Miss. I want to see you. I have an important message.'

'You're more than welcome! You can visit me at any time. It would be an honour.'

'No! No! I want the honour of having you visit me at my home.'

A female intelligence officer?! That I doubted. I'd never heard a female intelligence officer with a beautiful voice, and I'd heard loads of them. I said:

'The honour would be mine!'

'Fine! I'll be waiting for you, tomorrow evening. Eight o'clock. Eight precisely. I live on Farm Street near the *Dorchester*.'

'I know the street.'

'The name of the building is Wellington House. The top floor.'

'See you then!'

A mutual Afghan friend?! Lana?! A penthouse in Mayfair. The message in the pub was apparently the stick. And now it's the carrot's turn. Will Lana be the carrot? Kathy's voice interrupted my thoughts:

'Younus says you're not to forget your lunch appointment. You should leave now to get there on time.'

At a table beside the river I found the press attaché waiting for me.

He warmly embraced me. I embraced him even more warmly. I called the waiter and the attaché immediately said:

'Today, you're my guest.'

I smiled and said:

'It would be churlish to refuse.'

The food came. The drinks came. The attaché began to speak:

'I got your message. I'm grateful for your zeal for Arabistan X. The entire leadership values your stance.'

'Don't mention it, my friend. Arabism is our language, Arabism is our path, Arabism is our destiny. That has always been our watchword.'

'That is why we take such pride in you. You're the only journalist we trust in London.'

'That's very kind of you. However, I'm just a simple foot soldier in the ranks of the cause.'

The conversation dragged on. We moved from one topic to another, one rumour to another. The meal over, I made my excuses to leave. Before I stood up to go, the attaché handed me a large envelope as he smiled:

'A token gift for the children. It'll soon be the 'Id.'

I took it bashfully, saying:

'Thank you! Thank you! This will make the children very happy. These simple gestures are worth more than all the treasures in the whole world.'

What was this about the 'Id? The 'Id was more than three months away. What children? My marriage, which lasted nine months, only produced a divorce.

When I returned to the office it became clear that the 'token gift' was £100,000. No watches this time. God be praised! A very profitable day. I was skimming through the papers again when the phone rang and Kathy said:

'There's a man who insists on talking to you on the line.'

'Who is it?'

'He didn't say.'

'Did he say he has an important message?'

'So, you're a mind-reader now?'

'You know very well how good my sixth sense is. Put him on.'

On the line came an Arabistani voice oozing with insincerity:

'Mr Mass'oud?'

'Yes.'

'My name is Mamdouh Baroud'

'Baroud? God preserve us!'

Insincere laughs came down the line. The caller said:

'It's the family name. An old name. It goes back to my grandfather who was in charge of the gunpowder stores in the days of Sultan Abdul Hamid.'

'How honoured we are!'

'I am a national of Arabistan X. I'm one of your greatest admirers.'

'You know how much I admire Arabistan X.'

'You are the object of our pride and glory.'

'That's very kind of you.'

'I would like to talk to you about some issues concerning our nation, which is going through a critical turning point these days, as you well know.'

'A very critical turning point.'

'Indeed. For that reason I would like to benefit from your expertise.'

'Any modicum of expertise I might have is at the service of the cause.'

'When can we meet?'

'You're welcome to come here any time.'

'No! No! I would like to invite you to lunch at my home.'

This was an unconventional intelligence officer! Lunch at his home! I said:

'I would be honoured.'

'I live in the country. I'm a country yeoman. Ha! Ha!'

'*How pleasant the farmer's life.*'

'Ha! Ha! Ha! So, we'll lunch together on Saturday then.'

'I would be honoured.'

'Here's the address.'

Before going to sleep I dialled a number and on the line came the voice that owns me:

'Hello.'

'My love!'

Coquettishly she replied:

'My soul!'

'Do you remember that car you liked?'

'The Porsche?'

'The Porsche.'

'Sure, I remember. What about it?'

'I'm going to buy it for you.'

At the other end of the line there were gasps which my beloved could not stifle. Those gasps, those simple things, are more important to me than the world, than all the treasure in the whole world. I dreamt, that night, that I was eating endless dishes of blancmange. I hate blancmange. But in my dream it was delicious. I would have to ask my friend, Dr Basir Al-'Aref, what the dream meant.

Friday

As usual, I entered the office at ten o'clock. As usual, I opened the window. As usual I began to read the papers. And, as usual for a Friday, Kathy began her telephone conversation by saying:

'Thank God it's Friday.'

'Thank God.'

'You've got almost nothing on today. Except for Wajd.'

'When's she coming?'

'She asked me to ring her when you're ready to see her.'

'Tell her to come in an hour.'

Today's story which was hidden away was about the arrest of the leader of a prostitution ring. This 'Adnan Shahwan was a disgrace! He was sinking lower by the day. A prostitution ring! The son of a bitch! Tomorrow I'll have him commit suicide. I'll make him a butcher who kills himself with his own meat cleaver. The weirdest suicide in history. But let's talk about today! 'Tomorrow is in the realm of the unknown . . . All I have is today.' Today – this evening – was my date with Mademoiselle Lana. My irrepressible imagination had drawn for me a picture to make your mouth water. Not since my teenage years had I felt such anticipation before a date as I did this evening. Lana! Was that her real name? Life has taught me that there are no real names. There were always names behind names behind names. Wajd! Wajd, who would soon be here, had five real identity cards bearing five real names. How? Ask the officials who lust after her body. Even I've forgotten her first real name. Perhaps she has too. What does it matter? Names are just symbols signifying something. The thing itself doesn't change. There is nothing more stupid than fighting over names – the Arabistanis' favourite pastime.

A violent rush of perfume roused me from my linguistic reveries. I looked up to see a beautiful brown-skinned woman whose body burst forth where it should and contracted where it was suitable. A small doll made of concentrated sex! I said:

'Hello to my dearest beloved!'

'Hello to the man of my dreams!'

This had been true once. She had been my dearest beloved. And I had been the man of her dreams. But nothing lasts, particularly love. Of all human emotions none has a shorter working-life than love. So be it! I came to live this life, not to change it.

'Sit down! Sit down! I haven't seen you for ages.'

'Work!'

'Work! Our miserable fate in life. Any news?'

'Something that'll make you laugh.'

'God knows I need something to make me laugh.'

'I spent the whole night beating the British empire.'

'Well done! Give me the details.'

'Our dear mutual friend, Shaher Nattash.'

'What about him?'

'He invited me to one of his soirées. There, there was . . .'

'Wajd, you know I don't like news about parties. Give me the news of the beating.'

'After midnight, I found myself with a senior British officer.'

'How did you know he was a senior British officer?'

'I knew he was English because he looked English and I knew he was an officer because everyone called him "General"!'

'Wajd! No one was accusing you of being stupid. Didn't anybody call him by his name?'

'Shaher called him John. He treated him as if he was the most important person in the world.'

'Maybe he is. Maybe he is. Describe him to me.'

'Bald. A very long moustache. A moustache like the doorman at that Indian restaurant, The Bombay Palace.'

'A good description. So, let's get back to the beating.'

'After midnight I found myself with . . .'

'You've already told me that.'

'I'm sorry. You know how much I detest sleeping with those men. They're not circumcised and . . .'

'Wajd!'

'I'm sorry! I'm sorry! I just loath them, that's all.'

'An honourable and noble national sentiment.'

'Luckily I didn't have to sleep with him.'

'Why not?'

'Because he asked me to beat him.'

'So what did you do?'

'At first, I didn't know what to do. You know how much I hate violence.'

'An honourable and noble human sentiment.'

'But he kept on and on.'

'The inevitability of the inevitable'. What did you beat him with?'

'It became more sophisticated as time went on.'

'What do you mean?'

'I started with my hand. Then he suggested a belt. Finally, he suggested a shoe.'

'His shoe or yours?'

'My shoe.'

'What about the high heel?'

'When I'd got tired of beating him, just before dawn, there was blood all over his body. He was moaning in ecstasy and I needed a new shoe. His arse was like . . .'

'That's enough! That's enough! I don't want to know what happened to his arse. You have performed a magnificent service for Arabism. Now it's time for your reward. Pass by accounts and take £2,000.'

'Darling! Really! You know I'm not here for the money.'

'I know! I know! Soon we'll arrange something. At my place. We'll spend the whole night. Alone. But . . .'

'But what?'

'Come without any shoes on, please!'

'Wajd's laughter rang out as she left the office and I dialled Mike Pynchon's number. I said:

'Mike! I've got some news which is right up your street.'

'I'm all ears.'

'Do you know a bald general with a long moustache like that doorman at The Bombay Palace?'

'Sure! John Cromer. Head of sales at . . .'

'Ok! The man's been a victim of a physical assault. Arabistani aggression.'

'You're joking!'

I began to give Mike the full details while from time to time he would interrupt saying:

'You're joking!'

The call ended. I tried to write but my mental image of Mademoiselle Lana stopped me concentrating. I said to Kathy:

'What about taking the rest of the day off?'

'A brilliant idea.'

'I'll take you to lunch.'

'A tasty idea.'

'Get yourself ready.'

'Let's not go to an Indian restaurant.'

'No! We're going to the Olympus restaurant where the clientele can smash the plates. Book a table.'

'Are you in a Greek mood?'

'I'm in a mood for smashing something.'

With the Ouzo and the plates smashing around, Kathy began, almost magically, to take on the features of the unknown Mademoiselle Lana. I felt a sudden sexual desire. I asked Kathy:

'And after lunch?'

Immediately she said:

'My place or yours?'

'Your place.'

At precisely eight o'clock the grey-haired dignified English butler lead me into the depths of the penthouse. I looked around in astonishment. Eight million pounds sterling, at least. There were not many apartments in London like this one. An apartment?! That was a joke! I sat in one of the numerous sumptuous reception rooms contemplating the ivory statuettes as I sipped the champagne brought to me by the grey-haired dignified butler as soon as I had sat down. After a quarter of an hour, exactly, Lana entered. I was dumbstruck. She was completely different from how I had imagined her. She was neither more beautiful nor uglier. She was just different. There was something about her which made her different from all the women I had known in my life. How old was she? She could have been in her thirties; she could have been in her fifties. What did she do? She could have been a children's nanny; she could have been running a brothel. Was she a never-ageing vampire? Was she a witch? A vampire?! A witch?! In Mayfair?! Perhaps the champagne had begun to take effect. She wore a black caftan edged with real pearls and real diamonds. How much was it worth? More than the penthouse or less?

I stood up flustered and mumbling:

'Mademoiselle Lana! I'm so pleased to see you.'

'The pleasure is all mine. Please be seated! Sit down!'

The grey-haired, dignified butler came and placed a glass of champagne beside his mistress. His mistress?! Why did I use that word? Vampires again?! He replaced my empty glass with a full one. On the table he placed a small plate of caviar sandwiches. Caviar! I was at once reminded of Mike Pynchon. I smiled. Lana said:

'Is everything all right?!'

I said:

'I have a Scottish friend who is mad about caviar and whenever I see it I'm reminded of him.'

'Tell him to enjoy it before it disappears.'

'Disappears? What do you mean Madame . . . Mademoiselle Lana?'

'In Iran and Russia the sturgeon is becoming extinct. Unregulated fishing throughout the year. They don't distinguish between seasons. In Russia Mafia gangs run the operation, and in Iran . . . Aahh! What are we to do? If things continue as they are, caviar will soon disappear.'

Taking a sandwich I said:

'So, I should take my share before . . .'

Lana interrupted me:

'Your share? You've reminded me. I almost forgot. Your share is safe.'

In embarrassment I said:

'I was talking about caviar.'

'And I too was also talking about caviar. Caviar, my dear friend of the Scots, is of many kinds. Caviar one can eat, caviar one can buy things with. And caviar . . . Aahh! Forget it! Your share, of all kinds, is safe.'

This astonishing woman knows her own mind. In such circumstances, pretending to be a little stupid wouldn't be amiss.

'I was talking about this caviar in front of me.'

'There's no need to explain my dear Mass'oud. We understand each other perfectly.'

'Great minds . . .'

'Think alike.'

'And only fools disagree.'

She looked at me deeply and said:

'Madame Mafatin sends you her warmest regards.'

'Thank you. Do you know her?'

'One could say that. She apologizes for what happened in that public house in Wimbledon.'

I think Lana noticed my face had begun to redden. She went on:

'Men are innately violent. There is no justification for violence. Don't you think, my dear Mass'oud, that there is enough violence in this world.'

'Enough and more.'

'I have always been a lover of peace.'

'An honourable and moral stance.'

'I have always hated resorting to using force.'

'Using force is the enemy of civilization.'

'Quite! Quite! And we are civilized people, are we not? Civilized people do not have recourse to violence, threats or provocation, isn't that so?'

I was beginning to fidget in my seat. She continued talking. The grey-haired dignified butler continued to fill the glasses and bring more plates of sandwiches. While she spoke of her love of peace, my mind would keep on running away and coming back. In my whole life I had never been in such a strange situation. Lana said:

'Are you listening, my dear Mass'oud? I was talking about Bertrand Russell.'

Attempting, in vain, to conceal my confusion I said:

'Aahh! Lord Russell. The leader of the peace movement in Britain. He was a great philosopher and . . .'

Lana interrupted me smiling:

'The upshot of it all is that he was sleeping with his son's wife when he was over eighty-five.'

Was this young/old woman joking? Had she studied the sex lives of the philosophers as well as the sex life of the sturgeon?

I said:

'An astonishing vitality.'

'Intellectual dynamism is the source of sexual energy.'

I attempted to conceal my confusion by biting into another sandwich. Lana smiled and said:

'Don't believe all you hear about caviar.'

'About its becoming extinct?'

'About its other properties. Bertrand did not like caviar.'

She was talking about the philosopher–lord as if he had been her colleague, friend or lover. Was it plausible . . .

Suddenly she said:

'One thousandth.'

In astonishment I said:

'What do you mean?'

She said simply:

'Your share of the deal. It doesn't need a complicated calculation. Your share is one thousandth. A million dollars.'

Before I could get over the shock, she picked up a small silver bell and gently shook it. The grey-haired dignified butler appeared carrying a man's luxury leather attaché case. He handed it to his mistress who handed it to me, saying:

'A million dollars. In cash. You can open the case and count it now.'

In a state of agitation which I completely failed to conceal I mumbled:

'Thank you! I mean, don't mention it! I mean thank you. There's no need to trust! I mean trust is there! There's no need to count it!'

Mademoiselle Lana gave me a smile which chilled my heart and said:

'You're right! Trust! Trust is the main thing!'

More champagne. More caviar. Then she suddenly stood up and said:

'My dear Mass'oud! How I would love to have you stay for dinner. However, I have other guests coming at ten. In precisely seven minutes. I must be disagreeable and bring this historic meeting to a close.'

I stood up holding the luxury leather attaché case and thinking about the unknown guests who would be arriving in precisely seven minutes. Would they be leaving with luxury leather attaché cases? What was it with this woman? What was it with this apartment? What was going on?

At the door I stopped and said to her:

'I don't know how to thank you.'

She said:

'You can kiss me.'

As ever, she had completely thrown me. Did she mean what she said? Was she making fun of me? Before I could make up my mind she had placed her mouth on mine and pressed firmly. Strange feelings swept through my body, the strangest being that chill in my heart. When I had got my breath back she said:

'And now I can kiss you.'

The second kiss was more violent and longer than the first. Even stranger feelings were aroused and the chill moved to my spine. Before closing the door she said:

'The first kiss was from me. The second from Mafatin, my daughter.'

On the street I was buffeted by a cold wind which brought me back down to earth after the champagne, caviar, dollars and the kiss from the mother and the kiss from the daughter. Madame Mafatin was her daughter?! Was she having me on?! Why couldn't she be her daughter?! I had left my car in the care of the doorman at the Dorchester and I started to walk in the direction of the hotel. Coming towards me two men dressed in track suits appeared, jogging. Running at ten o'clock at night? And in a Mayfair side street? Who could ever understand these people? As they came closer I tightened my grip on the leather attaché case. You can never be too careful. It all happened in a flash. When the two men came alongside me, one of them pushed me violently backwards while the other tripped me up. I found myself flat on the ground. At the same instant, the earth split open and a third man appeared who snatched the case and ran off in the direction of the hotel. When I got to my feet, a blow to the face that had been waiting for me returned me to the ground. When I got up for the second time, the two men who had attacked me were nowhere to be seen, while the one who had snatched the case was running ahead of me with my attaché case, the million dollars, in his hand. I started to run after him. Before he turned the corner at the end of the street I saw a flash from the attaché case and heard the sound of a terrible explosion. I saw fragments of his body flying through the air falling with fragments of the case and fragments of glass which rained down on all sides.

Saturday

The car was passing through the meadows of the English countryside while I, in the back seat, passed through explosion after explosion. I hadn't slept a wink the night before. I couldn't believe that what had happened had actually happened, and in front of me. The kiss of the mother. The kiss of the daughter. The mixture of caviar, champagne and repressed desire. The case filled with death. I could have opened it and checked for myself. What if I had done?! What if I had blown myself up and the old witch as well. I tried to convince myself that what had happened in the penthouse had been a beautiful dream followed by a dreadful nightmare on the street. It was inconceivable for such a thing to happen in Mayfair. It didn't even happen in James Bond films. I must have imagined the whole evening: the penthouse, the grey-haired dignified butler, the old/young hag and the tragedy of the sturgeon, Bertrand Russell's vitality, the two kisses and the explosion. The morning press however had given me no room to escape into fantasy. News of the explosion was on the front pages of all the papers. A member of the IRA. Blew himself up before planting the bomb at an unknown target. Near the Dorchester. Maybe the Dorchester itself was the target. Oh, the

IRA! How many crimes have been perpetrated in your name? And me? Me? How did I get involved with that gang of killers. Where was my famous sixth sense? What about now? Now I was on my way to someone called Mamdouh Baroud. Baroud! His grandfather had been in charge of explosives stores. Hadn't I been hurt enough? Bullets, suitcase bombs! What was left? Weapons of mass destruction?!

Mamdouh Baroud was waiting for me at the door. He had a pallid complexion and was rapidly approaching sixty. The house was no palace. It was a cottage which had been added to over the years until it bore only a distant relationship with the original building. There was no sauna, or old French maid. Strange! An Arabistani who didn't like ostentation! Perhaps that was down to his aristocratic roots. He was not nouveau riche like most of my friends. His ancestors had served sultans.

At a small dining table the meal began. And Mamdouh began to speak:

'Mr Mass'oud, you are aware of the difficult circumstances which the nation is going through. You are aware that the situation is critical. You are aware that the peace process is faltering.'

'I think that the peace process is breathing its dying breaths.'

'Exactly! That's what I meant. Its dying. In such difficult circumstances it is the duty of us all to support our Palestinian brothers with all the strength we have.'

'This is a sacred duty.'

'But how can we support them? That is the question.'

He was not expecting an answer. And I didn't say anything. He went on:

'If one cannot exert pressure through war, then one has no other means but to exert pressure through peace. The stick or the carrot. Regrettably, we have lost, through successive ignominious defeats, any ability to use the stick. All that remains for us is the carrot. Are you with me?'

'I am with you. A very acute analysis.'

'Thank you. Arabistan X is trying to make Israel give concessions to our Palestinian brethren who have nothing to make concessions with because, in fact, they have already conceded everything. Are you with me?'

'I'm with you.'

'We in Arabistan X believe that it is our national duty to ask for more concessions on behalf of, and for the benefit of, the Palestinians. Don't get me wrong! I'm not talking about full diplomatic relations. No! No! Merely commercial facilities. There are, at the moment, sensitive and secret, very secret, negotiations between us and Israel aiming to make the Israelis give concessions to the Palestinians in exchange for facilities which Israel will obtain from us. Are you with me?'

'I'm with you right down the line. I celebrate such a noble nationalist spirit, Mamdouh Bey.'

'Don't mention it. It is our destiny. There is just one problem.'

'Which is?'

'Secrecy. At this stage, the negotiations must remain secret. If they were revealed now, everything would come to a standstill. And who would lose in such an eventuality?'

'Our Palestinian brethren.'

'Exactly! And I am sure that I can rely on you to avert this disaster.'

'Rely on me?'

'Yes. We in Arabistan X are aware of the extent of your self-sacrifice for the cause.'

'I am a simple foot soldier, Mamdouh Bey.'

'You are one of our most effective weapons.'

'What do you want me to do?'

'I'm asking you, begging you, to stop the press here publishing reports of these contacts at this stage.'

'I will do my utmost. However, you must realize, Mamdouh Bey, that I can only control what goes into *my* paper. I have no influence over other newspapers.'

'We, Mass'oud, realize the extent of your influence. There is no need to be so humble.'

'I can try and persuade them.'

'We're not asking anything more of you.'

The conversation turned to the pleasures of life in the English countryside. As soon as the simple lunch was over I made my excuses to leave. Mamdouh Baroud accompanied me to the car. He shook my hand and handed me a small envelope saying:

'This is just a little something for expenses. We are aware that the assignment will require certain expenses.'

Putting the envelope in my pocket, I muttered:

'Thank you. Thank you. I will serve the cause with all my power.'

I had the car pull up five minutes after leaving the cottage and took out the small envelope. Should I open it? Why not? A man can only die on the day appointed. No one can escape his destiny. If fate wishes to save me from dying in a suitcase bomb, I won't be dying as a result of a letter bomb. So be it then. Inside I found a cheque for £200,000 drawn on a Swiss bank. Luckily for me I had already opened an account in Switzerland before the banks there started asking 'Where did you get this?' The impudence of it all! You put your money in the bank and the bank won't give it back to you unless you tell them where you got it. But for the moment that wasn't important. What was important was keeping the contacts between Arabistan X and Israel secret. Mass'oud As'ad always kept his promises. My word is my bond!

In the evening I went to my friend, Shaher Nattash's party. There must have been at least three hundred people there. How could Shaher assemble this huge bizarre crowd? Society ladies and ladies of the street, ministers and pickpockets, the aristocracy and the working class, the elderly and adolescents, billionaires and paupers and everybody, apparently, having a good time. At the far end of the spacious room a group of Arabistani musicians was playing while a group of Western musicians was taking a break. Behind the singer sat the blind man playing a tambourine. Here and there blonde girls were dancing to the thud of 'Outside her Father's House'. Wajd smiled from a distance then disappeared like a ghost. Younus Abu Shakhtura was producing clouds of smoke around him. Champagne everywhere. Caviar, which apparently hadn't become extinct yet, accompanied the champagne. I was in a party mood. Yesterday I had been saved from a certain death. Today I had received a cheque for £200,000. Perhaps it was this party mood that led me, unusually for me, to talk to a beautiful blonde English girl who was making passes at me. Nothing, as a rule, terrifies me like a woman making a pass at me, no matter how beautiful she is. Making passes is the job of the hunter, not the prey. But this time I responded favourably. A look. A smile. A word. Champagne. Caviar. Laughter. A dance. An embrace. A small room in the big house. There was no resistance. Afterwards, as I smoked a cigarette, she was just leaving when she stopped at the door and said:

'Did you like the present?'

Confused, I asked:

'What present?'

'Me.'

'You're a present?'

'Absolutely.'

'What do you mean?'

'I'm a present from your friend Raf'i Rif'at.'

'That's generous of him. Thank him from me.'

'I don't think you'll be thanking him when you find out.'

'Find out what?'

'That I've got Aids.'

She left the room laughing guffawing shamelessly. Aids?! She had to be joking. Raf'i had to be joking. A very sick joke. Very, very sick! The son of a whore!

Sunday

At the president's house in Richmond the monthly meeting of the Central Committee of the Huristani Revolutionary Party was being held. The session began with the usual rituals. The president said:

'The Huristanis constitute an independent nation which is distinct from other nations.'

A committee member seated to his right said:

'Particularly from the bedouin, Arabistani nation.'

The president said:

'Which killed our glorious leader.'

A committee member seated to his left said:

'Long live the glorious leader!'

The president concluded the rituals by saying:

'Long live the Huristani Revolutionary Party!'

Afterwards the president looked into the faces of those present, and looked at me for a long time. He said:

'In the name of the great Huristani nation, the creator of civilization, I hereby open this meeting. Permit me, before beginning the proceedings to express, on behalf of the party, my deepest gratitude to Mass'oud As'ad for his contribution of the record sum this month of £100,000.'

The members warmly applauded. The president continued:

'Comrade Mass'oud As'ad is an example to us all, an example of keeping the embers of the revolution burning, and an example of revenge against the Arabistani scum who killed our valiant leader.'

The meeting ended two hours later. I left with my arm around the shoulder of my friend 'Adnan Shahwan. We swapped the latest gossip about the Arabistanis on our way to the White Swan where we met a representative of the Israeli embassy for the usual monthly meeting.

FOUR

The Psychiatrist

As his conduct degenerates so do his thoughts
And the delusions he entertains for reality he takes
Al-Mutanabbi

Identity Card
Full Name: Anwar Mikhail Mukhtarji
Known as: Anwar Mukhtar
Occupation: Psychiatrist
Age: 49
Wealth: $3million (approx.)
Place of Birth: Arabistan X
Place of Work: London
Academic Qualifications: BM (University of St Andrews); PhD (University of
                                St Andrews
Marital Status: Married
Children: One daughter

Monday
As I entered the clinic at eleven a.m. as usual, I was taken aback by my secretary,
Ruth, saying that Rafʿi Rifʿat had asked for an appointment to see me in the clinic
that morning. Rafʿi Rifʿat? !Rafʿi is a very dear friend whom I see every week,
sometimes twice a week. Why visit me at the clinic? Had he suddenly been struck
down by some sort of mental illness? I asked Ruth:
　　'When did he call?'
　　'At nine. Ten. Ten-thirty. He insists on seeing you as soon as possible.'
　　'What appointments have you got for me?'
　　'The actor.'
　　'When's his appointment?'
　　'At one.'
　　'And apart from him?'
　　'The journalist.'
　　'When's she due?'
　　'At three.'
　　'Can you put off both appointments till tomorrow?'
　　'I think that's possible.'

'Good. Cancel the appointments and tell Raf'i he can come now.'

After a few minutes, Raf'i entered my consulting room, lay down on the couch and began his deluge of words:

'Listen to me Anwar! And don't interrupt! Don't interrupt me! Just let me speak! You're surprised about me asking for an appointment to see you at your clinic. Don't deny it! Don't deny it. You're surprised. You're saying to yourself: This is my friend. My life long friend. I see him all the time. We spend evenings together. We drink together. We laugh together. We . . . Ok! Ok! Ok! You know full well the things we do together. I beg you not to interrupt me!'

'I wasn't going to interrupt you.'

'Don't you see? There you go interrupting me. Please, Anwar! In the name of friendship, I'm begging you to listen and not interrupt me. I am not here, for the present, as a friend. I've come as a patient. Do you understand? Do you understand? You can't reveal a patient's secrets. That's true isn't it? Don't interrupt! I know that's true. The Socratic Oath . . .'

'Hippo . . .'

'Don't interrupt! Fine! Fine! Hipposocratic. What does it matter? Hippo or Socco? What is important is the oath prevents you revealing a patient's secrets, isn't that so? Sure it is! That's what Doctor Roquefort assured me. I asked him once about a mutual friend. Just a question. Don't get me wrong, Anwar! I'm not a sponger. I don't want something for nothing. I don't sponge or freeload, as you well know. It was just a question about a friend. He wasn't even an important friend. Don't get me wrong! I think everyone's important. Everyone. Even the poor. My question was just a question. I was surprised when Doctor Roquefort told me: "The Socratic Oath . . ."'

'Hippo . . .'

'Ok! Ok! Hipposocratic. The Hipposocratic Oath. I told him: "Doctor! I don't want to discuss philosophy with you. I'm asking about a friend." He said: "I cannot answer your question because the Socratic Oath prevents me . . ."'

'Hippo . . .'

'Ok! Ok! The Hipposocratic Oath. Don't interrupt! Don't interrupt me, by the right of Hipposocrates. The Hipposocratic Oath prevents him. He said that every doctor was bound by this oath. They don't get their certificate unless they take the oath and are bound by it for the rest of their lives. Even psychiatrists! You are bound by this oath. And you won't divulge any of my secrets. Particularly to that bloody ass, the proprietor of the "Voice of Crime". I can't even speak his name. If his name crossed my tongue I'd be sick. But I think you know who I mean. Maybe he's a friend of yours. But I know you won't divulge any of my secrets to him, even if he pays you a £100,000. Particularly if he pays you £100,000. Remember, I'm a patient now. And you're the doctor. You're not my friend now. You're my doctor. And if you divulged one of my secrets, you'd be finished. Finished as a doctor. Any doctor who divulges his patient's secrets is finished. Especially in London. If you take the secrets out of London, what's left? The working classes, which used to be called the criminal classes, who live without secrets. As for the aristocracy, their lives are based on secrets. The Aristocratic Oath! Ha! Ha! The deals of an aristocrat are secrets. His love affairs are secrets. His girlfriends are secrets. If you take the secrets away from a gentleman, what have you got left? I'm asking you, by the right of Hipposocrates, what would be left of him? Don't interrupt me Anwar! Do you mind if I smoke in your clinic? You'll let me! Well done! Well done! That's a good principle. Particularly these days. When smokers are hounded and treated like lepers. Just a moment! Just a moment! I'm going to light a cigar. I don't need clippers. I bite the end off with my teeth. A very old habit. Don't interrupt me, Anwar! Please, don't interrupt. Don't say that biting the end off a cigar is the act of a sick man. Or a hostile act. Or indicates latent sexual leanings. Don't tell me that, please. As Professor Windbag once told me. I was at home biting off the end of my cigar with my teeth when this bastard says that biting off the end of a cigar with one's teeth is indicative of latent sexual leanings. He said that in front of guests. He eats my food, drinks my booze and then attacks me. Do you know what I did? After lighting the cigar I put it up his backside. From behind! His trousers got burnt, naturally. Then I kicked him out like you would a dog. And what happened after? Nothing happened. Attack is the best form of defence. I wrote to him threatening to take him to court if he didn't apologize. Via that famous lawyer, the Scorpion, Lord Stinger. And what happened? The coward apologized. Abjectly. In a personal letter, naturally. Do you want me to have the apology published in the press? Don't interrupt me, Anwar! Please! Please! I put a cigar up the bastard's backside and he apologizes. Accusing me of latent sexual leanings. Am I so afraid of him, his father and his mother to hide my sexual tendencies? Am I afraid of anyone? Don't tell me, Anwar, that you believe that biting the end off your cigar with your teeth is indicative of latent sexual leanings. Be warned! Remember, I'm smoking a cigar at the moment. Nobody's backside is out of danger. Ha! Ha! Just joking. The upshot is you can't divulge my secrets. And should you, I'd set the Scorpion, Stinger, on you. And you'd be completely finished. Finished totally, Anwar! I know you'll never divulge my secrets. Because you like me. And I like you. If I didn't like you, would I have given you the money to open your clinic? Would I have done that? I did that because I like you. And because of a long friendship. A lifetime's friendship. From our university days. Aahh! University! Do you remember our university days? You finished the course, but I didn't. You became a psychiatrist sought out by VIPs. From all over the place. The rich and famous Arabistanis seek you out because you're not living in Arabistan. And the rich and famous British seek you out because you're not British. The doctor to the stars! Do you have a single patient who is a nobody? Don't be humble. You've become a star psychiatrist sought out by sick stars. You've written four books, and the rest is yet to come. As for me, I didn't finish my studies. And what did I become? I became a mere billionaire. Can you appreciate the sufferings of a billionaire? You can't, of course. That's all to the good. Believe me! Listen, Anwar! Has anyone ever tried to rip you off? No! No one's tried to rip you off. And why has no one tried to rip you off? Because you're not a billionaire. Do you find on your desk every day a thousand letters from a thousand charities? No! And why not? Because you're not a billionaire. Does VIP after VIP ask to hire your private plane? No! And why not? Because you haven't got a private plane. And why haven't you got a private plane? Because you're not a billionaire. Do you know how much it takes a year to run a private plane? Three million pounds! You don't believe me?! Do you want the receipts? So you're relieved of this burden because you're not a billionaire. You're just a millionaire. Or a quasi-millionaire. Clara told me you gave her a necklace worth ten thousand pounds. That's a waste of money, Anwar. A waste of money not appropriate for a quasi-millionaire. And I'm not bound by an oath. I'm just a billionaire. I divulge secrets when I want, and keep them when I want. But I won't tell the story about the necklace to anyone. Especially Theresa. Where is your wife these days? I haven't seen her for ages. With her family in Brazil? Don't forget, at university I knew Theresa before you did. And when I realized you loved her, I willingly left the field open to you. You were cleverer than me at studying. But I was cleverer than you when it came to women. Admit it, Anwar! That's a talent which has nothing to do with money. Sexual attraction! Listen, Anwar! You must send me your bill after this session. You must! If you don't send the bill, you're not keeping your oath. Then it just becomes a conversation between friends. You have to be recompensed for your treatment. So that I can legally become your patient. I trust you as much as I trust myself. But my trust in myself has been shaken. Everyone I know has turned against me. Just because they realized I wasn't going to share my money with them. All my friends. No! No! That's an exaggeration. Most of my friends. But I'm sure you won't turn against me. Can I put the ash here? Is that an ashtray? It looks like a piece of jewellery. I've never seen such an expensive ashtray and I'm a billionaire. Ok! Ok! I'm glad you let me smoke. And that you don't consider biting the end of a cigar off with your teeth as indicative of latent sexual leanings. A fantastic cigar. Straight from Havana. From the friend of Comrade Castro. Don't get me wrong, Anwar! Comrade Castro is still a committed communist. But his friends are a different story. I'm involved in negotiations with the friend to open a hotel in Havana. That's another secret protected by the Hipposocratic Oath. Let me tell you another secret. Cuba has given me concessions and exemptions you'd never find in any capitalist country. Believe it or don't believe it! The site is free. Tax exemptions for twenty-five years. Imagine! Twenty-five years! But I didn't come here, Anwar, my dear old friend, to discuss business. You don't understand business. If you'd understood business you'd have been a billionaire hunted down by charities, orphans, widows, thieves, pimps, whores, con-artists, reputable institutions and disreputable institutions. But for the moment, no one is hunting you down. Except Clara, maybe. Why did you give her such a valuable necklace? Have you lost your mind? Don't you know what goes on inside a woman's head if you give her a valuable necklace. Women are filthy animals, Anwar. The filthiest animals in history. And the filthiest is Lola. My ex-wife. My late wife. How has she become my late wife? I'll tell you. I know you know her very well. I mean you knew her well in the past. Did you know that Lola was cheating on me? And who with? With my greatest enemy. My most dangerous competitor. Shukri Yasser. And how did I find out? Through a private detective who followed her until her infidelity was proved. If only she'd just been secretly unfaithful. No, she had to do it in public. That dirty bastard who owns the "Voice of Crime" found out about it. He tried to blackmail me. Do you know what I did? You'll laugh. I gave a beautiful young woman with Aids a considerable amount of money to sleep with the filthy bastard. And the donkey slept with her. Dreaming she'd been attracted by the lines on his forehead. He'll be dead in a few months. The late swindler. Lola will be dead in a few months. Don't worry! Don't worry! I don't believe in violence. Poison? A bullet? A car accident? No! No! I've told her a thousand times, infidelity means death. And she chose infidelity. She chose death. But it will be a death of a special kind. A crime that can't be punished by the law. Do you know what I did? You haven't worked it out yet? My secret weapon. The beautiful young girl with Aids. I sent her to that filthy bastard, Shukri Yasser. And he thought she fancied his potbelly. He slept with her. Several times. The virus must have been transmitted. And I think by now it's been transmitted to Lola. The late, Lola! Who chose infidelity and chose death. She could have told me and we could have separated without a scandal and without treachery. But she chose this fate for herself. I warn you against sleeping with her, Anwar! Ha! Ha! Just a joke. And I warn you against sleeping with Shukri! Or the other bastard! Ha! Ha! Just joking! You said Theresa was in Brazil? Is she Ok? Fine! Fine! I must be off now, doctor. My plane's at the airport and I have an important rendezvous in Rome this evening. Don't forget the bill! Give my regards to Theresa. And Lucy. How is Lucy? I haven't seen her for ages. Tell her Uncle Raf'i sends his best wishes. See you soon!'

As soon as my lifelong friend had left, I rushed to the bathroom and threw up. This congenital liar! He gave me the money to open the clinic?! He gave me a loan which I repaid at a rate of interest which was higher than the bank's. He knew Theresa before me?! No! He did not know Theresa before me. He was not cleverer than me with regards to women. That cleverness only came when he got rich. And what's all this about Aids? Was he lying? He had an insatiable desire for revenge. And I couldn't rule out the possibility that he had resorted to such a lethal stratagem. But why tell me about it? Why? Why? Was he expecting me to warn Lola? And if he wanted to warn her why didn't he do so himself? Was it just Shukri he wanted dead? And what was all that about the Hippocratic Oath? To tell the truth I hadn't even seen the oath since college. I'll have to look it up. I think it's in the association rule book, on the first page. Yes! Yes! Here's the bit talking about patients' secrets: 'Whatever, in connection with my professional practice or not, I see or hear, in the life of men, which ought not to be spoken of abroad, I will not divulge, as reckoning that all such should be kept secret.'

I don't think Hippocrates intended to protect a murderer. And I don't think my lifelong insane friend deserves the protection of the oath.

I called Lola immediately:

'Lola! I have to see you right away.'

Her voice was on the other end:

'Anwar? I haven't heard your voice for some time. I haven't seen you in ages. Did you know that the divorce . . .'

'Lola! I know! I know! And I want to see you straight away.'

'Now. I've got a date . . .'

'Forget the date. Come here at once.'

'To the clinic?'

'To the clinic annexe.'

The clinic annexe was an apartment directly above the clinic itself. You could enter by a separate door or via a staircase in the clinic. A comfortable arrangement for all concerned. Who would cast a second glance at a woman going into a building full of doctors' clinics? And who knew the clinic annexe even existed among all these clinics?

I sat and waited for Lola, going over what I was going to tell her. She was twenty-one when I met her. She was very beautiful and very innocent. Her real name was Lilian but everyone called her Lola. When was that? Ten years ago, more or less. Our relationship was somewhat strange. To a large extent the relationship was platonic. To a very large extent. I would protect her from all the filth surrounding me on all sides. From the corruption of this world. From the corruption of the job. From the corruption of human nature. From the corruption of daily life. Then one day Raf'i saw her with me. I was having dinner with her in a small French restaurant near Soho. He came up and introduced himself to her. And began to cast his net. The red roses. A trip on his boat. Love letters. Romantic gifts. And the innocent beauty succumbed. She married him despite my warnings. And now she had met another billionaire. The consequence? Death?

I was in the clinic annexe taking Dutch courage from a whisky when Lola

came in. She was still very beautiful and still seemed very innocent. She kissed
me on the cheek; I kissed her on her mouth. She said:

'What's going on? What do you want? I had to cancel a date. Shuki got
angry.'

'Shuki?!'

'Shukri. I call him Shuki.'

'Fine! You can make it up to Shuki later. Sit down. Would you like a drink?'

She sat down sipping champagne and looking at me. I tried to feel my way to
the subject in hand. I said:

'Lola! This is a delicate matter. It has to be dealt with in a clever and skilful
manner. It's difficult . . .'

She interrupted me:

'Anwar! I can't stay here long. What's the matter?'

'It's about Shukri.'

'Did I tell you we're going to get married? Did I tell you that I never knew
happiness until I met him? I've never seen a man in my whole life so courteous,
sweet and faithful . . .'

'Fidelity, Lola, doesn't exist. And, as you know, I'm speaking from the
position of one who knows about such things. A man who knows everything.'

'If infidelity is the rule, then Shukri is the exception.'

'No! No man is an exception to the rule. You're now making my task easier.
Recently, Shukri had a relationship with a young woman . . .'

She interrupted me vehemently:

'I don't believe it! I don't believe it!'

'This young girl carries the virus of a very serious disease . . .'

'I don't believe it! I don't believe it!'

'It is possible that the disease has been transmitted to him.'

'I don't believe it! I don't believe it!'

'And it is possible that the disease will be transmitted to you. Or maybe has
been transmitted.'

Lola fell silent. Then she looked at me angrily and said in a high voice:

'Anwar! Anwar! I could never have believed you could stoop so low. I know
you're still in love with me. And I know you were hoping that our relationship
would start up again after my divorcing Raf'i. But I never imagined you . . .'

I interrupted her decisively:

'Lola! Listen to me! My feelings for you, whatever they may be, have nothing
to do with what I'm telling you. I'm warning you. You could die! Are you
listening? You could die! I'm talking about Aids.'

'Aids?!'

'Yes'

'Shukri slept with a woman with Aids?'

'Yes.'

'How do you know?'

'I'm afraid the Hippocratic Oath prevents me from saying any more.'

'Is this woman being treated by you?'

'Lola! I can't answer that.'

Lola looked at me contemptuously and said, as if she were spitting:

'I hate you! I hate you!'

And left.

Tuesday

The day began with a session with a famous stage actor. Raf'i Rif'at was not wrong when he said I was a psychiatrist to the stars. And he wasn't wrong in his analysis of the reason. The British trust strange foreign doctors who don't know their friends and don't know their enemies. And the Arabistanis trust a British doctor, formerly Arabistani, who listens to his patients without judging them either morally or otherwise.

The stage actor's problem was stage fright. Every time he stood on stage he felt the well-known symptoms of anxiety: increased heart rate, dryness of the tongue, cold hands, feeling he's about to faint, feeling he'll do something crazy – destroy something, take off his clothes or die. Treatment had begun three months ago. I began with the problem itself. I didn't ask him to talk about his childhood. I don't waste much time on people's childhoods. Nor with Freudian complexes. Freud was a genius in his time, but all geniuses are eclipsed by time. All of them! Freud pointed us in the direction of many important things such as the unconscious and the language of dreams but then the party was over. The Greek myths he talked about are no more than myths. Condemning certain sexual practices was no more than an echo of the sexual taboos that prevailed in his time. I try to talk to my patients about the present. I discuss their current problems. What would I find in a patient's childhood? What would I find in any childhood? The usual stories, which are the same the world over and which don't change throughout history. There's the cruel father. There's the uncouth, loud-mouthed mother. There are orphans. There are stepmothers. There are happy families. There are miserable families. There is sexual abuse. There is rape. If every defective childhood produced people with psychiatric disorders there wouldn't be a sane person left on the planet. I told the famous actor:

'Mister Hammersmith! Haven't you read the book I gave you? There hasn't been an actor in history who, when faced with a crowd, did not feel afraid. Stage fright is a well-known phenomenon experienced by anyone who has to deal with a crowd of people.'

'But, Doctor Mukhtar, it's getting worse. At first there was just a moment's anxiety as I went on to the stage. Then a minute. Then minutes of anxiety. The crisis passed and everything was back to normal. But now, the anxiety begins before I even leave for the theatre. The anxiety barely leaves me before, during or after the play. Don't you see it's getting serious?'

'There's nothing serious. These are just annoying symptoms we can deal with. When did the symptoms get worse?'

'About three weeks ago.'

'But you felt an improvement after we began the treatment.'

'I felt a major improvement. But then there was a relapse.'

'We must discuss the causes of this relapse. And we won't find the cause on the stage.'

'What do you mean?'

'I mean we have to find out what happened in your life that led to this relapse.'

'There have been no major changes.'

'The changes don't have to be major. They just have to be enough to disturb you.'

'Nothing has happened to disturb me.'

'Try to remember what happened during that period. However, small and insignificant.'

'I can't remember anything in particular.'

'Don't rush. Take all the time you want to think.'

Silence prevailed for several minutes then Hammersmith said:

'The only thing I can remember is separating from Margaret around that time.'

'Who is Margaret?'

'My girlfriend.'

'You haven't talked about her before.'

'You haven't asked me about girlfriends. I never thought it necessary to drag her in to the conversation.'

'You can talk about her now.'

'It's a long and boring story, doctor.'

'It's my job to listen to long and boring stories.'

'The story began when we were in primary school. You could call it a story of childhood sweethearts . . .'

It was a long story and the session ended before we could get beyond the initial stages. Why the hurry? I asked the actor to try and write the story down. Writing, sometimes, helps focus ideas and yet, sometimes, confuses them.

After Hammersmith had left, Bustan Azhar, the well-known Arabistani woman journalist, came. Bustan! Meaning 'garden', it was a rather strange name. It was, however, her real name. I knew her father personally, and well, and knew that he had named her Bustan. It was this family link that had led Bustan to me.

And it was this link which had made me treat her for nothing. Was there anything about treating people for free in the Hippocratic Oath? Bustan was thirty, or slightly older. She took as much pride in her educational and intellectual sophistication as she did in her enchanting beauty. Bustan's problem was extremely simple. Or rather, describing the problem was extremely simple. A modern way of life in conflict with old values – the reason behind the nervous disorders of most psychiatric patients. The clash of civilizations. Rapid social change. Globalization. Cultural invasion. How can a middle-eastern girl who has had drilled into her head that she is the property of her husband, or the grave, cope with limitless sexual freedom? This was Bustan's story. This was Bustan's tragedy. She couldn't cast aside the old values neither could she sacrifice her new freedoms: the freedom to write, the freedom to go where she wanted, the freedom to speak and the freedom to love. And the consequence? The consequence was that she found herself in one predicament after another. I would listen to her, and talking about her predicaments helped her find a way through the problem. This is all a psychiatrist, any psychiatrist, can do: help the patient understand the situation he or she is facing.

Her latest problem was her burning passion for the famous newspaper editor, Sufyan Na'im. So where was the predicament? The predicament was that the editor was as old as her father. And married. And did not share her burning passion. The editor enjoys a beautiful body and a clever brain. And Bustan, were she to use her clever brain, would understand the nature of the relationship. However, she deals with the situation with her feelings, and her feelings are a long way from being rational. Her feelings have convinced her that her love for this middle-aged married man is reciprocated.

Bustan exhaled the smoke of her cigarette and said:

'If only he had the guts to do what he really wants to do. If he had the guts, the problem would be over. My problem, and his problem.'

'What do you mean?'

'I mean he wants to divorce his wife and marry me, but he lacks the courage required to do so.'

'How do you know he wants to divorce his wife and marry you?'

'Female intuition'

'Female intuition, like male intuition, cannot be relied on in the absence of evidence and proof. Has he told you that he hates his wife?'

'No.'

'Has he told you he's going to divorce her?'

'No.'

'Has he told you he wishes he could marry you?'

'No.'

'So then, how do you know?'

'I told you. Female intuition.'

'One of the most powerful instincts, in both women and men, is to believe what we want to believe.'

'Do you think I'm lying to you?'

'No. I think you're relating events as they are but interpreting them in the way you want to.'

'You don't think he loves me and wants to marry me?'

'I don't know. But I do know there is nothing to stop him divorcing his wife should he so wish.'

'I told you, he hasn't got the guts.'

'Or sufficient desire. A strong enough desire usually produces the courage required.'

'So, why does he continue the relationship?'

'Bustan! Any man with eyes would want to have a relationship with you.'

'Uncle Anwar! Uncle Anwar!'

'Even Uncle Anwar.'

'You mean he . . .'

'Bustan! I cannot know his motives. I haven't talked to him about the situation. Why don't you talk to me about your motives? What do you want out of the relationship?'

'What does any woman want when she loves a man?'

'There is no single answer. There are as many answers as there are women.'

'I think every woman wants to marry the man she loves.'

'That is a very loose generalization. A woman who wants to get married would not fall in love with a married man.'

'Uncle Anwar! Is love something one can decide? Can we fall in love when we want to and fall out of love when we want to?'

'Bustan! You're an intelligent woman with a strong personality, please don't try and tell me that you don't know what you're doing. Don't tell me that some unknown invisible power forced you to begin this relationship and is now forcing you to stay in it.'

'Do you think I deliberately complicated my life by getting involved with a married man?'

'A married man as old as your father.'

'As old as my father! As old as my father! Aren't you going to change the record?'

'It's not a record. It's a biological fact which you know, which he knows, which everybody knows.'

'Uncle Anwar! Don't turn Freudian on me. Don't tell me that I was in love with my late father. Don't tell me that my repressed sexual feelings for my father have finally found their release with a man as old as my father.'

'I wasn't going to say anything of the kind. The Oedipus Complex is just a myth. There is no need to go digging about in the depths of childhood. The editor is an extremely attractive man and has lots of relationships with women . . .'

'Please Uncle Anwar! I beg you! Don't believe those ridiculous rumours about him.'

'I wouldn't have to believe in them if it wasn't he himself who bragged about them.'

'That was before he knew me.'

'Maybe. The important thing is that it's perfectly understandable why women should like him. Have you ever heard of sexual charisma? Men, as well as women, have it.'

'It's not just a question of liking or charisma. I fell in love with him at first sight. For several months I loved him in silence, passionately. I thought it was just a one-sided love. Until one day he surprised me by asking me out. Then it was clear that the love was reciprocated.'

'There are no surprises in human relationships. During that period you must have given him messages which encouraged him to ask you out.'

'Messages? I didn't write anything to him.'

'I don't mean written messages. I mean those messages which a woman, any woman, sends to a man, any man, if she wants him to know she's interested in him.'

'Believe me, I did everything to hide my feelings.'

'Don't you think that hiding your feelings might, in itself, have been the message? A silent declaration.'

'Uncle Anwar! When did you become a poet?'

'Aahh! I was a poet once. For one month. At primary school. But let's get back to our friend. You liked him and you fell in love with him and he asked to see you. What makes you think that this was anything more than sexual desire?'

'Didn't you say yourself that he had a lot of relationships. He didn't need another.'

'The more the merrier, as the English proverb says.'

'Do you mean I'm just one among many others, just a body?'

'I mean that we cannot draw the conclusion that just because a man sleeps with a woman he is in love with her or wants to marry her.'

'Neither can we deny it.'

'That's true. It's best to keep one's options open. Maybe he loves you, and maybe he wants to have a good time with you.'

'Our relationship has now lasted eighteen months. If it was just a passing fancy it would have ended.'

'Passing fancies, though I love the expression, do not have a specific time span.'

'But I'm certain that he loves me. Uncle Anwar! I'm certain! If you could only see the way he looks at me. Hear the way he talks to me. If only . . .'

'Bustan! Don't you remember reading the story about the hunter who killed sparrows while all the time there were tears in his eyes? Don't look at the tears in people's eyes, look at what they actually do with their hands.'

'If you're trying to make me believe that the relationship is one-sided, I will never believe you. Never! Never! Never!'

'I'm not trying to make you believe anything. I'm trying to help you understand the full picture. The real picture. I don't want you to be disappointed if you find out that he has no intention of divorcing his wife or of marrying you.'

'When did you start reading the future?'

'I cannot. If you want to know the future, go and see my friend Basir Al-'Aref. I follow the present. If in the future there are new developments we can deal with them as they arise.'

'Uncle Anwar! You're not a woman. Women know these things. We know them through our intuition. I am absolutely certain that our relationship is deeper . . .'

Bustan can only cope with the modern way of life, sexual liberation, by linking it to the old values. A woman belongs to her husband, or the man who will become her husband. Bustan believes what she says when she swears her middle-aged Don Juan loves her. And next week, and the week after, and the week after that, we will resume the conversation but she'll never be convinced. She will only be convinced when she sees with her own eyes the middle-aged Don Juan with another woman, most likely another journalist. It is neither my right, nor my duty, to tell Bustan that I saw her middle-aged Don Juan with my own eyes with another woman just a few days ago. He was having lunch with her at a small restaurant. I wanted to ignore them but he greeted me warmly, kissed me in fact, and insisted on introducing me to his girlfriend. A judge cannot pass sentence on the basis of his own knowledge of the facts, neither can a psychiatrist.

My third and final appointment (and I try to avoid having more than three appointments a day) was with a star barrister. The hero of libel cases. A man who had earned a million pounds from some cases. Since reaching the age of fifty, this barrister had been feeling pangs of remorse. Aahh! Fifty! The age of wonders! The age of the awakening or death of a man's conscience. The age of the onset of old age or the return of adolescence. The age for a new wife or an old lover. The barrister, of course, did not know the cause of his problem. He was suffering from depression, but could think of no reason for being depressed. His financial situation was excellent. His marital life was excellent. His relationship with his children was excellent. His health was excellent. And he was a distinguished political figure (the Queen had knighted him two years ago). Nevertheless, he was experiencing a depression which grew worse by the day. He was taking antidepressants, but over time, as with all drugs, the effects had begun to wear off. His doctor had sent him to me. From the first month it became clear to me that modern life, the libel cases he dealt with, were in conflict with old values that were deeply ingrained in him, the values of justice, truth and the common good. A vicious circle! More cases, more money, more depression, more cases. I wished I could help him understand the only means of overcoming the depression: to resign. The decision had to be his. He had to reach it by himself. A psychiatrist who advises a famous barrister with an annual income of several million pounds to retire would soon find himself in a psychiatric clinic. I have no intention of entering a psychiatric clinic for the time being. In the future, perhaps! Not at the moment.

Sir Nigel laughed and said:

'How are you Doctor Mukhtar?'

'As well as can be expected. As well as can be expected. And how are you?'

'Worse than could be expected.'

'I read in the papers that you won another case this week.'

'I don't want to talk about the case.'

'Sir Nigel! We have to talk about the case.'

'I don't want to talk about that case. We'll talk about another case if you want.'

'Fine. Let's talk about another case.'

I knew perfectly well why Sir Nigel was unwilling to talk about the case. He had been representing one of the tabloids, which had published a deliberately false report libelling a famous footballer. The footballer had taken the paper to court. The paper had hired the services of Sir Nigel who managed to give the player a hard time in court, making him appear like a complete imbecile before the jury. He had provoked him by asking really devious questions. The jury found the paper innocent – a paper which had been anything but innocent. The press published a picture of the player with his wife beside him in tears. The player lost everything he owned on the case. And Sir Nigel didn't want to discuss the case because he didn't want to know that the wife's tears were the cause of his depression. Sir Nigel wanted to talk about other cases in which those he had defended had been wrongly condemned and were completely innocent. Fine! Why the hurry? Lets talk about other cases.

Wednesday
I spent the whole day at the University of Lobster. I was attending a seminar on the topic: Sex between Humans and Animals – towards a better understanding.

I would not have wasted my time on such a conference had not one of my patients committed suicide after his dog, with whom he had shared his bed, died. The dog had been the same breed as Lassie and had indeed shared his bed in every sense of the term. In a world of increasing sexual liberation, a psychiatrist has to keep abreast of all sexual activity, even human–animal.

The seminar began with a statistical study prepared by a team from Standard University. It was called: 'Post Kinsey: the new picture'. In brief, the research said that the data of the pioneering sexologist, Kinsey, on sexual contact between man and animals were widely inaccurate. The research said that such contact was many times more frequent than the small percentage cited by Kinsey. The study added that such contact was not confined, as the famous sexologist had imagined, to young adolescents in rural and agricultural regions. According to the latest study, the major cities had become the principle loci for such practices. The study concluded that at least one in every thousand of the population of a major western city had experimented at least once with some kind of human–animal sexual practice.

The second study was about sexually transmitted diseases between humans and animals'. More bad news. The incidence of disease was much higher than expected. The third study was entitled: 'Human–Animal Sex and the Law'. The study called for changes to rigid laws that hadn't been changed for centuries and for the passing of 'more broad-minded' legislation. In any case, broad-mindedness is necessary. The most curious part of the study was that which dealt with 'how to determine the gratification enjoyed by the animal party in the sexual relationship'. More wonders! When the day came to a close I looked at every animal I saw on the way home with a great deal of caution. Even my small dog, Bambi, who greeted me in her usual fashion when I got home received a lukewarm response from me. Who knows what goes on in a dog's brain? How could I be sure that her welcome did not contain an element of sexual gratification?

At home, I found my daughter, Lucy, immersed in a book by Jung. Lucy was studying psychology and intended to become a psychiatrist. The Oedipus Complex?! Lucy, as usual, wanted to talk to me about me and my relationship with her mother. Perhaps she thought she could begin her professional life as of now. She said:

'I spoke to Mum today. She sends you her regards. She says she won't be coming next week.'

'Lucy! I've told you many times before that your mother and I have agreed that she should spend four months in Brazil. She won't be coming home next week. She'll be coming home in two months.'

'But I don't understand . . .'

'You can't understand at your age. You'll understand when you grow up.'

'Don't forget that I can understand complex psychological theories.'

'I'm not talking about a psychological theory. I'm talking about a human relationship. No two human relationships are alike. The relationship between your mother and me is going through a difficult phase.'

'Isn't the solution that you should both sit down and talk about it honestly together? Isn't that what you advise your patients? That they should confront their problems instead of running away from them?'

'No one is running away from a problem. We've discussed it a thousand times. With the utmost honesty. All that's left is to take the decision. Is the marriage to be changed into just a comfortable arrangement or should it be terminated altogether.'

'But you both love . . .'

'Lucy! It has nothing to do with love. The marriage has lost its magic and if . . .'

'A psychiatrist talking about magic?! A voodoo witch doctor?'

'You know what I mean. We can stay in a marriage without magic. We can look for magic without marriage. No one can take such a fundamental decision in a hurry. We need, your mother and I, some respite to give it more thought. We'll reach the right decision. Believe me!'

'The right decision is that you live together again with the old magic.'

'Oh! Lucy! Lucy! Do you still believe in Santa Claus? Do you still believe he comes down the chimney, leaves his presents under the tree and then goes back to Lapland? Now that is magic! Can you bring it back into your life?'

'I never stopped believing in Santa Claus for a single moment.'

'And I believe the Pope's a Protestant.'

Lucy laughed and went back to her book.

I found several messages on the answer machine. Most of them from friends. Most of them routine. But some of them insisted I phone as soon as I got the message. I began with Lola. Her voice, choked with sobs, came on the line:

'Anwar! Anwar! I'm sorry! I'm really sorry! Please forgive me. The dirty bastard admitted it.'

'Lola! Calm down! What's happened?'

'I came straight out with it and accused him of being unfaithful. At first he didn't want to admit it. Then he did. He said it was just a fling and didn't mean anything. Can you imagine?! I loved him. I was going to marry him. And he was having flings. Do you know what I'm going to do, Anwar? I'm going to kill myself. It's the only solution.'

With growing apprehension, I said:

'Lola! Lola! Calm down! Stop all this childish talk. Let's meet and talk about it.'

'I don't want to become a psychiatric patient.'

'There's no need for you to become a psychiatric patient. We'll meet as friends. I have to make sure you're all right.'

'All right?! I've lost the greatest love of my life and you're talking about whether I'm all right?!'

'Fine! We'll talk about the greatest love of your life, if you want. The important thing is that I see you.'

'I'll think about it.'

'Promise me you won't do anything silly.'

'I won't do anything until I've consulted you.'

'When shall I see you?'

'I'll call you soon.'

'Promise?'

'I promise!'

I answered the second call. Raf'i's voice burst forth:

'Anwar! Anwar! I've missed you. I haven't seen you for ages. Have you heard the news? Amazing news! Lola and Shukri. She's left him. Split up with him. Kicked him out like a dog. Why? Do you know why? She confronted him with his infidelity. The fool admitted it. The ass! Would any sane person admit to an affair? I ask you, Anwar, would a sane person do that? Have you ever, in your whole life, ever admitted to an affair? What's important is that the fool's admitted it. And they've split up. The question remains: Who told Lola? A question I can't answer. It's impossible that you were the source. Impossible! The Hipposocratic Oath! I don't know how she found out. What's important is that she did. Rest assured, Anwar, I have no suspicions about you. I trust you more than I trust myself. But now I know you're asking yourself how, using Aids, I could kill Lola and Shukri. I know you're asking yourself. I know you're surprised. Your friend. Your lifelong friend, Raf'i Rif'at !Killing someone? Is that rational? Do you record your phone calls, Anwar, the way that filthy bastard, the proprietor of the "Voice of Crime", does? And even if you did, what could you do with it? The Hipposocratic Oath applies to phone calls too. Isn't that so? Sure it is! The Scorpion himself told me that. The question remains: is it rational for me to kill my ex-wife and her lover? Maybe! But how do we know? How can we be sure? The incubation period. Isn't that the term you doctors use? The incubation of the virus takes several months, from three months to a year. That's what the specialists told me. In six months the truth will be known. Was I joking? Did I send a perfectly healthy, beautiful young woman and just claimed she was infected with Aids? Do you think I was just joking? What's important is that Lola has split up with Shukri. Now, both of them are worried. Worry, in itself, can kill. Aahh! The third one! I forgot that bastard who owns the "Voice of Crime"! He's going to die as well. No! No! I was really only joking. Just one of Raf'i's famous little jokes. But you must appreciate, Anwar, that there's a very strong possibility that I'm not joking. It's not hard to find a beautiful young woman with Aids. Shall I tell you how? No! No! I don't think you require such services. You're a civilized psychiatrist. While I'm just an uncivilized billionaire. Who believes in revenge. Who believes in little jokes. You'll have to wait six months to find out. Till we all find out. In the meantime, don't forget the Hipposocratic Oath. See you soon! Bye!'

This dangerous sadistic lunatic! I swear, if Lola ever develops symptoms of the disease, I'll tell the police what happened. And to hell with Hippocrates and his oath!

The third call was from the star of stars. Niran! The Arabistani nation's film and TV queen of seduction. Its most famous and most lusted-after actress. Niran came from her home capital once every four months to spend a whole day with me. And what was Niran's problem? The usual problem. A modern way of life in conflict with old values. The modern way of life is the way of life of any star anywhere in the world. Friends. Lovers. Producers. Directors. Expensive gifts. Wealth. But the old values are the values of her poor family. A very poor family. And one of the values of this very poor family is that the poor always remain poor. And if they become rich, their riches will not last but will go as suddenly as they came. In the twinkling of an eye. Or by witchcraft. Or a vile plot. Everything will vanish into thin air and the poor young girl returns to her misery. Niran does not believe, on the emotional level, that she's living a real life. She thinks she's living a transient dream. A dream of wealth. A dream of fame. A dream of men. She believes the dream will suddenly end. Most probably by means of witchcraft. Every time she comes to London, she spends a whole day with me discussing her fears and a whole day with my friend, Basir, the astrologer, warding off black magic. Her alluring voice came on the line:

'Doctor! I'm sorry! I came this time without an appointment. There's an urgent problem. Very urgent. I want to see you as soon as possible. Tonight!'

'Niran! Tonight?! I'm just about to go to bed.'

'Tomorrow, then.'

'I can't see you in the morning.'

'After lunch, then. Please, Doctor. The problem is urgent. I'll come at two.'

'Come at three.'

Before falling asleep, the image of Niran filled all my senses. Her exploding body. Her radiant face. Her seductive voice. I felt desire enflame my body, from head to toe. The return of adolescence! But what about you, old grandfather Hippocrates? How about a compromise? 'I will [. . .] abstain [. . .] from the seduction of females or males, of freemen and slaves.' I promise I'll never seduce a man or molest a slave. What do you say?! And women?! Ok! I'll never seduce a woman, but I won't stop them seducing me. That's a reasonable agreement, isn't it? Things have changed a lot since your days, illustrious grandfather. The old values have to change a little bit at least. A little bit.

Thursday
The first appointment was with a businessman who was becoming an alcoholic. I don't know if the businessman would keep on seeing me if he knew I drank half a bottle a day. I wasn't going to tell him unless he asked. I'm trying to train the businessman to become addicted in a systematic manner. Addiction in the Churchillian manner. Churchill would drink more than twenty alcoholics but nobody ever accused him of being an alcoholic, because his addiction was systematic. Willie Brandt, the former West German chancellor, would drink a bottle and a half of brandy every day. The people used to call him 'Brandy Willie'. But despite that, he didn't let addiction ruin his life. Systematic addiction.

I tell the businessman:

'Listen Mister Haksel! There are only two ways to deal with addiction. The first is that you give up alcohol once and for all. Once and for all! In that event you can go to a specialized clinic where they'll dry you out, as they say. Three weeks of tranquillizers, sleeping pills and deep sleep. Then you come out "a good boy".'

'My problem, doctor, is that I don't want to be "a good boy".'

'That's what I expected. I must tell you, frankly, that the statistics don't support "the good boy" idea. According to the statistics, of those who are treated for alcoholism in clinics no more than ten per cent turn out 'good boys'. The remaining ninety per cent go back to the bottle. Take, for example, all those famous actors who become alcoholics and go into clinics. They all go back to the drink. And alcoholic actresses.'

'So what should I do, Doctor Mukhtar? I don't want to be finished off by alcohol. And I don't want to give it up and become an object of pity and commiseration. And I don't want the business empire I've built up over thirty years with sweat and tears to collapse.'

'There is nothing to make that a foregone conclusion, Mister Haksel. The second practical option is that you learn to live with your addiction. My father once told me, when I was in my teens: "the bottle cannot be neutral. You will either be its master or it will be your mistress." My father was right.'

'My father told me something similar.'

'Your father was right.'

'But how? How does one stop one's servant becoming one's mistress?'

'Aahh! Now we're getting to the heart of the matter. It needs a certain amount of discipline. A reasonable amount. But not to be compared with the superhuman discipline required to give up alcohol entirely.'

'And how is one to obtain this amount of discipline?'

'Discipline, like most things, is a habit that comes with practice. Let me first explain to you the difference between alcoholism and excessive drinking. People only call someone who drinks too much an alcoholic when three indicators appear . . .'

'I thought that anyone who drank too much was necessarily an alcoholic.'

'He may be an alcoholic, then again he may not. Let's take the three indicators. The first indicator is to do with work. The alcoholic doesn't turn up two or three days a week, or even more. If he is not like you, that is, the owner of the company, his repeated absences will soon lead to his dismissal. If the alcoholic is his own boss, he will soon find himself without clients. Who can have confidence in a surgeon who's drunk? And who can have dealings with a lawyer who turns up drunk in the courtroom? The golden rule is: don't let the bottle interfere in any way, in any way, with your work. Do your job first, then drink as much as you want.'

'I try to do that but I'm not always successful. Sometimes I have an overwhelming desire to have a drink in the mornings.'

'Don't fight the desire. Put it off. Put it off until you leave work. The second indicator of alcoholism is the deterioration in family relations. When someone who drinks too much starts beating his wife or children you can draw the conclusion that he's entering the alcoholic stage. The second golden rule is: don't let the bottle poison your relationship with your family. If you feel a strong thirst coming on, go somewhere far away to drink and don't come back to your family until the thirst is over.'

'The fact is, Doctor, I only came to you after I'd threatened my wife with divorce.'

'The alarm bell! But you can put the situation right. The third indicator is a deterioration in social relations. When people begin to avoid inviting you, when friends start making their excuses, when . . .'

Mr Haksel left with signs of satisfaction on his face. I don't know if he'll be successful in controlling his addiction, but his chances of success with me are greater than his chances in a clinic. I have to deal with my patients honestly. I could have sat with him for months and years on end talking about the layers upon layers of complexes that drove him to addiction. What complexes?! Science has proved, almost conclusively, that addiction is linked to one's genes and has no definite link with any psychological complex. Many people with psychological complexes don't drink and many people who drink don't suffer from any psychological complexes.

The second patient came. The bishop. The bishop's problem was that he was in love with a younger man, an adolescent to be precise. In the past, the bishop had had similar relationships but had managed to keep them secret. But now he realized he was deceiving himself and others and had had enough of it. He wanted to make a final decision. The bishop was a highly educated man so I saw no need to beat about the bush. I said:

'Your problem is the traditional problem: the clash between new ways and old values. I don't intend to waste your time or mine. The only solution is to renounce the ways or renounce the values.'

'How can I renounce the one true love of my life?'

'I do not know what is the one true love of your life. If the church was this love, then priority will have to be given to the church's values. I can't make a decision for you. No one can take the decision for you. This is your decision alone.'

'But Doctor . . .'

The bishop left despondent and dejected. The third patient arrived, the un-merry widow. The only problem of any kind that this almost youthful, almost beautiful millionairess suffered from was boredom. It was boredom that led her into numerous social and charitable activities, and it was boredom that led her to my clinic. I did nothing but listen and express a great deal of sympathy. Lady Kidding began, as usual, with her health problems:

'My health, Doctor Mukhtar, my health is beginning to deteriorate. Would you believe I've lost three pounds this week? I've completely lost my appetite. I eat only with difficulty. Then there's the constipation. This gets worse by the day. No medicine does any good. Neither do bran cakes. When the constipation and the haemorrhoids come together the situation is tragic. Then there's the sleeping problem. I wake up three times a night. At least. Is that normal, Doctor? Don't tell me that's normal. I used to sleep like a child. But now, I'm tossing and turning all night. I don't want sleeping pills. There is a danger of addiction, isn't that so Doctor? Then my allergy! My God! My God! My allergy these days is killing me. I tell you, killing me. Look at my eyes. Look at my nose. I can't breathe. I can hardly speak. Have you noticed how my voice rattles? And on top of all that there's the arthritis . . .'

I commended the aristocratic widow's bravery in the face of such medical disasters. She then turned to her second favourite topic, the servants:

'Did you know that my maid left me this week? She left, all of a sudden, without giving notice. And I'd treated her like my own daughter. No one could imagine how kindly I treated her. And she leaves me, out of the blue, without any notice. She must have found some man who sweet-talked her into leaving me. A man who'll trick her and take everything she saved while working for me. And when that happens, what's she going to do? She'll be back. Crying and saying sorry and asking me to take her on again. But I won't be taking her on. I treated her like I treat my own daughter. She has no respect for my position. She can go and work somewhere else. I won't be extending to her the hand she has bitten.

And on the same day, the chauffeur comes to me and says that his circumstances have forced him to leave my employ. What circumstances? Do you think he seduced the maid to leave me so that he could get his hands on her savings? I'm certain of it. It was my mistake for employing him. A terrible mistake. I should have realized that his long hair, tight trousers and his acting like a gigolo were warning signs. I'm now paying the price for my mistake. He went without giving notice either. Are my problems with these people over? Then the cook sends me a letter asking for a rise. But what has the cook got to do? I've already told you that I've lost my appetite . . .'

I congratulated her on her steadfastness in the face of successive acts of treachery and bad servants and advised her to be more cautious in future when taking on new staff. She then turned to her third favourite topic, her lady and gentleman friends:

'I have no idea what's happening to people's sense of taste these days. What has happened to people's sense of taste, Doctor? It's completely disappeared from people's lives. There's not one gentlemen nor one lady among them. Can you imagine?! I invited a group of gentlemen and lady friends for tea and one of them comes wearing a dress more like a bathing costume. Can you imagine?! And she's sixty! Can you imagine?! But for the shame of it, I would have asked her to go up to my bedroom and choose a robe to cover her nakedness. I pretended I hadn't noticed anything. Worse was her lover. He comes wearing a T-shirt. Can you imagine?! A T-shirt with the picture of a Rock 'n Roll singer on it. Can you imagine?! An old man wearing a shirt for a teenager. I tell you, taste doesn't exist any more. Worse still was the guest who expressed displeasure at the absence of cucumber sandwiches. Can you imagine?! A guest in my home trying to score points with me about . . .'

I assured the aristocratic widow that I was wholly in agreement with her about the decline in standards of taste. I asked her to adopt forbearance in a world of riffraff and gave her a new medicine for her constipation. She left laughing. A psychiatrist giving out medicine for constipation?! Why not?! When constipation becomes a psychological problem the cure has to come from a psychiatrist.

I decided to telephone my friend, the astrologer, before Niran came. It is our practice to exchange information about our mutual clients. I said:

'Hello there, Doctor Basir.'

(In fact he wasn't a doctor, but insisted on the title.)

'Hello, Doctor Anwar. We've missed you.'

'So have we. Has Niran been to see you?'

'Yes.'

'What's the problem this time?'

'The problem, this time, is a genie.'

'A genie?!'

'A genie.'

'What do you mean?'

'I mean a genie has possessed our beautiful actress.'

'Did you manage to exorcise it?'

'I'm still trying. By the way, Anwar, can you see Heather?'

'Your girlfriend?'

'Yes.'

'What's her problem?'

'It's best if she tells you herself. I think she needs a psychiatrist.'

'Fine! I'll see her.'

'When?'

'I'll ask my secretary to check my appointments and contact her. I'll see her at the earliest opportunity.'

'As soon as possible.'

'Fine! I'll try and see her tomorrow.'

Niran arrived. The person who had chosen Niran, meaning 'fire', as her stage name had been spot on. (Her real name was Durriya, but that was another story.) Everything about Niran was aflame and burning. If I didn't know that she was thirty-six, I would have said she was twenty-six, or even sixteen. Despite the late-night parties, despite the studio lights, despite the fact that she didn't take any form of physical exercise, her body was as firm as a champion runner. Some people are born with the gift of beauty and the gift of eternal youth, while some children are born middle-aged. Science does not know why and I'm not going to try to find out. I acknowledge my inability to understand many of the things with which this planet teems with. I take things as I see them. Niran lay down on the couch and began to smoke in silence. She finished her first cigarette, lit a second and began to speak:

'I'm sorry to disturb you, doctor, but I had to see you. Imagine, my fiancé has finished our relationship. We were about to get married.'

'That's not a problem. You'll find another fiancé.'

'But I love him, Doctor. I'm madly in love with him.'

'Niran! You say that about every new fiancé.'

'But this one's a real find. A real find, Doctor! He owns a huge company. He's handsome. And what's more he's . . .'

'Niran! When will you understand that you're the real find and that you can choose any man you want?'

'Doctor! You're just being nice to me. You know that isn't true. Look at me! Look at me! I'm starting to turn to flab. Who's going to want an old woman?'

'There is, at least, one admirer guaranteed.'

'Who, Doctor?'

I laughed, but did not reply. She said:

'You're just trying to be nice to me again. But anyway, I'm grateful. You must understand, Doctor, I can't go on losing fiancé after fiancé after fiancé.'

'It was always your decision. It was you who got rid of them one after the other.'

'You're mistaken, Doctor. Believe me! Believe me! Whenever I fall for a man and we become close, something strange happens. Something beyond my control. Suddenly I notice he has started to hate me. Suddenly, I notice . . .'

'And you believe this is to do with black magic?'

'Is there any other explanation? When a man is in love with you one day and can't even bear to look at you the next, is there any other explanation? And when you agree in the evening to get married and make detailed plans and he comes in the morning and says circumstances prevent him from getting married, is there any other explanation?'

'There are a thousand and one explanations.'

'How?'

'Maybe he was telling the truth. Sometimes things that seem perfectly rational when one is under the effect of alcohol cannot stand up to the cold light of day. Maybe he noticed you weren't serious when talking about marriage. Maybe . . .'

She interrupted:

'Maybe it was the black magic that made him hate me. Do you know the effects of magic? The person bewitched looks at a beautiful woman but sees the face of a monkey. A real monkey! A chimpanzee! That's what people who know about these things told me. Imagine my face being turned into that of a monkey. My face!'

I couldn't stop myself laughing. It's very bad practice for a doctor to laugh at anything a patient says, but for the life of me, I couldn't imagine, with respect for all magicians down the ages, how Niran's face could be changed into that of a monkey.

Niran carried on at full tilt:

'You're laughing! You're laughing! You wouldn't be laughing if it happened to you. Are you challenging me? Do you want me to do something that will make you see your wife's face transformed into that of a monkey?'

'An amazing idea, Niran. I don't hate monkeys. And this week I attended a seminar on sexual relations between humans and animals.'

'Animals? Animals! These westerners, they're all animals.'

'Maybe that's why magic has no effect in the west. If one of them saw his girlfriend's face changed into a monkey's, he'd love her even more.'

'Doctor! Stop playing around! I am suffering from a real problem. I need your help. When Simsim went . . .'

'I'm sorry? Simsim?!'

'Aahh! Hosam! My fiancé I was telling you about. When he went, the world closed in on me. I seriously thought about killing myself. Do you know what happened the night he left me?'

'What happened?'

'We were together. As you know, he was my fiancé and we were going to get married, and we were together. You understand my meaning?'

'Naturally. You considered yourselves as good as married.'

'Exactly! Exactly! Then suddenly, I felt I wasn't with just one man. Suddenly, I felt things inside me . . . I can't describe what I felt. You'll never believe me anyway.'

'Niran! I believe everything.'

'Fine! Fine! I'll be frank with you. There was another man, a genie inside me. Are you going to laugh?'

'I'm not going to laugh.'

'Do you believe me?'

'Carry on.'

'There was a genie inside me. I felt him inside me. Do you understand what I'm saying?'

'I understand.'

'Simsim felt him too. I mean, Hosam. Here is the tragedy! Hosam felt the genie and suddenly began to scream. He was screaming at the top of his voice. He left his clothes and ran naked into the street. Do you believe me?'

'Why wouldn't I believe you?'

'After he'd gone I heard a voice laughing in the room. I couldn't see anything but I heard this voice laughing. Then I heard a voice whispering in my ear. Do you believe me, Doctor?'

'I believe you. Stranger things than laughing and whispering happen.'

'Do you know what he said . . . what he said?'

'The genie?'

'The genie.'

'What did he say?'

'He said: 'I'm going now. But I'll be back if I ever see you with another man. And I'll cut off . . .'. I can't repeat the word, Doctor. You know what he meant.'

'The meaning is perfectly clear. He'll castrate the next man he sees you with.'

'Exactly! Exactly! Do you know what that means, Doctor? It means I'll never get married. Never! I'll be left on the shelf. I'll be an old maid. The genie will come if a man comes close to me and he'll cut off . . . You know what I mean. What am I going to do? Suicide is the only way out.'

'Niran! Did you enjoy being with the genie?'

'Doctor! Doctor! What kind of question is that?'

'Ok?!'

'It was a completely different experience from . . . from . . .'

'From sex with a man?'

'Yes.'

'Niran! Do you want the genie to come back?'

'Doctor! Doctor! How can you ask me a question like that? I want to get married and have children before its too late. What am I going to do with a genie?'

'Niran! Maybe the genie was just joking with you. He did it just the once and has no intention of coming back.'

'But what if he does come back?'

'Niran? When you were with another man did . . .'

'Doctor! Doctor! How can you ask me such a question? What happened happened only last week. And Hosam was my fiancé. Do you think that I . . .'

'We'll only know if the genie's threat is true if we conduct an experiment.'

'Meaning? You mean . . .'

'Niran! It's now five o'clock. I finish my work in the clinic at five on the dot.'

'But, doctor, I'm leaving tomorrow. You have to find a solution straight away.'

'What do you say to resuming our conversation somewhere else?'

'Where?'

'In the clinic annexe.'

'Where is the clinic annexe?'

'The clinic annexe is the comfortable apartment above the clinic. Let's go up and continue our conversation.'

Niran left the clinic annexe after midnight. We conducted a practical experiment and the genie did not come. Or perhaps he came but did not carry out his threat. I had never seen a woman act like her before in bed. Perhaps the genie lives in her permanently and is active when the need arises. The important thing is that she left convinced the genie was only joking with her and that without any fear she could look for another fiancé. Aahh, old grandfather Hippocrates! It was part of the treatment, a very necessary part. Psychiatry is a unique type of medicine. You have to use anything if you think it will work. I didn't seduce her, grandfather Hippocrates. I swear to you! And in truth, she did not seduce me. The truth is that it was the genie who did everything. You must understand, grandfather, Hippocrates, that Niran comes from a very poor and a very conservative family. She can't have sex with a man unless she's convinced herself that he's her fiancé or . . . or . . . or . . . that sex is the only cure.

Friday

The first patient was a famous British journalist – it seems that this was the week for the press! – who wrote for the gutter press. Recently he had begun to suffer from insomnia. He wanted to talk about his childhood. All patients want to talk about their childhoods. Freud's lethal legacy! The tabloid journalist was astonished when I told him that I would not talk to any patient about any subject until after they'd had a full medical examination at a state-of-the-art medical centre. He tried to get out of this condition by saying he had regular check-ups. I stood my ground. He only became convinced when I explained to him that a complete medical examination often showed up a physical cause for a patient's problems, saving the patient and me a great deal of trouble. I added that the exhaustion he was complaining of could be the result of a physical illness which had nothing to do with the subconscious mind, his childhood or the unconscious. I sent him to a specialist medical centre I have dealings with and said I would arrange an appointment with him as soon as I received the report from the centre.

The second patient was a a fifty-year-old woman professor who had fallen in love with one of her students who wasn't even twenty. Nothing had happened between them yet but she felt that it was about to happen. For more than five months she had been coming to me and talking to me about it. My own impression was that *it* would never happen. My decided impression was that this tempestuous love, which was turning her life upside-down, was one-sided. Rather than coming to terms with life at fifty, she had fled into a love affair with a twenty year old. Ok! I think we'll need another five months before she understands the reality of the situation. Until that time, it is my duty to devote my undivided attention to the professor as she speaks, with rare eloquence, about a sexual contact that hasn't happened, and is unlikely to happen, and the tortured conscience it has caused her.

The third patient was my friend, Sufyan Na'im, the grey-haired editor. Didn't I say this was the week for the press! Sufyan Na'im was Bustan's boyfriend. I hesitated before giving him an appointment. But I decided that the best way for me to explain to him why I couldn't accept him as a patient was to tell him myself, at the clinic. As soon as he entered he began talking about a serious marital problem. He went on to say that he didn't have any psychological problems himself, but he wanted to consult me about his marital problem. I told him I would be more than happy to give him some advice but that I could not. He seemed rather surprised. I told him that the conventions of the profession made it difficult for me to treat a friend. There has to be a degree of objectivity which is impossible when the patient is a friend of the doctor. I managed to persuade him with difficulty and gave him the name of a colleague who specialized in marital problems. I hope Bustan doesn't get to hear about the grey-haired man's marital problems. If she did, she'd be convinced he was on the point of divorcing his wife to marry her. The truth was that he was more than concerned to keep the marriage going and that it was his wife who was getting restless. I hope my colleague tells him what I can't: putting the girlfriends on hold for a while should restore peace to the marital home.

Heather, whom Basir – Sorry! Doctor Basir Al-'Aref! – had insisted I see as soon as possible, arrived. I said to her:

'Heather! You don't look as if you need a psychiatrist.'

'I think you're right.'

'So why did you ask to see me? And with such urgency?'

'It wasn't me who asked. It was him.'

'Ok! So why did he ask?'

'Because he thinks I've started imagining things. That I'm losing my mind.'

'We all imagine things but it doesn't mean we're losing our minds.'

'But I'm not imagining things.'

'Ok! So what's the problem?'

'The problem, Anwar, is that your friend is going mad.'

'Basir?!'

'Basir.'

'How?'

'You know that what we do is based entirely on collecting information, intuition, a few harmless tricks, selling hope to people and . . .'

'I'm well aware of the nature of what you do.'

'Recently, Basir has started believing that he's a medium and that he can have dealings with people from other worlds.'

'You're joking!'

'I'm not joking.'

'Basir? I know that deep down Basir is laughing at those clients for whom he arranges meetings with the spirit world.'

'True. But things have changed recently.'

'What do you mean?'

'He firmly believes that he can contact genies, and one genie in particular, he says, has become one of his dearest friends.'

'Basir is friends with a genie?!'

'That's what he says.'

'And what have you done?'

'I told him frankly that he was losing his marbles.'

'And how did he react?'

'He sent me to you. He says I'm paranoid. He says his friendship with the genie has had no ill effect on his mental powers.'

'Heather! Let us suppose he is a friend. What do you find disturbing about this relationship?'

'He hasn't slept with me since the genie came on the scene.'

'Aahh!'

'But that's not important. I mean that doesn't scare me. He's started spending hours on end alone with the genie. He doesn't offer any advice to a client until after consulting the genie. If this carries on, your friend's going to end up in a mental hospital.'

'I think you're right.'

'So what can we do to avoid it?'

'The golden rule in psychiatry is that there's no point in treating a patient unless he realizes that he's got a problem and unless he asks for the treatment himself.'

'Basir won't admit there's any problem.'

'So, we can't help him.'

'Anwar! This is your friend! How can you just let him decline into madness?'

'I can't help him if he doesn't want to be helped.'

'So what am I going to do?'

'Try and get him to see another psychiatrist apart from me. It would be difficult for him, and for me, for him to admit to me he has a problem. It might be easier with another psychiatrist.'

'And if he refuses?'

'We'll just have to be patient . . . and pray.'

I spent the evening at the house of my friend, Shaher Nattash. As usual, there was a noisy party going on. And, as usual, there was a bizarre mix of guests. I was trying to listen to an Arabistani singer when Shukri Yasser suddenly pounced on me, took me into a corner and started talking:

'Anwar! I've missed you. I haven't seen you for ages. Listen! I've got an interesting story for you. You're a psychiatrist and you love interesting stories. Do you want to hear it? I'm sure you'll like it. Let's call it the story of the Two Billionaires: "Billionaire One" and "Billionaire Two". Now, Billionaire One likes grabbing things from people, from anybody, but particularly Billionaire Two. A very bad habit! Billionaire Two was on the point of buying the Star hotel – you know the Star hotel?! – when Billionaire One comes along like a hawk and snatches the deal out of his hands. By devious means. Foul means. Naturally, Billionaire Two is annoyed . . .'

A this point, a beautiful young blonde woman came up to us and interrupts Shukri:

'Shukri! Isn't this Anwar Mukhtar? The famous writer?'

Shukri, who was annoyed to have had his story interrupted in this manner, replied rudely:

'Yes! The very same! Anwar! Let me introduce you to Jessica.'

Jessica leapt in:

'Doctor Mukhtar! I'm so pleased to meet you. You can't imagine how much I like your books. Especially *The Voodoo Doctor*. You can't imagine . . .'

Shukri broke in:

'Jessica! I'm having an important conversation with the doctor. Go and play somewhere else. You can tell him how much you admire him some other time.'

Jessica looked at me as she said:

'Ok! Ok! May I have your visiting card, Doctor? May I get in touch with you?'

The beautiful blonde went away after taking my card and permission to contact me whenever she wanted. Shukri returned to his story:

'I was saying that Billionaire One had snatched, in a completely illegitimate manner, a deal out of the hands of Billionaire Two. Now, Billionaire Two decides to get his own back on Billionaire One. A bad habit, revenge. He decides to take the most valuable thing Billionaire One has. The absolutely most valuable thing. And his most valuable thing is his beautiful young wife. It isn't difficult. With a little cunning Billionaire Two begins a relationship with Billionaire One's wife. Now, Billionaire Two is very keen that Billionaire One should find out that his wife is being unfaithful. When Billionaire One hears the news, he goes crazy. So far, everything is perfectly normal. A snatch for a snatch. One for one. A wife for a hotel. But it gets a little bit more complicated when Billionaire One's wife asks Billionaire Two to marry her. An annoying case of being madly in love. This hasn't been part of the plan. Billionaire Two now has to find a way of getting rid of the wife who, once he's got his own back, is becoming a burden. The director doesn't have a screenplay. One day, Billionaire Two is in his office when a beautiful young girl comes in. She's a volunteer at an Aids hospice and she asks for a donation. Now, Billionaire Two knows just how Billionaire One thinks. He gives the young girl a huge donation for the hospice and an even bigger amount in return for her involvement in a truly diabolical plan. He asks her to go to Billionaire One to ask him for a donation for the Aids hospice. He also gets her to tell Billionaire One that she's got Aids herself. So, as soon as Billionaire One hears she's got Aids, his instinct for revenge springs into action and, in return for a vast amount of money, gives her two specific tasks to do. The first is to sleep with a journalist who's been trying to blackmail him. The second is to sleep with Billionaire Two. Now, somehow he lets his wife know that Billionaire Two is sleeping with a young woman. So the wife of Billionaire Two decides to leave him. And so everybody's happy. Billionaire Two has got his own back on Billionaire One who thinks he's got his own back on Billionaire Two. And nobody gets hurt. And they all lived happily ever after. What do you make of that?'

Before I could reply, Shukri Yasser left me, guffawing at the top of his head as he did so. I felt an immense burden had been lifted from me. Lola, therefore, did not have Aids. The whole thing had been a practical joke between a couple of billionaires. I went to the nearest phone, talked to Lola and asked her to come and see me the next day in the clinic annexe.

Saturday

As was usual every Saturday, I spent most of the day writing. My books have brought me the fame and money that the clinic hasn't. My fist book was called *The Old and the New: choose one.* In the book I expanded on my doctoral thesis: many psychological disorders arise from the clash between the modern way of life and old values. If we let go of either the modern way of life or the old values, the disorders disappear. The book created a storm and was translated into several languages. My second book was called *The Voodoo Doctor.* In it I attacked all of Freud's concepts and compared them to voodoo medicine. The second book outsold the first and created a convulsion in scientific circles. My third book was not terribly successful as the subject did not interest the western reader. It was called *The New Gypsies: arabistanis in europe* and dealt with the psychological problems which Arabistanis living in Europe suffer from. My fourth book sold tremendously; within a few weeks it was a bestseller in several European capitals. The book was called *Sex . . . As a Treatment,* and it dealt with a number of psychological problems that can be cured through a healthy sexual relationship. I'm working on my fifth book. I haven't chosen a title yet but its subject matter is taking shape by the day. The book will include a reworking of the theory contained in the first book: in most cases, its difficult to abandon old values once and for all, or abandon modern life in its entirety. What is needed is a compromise, a way to harmonize the modern way of life with old values. Concessions from both sides! I think I'm going to call the book *The Compromise.*

In the evening, Lola came in all her radiance. I told her that she had nothing to fear about having Aids. I couldn't give her the details. The Hippocratic Oath! We celebrated together. The celebration lasted a long time. Then, without any premeditation, we found ourselves in bed together. *Sex . . . As a Treatment!*

Sunday

As usual for a Sunday, Lucy and I had lunch together. Lucy had chosen a beautiful restaurant by the river. Luckily, she didn't raise the question of her mother. All our conversation was about psychiatry. Lucy treated me like a professional colleague, as equals. And why not? If I was going to call the Great Professor a 'Voodoo Doctor' why shouldn't I let my daughter raise objections to some of my theories? She'd see they were valid in time. Why hurry?

At home in the evening I was forced to see the beautiful blond girl I'd met at Shaher's party. She had phoned a number of times saying she had to see me at once. Her voice was hysterical. I took her insistence as a warning bell, which made me abandon the principle I'd adopted my entire professional life always to treat patients at the clinic, never at home. Jessica arrived pale and in a confused state. Without preliminaries she blurted out:

'I had to see you as soon as possible. I'm telling you the truth, as soon as possible. I think Shukri has told you about me. It's clear he's been talking about me. I think it's my duty to tell you. I don't know why I'm telling you. I think you can do something, anything. You've just got to do something.'

'Jessica! Calm down! Tell me what's going on. I can't understand what you're going on about.'

'I told Raf'i that I had Aids and he sent me to . . .'

'I know the story. And I sent you to . . .'

'Ok! Ok! You only know part of the story. The whole truth is that – and neither you nor Shukri know this – is that I do in fact carry the Aids virus.'

The world suddenly span round. I whispered:

'Jessica! Jessica! What are you saying?'

'I'm telling you I've got Aids. All the tests say so.'

I don't remember Jessica leaving. All I remember is that I spent the whole night between the bed, where I sweated profusely, and the bathroom where I kept throwing up. Nothing is worse than dying from Aids. Nothing!

FIVE

The Astrologer

They talk much of the influence of the stars on man
But what, pray, of man's influence on the stars?
Al-Mutanabbi

Identity Card
Full Name: Basrawi 'Alwan Ma'aruf
Known as: Dr Basir Al-'Aref
Occupation: Astrologer
Age: 53
Wealth: $23million
Place of Birth: Arabistan X
Place of Work: London and throughout the world
Academic Qualifications: BA Psychology (Tariq bin Ziyad University); MA Psychology (University of Liverpool); PhD (forged) in Spiritual Studies from the University of Delhi Port (non-existant)
Marital Status: Single
Children: None

Monday
I began the day, as usual, by writing my weekly article for the *New Man*. As a title I'd chosen: 'Your Star Sign in Seconds'.

Aries, 21 March–20 April
Most Significant Characteristics: active, love of adventure, excessive sexual energy.
Most Significant Problem in Life: fiercely, at times lethally, competitive.
Basic Personality Flaw: selfishness.

Taurus, 21 April–20 May
Most Significant Characteristics: patience, persistence, loyalty.
Most Significant Problem in Life: boring other people.
Basic Personality Flaw: lack of imagination and originality.

Gemini, 21 May–21 June
Most Significant Characteristics: *ambitious, active, anxious.*
Most Significant Problem in Life: *weak constitution and associated illnesses.*
Basic Personality Flaw: *indifference to the feelings of others.*

Cancer, 22 June-22 July
Most Significant Characteristics: *intelligence, charm, attention to detail.*
Most Significant Problem in Life: *over-sensitivity.*
Basic Personality Flaw: *depressive tendencies.*

Leo, 23 July–23 August
Most Significant Characteristics: *courage, love of power, obstinacy.*
Most Significant Problem in Life: *exaggerating problems.*
Basic Personality Flaw: *arrogance.*

Virgo, 24 August–22 September
Most Significant Characteristics: *flexible, practical, adaptable.*
Most Significant Problem in Life: *difficulty in relaxing.*
Basic Personality Flaw: *no capacity for leadership.*

Libra, 24 September–23 October
Most Significant Characteristics: *self-confident, clever, good-looking.*
Most Significant Problem in Life: *inability to understand the feelings of others.*
Basic Personality Flaw: *over-sentimentality.*

Scorpio, 24 October–23 November
Most Significant Characteristics: *sensitivity, hardworking, fidelity.*
Most Significant Problem in Life: *susceptible to all forms of addiction.*
Basic Personality Flaw: *inability to admit a mistake.*

Sagittarius, 24 November–21 December
Most Significant Characteristics: *love of freedom, enthusiasm, spirit of adventure.*
Most Significant Problem in Life: *allowing stronger personalities to decide their fate.*
Basic Personality Flaw: *no sense of decorum.*

Capricorn, 22 December–20 January
Most Significant Characteristics: *ambitious, self-renewing energy, capacity to cope with hardships.*
Most Significant Problem in Life: *extreme shyness.*
Basic Personality Flaw: *avarice.*

Aquarius, 21 January–19 February
Most Significant Characteristics: strong personality, independence, principled.
Most Significant Problem in Life: using other people.
Basic Personality Flaw: inflexibility.

Pisces, 20 February–20 March
Most Significant Characteristics: creative, peace-loving, spiritual.
Most Significant Problem in Life: over-sensitivity.
Basic Personality Flaw: sudden mood-swings.

Good! I've read hundreds of books (maybe more) on the signs of the zodiac. I spent a whole year studying them and have written four best-sellers on the subject. Not a day goes by without my reading a client's horoscope (using a computer which produces reams and reams of the stuff). Do I really believe, deep down, in astrology? Do I really and truly believe the things I write and say to people? The answer is, most definitely, No. Believing that the position of the heavenly bodies at the moment of birth has an effect on the newborn child is a delusion and has no scientific basis, despite its being a delusion going back thousands of years. But then again, the answer is a most definite Yes. I believe in astrology and its enormous, I repeat, enormous, effect on people's lives. Why? The power of suggestion! Ninety per cent of my work is based on suggestion. Everyone, I repeat, everyone tends to adopt the characteristics they think their star sign imposes on them. Those born under Leo tend to control others, Pisceans search for an artistic identity and Taureans never lose hope, whatever the obstacles. Why? Because these are the characteristics of their star signs and their star sign, in their eyes, holds their inescapable destiny. A few years ago, a university in Europe carried out a statistical study using a sample of 50,000 people. The study clearly showed that certain star signs predominate in certain professions: many politicians were born under Leo, many actors were born under Pisces and many businessmen were born under Aries. Why? The power of suggestion! All my clients without exception, I repeat, without exception, believe in astrology. If people did not believe in astrology today, I would just be a poor lecturer in some obscure Arabistani university.

My first client this morning has not come to have an astrological reading. He has come to me for help getting back into power after it was taken from him in a military coup in the same way that he himself had originally seized power. Before talking about this client, I should say that fifty per cent of my success is down to good information, detailed and accurate information. The remaining fifty per cent is down to my spiritual gifts – spiritual gifts which have flourished since I was ten years old. They include: clairvoyance, mind-reading, palmistry and the ability to converse with unseen powers. In my office here I have information about important Arabistani figures which, in terms of the accuracy of the information, is better than that held by the biggest intelligence services (and better than that in the possession of my friend, Mass'oud As'ad!). In the Information Bureau I have fifteen people working for me, eleven are geniuses at intelligence gathering and the other four are computer whizz-kids. Thanks to the information collected by my intelligence analysts from open and hidden sources (as is the case with any intelligence-gathering service, newspapers and magazines are the most important source) and thanks to the computerized data organizing and indexing systems, I can find out in seconds, I repeat, seconds, everything that can be known about any potential client (and a potential client, in this context, means someone extremely rich). In the information centre I have substantial data on 5,000 individuals. This list includes every, I repeat, every Arabistani who is in a position of leadership, at the pinnacle of power. It also includes every, I repeat, every Arabistani worth more than $200 million. These men and women constitute the market palace where I sell my wares. And what are my wares? In crude and simple terms, I deal in hope. I sell hope to those looking for it. And to give a person hope I have to know everything about them. And I charge a great deal in return for hope. Why not? Most of those who pay me a great deal obtained a great deal with no effort on their part. I know in detail, I repeat, in detail, the problem of the respected client who is doing me the honour of visiting me for the first time.

I stood up to embrace the admiral and repeated:

'Hello, Your Excellency, Mister President. My humble office is honoured by your presence, Your Excellency, Mister President.'

The admiral smiled as he mumbled:

'President?! That was in the past.'

Immediately, I said:

'It was in the past. But the past shall return. I repeat, Your Excellency, Mister President, the past shall return. And you shall return to your homeland sooner than you can imagine. Before Your Excellency arrived, I was contemplating the crystal ball. The time for your return is sooner than you imagine.'

Signs of joy mixed with a certain astonishment appeared on the admiral's face. I resumed the onslaught:

'You shall return victorious and triumphant to your homeland which is awaiting you with impatience.'

What is the difference between 'victorious' and 'triumphant'? I don't know. I don't think the admiral knows either. But what I do know is that he liked the expression. I said:

'Come with me, Your Excellency, Mister President, into the Crystal-Ball Room. And you shall see and hear everything for yourself.'

I designed the Crystal-Ball Room myself in the same way that I designed

everything, I repeat, everything in my office. The Crystal-Ball Room is full of
mirrors. The ceiling, walls and floor are covered in mirrors. There are hidden
spotlights and concealed vents for a gas which calms the nerves. The only
furniture in the room is a table – itself a mirror – and two chairs. On the table is
the biggest crystal ball in the world. I had had it specially made in Germany.

I entered the room with the admiral and asked him to sit down in front of me.
In the meantime, Heather, my girlfriend and business partner, began to toy with
the lights: darkness, then a bright light, then subdued lighting. And the gas began
to flow through the vents. I pressed a button under my seat and the crystal ball
slowly began to fill with smoke. Under the influence of the lights and the smoke
billowing in the crystal ball, the admiral was prepared to believe anything. I
contemplated the crystal ball for some minutes without uttering a word. I closed
my eyes then opened them. (Following an operation in Sweden, my eyes had
doubled in size, so too had their effect.) I said:

'Your Excellency, Mister President! I see the image of a man dressed in
military uniform. I am not familiar with military ranks but I see on his epaulette
an aeroplane, two stars and . . .'

The admiral interrupted:

'A colonel.'

'Yes. A colonel. He wants to send a message to Your Excellency via me. A
telepathic message, naturally. Firstly, I will ask him his name then convey to you
all he has to say.'

I fell silent contemplating the crystal ball, then said:

'The colonel is unwilling to divulge his name, Your Excellency, Mister
President. He says you will know who he is when I tell you the message is from
"Miftah".'

As soon as he heard the word 'Miftah' the admiral let out a faint cry. I began
again:

'Miftah, Your Excellency, Mister President, wants to tell you that everything
is almost ready. Just a few difficulties with "Murjan" and "Ruman" remain
but . . .'

Another cry from the admiral interrupted me but I ignored it. I continued:

'The comrades are working out a deal with them. As soon as the deal is done,
everything will be ready for Your Excellency's return.'

The admiral opened his mouth, but he couldn't speak. I said:

'Miftah thinks, Your Excellency, Mister President, that they could make a
move in three months, maybe less. But caution is necessary, extreme caution.'

I ushered the admiral, who was still feeling the effects of the successive
shocks, back into my office where Heather gave him a glass of aniseed cordial.
(According to the Information Bureau, aniseed cordial was the admiral's
favourite drink.) He sipped from the glass as he said:

'Doctor Basir! This is astounding! This is unbelievable! I have heard much of your spiritual powers, but had I not seen them with my own eyes, I would not have believed. A truly astounding thing!'

With the utmost humility, I said:

'Gifts are from God, Your Excellency, Mister President. I merely put them at the disposal of those of His servants who deserve them, the champions of liberty and national dignity, such as yourself, Excellency.'

'I don't know what to say. I really can't . . .'

I interrupted politely:

'Your Excellency, Mister President! Let us leave gratitude until the crisis is over and Your Excellency returns to the homeland. As you have heard, there remain obstacles to be overcome. However, I would reassure you that I will overcome them. I will use all my spiritual powers . . .'

The admiral interrupted:

'What are you going to do, Doctor?'

'I shall conduct a special night sitting during which I will direct electro-magnetic spiritual forces against the despicable enemy who usurped your power, Your Excellency. I shall concentrate on destroying his morale, I repeat, destroying his morale. Spiritual, psychological war, Your Excellency, Mister President, is a lethal weapon. In a short time, the vile animal will lose his self-confidence, lose it for good. And then everyone will see, I repeat, everyone, an obvious change in his behaviour. Then, and only then, will Your Excellency be in a position to give the green light to your supporters.'

'Doctor Basir! I don't know how . . .'

'However, you must help me, Your Excellency, Mister President.'

'I'm at your command, doctor. Just say the word.'

'You're too kind! You're too kind! Every evening, I repeat, every evening, I want you to focus your thoughts on the accursed enemy. Have a photograph of him in front of you to help focus your thoughts. I want you to look at the photograph and say in a loud voice, I repeat, a loud voice: "You are just a usurper. I am the legitimate ruler. I am the legitimate ruler. I am the legitimate ruler". You must say this, in its entirety, ninety-nine times, ninety-nine times exactly. I want you to start at exactly nine o'clock, I repeat, exactly nine o'clock. And I will start at that time as well. With your and my efforts, the vile animal will lose all power to resist, and will fall like a rotten fruit to the ground.'

The admiral put his hand in his pocket and pulled out his cheque-book and opened it mumbling:

'Doctor Basir! I don't know . . . I don't know . . . I don't know . . .'

I interrupted him:

'Your Excellency, Mister President! There is a box in the Charity Room. Go there, write a cheque for the amount you see fit and place it in the box. All proceeds from the box are used for charitable works, I only take my expenses. No one to whom God has granted spiritual gifts may profit from them personally in any way, I repeat, in any way.'

The admiral went into the Charity Room, came out, and then I accompanied him to his car. When I returned, I found Heather smiling. I said:

'Everything went as we had wished. How much do you think the news of his return to power was worth?'

'Thirty thousand pounds?'

This Scottish woman! This congenital Scottish skinflint! I said resentfully:

'Heather, are you crazy? I spent twice that amount to find out the code names of the officers he's dealing with. I think His Excellency, the President, will donate no less than a quarter of a million dollars to charity.'

'I don't think so.'

'Do you want to bet?'

'It would be easier just to open the box.'

'And take the money going to charity?!'

We laughed and opened the box. The admiral was clearly stingier than I'd expected, but more generous than Heather had thought. The cheque was for £150,000. A good start to the day, I repeat, a good start.

My second client was Mrs Faa'iqa, the richest woman in Arabistan X. Minutes before she arrived, Heather prepared a small index card for me which reminded me of the basic information I'd carefully studied beforehand. I read the card:

Name: Faa'iqa.
Age: Sixty-five. (Claims to be forty-one.)
Wealth: $450 million.
Problem: Thinks her young husband is about to marry another woman. (In fact
   he has married another woman, but Mrs Faa'iqa does not know.)
Reason for visit: Separate the husband from his young amour (new wife).
Technique trusted by client: Reading coffee grounds.

Cases like Mrs Faa'iqa's came to me with deadly monotony, I repeat, deadly. An old rich wife buys a handsome young man with money who, having got what he wanted, goes after a beautiful young wife. The aged wife has no other way to keep him with her but to seek the help of supernatural forces. And her humble medium is Dr Basir Al-'Aref. A little hope does no harm, I repeat, does no harm, and may be beneficial. And for Mrs Faa'iqa I had prepared a huge dose of hope, a dose which would never have occurred to her.

I rose and welcomed her with exaggerated respect, saying:

'You are radiant, My Seraphic Lady. You have honoured this office and its occupier.'

Mrs Faa'iqa, who apparently had never been addressed with such a title, smiled in evident pleasure. She said:

'I have heard much about you Doctor Basir. A very great deal! Mrs Raja' told me . . .'

Nothing, I repeat, nothing, is more boring to me than hearing tales of my miracles and wonders, and the way people spice them up. Nevertheless, I listened to Mrs Faa'iqa, giving the impression of being deeply interested. After a few minutes, Heather came in with two cups of Turkish coffee. She placed one cup in front of me and the other in front of Mrs Faa'iqa who stopped talking to scrutinize Heather. She asked:

'Your wife?'

'My fiancé.'

'A beautiful woman.'

'Thank you. Only the beautiful can recognize beauty.'

'Is she English?'

'Scottish.'

'But you spoke to her in English.'

I had discovered, God how stupid I am sometimes, that My Seraphic Lady did not know the difference between England and Scotland. I said:

'She is in fact English, but lives in a town called Scotland. An English town.'

'A very beautiful woman.'

I was somewhat apprehensive. Did Mrs Faa'iqa have tendencies the Information Bureau hadn't managed to discover. I said:

'My Seraphic Lady! Beauty is important, but intelligence is more so. And when the two are combined in one woman, I repeat, in one woman, like you, my Seraphic Lady, such a woman is a rarity, I repeat, a rarity, a priceless jewel. Who values such a woman in these decadent times, these times of treachery and perfidy?'

I'd hit the target. The bull's eye. Mrs Faa'iqa's cheeks blushed. I resumed the onslaught:

'The world has gone rotten My Seraphic Lady, gone rotten once and for all. No one can trust anybody, I repeat, anybody. One cannot even be safe from the evil of those one has treated well.'

Mrs Faa'iqa nodded vehemently in support of the harsh judgements I continued to rain down:

'We live in a jungle. No one can feel safe. There are enemies everywhere. Treachery from all sides. Worse than that . . .'

I noticed that Mrs Faa'iqa had finished sipping her coffee and had turned it upside down on the saucer in a smooth, automatic movement which indicated she had done it a thousand times before.

'What is worse, such treachery comes from those closest to us. Please hand me the cup, My Seraphic lady.'

I spent a few minutes contemplating the cup in silence. Then I looked at her and began to speak slowly:

'I see the image of a man. A brown-skinned man. Of medium build. A thin moustache. About thirty years of age. About the same age as you, My Seraphic Lady. Now I'm trying to make out his name. A ... Ahmed! Yes, that's his name!'

Mrs Faa'iqa gasped on hearing the name. I ignored her and carried on:

'I see a woman beside him. A cheap, disgusting woman. Please forgive me, My Seraphic Lady, when I say that the woman I see in the cup next to Ahmed is a woman of the streets, I repeat, a woman of the streets. This filthy woman is plotting against you with Ahmed.'

I fell silent for a while contemplating Mrs Faa'iqa's face as it reddened then grew pale. I said:

'They want to conclude some sort of agreement. I can't read in the cup what sort of agreement it is. A company. Commercial premises. A deal. A marriage. I don't know. What is clear is that there is a conspiracy and you, My Seraphic Lady, are the victim, I repeat, the victim.'

Mrs Faa'iqa's quiet sobs quickly grew louder. Between her wails she mumbled:

'You're right, Doctor Basir. Everything you say is true. One hundred per cent true. Ahmed is my husband, Doctor, and he wants to marry this cursed woman. After all I've done for him, more than I've done for anyone. After I gave him the most precious thing I possessed. After ...'

I interrupted her:

'Do not give up hope, My Seraphic Lady. Don't give up hope. We will stop the traitor in his tracks. Come with me to the Room of Separation.'

The Room of Separation was designed to my own specifications. It was specially equipped to carry out the rituals necessary to split up a pair of lovers. The walls, ceiling and floor were pitch black, the colour of mourning, the colour of separation. Apart from the hidden gas vents, there were only two chairs and a small screen. I asked Mrs Faa'iqa to sit down on one of them. I said:

'Pay attention, my Seraphic Lady. I want you to concentrate. I want you to use all your powers of concentration. Look at the screen and focus your thoughts on Ahmed and the vile woman with him. I will concentrate with you and will use all my magnetic powers. Concentrate! And look!'

In the meantime, through an invisible small hole, Heather was showing slides which had been carefully prepared beforehand. On the screen there appeared the image of a man clinging to a woman. The details weren't clear, deliberately so.

But it was a picture of her husband and the woman was his lover (I mean, his new wife).

Mrs Faa'iqa began to breath heavily, uttering incomprehensible words. I said decisively:

'Please, My Seraphic Lady! I'm sorry! I would ask you not to make a sound. Concentrate your thoughts in silence and let me do my work.'

I looked at the screen and said in a a loud voice (amplified by the microphone, which I could turn on when required, hidden in my coat collar).

'I command you, Ahmed son of Zuhra . . .'

Mrs Faa'iqa shrieked on hearing his mother's name. I looked at her angrily and continued:

'I command you, Ahmed son of Zuhra, by the spiritual power subjected to me by the lords of the underworld. I command you to leave the woman Nahid daughter of Sakina . . .'

Mrs Faa'iqa cried out, again. I ignored her and went on:

'I command you by the spiritual power subjected to me by the servants of the celestial signs of the zodiac . . ..'

I went on like this for about five minutes. As I did so, Mrs Faa'iqa was weeping and shaking violently. Gradually, the image of Ahmed son of Zuhra faded from the image of Nahid daughter of Sakina until it finally disappeared entirely.

I lead Mrs Faa'iqa, who was clearly agitated, back to my office. I said:

'Calm down, my Seraphic Lady. Calm down. I will continue my spiritual campaign until the separation, but you must be patient. It will take a few weeks.'

Trembling, Mrs Faa'iqa said:

'Doctor Basir! I can be patient for months if necessary. Now, and only now, I know I will win the battle. Now, and only now, I know why everyone calls you the king of the spiritualists.'

I smiled and said:

'You're too kind! You're too kind!'

'The greatest thing about you, doctor, is that you give every penny you get to charity. Don't deny it! Don't deny it! Mrs Fawziya told me that she . . .'

I interrupted her:

'Such gifts come from God, my Seraphic Lady, and their fruits are for the poor and needy.'

Mrs Faa'iqa smiled and said:

'Where is the Charity Room?!'

I summoned Heather and asked her to accompany Mrs Faa'iqa to the Charity Room and to leave her there on her own. When Mrs Faa'iqa came out I accompanied her to the door to say goodbye. I then returned to the Charity Room where Heather was mumbling in astonishment:

'Look at all this money! In cash! In cash! She couldn't get it into the box so she left it beside it. At least a hundred thousand pounds. In cash! How can a woman walk around with so much cash on her! Is she mad?'

'You're the mad one, my Scottish beauty, driven mad by miserliness.'

I went back to my office to gen up on the coming days' clients when the Scottish woman interrupted my private thoughts with a phone call:

'We've got a charity case. Do you want to see her?'

I don't usually see anyone without at least a week's notice so that all the necessary information can be collected. However, it sometimes happens, I repeat sometimes, that someone unimportant comes to my office, someone we don't have a file on, some poor man or woman. When I'm in the right mood, I see such people, whom I refer to as charity cases, because I'm giving instead of taking. A spiritual Robin Hood, who takes from the rich to give to the poor. Heather came in and gave me a small card which I read quickly. I said:

Send her in.

A young woman came in. It was very clear that she was very Arabistani. It was also clear to the observant eye, I repeat, the observant eye, that she was in the early stages of pregnancy. It was also evident from her clothes that she's wasn't on *Fortune*'s list of the world's richest people. I gave her a lukewarm welcome and said:

'Please sit down.'

She put her hands on her lap and said almost inaudibly:

'Doctor Basir! I don't have an appointment. I'm sorry. I'm desperate. I don't know what to do. I've heard so much about you and about your charity work and what you do for . . .'

I interrupted her:

'Salwa! Give me your hand!'

The young woman was astonished to hear her name. She had forgotten she'd written it down herself just a minute beforehand on the card that Heather had brought in.

I said:

'The left one! Your left hand!'

I contemplated her hand, looked up at her and said:

'You're Sagittarius, aren't you?'

Her astonishment increased. She had forgotten she'd written her date of birth down on the card. I studied her hand for two or three minutes then said:

'Salwa! You can't keep it.'

She couldn't stifle her cry. I went on:

'In the future, God willing, you will have children, two boys and a girl. But after you're married. This boyfriend of yours will never marry you.'

Another cry came forth, louder than the first. I said:

'Salwa! Listen to me! He's gone. He won't be back. I repeat, he won't be back.'
With a rattle in her throat she said:
'What am I going to do then, doctor? In my situation . . .'
I let go of her hand. I reached into a drawer and pulled out an envelope containing £5,000. I gave it to her and said:
'Take the envelope. Have an abortion. Wait until the right man comes along. The right husband, I repeat, the right husband.'
She took the envelope and mumbled:
'Doctor Basir! I don't know . . .'
I interrupted her:
'Goodbye.'
Salwa left and I thought about the book written by my friend, Anwar Mukhtar, *The New Gypsies*. She was one of them. And a Sagittarian. The love of freedom. A tendency to give in to stronger personalities. And this was the result!

Tuesday

For over a month, Mr Buhanas has been asking for an appointment and I've let him wait all this time. I've been expecting him to visit ever since his wife died seven months ago. I knew that, sooner or later, he'd be coming to see me. I'd heard that he'd visited every famous medium in Europe and America. I was sure my turn would come. And what does Mr Buhanas want? He wants to talk to his wife, I mean his wife's spirit. And why this growing desire to speak to a woman who is dead after spending more than forty years talking to her when she was alive? The reason was something that no medium, I repeat, no medium, before me had been able to unearth. As a consequence, none of them had been able to give the answer Mr Buhanas was looking for. The reason was simple: Mr Buhanas wants to know if his wife died from natural causes or committed suicide. Why, then, didn't he ask for a post-mortem? The answer is simple: a post-mortem could have led to a scandal that neither Mr Buhanas nor his financial advisors wanted. And what had really happened? In fact, she had killed herself with a fatal dose of sleeping pills. And how did I know that? My friend, Anwar Mukhtar told me. And how did he know? The late Maa'isa had been one of his clients. He had been treating her for depression which she had suffered from since finding out she had lung cancer. It hadn't been detected until after it had spread and was untreatable. On her last visit she had told Anwar she didn't want to wait and spend months in pain and had decided to end her life. But why should Anwar divulge his patients' secrets to me? Because we share secrets, a practice extremely beneficial for both of us. Mr Buhanas was now suffering deep remorse. He believes he failed his wife by being away on the night she died. Mr Buhanas cannot be in peace unless he is sure his wife died of natural causes. A man has a right to live in peace, and he will find that peace with me.

Mr Buhanas came in and I jumped to my feet to greet him:

'Hello, Your Excellency, Pasha, hello.'

Mr Buhanas was no Pasha. Nor did I have the slightest idea, I repeat, the slightest idea, why I was using the word 'Excellency'. However, the visitor seemed more than happy with his title. He smiled and said:

'Hello, Doctor Basir. I've heard a great deal about you. His Excellency, the Minister told me . . .'

I listened to the tale of my usual marvels and said:

'Such gifts are from God, Your Excellency, Pasha. Gifts I put at the disposal of His servants. I am just a channel, just a postman conveying the messages of the spirits to those they love.'

As usual, I'd hit the target. Mr Buhanas cleared his throat and with some embarrassment said:

'In truth, Doctor, I came her today to . . .'

I interrupted him firmly but politely:

'Your Excellency, Pasha! From the outset, I would ask you to understand that I can't promise anything, I repeat, anything. I cannot make the spirits appear. All those who say they can do such a thing are lying, I repeat, lying. All I can do is create the right atmosphere. And should a noble spirit, any noble spirit, wish to appear they are more than welcome. Do not give credence to any charlatan who claims to be able to make the spirits manifest themselves.'

'In truth, I've noticed from previous experiences that . . .'

'You've noticed, Your Excellency, Pasha, that some alleged mediums promise much but do not deliver. They'll give you some sort of obscure and vague patter and claim its from this or that spirit.'

Signs of amazement appeared on Mr Buhanas' face. I developed the attack:

'But you'll find nothing like that with me, Your Excellency, Pasha. All you'll find is the truth. I'll try, but I'm not promising anything. A spirit may come, then again it may not. In advance, I must say that I do not wish to know which noble spirit you wish to contact, because this knowledge will be of no use to me, I repeat, of no use. If the noble spirit is prepared to appear and send a message then it will appear. So let us move to the Spirit Room, Your Excellency, Pasha.'

The Spirit Room was without question the jewel of all the rooms. I had spent a great deal of time, effort and money on its design. The walls, ceiling and floor were covered in pure white marble. The lights could shine onto the marble any colour I chose. There was a hidden tape recorder which could produce any sound, I repeat, any sound you could imagine, from the human voice to music, bird song or the roar of a lion. In addition to the hidden gas vents, there were other vents for the fragrances of perfume or incense. There was also a projector which could show any image, I repeat, any image I wanted on the ceiling, walls or floor.

I ushered Mr Buhanas into the Spirit Room. There were nine chairs laid out in a circle. Some of the employees from the Information Bureau were sitting on the chairs. They were each wearing a white robe and a white turban.

I sat Mr Buhanas down beside me and whispered in his ear:

'Your Excellency, Pasha! All these you see before you are spiritual mediums who have been carefully chosen by me. And I, in all humility, possess not inconsiderable spiritual gifts. It appears to me that you also have the gift. Now, I want you with your left hand to take the hand of the person sitting next to you and with your right hand hold mine so that the spiritual circle is complete. After that I want you to concentrate all your thoughts, I repeat, all your thoughts, on the noble spirit you wish to contact.

In the meantime, Heather had dimmed all the lights and put on some soothing classical music. From one of the vents in the room there wafted the perfume 'Sauvage', the late wife's favourite perfume. I felt Buhanas' grip tighten when the perfume wafted in. Suddenly, from somewhere in the ceiling a women's voice could be heard saying:

'Noo-Noo!'

'Noo-Noo' had been Mr Buhanas' wife's pet name for him and was derived from his first name, Nabil. It was a pet name which was known only to a few of their closest friends. Mr Buhanas began to sob quietly. The voice from the ceiling continued:

'Noo-Noo! I can't stay here long. I've been allowed a short visit. All I want you to know is that I passed over in my sleep, quietly and peacefully. There's nothing for you to worry about. God forbid! Noo-Noo! Say hello to the children for me. Give Bousbousa a kiss from me. Goodbye!'

Bousbousa was the pet cat the late wife had left. And her voice had in fact been that of the famous film star, Niran. I had recorded the words, which had reduced Mr Buhanas to tears, the week before when she'd visited me. I'd recorded them on a machine which can change the tone and intonation of a person's voice. I turned the lights back on. Mr Buhanas' restrained sobbing had become floods of tears, tears of joy.

I took Mr Buhanas back to my office and the usual lecture began:

'Doctor Basir! It was astonishing! Incredible! Unimaginable!'

With my usual humility, I said:

'Believe me, Your Excellency, the Pasha, I know nothing about what transpired. I do not know who the spirit was that spoke and I have no idea what Noo-Noo or Bousbousa mean. I do not understand the content of the message.'

'But I understood everything. Everything! It was the spirit of my late wife, without a shadow of a doubt. Didn't you smell the perfume "Sauvage"?'

'I did smell a perfume but I didn't know what it was called. Very often a spirit comes with a fragrance it likes. Sometimes, I smell the aroma of food.'

'It was my wife's perfume. It was the only perfume she used throughout our married life. It was my wife's spirit. There's not the slightest doubt about it. No one but her could have known the things she said. Doctor Basir! I don't know how . . .'

I interrupted him:

'Your Excellency, the Pasha! I did nothing. The noble spirit came because it wanted to and it had permission.'

'But I've tried before, loads of times, but nothing . . .'

'The gifts are from God.'

He took out his cheque book as he said:

'I have heard about your work for charity and I'd like to . . .'

I interrupted him:

'Put as much as you want in the charity box in the Charity Room. I will make a donation in the name of your late wife . . . By the way, what was your late wife's name?'

With great pleasure, he said:

'Maa'isa. Maa'isa Khoukhi.'

He went to the Charity Room then returned. I accompanied him to his car. Heather was waiting for me in the Charity Room. I kissed her warmly and said:

'Heather! You were brilliant! The timing was amazing. Even I believed that a noble spirit had given us the honour of a visit.'

'Who knows? Maybe there was a noble spirit.'

'What about the cheque?'

'A hundred thousand pounds.'

'Not bad!'

I had just begun to write my weekly article for the magazine *Ma Belle* having chosen the title, 'How to Read Your Palm in One Minute', when Heather came in. She said:

'There's someone who wants to see you straightaway.'

'But I'm busy at the moment. I've got my weekly article to write.'

'He says you know him very well and you'll let him in as soon as you hear his name.'

'What's his name?'

'Colonel Saqr Al-Fantir. The military attaché of . . .'

I interrupted her:

'Send him in!'

The colonel wasted no time on pleasantries. As soon as he'd sat down, he said:

'I have a message from His Excellency, the President.'

'I am at His Excellency's command. And at yours.'

'His Excellency wants you to visit Arabistan X and to arrive on Thursday. His

Excellency has informed me that he will send his private plane to . . .'

Without thinking I shouted out:

'No! No! No!'

The colonel was surprised. I said:

'I don't want a private plane. There are regular flights everyday and I can be with His Excellency at the time specified.'

'But the plane is . . .'

I interrupted him:

'My dear Saqr! Please! I beg you! Tell His Excellency that I will be in his flourishing capital on Thursday morning.'

'Fine! What about expenses?'

I laughed and said:

'Expenses? His Excellency has been a friend for more than fifteen years and has done me a lot of favours. We don't have expenses.'

The colonel left. I began thinking. My relationship with His Excellency did indeed go back a long way. He had visited me a number of times at my office before taking power. And I had visited him a number of times in his capital after he took power. But this was the first time he'd contacted me in about eight years. What did he want now? In the past there had been the usual requests: a woman he wanted to fall in love with him, some jealous rival he wanted to stop in his tracks. But what did he want now? I don't think any woman, I repeat, any woman, would refuse him now, nor, according to the Information Bureau, was there any sign of a possible conspiracy. And why Thursday in particular? I asked Heather to prepare a dossier for me on the hundred most important people in Arabistan X. I also asked her to get my friend, Mass'oud As'ad, on the phone for me.

His loud laugh came on the line:

'Doctor Basir! This is a miracle! I was just thinking about you. I was just about to call you. This is what you call 'telepathy' isn't it?'

'It is indeed. Massoud! I need your help.'

'You know I'm always at your disposal.'

'His Excellency, the President of Arabistan X wants to see me.'

'So, you'll be getting a Rolls Royce.'

'There's a problem.'

'What is it?'

'I don't know why he wants to see me.'

'Why don't you ask your crystal ball?'

'Mass'oud! I'm being serious. Have you got any information about anything that could be worrying His Excellency?'

'I think it's the usual problem.'

'What problem?'

'Sex.'

'I don't think he's got any sexual problems.'

'I tell you it's got to do with sex.'

'What's sex got to do with me? He's got loads of doctors.'

'Ah! Doctors! You've reminded me why I was thinking about calling you. I want you to read my palm.'

I laughed for a long time and said:

'At last! At last! I've finally convinced you of my spiritual powers.'

'Basir! I've never doubted your spiritual powers for one moment.'

'What's on your mind?'

'Nothing in particular. I just want you to read my palm. That's all.'

'With pleasure. Come round tomorrow.'

'What time?'

'Whenever you want. It'll only take a few minutes.'

I tried to get back to the article but my mind was distracted, wandering off to His Excellency and the urgent problem that required my presence on Thursday. And the private plane! Luckily, the colonel had not insisted on the private plane. Had he done so I would have refused most adamantly, I repeat, most adamantly. Why this fear of the private plane? It's a matter of life and death. I will die, I know for certain, on board a private plane. And how do I know that? Aahh! I found out by chance. One of the sacred rules, I repeat, sacred rules among astrologers is that they are not allowed to find out their own destiny. Another of the sacred rules, I repeat, sacred rules among astrologers is that they're not allowed to discuss a client's death with him even when the signs of that death are visible on the palm or in the crystal ball. So, how did I know, then? Pure chance. I was on my annual visit to my great teacher, the king of astrologers and magicians, Guru Mungo Jitni in Bombay. When I told him in passing that I'd come by private plane, I was startled by the Guru's reaction. He had read my horoscope and my palm dozens of times. So why did his face suddenly turn ashen coloured when he heard the words 'private plane'? I asked him:

'What's wrong, master?'

He said:

'From now on you must not fly on a private plane.'

'Why not, master?'

'I cannot tell you the reason.'

'So, it's to do with my death?'

'You can conclude what you like. But you must never, never, never fly on a private plane whatever the circumstances or situation.'

Luckily, the colonel had dropped the idea of the private plane. To date not a single one of Guru Mungo Jitni's prophecies has been proved wrong.

Wednesday
Today I finished my article 'How to Read Your Palm in One Minute'. I added a diagram to help explain the lines:

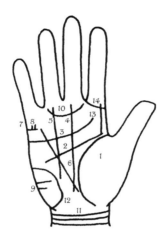

1. The Line of Life
This line is the most important and almost everybody has heard of it. If the line is clear and without interruption or curvature it means the person will be healthy and active with a long life ahead of them – the further the line goes down the hand, the longer the person's life will be. But when the Line of Life is broken or zigzags it means the person's health is poor and they are susceptible to various diseases and illnesses. When the line suddenly breaks off completely and then starts again, this means the person will have a serious accident or a potentially fatal illness.

2. The Line of the Mind
This is the line which determines whether the person is ruled by emotions or by logic and intelligence. The closer this line is to the Line of Life the more cautious the person will be, avoiding adventures and preferring things to stay as they are. The further this line is from the Line of Life the more the person will incline to adventure and risk taking (and gambling). The longer and clearer the line, the greater the person's powers of concentration and ability to handle intricate details. A faint or wavy line means that the person is unable to take rational decisions and is more likely to leave his fate in the hands of others.

3. The Line of the Heart
In a very small number of palms this line cannot be seen at all or is completely

merged with the Line of the Mind. In such cases, the mind is in complete control of the heart. When the line is distinct and strong, this means that the person is capable of generosity and love and will make an excellent wife or husband. When the line is faint, this means the person is introverted and is unable to interact and deal with other people easily.

4. The Line of Fate

This line is only visible in approximately fifty percent of people. Absence of the line indicates that the person is unable to control his own destiny and allows his life to go on without direction. When the line is visible it means that person takes all the decisions which affect his destiny himself and is able to shoulder responsibilities. The deeper the line, the more independent the person and the less he needs other people.

5. The Line of the Sun

Some palm readers call this line the Line of Success since it is frequently linked to hope, optimism and pleasure. The more visible the line, the greater the person's standing, renown and happiness. Absence of the line means that any endeavour the person undertakes will be mixed with frustration and disappointment.

6. The Line of Health

The absence of this line is extremely good news as it means the person will have excellent health throughout his life. When the line is visible and is clear and unbroken it means that, on the whole, the person will enjoy good health. However, when the line is faint or broken it means the person is not in the best of health. When the line suddenly breaks this is an alarm bell warning of an incurable illness in the near future.

7. The Line of Marriage

When this line is clear and continuous it means the person will marry once and, in all probability, happily. When the line divides into two clear main lines it means the person will marry twice and both marriages will, in all probability, be happy. When the line divides into three or more lines it means the person will have difficulty in maintaining a stable relationship with someone of the opposite sex and his life will probably be full of transient relationships.

8. The Line of Children

Contrary to what many amateurs and charlatans imagine, both in the East and the West, this line has nothing to do with the number of children a person will have. Instead, the presence of this line gives us some idea about to what extent the person will be able to deal with children. When there are several straight lines this means the person likes children and can give them a lot of happiness and attention. When the lines are broken this means the person finds difficulty in dealing with children and in giving them love and affection.

9. The Lines of Travel
These lines indicate the extent to which the person wants stability or to keep on moving. The greater the number of lines, the greater the number of important journeys in the person's life.

10. The Lines of Sensitivity
These are not lines in the strict sense of the word. Rather, they are signs which are difficult to make out except to the expert eye. One sign is similar to the mathematical + sign and the other is similar to an arc ∩. Their presence is decisive evidence of the person's latent spiritual gifts including dreams which foretell the future, telepathy and, in rare cases, mind reading.

11. The Lines of Fortune
These lines are also not lines in the strict sense of the word. Rather, they are signs which can be made out on the back of the hand. Some of these signs are in the form of a square □. The greater the number of squares, the greater the good fortune of the person. The fewer the number of squares, the less fortunate the person will be. In rare cases, there are signs in the form of a triangle △. When such a sign is apparent it is indicative of extraordinarily good fortune.

12. The Line of Intuition
Again, this is not a line in the strict sense of the term. It is in the form of a horseshoe and cannot be detected by amateurs. When this sign is present it indicates the person has unusual powers of intuition such that he is able to judge a person correctly and accurately on first meeting them. Most mediums have this sign on their palms.

13. The Line of Wealth
This line is perhaps the line which most people are keen to see and interpret. It is also perhaps the easiest line to read. When the line is strong, deep and continuous it means the person will be rich and an outstanding businessman. The more faint and less clear-cut the line, the greater the financial problems which the person will encounter time and time again.

14. The Line of Spiritual Powers
This line is invisible to the naked eye. Therefore, professional palmists use a

magnifying glass and sometimes even a special grey powder in addition to the
magnifying glass in order to be able to see the line. My advice to the reader is not
to waste valuable time in looking for this line. If the line is there, the person will
most probably be a professional palmist or a renowned fortune-teller.

I finished the article. The first client arrived. It was a very routine case: a
wealthy Arabistani who has failed in all his attempts to find treatment for his
arthritis and is now looking for a spiritual cure. All I did was concentrate and put
my hand on his forehead for ten minutes. At the end of the ten minutes the
patient swore he felt a great deal better. And why not? I repeat, why not?
Suggestion can work miracles. Before he went, he left the usual envelope on my
desk, an envelope containing £3,000.

As soon as he'd gone, a strange man came in wearing a simple plain white
robe. He had a long white beard, but no moustache, and on his head there was
a turban. I was surprised when he came in. He must be a charity case. But why
had Heather let him in? I was just about to call her to reprimand her when he
said:

'O Basrawi! She has done no wrong. She did not see me.'

Didn't see him?! I didn't know what he meant but didn't want to ask.

The strange man continued:

'O Basrawi! I have a message. A friend wishes to meet you. An earthly friend,
one of our terrestrial brothers, the genies.'

I started to laugh. He interrupted me:

'Laugh later should you wish so to do.'

I said:

'Our genie friend is welcome. I would be honoured by a visit anytime.'

'He cannot come without an invitation.'

'Tell him he's welcome.'

'The invitation has to come from you, personally.'

'How?'

The old man left a piece of paper on my desk and left the office trailing clouds
of incense behind him. Where did the incense come from? He had scarcely left
the room when Heather called me:

'Who was that strange man who just came out of your office? How did he get
in?'

'I was going to ask you the same question.'

'I've been here the whole time and didn't see anyone go in. I've got your
friend Mass'oud As'ad with me.'

'Show him in.'

Mass'oud entered preceded by his loud laugh and said:

'Doctor Basir! What's got into you? Have you started seeking the help of other spiritualists? Who was that dervish in here with you?'

'A postman. He had a message.'

'Where from?'

'The material world.'

'I thought you were in permanent contact with the material world.'

'That's what I thought. Since I was an adolescent I've been receiving telepathic messages from genies when they wanted to send them.'

'So why did this message come via the postman.'

'I don't know.'

'What does the message say?'

'Mass'oud! Let's leave this for the moment. Why this sudden urge for me to read your palm?'

Without saying a word, Mass'oud gave me his left hand. I contemplated it for a few minutes. In his health line I saw a grave warning, a very clear grave warning, a harbinger of a fatal health crisis. I tried to hide my feelings as I said:

'Mass'oud! When did you last have a medical check-up?'

Mass'oud sighed and answered:

'So, it's definite.'

'What's definite?'

'A long story.'

'Is there anything I can do?'

'I don't know. Maybe in the future.'

'But promise me you'll have a thorough examination, I repeat, thorough.'

'I don't see any need for that.'

'Promise me in any case.'

'I promise. I'll have a word with Anwar Mukhtar. He's the expert on health centres.'

Mass'oud left frowning. Heather reminded me I had to go to the airport right away. For the tenth time she asked:

'Why don't you take me with you?'

For the tenth time I replied:

'Because I need you here. I can't do anything without the information you send me, you and the team.'

When the plane took off, from my pocket I pulled out the note that the amazing man had left me. It was written in a beautiful hand, almost as if it had been printed. At the top was the following: Incantation for the Summoning of Atawit Ben Shaltikh. I smiled. So this was the name of my new friend: Atawit Ben Shaltikh. I carried on reading: 'I call upon you O Shamkhita, O Tamitha, O Shamkhutiya, O Madhur, O Ramutif, O Hajlatif, O Yakifiyal to bring Atawit Ben Shaltikh to me at once'. I don't know when I fell asleep but I was woken up by the voice of the stewardess:

'Doctor! Doctor! Don't you want dinner?'

Thursday, the Capital, Arabistan X

The flight was eventful. As soon as I'd finished dinner the free consultations began. Stewardess after stewardess came up to me asking me to read their palm. There was an exceptionally beautiful stewardess, I repeat, exceptionally, who was called Hasna'. I said to her:

'Hasna'. Your palm needs more time to be read properly. Why don't you come and see me tomorrow evening?'

She said simply:

'Where?'

I said:

'I'll be at the Four Seasons. Eight o'clock?'

Hasna' smiled, nodded and left.

After a fitful nap, the hotel receptionist rang to say that General Salamayn Salem wanted to see me at once. I asked him to send him up. General Salamayn Salem was head of intelligence in Arabistan X. I'd had many dealings with him on matters of mutual benefit, including magnetic hypnotism and the spirits of the dead. His superior, His Excellency, had been more than generous with me. The general embraced me warmly and said:

'I hope you're comfortable.'

I looked around at the luxurious hotel wing looking out over the blue waters of the Gulf and said:

'Luxury, perfect luxury. This isn't the wing of a hotel, it's a palace, I repeat, a palace.'

'His Excellency has ordered that all our facilities be put at your disposal. There are two cars at the entrance for your use.'

'One would be enough.'

'Who can say? One should be kept in reserve.'

I said:

'General! Do you know why His Excellency wishes to see me?'

The general smiled, saying:

'There are many things I know about His Excellency, and many things I don't know. One of the things I don't know is the reason for your visit.'

Laughing, I said:

'And what about your intelligence?'

'We carry out intelligence work for His Excellency, not about him.'

'Naturally! Naturally!'

'He'll tell you himself. He'll be seeing you this evening at eleven o'clock precisely. I'll pass by at ten and we'll go to the tent together.'

'The tent?'

'Yes. His Excellency is out of town.'

'I'll be waiting for you.'

The general left and I found myself uncharacteristically, I repeat, uncharacteristically unable to concentrate. My thoughts wandered from genies to stewardesses, from His Excellency to the head of the intelligence services. I tried to read the dossier I'd brought with me but couldn't make head or tail of it. I tried to write a chapter of my forthcoming book, *The Secrets of Numbers*, but I couldn't write a single word. I spent the time zapping between the satellite TV channels until Hasna' arrived. I read her palm, then I read the rest of her body. The time passed without my noticing until my reading was interrupted by the ringing of the phone. The receptionist was on the other end telling me that the General was waiting for me in the lounge. I asked Hasna' to stay until I'd disappeared after which she was to disappear as well.

His Excellency received me in his tent which was much bigger, I repeat, much bigger than my spacious hotel wing. He embraced and hugged me warmly and at the top of his voice said:

'Doctor Basir! It's been a long time!'

I said:

'We have missed your radiant countenance, Your Excellency.'

He said:

'I'm getting old, Doctor.'

I said with a smile:

'That's not true. Who's been telling you that.'

His Excellency smiled broadly and said:

'Air stewardesses. Beautiful air stewardesses.'

He must have noticed that I couldn't hide my astonishment. He quickly went on:

'I was just joking.'

Just joking! I now understood the purpose behind the two cars at the hotel entrance. God, how stupid I am sometimes! I was waiting for His Excellency to tell me the reason for my visit but he was in no hurry. The bitter coffee came, then the sweet tea. The bitter coffee returned as did the sweet tea. His Excellency said:

'Any news from London?'

'Nothing's changed, Your Excellency. It's just the same as ever.'

'No, Doctor. London in the days of my youth was far better than it is today. London has turned grey, as have we all.'

His Excellency fell silent then suddenly said:

'You promised your girlfriend a Rolls Royce. You'll have it next week. And you promised her a country estate in Scotland costing half a million pounds. You'll have the money next week.'

In astonishment, I said:

'Was it Heather who . . .'

Laughing, His Excellency interrupted me:

'No, Doctor! the crystal ball! The crystal ball told me! How I know doesn't matter. Walls have ears as General Salamayn says.'

Disturbed, I said:

'Your Excellency, I repeat, this is unbelievable generosity. I don't deserve . . .'

He interrupted me:

'In exchange, all I want is something very simple which will not be beyond your great spiritual powers. Something I know you can do easily.'

Breathing with difficulty, I said:

'All my limited gifts are at . . .'

He interrupted me again with a voice as sharp as a sword:

'Your limited gifts are of no interest to me. What I am interested in is that the Brazilian team loses tomorrow's match against our team.'

The shock silenced me. This was the first time, I repeat, the first time, I had been asked to arrange the defeat of a football team, let alone the best team in the world. I said:

'But . . .'

His Excellency's features changed. He was no longer the old friend joking with me. In a voice that sent shivers through my body he said:

'Doctor Basir! If the Brazilian team loses, I'll give you the car and the house. However, if our team loses, I'll ask General Salamayn to take you swimming in shark-infested waters.'

Swimming?! I don't know how to swim. And in shark-infested waters?! Was His Excellency joking? From his face it didn't look as if he was joking.

I said:

'But I can't . . .'

Again he interrupted me:

'My faith in you is blind. My faith in you knows no limits. You must excuse me now, it's time for me to go to sleep. I told you I'm getting old. General Salamayn and his department are at your disposal.'

The general took me back to the hotel wing and said that he would do anything I asked him to. I told him truthfully, I repeat, truthfully that I didn't know what my next move was going to be and that I would be spending the whole night planning. I asked him:

'When does the match start?'

'Tomorrow. Four in the afternoon.'

I said:

'Come at two o'clock. I hope by then I'll have come up with a plan.'

He said:

'Till then will you be needing anything?'

'Two direct phone lines and two fax machines.'

The General laughed and said:

'Good God! That's what I'd thought you'd want. In this small room here you'll find everything you'll need.'

As soon as the general had gone, I dialled and said to Heather:

'Heather! Listen! Listen carefully! This is an emergency, I repeat, an emergency. I want you to get the team together, the whole team, I repeat, the whole team, one by one. I want to know everything there is to be known about the Brazilian football team which will be playing here tomorrow. Yes! Yes! The national team! I want to know everything. About every player. I repeat, everything about every player. Don't leave anything out. Girlfriends, lovers, drugs, mothers, fathers, children, scandals, financial deals. I want everything. I'll be beside the fax all night, I repeat, all night.'

After three hours, the first fax arrived. They kept on coming until morning and I devoured each one as it arrived.

Friday, the Capital, Arabistan X

The day began with the faxes piled up in front of me. In my brain I had enough information on the Brazilian team to write a book. But a plan hadn't taken shape. What was I going to do with all this information? I decided to take a nap and think about it later. Absent-mindedly, I picked up the note which the strange man had given me and began to read it aloud. Before I'd finished I fell into a deep sleep. A very strange dream began, I repeat, very strange. I was in a room which looked like my office in London. In front of me was a handsome young slave, the colour of a red rose with rose-coloured hair down to his shoulders and wearing a rose-coloured, diaphanous gown. The rose-coloured young slave smiled and I saw his slightly pointed teeth, as white as pearl.

He said:

'Haven't you worked out a plan yet? It's very simple. Listen . . .'

At precisely two o'clock, General Salamayn arrived and as soon as he came in said:

'We are at your command. Myself and my department.'

I said:

'I want a man right this minute who can speak Portuguese.'

'Portuguese?! Why?!'

'It's a Brazilian team.'

'And you want someone who speaks Portuguese?'

This highly regarded head of the intelligence services doesn't know that the Brazilians speak Portuguese. I think such things must be outside his sphere of competence. I said:

'I want someone, as soon as possible, who speaks Portuguese.'

The general thought for a while then said:

'There are several Portuguese companies. There are a few Portuguese officials.'

'So, hurry up and get me one of them. Make sure he's reliable and that he won't talk.'

In less than an hour, General Salamayn was back with a Portuguese sea captain. I asked him to write two letters in Portuguese, and I asked him to write clearly. The man did as I had asked then left. I turned to General Salamayn and said:

'Everything, I repeat, everything depends on timing. Twenty minutes after the start of the match, I want the Brazilian goalkeeper to get this letter. I want him to read it straight away and not put it aside till later. I repeat, he must not save it for later. Now, forty minutes after the start of the match, I repeat, forty minutes, I want the Brazilian centre-forward to get this letter which he must not put aside till later. Can you arrange that?'

General Salamayn smiled and said:

'Easily. Very easily. Isn't there anything else?'

'Can you have all phone lines to Brazil cut off as soon as the centre-forward gets the letter. Cut them off for half an hour.'

'That can easily be arranged.'

'Good! That's everything.'

General Salamayn looked at me in amazement and said:

'Don't you want to be there at the stadium? His Excellency has arranged a box for you so that you can see everything but without being seen by anybody.'

'I would be grateful if you would convey my thanks to His Excellency. However, there's no need for me to be there. I'll keep an eye on things from here via the television.'

'And the spiritual influences? The magic?'

'I can do everything required from here. The important thing is that you carry out everything I've asked you to do, to the letter, I repeat, to the letter.'

General Salamayn left and I spent the time before kick-off pacing up and down the wing of the hotel. I had never seen, nor had anticipated seeing, a match of such importance. The Brazilian team losing would mean a Rolls Royce and a country estate. The Brazilian team winning would mean me being thrown to the sharks – an end unworthy of an illustrious astrologer.

The match began much worse than I had expected. After just seven minutes, the Brazilians put the ball in the Arabistani net. A cloud of anxiety crossed His Excellency's face as he followed the match in the stadium. Behind him stood General Salamayn with his face a mask of stone, betraying no emotion whatsoever. Twenty minutes into the match I saw the Brazilian goalkeeper take the ball off the linesman who also handed him a white piece of paper. The goalkeeper read the note and began to talk to the linesman who snatched the note back and disappeared. Exactly two minutes later the Arabistani team attacked and scored. The crowd went wild. Even His Excellency forgot his sense of dignity, rising to his feet clapping and shouting. On the Brazilian goalkeeper's face were signs of astonishment mixed with anguish. Ten minutes after their first goal, the Arabistanis scored again. The crowd roared. A few minutes after that goal, the Brazilian centre-forward was given the message as he was handed the ball. Play continued, but it was obvious the centre forward was too preoccupied to lead the attack. The Arabistanis managed to score again. At half time, the goalkeeper and centre-forward were seen running out of the stadium. The second half began with substitutes for the goalkeeper and the centre-forward. The game ebbed and flowed but the result remained the same. At full time, the Arabistanis were the winners.

The whole capital turned into a carnival: cars sounded their horns, women ululated, men danced. My car made its way with difficulty to the airport. Beside me General Salamayn was guffawing away saying:

'You did it, Doctor Basir! You did it! Magic in Portuguese!'

I smiled but made no comment. The general took an envelope out of his pocket and handed it to me. He said:

'With His Excellency's compliments. A quarter of a million pounds. You'll get the rest next week. And the car.'

I took the envelope and said:

'Please tell His Excellency that I'll never forget his kindness for as long as I live. I repeat, for as long as I live. Please tell him how happy I am that he asked me to carry out this task and that he thinks so highly of me.'

The general started guffawing again and I said:

'General! May I ask you a question?'

'Please do.'

'Was His Excellency joking when he said he'd have me thrown to the sharks if I failed?'

The general continued guffawing and ignored my question. He said:

'Magic in Portuguese! Whatever next!'

I did not think it appropriate to tell the general that the message which the goalkeeper received consisted of a single sentence: 'Mariana is sleeping, right this minute, with Paulo.' Mariana was the goalkeeper's wife and Paulo was his closest friend. As for the message to the centre forward, it said simply: 'Mario has crashed the car and is in intensive care.' Mario was the player's only son. The general had not been wrong when he'd described what happened as being magic in Portuguese. Is not magic a means of influencing people without their knowing?

Saturday, London
I spent most of the day in bed. I needed rest after the immense nervous strain and the long flight. Heather was next to me in bed doing everything she could to try to arouse me. All her efforts, however, were in vain. On the return flight, every time I'd dozed off, I repeat, every time, I'd dreamt of the handsome rose-coloured young slave who told me in every dream, I repeat, every dream: 'You must stay away from Heather.' She eventually gave up. I began to write and she went off into the lounge to read.

Sunday
Heather went out to visit one of her girlfriends in the suburbs and I remained on my own in the apartment. I decided to continue working on my new book. I began: *The Secrets of the number 9.*

The number 9 is the king of the secrets of numbers. Suffice to say that when 9 is multiplied by 9 or any other number and the numbers in the product are added together the result always equals 9.

For example:
$$9 \times 1 \ = \ 9$$
$$9 \times 2 \ = \ 18 \ = \ 8 + 1 \ = \ 9$$
$$9 \times 3 \ = \ 27 \ = \ 7 + 2 \ = \ 9$$
$$9 \times 4 \ = \ 36 \ = \ 6 + 3 \ = \ 9$$
$$9 \times 5 \ = \ 45 \ = \ 5 + 4 \ = \ 9$$
$$9 \times 6 \ = \ 54 \ = \ 4 + 5 \ = \ 9$$
$$9 \times 7 \ = \ 63 \ = \ 3 + 6 \ = \ 9$$
$$9 \times 8 \ = \ 72 \ = \ 2 + 7 \ = \ 9$$
$$9 \times 9 \ = \ 81 \ = \ 1 + 8 \ = \ 9$$
$$9 \times 10 \ = \ 90 \ = \ 0 + 9 \ = \ 9$$

People for whom the number 9 is the main number in their lives, and we explained in the previous chapter how to find out the main number from a person's date of birth, enjoy numerous spiritual gifts. Very often you see such people involved in humanitarian work or giving a great deal to others. Although such individuals are able to forget the hurt done to them, they find it difficult to accept any form of criticism.

For numerologists, the number 9 symbolizes many things: it symbolizes mankind itself, it symbolizes survival and steadfastness, and for sorcerers it symbolizes the Devil. The Devil?! Why?! The Devil's number, 666, is well-known. If we add the numbers up, we get:

$$6 + 6 + 6 = 18 = 1 + 8 = 9.$$

At this point I had the irresistible desire to utter the incantation. I began to read aloud: 'I call upon you O Shamkhita, O Tamitha, O Shamkhutiya . . .' No sooner had I finished reciting, when I found the handsome rose-coloured young slave whom I had seen in the dream standing in front of me smiling and saying:

'I am Atawit.'

He held out his hand to me and I held out mine to him. When our hands touched, I felt a sudden charge of electricity and lost consciousness. When I came round, I found myself lying on the bed with the handsome rose-coloured young slave pressing his lips to mine. He then whispered:

'Don't be afraid! Don't be afraid! You only faint the first time.'

The Businessman

There is no glory in this world for those who lack wealth
And for those who lack glory there is no wealth
Al-Mutanabbi

Identity Card
Full Name: Harbi Boukhshamin Al-Hurayabibi
Known as: Hi Baby
Occupation: Businessman
Age: 43
Wealth: $750million (approx.)
Place of Birth: Arabistan X
Place of Work: Throughout the world
Academic Qualifications: BA Business Administration (Stanford); MA Business Administration (Harvard)
Marital Status: Married
Children: One son

Monday, New York
I spent the morning, the whole morning, with lawyers, discussing another court case brought by a consumer watchdog against the Camelburger chain. They were claiming that consumers were being hoodwinked into thinking that they were only eating camel meat whereas in fact they were eating a mixture of all sorts of meats. The Camelburger chain, of which I am the sole proprietor, has never claimed, at all, that the burgers are made only from camel meat. The chain has merely implied, through its name, that that was so, and has never said anything to the contrary. I am against fraudulent trading practices. My late father taught me never to lie, whatever the circumstances and whatever the motives. Everyone who has dealings with me can testify to my probity. The idea for Camelburger came to me during my student days at Harvard. I had proposed a seminar topic: 'The Creation of New Outlets for the Sale of a New Type of Burger Manufactured from Camel Meat'. It was just an idea. I prepared the usual paper with the usual data, the usual statistics and the usual questionnaires. I was surprised when I saw the professor paying a great deal of attention. I was surprised when I saw my colleagues asking question after question. Afterwards, I spent a number of years conducting trials with a team of chefs in Switzerland and an international team

made up of an American chef, an Indian chef, an Arabistani chef and a Swiss (French) chef. In the end, we arrived at the optimum formula: one quarter camel meat, one quarter lamb, one quarter beef and one quarter chicken. And, after countless trials, we arrived at that blend of spices which gives the Camelburger its distinctive colour and distinctive taste. I opened one outlet and it was an unparalleled success. This was followed by numerous outlets in every Arabistani capital. The craze then moved to America. Within ten years I had opened more than 5,000 outlets. Camelburger became a household name. Profits flowed in through the franchises which I would generously award in exchange for generous amounts of money. It proved my theory, the principle source of my wealth, which is that in the world of business you can't amass millions without new ideas, new products, new marketing methods, new ways of advertising. Yet success has its price. In the United States, you can't become a millionaire without being pursued by lawsuits. And you can't become famous without being hounded by the press. The Camelburger had made me a famous millionaire. Americans can't pronounce my family name – Al-Hurayabibi – so it was quickly changed in the press and on television to 'Hi Baby'. I liked the name. Mister Hi Baby! Why not? A new and original name. The lawyers assured me that the latest lawsuit would fail in the same way that the previous lawsuits (twenty-six of them!) had failed. We weren't selling bad meat and we weren't lying. If some consumers wanted to believe that Camelburgers were only made out of camel meat that was their business. Does anyone know what a hamburger is made of? More than half of it is fat, intestine and gristle. We would not be losing the latest lawsuit. Nevertheless, my legal team wanted to settle the case amicably. I told the leader of the team:

'Mister Legaleagle! As long as we're going to win the case, why don't we go to court?'

'We can if you want, Mister Hi Baby, however, I don't recommend going down that route.'

'Why not?'

'The consumer watchdog that filed the suit is very well-known and highly respected in consumer circles. The suit would create a big media frenzy which would go on for as long as the case lasted. I think we would win the battle but lose the war.'

'What do you mean?'

'I mean that the media frenzy could affect sales, and affect them seriously.'

'And we don't want that.'

'And we don't want that.'

'Does anyone have a specific proposal?'

'There is a proposal from the watchdog's legal team.'

'Which is?'

'Dropping the suit in return for an appropriate financial settlement.'

'That's daylight robbery!'

'The team does not look at it like that.'

'And how does the team look at it?'

'This is a charitable group with irreproachable social aims and the lawyers consider that any additional income which would help the group achieve its goals is legitimate.'

'Even if it's the proceeds of a robbery?'

'Mister Hi Baby! We lawyers try to avoid provocative words.'

'Very wise! Very wise! Did they specify the amount?'

'A million dollars.'

'That's daylight robbery.'

'That's what we told them.'

'And what was their reaction?'

'After difficult negotiations, we agreed on half a million. That's if you agree, naturally.'

'And you're suggesting I agree?'

'That is the unanimous view of the team.'

'Mister Legaleagle! This mustn't be seen as a defeat for us. Firstly, the case must be dropped unconditionally. Afterwards, once the case is dropped, the money will be given in the form of a donation. A donation! A donation to the watchdog with no strings attached.'

'Mister Hi Baby! You should have been a lawyer.'

'What do you mean?'

'I mean that's exactly what we managed to impose on them. The case will be dropped, quietly. After three months the donation will be made, quietly. No publicity, no comments and no statements.'

'Well done! Get things moving immediately.'

There can be no justification for delay in making a decision. I think that the decision made is the right decision. I could think matters over for a week, a month or a year but more thinking doesn't mean more wisdom. All that thinking for a long time does is waste a lot of valuable time. And I'd already wasted enough of my valuable time with the team of lawyers.

As soon as the lawyers had gone, my meeting began with Mr Yama Shuftu Yama, who had come from Tokyo especially. We had decided to settle the question of the desert ships at this meeting. Don't get me wrong! I don't mean those ships of the desert I turn into burgers. I'm talking about the idea I had that Mr Yama Shuftu Yama liked so much he's going to put up half of the capital. My latest idea! The desert ship is a cross between an ordinary car and an ordinary boat. It will look pretty much like a boat and its engine will be pretty much the same as a car engine. And it won't go on wheels but on skis. The field study indicated that we could sell 6,000 in the first year alone. Our target market is rich adolescents, who, in the oil capitals of Arabistan, are by no means hard to come by. The meeting with Mr Yama Shuftu Yama was not without its problems. The man was over eighty and you had to shout to make him hear. He had brought twenty aides with him and would not make any decision without consulting all of them. My spacious hotel wing was jam-packed with these flat-nosed people. Just joking! In truth, I have a great deal of respect for the Japanese, and for this old billionaire, particular respect. The meeting lasted seven hours, at the end of which we managed to reach an agreement. We decided to sign the initial agreement in New York and the final contract in Tokyo, as soon as the lawyers have finished going over the details.

Whenever I visit Tokyo, Mr Yama Shuftu Yama invites me to one of those well-known Geisha houses, to an evening's entertainment which will cost thousands of dollars. The favour had to be returned. There were no Geisha houses in town, but I had a lot of girlfriends – one in particular was Wendy Palmer, a theatrical agent for the stars of stage and screen, or more accurately, for young girls dreaming of becoming stars of stage and screen. The stars of the future! Starlets! I called her and asked her to get together as many girls as possible for a party I was giving for my Japanese guest that evening. Mr Yama Shuftu Yama would have to be made aware that there existed in the world a people no less generous than the Japanese.

I had hired the single-storey main wing of the hotel especially for the party. Wendy came at eight-thirty. Mr Yama Shuftu Yama and seven of his aides came at nine. The musicians came at nine-thirty. The girls came at ten. Twenty-seven stars of the future. Twenty-seven females to nine men. Not a bad ratio. The party began noisily: the noise of the musicians and the noise of the girls who were forced to shout to make Mr Yama Shuftu Yama hear. After a while, the ratio changed. As soon as the girls found out that among the things which Mr Yama Shuftu Yama owned was a film company, all attention was directed at him alone. The aides were left talking among themselves. Only Wendy remained with me, an old friend with whom a physical relationship had become a platonic one several years before. Mr Yama Shuftu Yama had begun to take on a new lease of life. He was dancing with star after star, dancing everything from Rock 'n' Roll to the Tango. The night wore on. Wendy began to kiss me. I began to kiss her. She began to pull me towards one of the rooms in the spacious wing. I began to let her pull me. Before going into the room, I glanced back into the salon. The band was playing jazz and the aides were assembled as if a board of directors. As for Mr Yama Shuftu Yama, he was being carried, like a corpse, on the shoulders of the girls towards another room. A disturbing idea took hold of me: he had died of dancing. Let him die later, after signing the final contract. For the moment, I had to make sure he was all right. I tried to go and see to him but

Wendy pulled me forcibly into the room and locked the door. There is nothing to equal the weakness of a gentleman in the face of an old girlfriend.

Tuesday, New York
I had breakfast, rather late, with Mr Yama Shuftu Yama who seemed thirty years younger. Evidently he hadn't had a heart attack, fainted or suffered from exhaustion. We exchanged warm greetings and signed the papers. He thanked me for my hospitality which he 'would never forget' and we agreed to meet in Tokyo in the near future.

My second appointment was with a reporter for *Business Stars*, the business magazine with the largest circulation in the world. The magazine had decided that I was to be the main story in a coming issue, with my picture on the cover subtitled: 'Hi Baby – the Man Who Turned the Camel into a Gold Mine'. The reporter arrived. Deborah Cousins. She was a pleasant surprise. I hate surprises but I make an exception for pleasant ones. In her thirties. Very pretty. Slightly brown-skinned. Probably one of our Jewish cousins. I've got nothing against the cousins, whether male or female. I'm a businessman, not a politician. Trade dissolves political differences and brings with it prosperity, joint projects and harmony. I soon realized that Deborah, though pretty, was not blessed with a great deal of intelligence. I don't look for intelligence in women. I look for intelligence in Harvard professors. I look for exciting sex in women and, sometimes, friendship. There's nothing wrong in mixing friendship with sex, occasionally. Deborah began to ask me about my childhood. If I told the truth, they wouldn't publish a single word. I don't believe in lying, but I do believe in embellishment. Reality, in certain circumstances, requires embellishment. This is what I did. I said:
'Ms Cousins! My childhood . . .'
She interrupted me gently:
'Call me Deborah!'
'Ok! My childhood, Deborah, arouses in my mind many conflicting images, many dreams and nightmares, many images of heaven and hellfire. Take what happened with the wolf, for example. I was . . .'
Deborah suddenly gasped:
'The wolf?! Something happened to you with a wolf?!'
I said calmly:
'I was ten years old. I was looking after the camels of the tribe. Imagine a ten-year-old child looking after five hundred camels. I was on my own. My only weapon was a small stick. I'll never forget that day as long as I live. When the hungry wolf attacked . . .'
Deborah gasped:
'A hungry wolf!! This is exciting! Very exciting!'

'He looked as if he hadn't eaten for weeks. What was he going to do? What do you think he would do? He left the camels alone and pounced on me. He chose the weakest and tastiest victim. The flesh of a ten year old child is most tender.'

Deborah gasped and began to repeat:

'Good God! Good God! What happened?'

'The wolf's face was right above mine. His fangs were aiming for my neck, right at my neck. I threw myself to the side, but his fangs sank into my arm. Look here! Look here!'

I revealed an old scar on my arm. (It had been inflicted by the frond of a palm tree which had had its leaves stripped off for one of my late father's lessons to teach me discipline and attention to detail.)

Deborah gasped:

'Good God! Good God! What happened then?'

'A miracle, Deborah . . .'

She said suddenly:

'Call me Debbie!'

'A miracle, Debbie, I was saved by a real miracle.'

'A miracle?!'

'Blackie. The black camel.'

'Blackie?!'

'Yes. The male of the herd. You must know, Debbie, that a herd is made up of she-camels and one male, just one male. Blackie was the male.'

Deborah gasped and said laughing:

'Wow! Wow! Wow! One male and five hundred females! Now I know who taught you how to deal with women. You learnt it from your camels. Ha! Ha! Just joking! Tell me what happened.'

'Blackie began to bray. He made a sound like thunder. Have you ever heard a camel bray? You haven't? Of course. And I don't think you want to hear a camel bray. A roaring sound like thunder. Just like thunder. The wolf turned to where the sound was coming from. In a second, in one second, Debbie, Blackie's teeth closed on the wolf's neck. I heard the sound of bones breaking. The wolf fell to the ground dead. Then, I fainted. Blackie, that dear, dear animal, began to lick my face tenderly until I came to.'

Deborah gasped in a manner not very dissimilar to a camel's bray and said:

'Oohh! Oohh! A camel killing a wolf! That's so exciting! Does that always happen?'

'You must be joking. That's the first event of its kind in history. And it'll probably be the last. Usually, it's the wolf that kills the camel. The wolf attacks the camel in the stomach, the softest part of the body. I'll never forget what Blackie did for me as long as I live. Do you know what I did? After he died, I had a statue made of him and had it erected in the biggest square in the capital. I made Blackie the logo of all my enterprises. Take a look! Take a look!'

From my wallet I took out a picture of a huge black camel and handed it to Deborah as I mumbled:

'Look how awesome he is! How beautiful! How handsome!'

I began to dab at an imaginary tear with my handkerchief. Deborah's gasps began to intensify then a flood of real tears began to flow as she moaned:

'Oh! Blackie! Oh! Blackie! You noble creature! You unique creature! Mister Hi Baby . . .'

I interrupted her:

'Let's drop the "Mister", please!'

'Fine! Fine! Hi Baby! You are a rare example of loyalty. An example it's impossible to find these days.'

I continued to dry my imaginary tears and returned the picture to my wallet. I said:

'Whatever I do, I'll never match a tenth of his loyalty. He risked his life to save mine.'

The interview lasted over four hours. It was full of gasps, sighs, tears and laughter. Suddenly, my private, very private, secretary, Barsam Marsam, the only person to accompany me on my travels, appeared to remind me that it would soon be our takeoff time for London and we had to leave the hotel within the hour.

Without thinking I asked Deborah:

'Debbie! Why don't you come with me?'

'Me?'

'You.'

'Where to?'

'London.'

'You're joking, aren't you?'

'I'm not joking. And there's no time to think about it. We have to leave for the airport within the hour.'

'But . . .'

'I'll arrange everything. You'll be my guest.'

'It is a tempting idea.'

'You know what Oscar Wilde said was the only way to deal with temptations.'

'Give in to them?'

'Exactly.'

'It is a very tempting idea.'

'So, give in to it.'

'But . . .'

'I told you I'll arrange everything. You can come back to New York whenever you want. You can spend a night, a month or a week in London.'

'What about two nights?'

'That's your decision. We've only got an hour left.'

'I think I can get home and fetch my passport and case in an hour.'

'Great! Really great! Barsam will arrange a car and driver.'

Barsam did indeed arrange everything. When the plane took off, Deborah was seated beside me in first class. In first class there was only us, Barsam, in a seat a long way off, and an old married couple holding hands.

Wednesday, London

The flight was unbelievable. Champagne came, then caviar. More champagne, more caviar. Barsam had, as usual, given each hostess a gift of $1500. And, as usual, we received better than normal service. Deborah began to drink. And gasp as she listened to more of my desert adventures. The scorpions I would eat when hungry, the hyena which suckled me, once, and saved me from dying of thirst, the ghouls, the genies. Then dinner was over. The lights dimmed. The old married couple slept still hanging on to each other's hands. The champagne continued to arrive. I said to Deborah:

'Debbie! Have you ever heard of the Mile-High Club?'

'The Mile-High Club? I don't think so. What is it?'

'You've never heard of it at all?'

'No. What about it?'

'It's a club for the élite. La crème de la crème! The club with the fewest members in the world. Only a few get in. Less than a few.'

'I'm dying of curiosity. What is this club?'

'Do you really want to know?'

'Yes.'

'Really and truly?'

'Hi Baby! You're a rogue! Really! Really! Really!'

'Ok! "Mile-High" refers to height, from the ground. Aeroplanes. Now do you understand?'

'I don't understand anything.'

'Do you really want to know?'

'Really! I swear . . .'

'There's no need to do that. I believe you. The members of this club are la crème de la crème. People who have made love on an aeroplane.'

Deborah gasped and said:

'You're pulling my leg, aren't you?'

'I'm not joking. It's a real club. With a real secretariat. And a secret list of members. And an annual masked ball.'

'How many members are there?'

I laughed and said:

'That's secret information. You're not a club member. If you were . . .'

She interrupted me:

'You mean . . .'

I interrupted her back:

'Yes. Didn't you see the film *Emmanuelle*?'

'You mean . . .'

I said simply:

'Yes.'

'Now?'

'Yes.'

'On the plane?'

'Yes.'

'Hi Baby! Did anyone ever tell you you're crazy?'

'Lots. What do you say?'

'Now? On the plane?'

Fine! The lights were low. The old married couple were asleep. Barsam was keeping the hostesses busy. The washroom was big enough. Deborah gasped and gasped and gasped and gasped as she entered the Mile-High Club. An unforgettable flight.

After a brief sleep, the day's agenda began with meetings with British businessmen wishing to obtain Camelburger franchises. In reality, there was nothing to negotiate. All they had to do was accept all the terms of the franchise contract. I had already closely vetted each of them to make sure their financial status was sound. There were five customers. They came one after the other. Each of them signed the contract and signed a cheque for the first instalment. Each of them went out with the contract under his arm as if they were carrying a priceless treasure. And each of them was indeed carrying a priceless treasure. So far, thank God, not one of my restaurants has lost money, not a single one.

I gave Deborah £20,000 in cash and sent her off shopping with Barsam. Deborah gasped – I'll have to call her the 'Gasping Woman' – as she took the money. She said:

'Hi Baby! Did anyone ever tell you you're crazy?'

'Yes. The members of the Mile-High Club.'

'Hi Baby! You're a devil! A cunning devil! You know how to get innocent young girls drunk and take advantage of their good nature.'

I gasped, but said nothing.

I spent the afternoon in a meeting of the board of The Crimson Desert Bank. The aged Arabistani chairman of the board was no younger than Mr Yama Shuftu Yama. The chairman opened the meeting as usual then fell asleep on his seat, leaving me to chair the meeting. The bank has shareholders from seventeen countries, and the board has members from nine countries. I presented a summarized report of the banks activities for the past six months. Net profits were more than $150 million and the year was only halfway through. I received the usual congratulations and the discussion, for the most part, was as usual in the form of praise for my own humble self. However, I was surprised by a discordant voice from a new member of the board, Sabouh Al-Dirhaman. He asked to speak but instead of the customary commendation he said things I had never heard before:

'Mister Harbi! You say that the Islamic Investments Department has experienced a major expansion in its activities and that most of the profits come from . . .'

I interrupted him:

'That is correct.'

He said:

'But we don't know the details of these investments.'

'What do you mean?'

'I mean we know the amount invested, we know the profits but we don't know where the money is invested.'

'That, Mister Sabouh, is secret information.'

'Even for members of the board?!'

'I believe that the honourable members of the board have always received the information they require. However, as a matter of principle, we don't go into the details of investments, whether Islamic or otherwise.'

'For ordinary investments the details aren't important. I am with you one hundred per cent. But for Islamic investments the situation is different. The issue is a matter of conscience. We have to know . . .'

I rudely interrupted him:

'Do you think we're using these investments to buy casinos in Las Vegas?'

The member's face reddened, and with an irritation he made no attempt to hide said:

'Mister Harbi! My apologies! It was not my intention to cast doubt on the integrity of the bank or its board. However, you must bear in mind that this isn't my money or your money. It is the money of Muslims who want to put it into halal investments. It is a question of conscience.'

'You are correct. And because it is a question of conscience, and with a clear conscience, we created the Islamic Law Monitoring Committee. Every Islamic investment is submitted to the Committee.'

'Forgive me Mister Harbi. If the Monitoring Committee is informed of the details of the Islamic investments, why are these details kept hidden from the Board?'

'Mister Sabouh! You are a new member of the Board and this is the first meeting you've attended. In time you'll understand how the bank operates. We do not submit figures to the Monitoring Committee. We submit the nature of the investment. Let us suppose we wanted to invest in a diamond mine which had not begun to . . .'

I was interrupted by the honourable member of the Board. I, interrupted! I who had never been interrupted by an honourable member before! Interrupted by the honourable member who had reminded me that it was not my money. The honourable member would have to be put in his place. The honourable member who was now shouting:

'In my opinion, members of the board must be given all the information they want . . .'

I cut him off sharply:

'Mister Sabouh! Are you an expert on Islamic law?'

'No. But . . .'

'Do you think that our investors will be more confident of your opinion, which has no grounding in Islamic law, than in the opinions of revered religious and legal scholars?'

'But I'm asking for the figures, not the . . .'

I interrupted him decisively:

'I think the topic has been sufficiently discussed. We are ready to vote. I would ask honourable members of the Board who feel that details of Islamic investments should be submitted to the Board to raise their hands.'

Every hand remained in its place, except for the hand of Sabouh Al-Dirhaman, which was held up and remained in the air as a clear challenge.

I ignored his hand and said:

'Excellent! I think the matter is settled, almost unanimously. We will continue with the current policy until our most honourable Board decides otherwise.'

In my own mind I had decided to get rid of this new member. In my own mind I had decided that he would have to be anaesthetized so as not to be aware of the coming danger. I smiled broadly and looked at the respected member and said:

'Nevertheless, the point you have raised, Mister Sabouh, is valid, extremely valid. I will arrange a meeting for you with the Monitoring Committee which will explain many things to you. And I will arrange another meeting with the Director of the Islamic Investments Department who will answer all your questions. If you still have any questions thereafter, I will answer them myself.'

I was, naturally, not going to do anything of the kind. But my words had made a favourable impression on the honourable members and had calmed the rage of the meddlesome member, at least on the surface. The usual discussion continued, then I handed the chair to the chairman who announced, as usual, that the meeting was closed.

In the evening Deborah came wearing one of the new dresses she had bought that morning. It was a tantalizing dress which revealed practically everything. I decided, as soon as I saw the dress, to take her with me to the party being given by my friend, Shaher Nattash. Shaher is a very charming character. He had had a novel idea, which had made him one of the wealthiest people around. Further proof of my theory that you can't get immensely rich without original ideas. And what was Shaher's idea? Investing in parties! Every night, every night! Shaher holds a party to which everyone is invited: rich and poor, the famous and the unknown, film stars and socialites, literati and the political élite and lots of beautiful girls of every nationality. He serves the best food and the best wine. There's a group of Arabistani musicians and a western group. When this large number of people meets in an atmosphere oiled with hard liquor, wine and music a vast number of deals, both large and small, inevitably take shape. A deal between a bank proprietor and an investor, another between a film producer and a female film star, a third between one billionaire and another billionaire. Gradually, Shaher had become a shareholder in a number of major companies without paying a penny. He hears news of a deal concluded in his house before anyone else. And there's always a bank manager willing to grant the necessary loans. Shaher's parties have become an integral party of London's business life. I think that, aside from stock exchanges, no place on earth witnessed as many deals as Shaher's parties. The large house was now a cacophony of music teeming with dozens of guests. Shaher greeted me with a hug and kisses and swore that the party was in my honour. I gave the impression of believing him. Deborah began to listen attentively to the Arabistani music. I decided the time had come for her to learn eastern dance. Shaher immediately volunteered to teach her and he took her into the middle of the room. Suddenly my friend, Raf'i Rif'at bounded up to me:

'Hi Baby! Hi Baby! what a pleasant surprise! When did you arrive?'

'This morning.'

'Why didn't you tell me?'

'I was sure I'd be seeing you here. Anything new?'

'Of course! Of course!'

Raf'i pulled me into one of the small rooms scattered throughout the house and closed the door. He took out a cigar, bit the end off, lit it and launched into his well-known verbal deluge:

'Listen Hi Baby! I'm talking to you! This is an unmissable opportunity. I tell you, unmissable! Are you listening? A rare investment opportunity. I haven't told anyone about it yet. There are loads of eager investors but I haven't offered it to anyone. I told you it's a rare opportunity. A five-star tourist hotel in

Havana. Havana! The capital of Cuba! Did you hear me? A new tourist paradise. Thousands of tourists flooding in every hour. From all over the place. There's someone close to President Castro. His friend. I can't tell you his name at the moment. I might tell you later. What's important is that this friend has arranged . . .'

The deluge continued as I feigned interest. I did not think investing in tourist hotels anywhere was an idea that merited such enthusiasm. Everyone is investing in tourist hotels. The profits are guaranteed but modest, even in the most successful hotels I own. Real money only comes with new ideas. I seized the opportunity of Raf'i lighting another cigar to escape from the room promising that I would give the matter serious thought.

When I returned to the main room, everyone was standing in astonishment watching Deborah dancing a sensual eastern dance as if she had grown up in the house of Tahiya Kariyuka, the famous Egyptian belly-dancer. I left Deborah to dance and slipped out of the house. At the hotel an old girlfriend was waiting for me, a girlfriend with whom my relationship had become a platonic friendship several years ago.

Thursday, London

This morning, my friend Shukri Yasser came to see me and we talked about the new industrial project we're planning to get going together: '*Bushuts* You Only Use Once'. Disposable *bushuts*! In fact you could use them three or four times. One of my amazing ideas. I noticed that the wearing of *bushuts* had been on the increase in Arabistani capitals, particularly in the oil states. The reason being cultural and civilizational identity. (Money knows no identity, but that's another issue!) I noticed that a lot of Arabistanis were buying *bushuts* but only wearing them occasionally, once a year or once in a lifetime, when they get married usually. This is where the idea sprang from: making a cheap *bushut* which can be worn once or twice and then thrown away. The technology to be used came, as usual, from Japan. After a lot of research and many experiments we'd reached the development stage. To look at, a disposable *bushut* is not much different from an ordinary *bushut*. You'd need an expert eye closely examining it to tell the difference. Shukri Yasser, like me, was mad about new ideas. A few years ago I'd started the first company for the hiring out of *bushuts* with him. For a very modest sum you could hire an expensive luxury quality *bushut* for a night or a week. The idea was hugely successful and very profitable. However, as usual, imitators pounced on such a successful idea. Shops for hiring out *bushuts* appeared all over the place. We pulled out of the market. I'm sure imitators will pounce on our new idea but by the time they've caught up with us we'll have made huge profits and moved on to even newer ideas. I reviewed the latest developments with Shukri and we decided to meet in Tokyo to select the colours and begin production.

My second appointment was with Mass'oud As'ad, that notorious extortionist and owner of the rag the *Voice of Truth,* who called himself the founder of the expatriate Arabistani press. This scoundrel has tried to blackmail me a number of times without success. Once he published a picture of me with a woman in a night club so I sent him a photo of me and the women with us both naked and asked him to publish it. Once he ran a story about a secret deal I had going and threatened to publish the full details, so I pre-empted him by making everything public at a press conference. However, I began to realize that this man who failed to blackmail me could give me useful information and I began to co-operate with him on that basis. He has information for sale, I buy it. A comfortable and profitable relationship for both parties. The scoundrel knows I'm not interested in sex scandals or family dramas. Nor stories about alcoholics and drug addicts. All I'm interested in is the business secrets of specific individuals. He sat down and drank coffee. The morning bulletin began. I interrupted:

'Mass'oud! I heard all the morning's news before you came. I'm not interested in who's in bed with the Zionist Entity and who's fighting it. I'm not interested in arms dealers or white-slave traders. I don't want to know which fat cat is sleeping with his maid. My request is very specific.'

'I'm at your command, Mister Hi Baby.'

'There's a new member of the board of . . .'

He interrupted:

'A troublemaker. Sabouh Al-Dirhaman.'

I looked at him in wonder. He laughed saying:

'Walls have ears. And people too. He's threatened to have you thrown off the board. He's repeated the threat on more than one occasion in public.'

'The bastard! The filthy bastard! I'm the majority shareholder and I control the majority of the votes. How does the bastard intend to get rid of me?'

'He intends to create a big fuss culminating in a shareholders' revolt and your resignation. He wants to raise the issue of Islamic investments. He says he has definite and reliable information proving that the money that pious Muslims are paying to the bank to invest in areas returning a halal profit is going in directions far removed from . . .'

I interrupted:

'Ok! Ok! He must be an extremist. I want all the necessary information about this bastard.'

'You mean, Mister Hi Baby, that you want all the information necessary to destroy the reputation and credibility of Sabouh Al-Dirhaman.'

'You understand me perfectly.'

'But there are many difficulties which . . .'

'I understand them perfectly. How much?'

'I don't know.'

'What do you mean?'

'As yet, I haven't got my hands on the information you need. There are a lot of rumours. Things said which are unconfirmed. There would have to be a thorough investigation to get . . .'

'A hundred thousand pounds.'

'Two hundred thousand.'

'A hundred and fifty thousand. Final offer.'

Mass'oud As'ad took the cheque, shook my hand and left. After he'd gone I went into the washroom and the hand he had shaken I rubbed with eau de cologne until it turned red.

My next appointment was with my private doctor, Professor Giles Midland. For a long time, I had been discussing with the professor the idea of donating a ward to the hospital he practices in, a ward bearing the name of my father in order to immortalize his memory. The professor had previously suggested creating a coronary care wing but I had refused. He had come back with the idea of an oncology wing but I had refused. During our meeting I told him my final decision: the wing must specialize only in those diseases my late father suffered from. The professor agreed and left with the cheque in his pocket for half a million pounds to be used to build a new wing at the 'Cynic Clinic' hospital. The wing would be called the Shaykh Abu Khashmin Al-Hurayabibi Department for the Treatment of Constipation, Haemorrhoids and Fistulae.

Deborah came in wearing another alluring dress. She kissed me, gasped and said:

'Hi Baby! Hi Baby! The party was brilliant. Do you know, I danced until the morning. The morning!'

'Everybody liked the way you danced.'

'Really? You're just saying that. Really?'

'Really! I've never seen a dance like that in my life.'

Deborah gasped and said:

'Really?'

'It was a dance straight out of *A Thousand and One Nights*.'

'I had no idea it was getting so late. I looked but couldn't find you. Where did you disappear to?'

'I didn't disappear. By midnight I was really exhausted so I went back to the hotel and went to bed. I knew you were safe among friends. By the way, when do you want to go back?'

'Go back?'

'Have you forgotten you only came for two nights?'

'I haven't forgotten. But can I change my mind? Can I stay another two nights?'

'With pleasure. I'll arrange things with the hotel. I'm leaving tonight as you know.'

'Hi Baby! Promise me you won't get angry. I want to tell you something, but promise me you won't get angry.'

'I promise. I won't get angry.'

'Really? Really?'

'Really!'

'During the party I met a man, a real gentleman, who gave me . . .'

I interrupted her gently:

'Who gave you a red rose and invited you to a romantic dinner this evening on his boat on the river.'

Deborah gasped and said:

'How? How did you know?'

'Raf'i is a very old friend of mine. He still believes in the romantic approach for dealing with beautiful young women.'

'Would you be angry if I stayed with your romantic friend for a day or two?'

'On the contrary. I would be pleased. More than you could imagine.'

Raf'i's romanticizing had saved me. I had been afraid this gasping cousin would become a heavy burden it might have been difficult to get rid of. There's nothing worse than a woman who's got what she wants. I invited her to lunch at The Equatorial Forest restaurant. The place was filled with animals, thunder, lightning and roaring. Deborah looked around her with the amazement of an innocent child and gasped whenever a lion roared.

After lunch I went to visit my famous friend, Basir Al-'Aref, in his famous office with its variety of amazing rooms. He received me most warmly. His girlfriend, Heather, received me with a warm hug – an old fling which had become platonic; you know the rest! For over a year, I'd been discussing with Basir a fascinating new idea: the 'Genie Buster'. I had noticed that a lot of wealthy Arabistanis were terrified of genies interfering in their lives. I'd also noticed that they were willing to pay a lot of money to protect their lives and money, particularly their money, from such negative interventions. I'd agreed with Basir to manufacture a device called a 'Genie Buster'. About the size of a transistor radio, it would have intricate pictures of devils and genies on the outside and a recording of Basir chanting a terrifying and incomprehensible incantation inside. Each device would have Basir's signature guaranteeing to exorcise any house of its evil spirits. Producing each device wouldn't cost more than twenty dollars but you could sell them for more than twenty thousand. We'd made a lot of progress on the design and Basir was as enthusiastic about the idea as I was.

Today, however, I noticed that his enthusiasm had begun to evaporate. After deep thought, he said:

'Hi Baby! I've had second thoughts.'

In astonishment, I said:

'Second thoughts?! Now?! What do you mean?'

'There are genies and genies.'

'I'm sorry?!'

'I mean you can't treat all genies the same. There are good ones and bad ones.'

'Good ones and bad ones?! Basir! Doctor Basir! We're talking about a business project which has got nothing to do with genies, good ones or bad ones. We're selling people an idea, no more no less.'

'That's true. But some of our genie friends don't like the idea.'

Some of our genie friends?! What was going on in Basir's head? From the very outset both of us knew that we were making a device that didn't repel anything, not even insects. What had happened? I said:

'Basir! I beg you! Don't play around with me. I don't joke when it comes to business. I joke about everything except business.'

'Hi Baby! I'm being serious. Perfectly serious. Some of the genies, in whom I have great confidence, have advised me to abandon the idea.'

'Abandon millions of dollars?!'

'That's the advice I've been given.'

With an anger I made no attempt to suppress, I said:

'And are you allowed to tell me how you received this advice? By fax or the Internet?!'

Basir's face reddened and in a trembling voice said:

'I beg you! I beg you! I can't tell you.'

'Am I to understand that you're pulling out of the project for good?'

'Yes. That is my decision. There's no going back on it. I'm sorry for all the trouble I've caused you. As regards costs . . .'

I interrupted:

'There's no trouble. There are no costs. I'll just develop the idea with another astrologer who doesn't take advice from genies.'

I said this to put Basir's mind at rest. The truth of the matter was that his decision meant the idea was dead. No other astrologer was as well-known to Arabistanis as Basir. Consumers wouldn't have confidence in a device guaranteed by any other astrologer.

Every time I visit Basir he asks me to choose the name of a woman who is playing hard to get and assures me that he will break down her resistance. As usual, he took me into the Room of Lovers. We stood in front of a huge thurible giving off a black smoke which made one dizzy. As usual I wrote Galnar's name on a piece of paper, folded it and handed it to him. As usual, Basir took the piece of paper and threw it on the thurible without reading the name. He stared at the thurible for a while then said:

'The outcome is guaranteed. She will come to you herself. Out of the blue, she will telephone you.'

Heather came down to see me out and I said:

'Heather! What's wrong with Basir? What's going on?'

A cloud of sadness passed over the beautiful Scottish face and she said:

'Hi Baby! Your friend's in trouble. He's started thinking he can talk to genies. He thinks one of them is his friend.'

'Heather! That's a dangerous sign. A very dangerous sign. What are you going to do?'

'I can't do anything. Whenever I talk about it he says I'm mentally disturbed and need help.'

'Heather! Be careful.'

'I'm trying to. I'm trying to.'

That evening, Deborah said goodbye with a rough, warm kiss. She then whispered in my ear:

'I hope first class is full.'

I laughed and took from my pocket a small card and put it in her hand. Intrigued she asked:

'What's this?'

'The address of the Mile-High Club. Remember, the address is top secret information. Only members can have it.'

She looked at me in total amazement and said:

'The address of the club?! The Mile-High Club?! So, you weren't joking?'

'I wasn't joking. That's the club's address. I'll see you at the annual reunion.'

As she left the hotel wing, Deborah was still gasping.

Friday, the Capital, Arabistan X

As soon as I reached the hotel, I spoke, as usual with my wife, Douyahya. Whenever I'm back home I spend one day of the week with her, Friday. And when I'm away I phone her once a week, on Friday. Douyahya is a cousin, I mean, a real cousin. I chose her, with the utmost care, after I'd finished my studies and had gone into business. I made a detailed feasibility study of the pros and cons of all the potential candidates and settled on her. She's fairly intelligent, not bad looking and has a high-school certificate. After drawing up the marriage contract but before the wedding, I explained to her the rules of the game in detail. I told her she could back out before anything happened. I told her I would be living in my own villa and she would be living in her own villa. If there were children they would have their own villa. All her material needs, without exception, would be met. She could finish her education and take up any pastime she chose. She could spend her time sleeping, playing chess or reading Aristotle. We would meet once, just once a week. We would have sex once, just once a week. The other days of the week were not her business. Nor were other aspects of my life. No investigations and no interrogations. She accepted the conditions and everything went perfectly. I think I began to love her in my own special way. And I think she began to love me in her own special way. Then a son came along, Muharib. I put him in his own villa with three governesses to look after him: one from Japan (to teach him all things technical), one from Sweden (to teach him physical education) and one from Arabistan (to teach him cultural identity, etc.). All of them had PhDs in education. Careful planning produced the desired results and Muharib began to distinguish himself in a number of fields, particularly in Arabistani poetry. For his birthday, I promised him I would ask a famous poet to take him under his wing and organize a poetry evening here, a poetry evening attended by the prime minister himself and no less than five thousand guests from the worlds of intellectual thought, literature and culture. After I had finished talking to Douyahya I began to talk to Muharib who was yelling:

'Papa! Papa! I've written a new poem.'

Pleased, I said:

'Let's hear it, son. Let's hear it!'

'It's called "My Father on the Aeroplane".'

'Ok! Let's hear it.'

'My dear father travelled
He took his suitcase
He went to the airport
With him his suitcase
With him his passport
He travelled
He travelled by plane
There were passengers on the plane
There was a captain on the plane
There was my father on the plane
My father was on the plane.'

'Brilliant! Brilliant! Get yourself ready for the poetry evening, son.'

'When papa?'

'Soon. Soon.'

I brought the conversation to a close and received an old friend from my student days at Stanford, Sabir Hayir, under-secretary of state for culture in Arabistan X. He told me the poetry evening plans were going well and preparations were in progress. He told me that the famous poet Ken'an Filfil would be taking Muharib under his wing, the first fruits of which would be appearing in the next issue of the *New Poetic Prowess*. He assured me that the Minister of Culture had the promise of the Prime Minister that the poetry evening would receive his patronage and that the date would be fixed shortly. I thanked my old friend warmly. Before he left the wing of the house, I put an envelope containing 100,000 dollars in his pocket as I whispered in his ear:

'For the children. The *'Eid* is just around the corner.'

Sabir tried to give the envelope back, saying:

'You shouldn't have, Harbi. You shouldn't have.'

I put the envelope back in his pocket, saying:

'You're right! One shouldn't return a gift!'

This was a trifling sum to pay for a talented child to find his way in life laid out for him as I had found my way laid out for me, thanks to my late father.

After Sabir had gone, Dr Za'il Bahran, head of the High Commission for Poetry and Prose in Arabistan X, came to see me. He was happy when I told him I had decided to put half a million dollars at the Commission's disposal provided it was used to award an annual prize to the best collection of poetry published by a poet under the age of twenty. I told the head of the commission that the prize would be called the Muharib Poetry Prize. Dr Za'il thought that Muharib was the name of my late father until I explained to him that it was the name of my son. Dr Za'il accepted my sole condition: Muharib would present the prize in person to the winner. After Dr Za'il had left, I felt a deep psychological satisfaction. I had guaranteed Muharib's place in history, whether through his poems or through the prize.

I asked Barsam to call Galnar and tell her I was willing to appear for a second time on her programme, *The Eyes of the World Are Upon You*. Since appearing on her programme four years ago, the image of her had practically never left my mind. All my attempts to lure her into a more intimate relationship had failed. All gifts had been returned to me, with expressions of deep gratitude, even the Mercedes. Barsam returned with another courteous excuse. Apparently the pieces of paper bearing her name burnt in Basir's thurible had not enflamed her heart. The path of love is indeed long, as my late father would say after every rhyme-free Nabati poem he recited.

The correspondent of *Business Secrets* came for an interview about my latest commercial and industrial projects. The interview was going well until the correspondent began to talk about Islamic investments. Why all this sudden interest everywhere in Islamic investments?

The correspondent said:

'Mister Harbi! Everyone knows that the Crimson Desert Bank was a pioneer in the field of Islamic investments but . . .'

I interrupted him:

'Thank you. This is something that even our enemies, if we had any enemies, would be the first to admit, even before our friends. We were, thanks be to God, one of the first banks to break into this field. And we've been followed, may God be praised, by many other banks.'

'Mister Harbi! That is true. But a lot of questions are beginning to be asked about . . .'

I interrupted again:

'A lot of questions being asked?! What questions?!'

'About the bank's Islamic investments.'

'We at the Crimson Desert Bank believe in complete openness. We are transparent to an unbelievable extent. You can say, without reservation, that we are the pioneers in transparency in Arabistani banking.'

'That will make my job easier. Let's begin with the first question. Where are the Islamic investments targeted?'

'My dear friend, now you're putting me in a very embarrassing position. Transparency applies to all the banks activities, but not the secrets of its clients.'

'But the question is being asked by the clients themselves.'

'What do you mean?'

'I mean that a number of investors have contacted us asking about how their money is being invested.'

'This is a very clear matter. The money is invested in fields permitted by Islamic law. No interest-charging transactions. No investments in night-clubs or hotels which serve alcohol or pork. Any issues we're not certain about we submit to the Islamic Law Monitoring Committee.'

'Could you explain that in more detail?'

'With pleasure. Sometimes it's not clear if an activity is tainted by interest or is free of it. These are difficult questions of Islamic jurisprudence which neither you nor I can judge. For a clear conscience, all commercial activities of this kind are submitted to the Monitoring Committee.'

'Could you give me any examples of such commercial activities.'

'At the moment, no specific examples come to mind. However, the Head of the Monitoring Committee responds to such questions on a regular basis and has the reference works to provide detailed . . .'

The correspondent interrupted me:

'All this is true. But that's not the problem.'

'Where is the problem?'

'The problem, as they put it, is that the Islamic Investments Department is supervised by you directly. In other words, officials in that department answer to you alone.'

'Let's suppose that that is the case. Where is the problem? Isn't that what I'm delegated to do?'

'To be frank, Mister Harbi, people are saying that some of your investments have certain question marks about them.'

'Question marks?! What do you mean?!'

'I mean . . .'

I interrupted him angrily:

'So, I'm investing Muslims' money in casinos, strip clubs and bars?'

The correspondent gave no sign of embarrassment but continued calmly:

'No! No! Perish the thought! You couldn't do such a thing. What is being asked is a completely different question.'

'I hope you'll enlighten me then.'

'People say that you choose financial institutions suffering from liquidity problems and you offer them loans at rates of interest much higher than market rates. This is what has enabled you to make the extraordinary profits you've made.'

'And I keep them for myself?!'

'No! No one is saying that. Everyone knows that the profits are distributed to investors. That isn't the problem.'

'Where is the problem then?! Please tell me!'

'There are experts who believe that this is not a sound investment and that the financial institutions you have granted loans to will collapse one after the other. And when they do collapse, the lifetime savings which investors, in their tens of thousands, have put at the bank's disposal will disappear.'

'Did you get this information from Sabouh Al-Dirhaman?'

He blushed and I realized I'd hit the target. I said:

'I don't want to talk about that creature. I'll let his vile deeds speak on his own behalf. All the shareholders will know, in the very near future, what he's really like and his malicious intentions. However, as some people with sick minds have been taken in by what he's been saying, I find myself forced to speak to you, for the first time, about our Islamic investments. We are currently building a huge hotel in Chechnia. You've heard of Chechnia? A hotel which won't be selling alcoholic drinks. I believe the people of Chechnia are Muslims and deserve some help from us in giving their economy a boost. We are currently building three hospitals in Afghanistan. I believe the Afghan people are Muslims and that investing in a hospital is legitimate. We have previously set up rabbit farms in Indonesia and an ostrich farm in Malaysia. Do you want the documents?'

The correspondent was silent for a while then said:

'Is it likely that a hotel in Chechnia and hospitals in Afghanistan will make a profit?'

'No investment makes a profit from day one. That's the golden rule of business. In the medium term, and I'm not saying long term, these projects will be very profitable.'

Barsam came in to remind me that that it would soon be time to take off for Bombay. I showed the correspondent to the door of the hotel wing. I whispered in Barsam's ear to escort the correspondent to the hotel entrance and to give him an envelope containing twenty thousand dollars. I don't think the curious correspondent will turn down the money, seeing as it was an investment in a non-Islamic field.

Saturday, Bombay

The service on the plane was, as usual, splendid. And one of the air hostesses was more than splendid. In addition to the usual gift, I asked Barsam to give her a diamond ring worth five thousand dollars. By happy coincidence, it turned out she was staying in the same hotel as me and agreed, in gratitude, to have dinner with me.

My first visitor came, Guru Mungo Jitni. For two years I'd been discussing with him a new idea of mine: Your Luck Today – By Computer. In short, the idea was to design a minicomputer that the owner could use, once he'd programmed in his star sign and date of purchase, to find out how much luck he was going to have on every day of the year for the next twenty-five years. The computer would provide the information in several languages in both written and spoken modes. It was designed in such a way as to prevent the user from anticipating things: you could only find out what luck had in store for you on a given day on that day itself. There were immense technical obstacles which I'd managed to overcome in co-operation with specialist companies in Japan. All that remained was the software, the astrological information stored in the computer, and for that, a genius of an astrologer was needed. I had chosen the most famous astrologer in the world, Guru Mungo Jitni. He had agreed to be involved and had begun, in fact, to prepare the necessary data. The problem was that he had refused to accept a one-off payment and was insisting on a percentage of the profits. I hate arrangements that can lead to difficulties and a percentage in a project like this would lead to a thousand and one difficulties. Who would determine the profit? Would he accept the accounts I presented to him? What would happen if we disagreed? And who wants to fall out with an astrologer? I had decided that this meeting would be decisive. Either he agreed to the lump sum or I would be looking for another astrologer. As soon as he sat down, the guru said:

'Don't you want me to read your palm?'

'My palm? I thought star signs were your sole speciality.'

'Star signs, palm reading, the crystal ball, magic, both black and white, spiritualism, healing . . .'

I interrupted him:

'You remind me of a friend of mine who does all that. Recently, he has started talking directly to genies.'

'Genies? Where's the difficulty in that? I've been talking to genies since I was five years old.'

The guru fell silent and began to reflect, then he said:

'Have you got a problem? Would you like to meet a genie?'

I laughed and said:

'Thank you. We'd better concentrate on the projects of this world. In the past, we were talking about half a million dollars. I am prepared, now, to double that amount.'

'Mister Hi Baby! You're selling each computer at a thousand dollars. You're going to make tens of millions in profits and you want me to be satisfied with this trifling sum?'

'Guru Mungo Jitni! It is not a trifling sum, as you know full well. And I, as you know full well, am taking a huge risk. A very huge risk! To date, I've spent more than three million dollars. The idea could fail utterly. Maybe nobody will buy a single computer.'

The guru guffawed for a long time, then said:

'The stars assure me the computer will be a great success.'

'Haven't the stars also assured you that, if you refuse my offer, you won't get a single dollar, after all the work you've put in?'

'What do you mean?'

'I mean I could use the services of another astrologer. As for you, you couldn't sell the data to anyone. I, and I alone, am sole proprietor of the manufacturing rights. Your lawyer will have shown you the documents.'

The guru guffawed again (I'll have to call him the Guffawing Guru) and said:

'Mister Hi Baby! What's all this about? Rights? Lawyers? Remember, we're friends. This is between friends. Let's leave lawyers out of it.'

'Ok! So let's leave the percentage out of it as well. I've offered you a million dollars. Do you accept or refuse?'

The guru guffawed, opened his attaché case and took out a small crystal ball. He placed it on the table, knelt on the ground and began to look into the crystal ball.

I couldn't stop myself laughing. I said:

'Guru Mungo Jitni! Is the answer going to come from the crystal ball?'

He replied in all seriousness:

'Yes. Yes. Just give me three or four minutes.'

'Do you want me to go?'

'That won't be necessary. However, I would ask you to remain silent.'

I did remain silent while I watched the features of his face change in a strange manner as he gazed into the crystal. I couldn't decide whether I was in the presence of a brilliant actor or a gifted guru.

After a few minutes silence, he said:

'Two million dollars.'

'That's what the crystal ball thinks?!'

'That is the decision of the crystal ball.'

'And if I refuse?'

'The crystal ball is certain you won't refuse.'

'And how did the crystal ball reach this level of certainty?'

'The crystal ball said that, if you pay the money, you'll get something else in addition to the software.'

'Something else?!'

'Yes. Call it a bonus if you like.'

'And what is this bonus?'

'If you really want to know I'll have to return to the crystal ball.'

The guru guffawed and pulled out of his attaché case a candle which he lit and placed behind the crystal ball. He then sank to the ground and crouched gazing at the candle through the crystal ball. The candle gave off strange pungent odours and the features of his face were completely transformed. After a few minutes he blew out the candle and returned it to his attaché case. He guffawed and said:

'Sabouh Al-Dirhaman.'

He must have noticed the look of total amazement on my face. He must have noticed that I was suddenly unable to speak. He guffawed again and said:

'That's the bonus.'

In an almost inaudible voice, I said:

'What do you mean?'

The guffawing guru said:

'If you pay the money you will be rid, once and for all, of the meddlesome Sabouh Al-Dirhaman.'

In astonishment, I said:

'How?!'

'The details do not concern you.'

'Black magic?!'

'I told you the details are not you're concern.'

I made one of my quick decisions:

'Fine! fine! I agree.'

The guru guffawed and said:

'With regard to payment of the money . . .'

I interrupted him:

'I will deposit it in your secret account at the Montpellier bank in Zurich.'

I smiled as I watched the guru's features being swallowed up in astonishment, and said:

'Did you think you were the only one with a crystal ball?'

The guru guffawed and left. For some unknown reason, I felt a chill permeate my whole body.

My second visitor was Mr Masala who owned a chain of restaurants that was famous throughout India. This was our tenth meeting to discuss our joint project: canned *sambousa*. *Sambousa* is one of the most popular foods in Arabistan, and one of the hardest to cook. A few years ago I'd come up with the idea of canning it. You put the can in the oven for half a minute, open it and you're eating fresh *sambousas*. No mincing, no kneading, no onions, no headaches. I hadn't the slightest doubt of the success of the idea. The only remaining problem was the pig-headedness of Mr Masala who was beginning his usual lecture:

'Mister Hi Baby! We can put *sambousa* in tins. The purchaser can put the can in the oven then eat what's inside the can. But he won't be eating fresh *sambousa*. It will taste like *sambousa* made the day before.'

'Mister Masala! That's what you say every time. The problem is that you insist on having the canning done in India. I've told you time and time again that a Japanese company I have dealings with has solved the problem. Nowadays there are countless foods which come out of a can as if they'd just come out of the frying pan, completely fresh.'

'Maybe. Maybe. But I do not like the Japanese. I do not like dealing with them.'

'Who's asking you to like them? Who's asking you to deal with them? I'll be handling that side of things.'

'But I do not trust them. They might steal my recipe and start making *sambousa* themselves.'

'They can't do that. I'm the one who owns the legal rights.'

'Even if we overcome over this problem, there's another one.'

'Which is?'

'Is it logical to make the recipe up here, then ship it to Japan for canning and then ship it to Arabistan for retail?'

'And who told you that was the plan?'

'So what is the plan?'

'The factory will be in Arabistan. We're the only ones in the picture. You'll be responsible for the recipe, I'll be responsible for the processing.'

'And the technology will come from Japan?'

'Yes.'

'But can the Japanese make it so that the *sambousa* is fresh when the can is opened?'

'Yes.'

'Mister Hi Baby! Please forgive me if I tell you I don't believe it. We have been trying with a number of companies here and the results have been disappointing.'

'Mister Masala! Try it and see for yourself.'

I called Barsam over and whispered in his ear. He went to the servants quarters and came back with a small can and a candle (This must be candle week!). He lit the candle and placed the can over the flame until it was hot then opened it using one of those famous Swiss army knives. I handed Mr Masala the opened can and asked him to taste it. He put his fingers inside with the utmost caution and pulled out a *sambousa* which he looked at with the utmost caution. I said laughing:

'Have no fear! Have no fear! Eat it!'

Mr Masala began to eat the *sambousa*. He stopped and said:

'I don't believe it! I don't believe it! It's like it's just been cooked. It's fresh. Completely fresh. But the taste . . .'

I interrupted him:

'Let's leave the taste aside for the moment. It's not your recipe. When we use your recipe the taste will be excellent.'

Mr Masala began to bite into another *sambousa*. I realized, with absolute certainty, that the decision would come now or never.

I said:

'Mister Masala! Now you have tested the technology for yourself, what do you think?'

'To tell the truth . . .'

I interrupted him:

'The truth is you liked the *sambousa*. The truth is the *sambousa* is fresh. And the agreement is fresh and ready to sign.'

Mr Masala smiled and said:

'Fifty–fifty.'

I was fully aware of the fact that without the name Masala on the can the success of the project couldn't be taken for granted. I was also full aware that even if I negotiated with him for a hundred years I wouldn't be able to make him change his mind. I smiled and said:

'Fifty–fifty. I'll get my lawyers to finish off the details. When you visit us next month the agreement will be ready to sign.'

Mr Masala devoured the remaining sambousa and said:

'We must celebrate this happy occasion. What do you think?'

'In one of your restaurants?'

'No. At one of my homes. Eight o'clock tomorrow evening. What do you say?'

'Eight o'clock tomorrow evening.'

After Mr Masala had gone, I felt absolutely exhausted. I asked Barsam to hold my calls and not to wake me until after my female guest, whose name I'd forgotten, arrived. Barsam reminded me she was called Jackie, full name Jacqueline. I fell into a deep sleep full of strange dreams about a guru with a long moustache and a thick beard eating a viper as he looked at me guffawing, a guru called Mungo Jitni.

Barsam woke me at nine. I found Jackie, dressed in an Indian sari, waiting for me in the salon. Jackie was as Australian as a kangaroo but the eastern sari suited her so well you'd have thought she'd been born in it. I said:

'This is your host speaking. What can I get you?'

She laughed and said:

'So, you're going to do the same for me.'

The champagne arrived. The caviar arrived. When she had finished her fourth glass I asked her suddenly:

'Jackie! How did you become a member of the Mile-High Club?'

She blushed momentarily then said:

'How did you hear about the club?'

'You could call me a founder member.'

'And how did you find out I was a member?'

'We're in the land of magic, magicians and crystal balls. My crystal ball told me.'

'If your crystal ball told you, why are you asking me?'

'I want the details. My crystal ball didn't go into the details.'

'Mister Hi Baby! . . .'

I interrupted her:

'There's no need for the "Mister", please.'

'Hi Baby! You're a devil.'

'Jackie! You're a devil too. So let's hear the story.'

'There's nothing to tell. The usual story.'

'All stories about the Mile-High Club deserve a telling.'

'I didn't feel I was on a plane. Believe me. I was in a bedroom no smaller than my room at the hotel.'

'So, I take it you were on a private plane.'

'Ah ha! Your crystal ball again!'

'And who owned the plane?'

'The Maharajah.'

'I didn't think there were any maharajahs with private planes.'

'Well, we called him the Maharajah.'

'Jackie! You're a wicked woman.'

'Hi Baby! You're an inquisitive man.'

'You're right. Finish the story, or rather, start it.'
'There's nothing to say. It was a long flight and the Maharajah chose me.'
'And how many candidates were there?'
'There were twenty-seven hostesses.'
'And how many passengers?'
'Apart from the crew, there was just the Maharajah and three guards.'
'And what was the experience like?'
'Hi Baby! Have you no shame? How can you ask a girl a question like that?'
'I'll rephrase the question. Did you enjoy . . .'
She interrupted me:
'It was average. Very average.'
'Any other experiences in flight?'
'That was the first and the last.'
'Where there's life . . .'
'There will be aeroplanes.'
'What happened to the Maharajah?'
'I don't know. I stopped working for him.'
'Was it that bad?'
She laughed and said:
'That wasn't the reason. I was having a tempestuous love affair.'
'So you went after this other lover.'
'Exactly.'
'And this tempestuous love affair did not last?'
'Exactly. What about you?'
'Me? I haven't got a private plane.'
'So how did you join the Mile-High Club?'
'So, you've got a crystal ball as well.'
'Naturally. I learnt magic from the aborigines. Now, it's your turn. Tell me what happened.'
'It was a terrifying experience. It ended in tragedy. It almost killed me.'
'Wow! Go on! Go on! Tell me the details.'
'It was a long time ago. When I was good-looking and crazy. I mean when I was very good-looking and very crazy. I was a passenger on a communist plane. I mean a plane owned by a communist country.'
'Ok?'
'It was an internal flight. Less than an hour. It was a small plane, propeller powered. Don't ask me what type. I think it was Russian-made, a Tupolev, or Lopov or maybe even Khruschev. Something like that. It didn't have more than twenty seats.'
'It doesn't seem the appropriate backdrop for joining the Mile-High Club.'
'You're right. That's what led to the disaster.'

'Tell me! Tell me!'

'Ok! I was the only passenger. There was no hostess on board, just a male flight attendant.'

'You slept with a man?!'

'Jackie! Damn you! Wait till I've finished. The flight attendant was a man but the pilot was a woman. A very beautiful woman. The cockpit door was open and she was the only person in the cockpit. I told you the plane was very small. The pilot was really beautiful, despite the fact she was a communist. Anyway, I assume she was a communist. I wasn't really interested in her political beliefs. She had a lovely ar . . .'

'We don't need those details.'

'Ok! After take off, I told the flight attendant I wanted to speak to the pilot about an important matter. At first he was hesitant . . .'

'Then you gave him . . .'

'I gave him my extremely expensive Swiss watch. He went to ask her permission and returned with the necessary authorization. I went into the cockpit and shut the door behind me. She looked at me and smiled. I smiled suggestively, drew close to her and started to kiss her.'

'While she was flying the plane?!'

'While she was flying the plane. Then one thing led to another. I found my self sitting in the pilot's seat with her sitting on top of me holding the joy stick at the same time as . . .'

'I can imagine the situation.'

'Ok! The pilot was a passionate woman. She apparently forgot to keep an eye on the controls. She left the plane to its own devices. Suddenly, we realized that the plane was shaking and heading for the ground at a tremendous speed. At the last minute she managed to land in a field, a maize field. The flight attendant was killed and we had burns and bruises.'

'Do you expect me to believe a single word of all that?'

'I believed your story.'

'But your story is unbelievable.'

'Look! Look!'

I took off my shirt and turned round:

'The scars are still on my back. Can't you see them.'

In fact, the burns were the product of another of my late father's lessons. Jackie gasped (another gasping woman!) and said:

'You poor thing! You poor man!'

I have no idea why these scars arouse the sexual desires of every woman who sees them. Do woman have an innate sadistic streak. I'll have to ask the psychology professors at Harvard one day about this. I said:

'Jackie! Believe me, my back still hurts me. Only massage relieves the pain.'

As we went to the bedroom she was mumbling:
'You poor thing! You poor man!'

Sunday, Bombay
The morning began with a meeting with Mr Jildi to discuss another of my new
ideas: the New Aloes Wood. In the not too distant future, aloes wood will
disappear, disappear once and for all. Demand is on the increase and the trees
are being cut down. And prices are rising to fantastic levels. The price at the
moment for superior quality aloes wood is more than $10,000 a kilo. But
everyone in Arabistan wants superior quality aloes wood. It's an extremely
attractive market. Poor quality timber is being sold as aloes wood but that is
fraud and something I will not allow myself to do. Some aloes wood is being
filled inside with lead mixed with real aloes wood. That too is a deception I will
not permit myself. My new idea is the honourable one of calling things by their
real names. I'm not claiming to be producing an authentic aloes wood, I'm
claiming to be producing the New Aloes Wood. New aloes wood is exactly like
old aloes wood in colour, form and aroma (which comes from fragrant chemical
additives). I can sell the new aloes wood at five times the price of the old aloes
wood and make incredible profits. I have chosen Mr Jildi as a partner in the
project. At the outset he was hesitant. He was afraid that the new aloes wood
would compete with the conventional aloes wood, a trade that Mr Jildi almost
totally monopolizes. He was only convinced when I showed him a scientific
study prepared by a team of Harvard professors which proved that within
twenty-five years at the outside there would be no more aloes wood forests left.
Mr Jildi realized that the new aloes wood was the aloes wood of the future. At the
meeting we discussed a great many of the details. And we agreed to travel
together to Tokyo so that he could see the new aloes wood for himself and smell
its fragrance. Marketing would be done by Mr Jildi and Mr Jildi alone. In
addition to his marketing monopoly, he would own half the project, fifty–fifty.
Excessive generosity?! No! Pragmatism. The Arabistanis have confidence only
in the aloes wood imported by Mr Jildi. This fact Mr Jildi has understood as well
as I have.

In the evening I went to Mr Masala's party. There was a small number of men
and a large number of women. Real female stars. Actresses, singers and dancers.
The hospitality I had shown to Mr Yama Shuftu Yama paled in comparison. No
sooner had I entered than there before me was the guffawing guru standing like
Aladdin's genie. He took me aside and whispered:
'The matter is settled.'
In amazement I said:
'What matter?'
'Sabouh Al-Dirhaman.'

'What about him?'

'You will soon hear the news. Perhaps this evening.'

The guffawing guru fell silent for a moment. Then his features darkened until his face was almost black. He said:

'Galnar!'

I felt the chill return to my body. I whispered:

'What about her?'

'You desire her, but she refuses.'

'True. I'm beginning to have great faith in your crystal ball.'

'In that case you must also trust my warning. Do not go anywhere near this woman. Do not meet her, whatever the circumstances. Even if she insists. Even if she begs you. Beware of meeting this woman.'

Astonished, I said:

'Why?'

'Because the consequences will be . . .'

The guru fell silent, bowed his head and said:

'I am sorry! I cannot say more.'

The guffawing guru disappeared as Barsam came up to me holding his mobile phone. I looked at him reproachfully. He said:

'It's a very important call. From London.'

I took the phone and Mass'oud As'ad was on the other end.

'Hi Baby?! Please accept my deepest condolences!'

I asked:

'What's happened?'

'Your friend.'

'Which friend?'

'Sabouh Al-Dirhaman.'

'What about him?'

'He was in a car crash this morning when he left the hotel. My deepest condolences!'

I felt the world spinning round and the ground coming up to meet me. From afar I saw the guffawing guru raise his head from the palm of the beautiful woman whose fortune he was reading. He looked at me and smiled. When I made contact with the floor I imagined I could hear his guffaws carrying me nicely off into unconsciousness.

SEVEN

The Politician

The like of you there never again shall be
For the like of you shall only empires fitting be
Al-Mutanabbi

Identity Card
Full Name: Raymon Daher Abu Shawka
Known as: Abu Al-Faqir (Father of the Poor)
Occupation: Leader of the Absolute Equality Party and Minister
                                 of Tourism & International Co-operation
Age: 46
Wealth: $50million (approx.)
Place of Birth: Arabistan X
Place of Work: Arabistan X
Academic Qualifications: BA Economics (University of Oklahoma) Diploma
                                 in Economics (University of Paris)
Marital Status: Married
Children: A son and a daughter

Monday
Before going to the ministry, I was visited at home by my personal party advisor, Ilyas Shahtout, who tried to convince me not to appear on the programme. That night I was to appear with Galnar on her popular programme *The Eyes of the World Are Upon You*. The programme was not normally broadcast from our country, but Galnar had decided to broadcast seven editions from here and had chosen me to start with. Ilyas said:

'Minister! Believe me, your appearance will serve no one's interests.'

'Whose interests do you mean?'

'Your interests, the party's interests or the country's interests.'

'Why not? I've done thousands of television interviews before. What's so new about this one?'

'I think this one will be different.'

'Why?'

'Galnar! This woman is evil. She has malicious intentions. For some time she's been collecting information about you from certain elements with which you are familiar.'

'Have they got anything to say that they haven't said already? Even in parliament?'

'But this will be different. Any viewer will have the opportunity to ask questions.'

I didn't tell Ilyas about the plan I'd worked out with the party's Special Operations Unit to deal with the situation. I said:

'So be it. I've got nothing to hide. I believe in democracy and letting people ask questions. People will ask me questions and I'll answer them.'

'This woman is going to create problems.'

I didn't tell Ilyas that I had asked the party's Special Operations Unit to prepare a complete dossier on Galnar which I had read carefully.

'There's nothing to worry about Ilyas.'

'It's up to you. I wish you luck.'

'Don't worry. And make sure you watch the programme.'

'Of course I'll be watching.'

On arriving at the office, my private secretary, Tina, informed me that the well-known businessman and owner of the famous Golden Vine hotel chain, Albert Zantout, had been waiting for me for an hour. I asked her to send him in. I greeted him warmly and apologized for being late. I knew perfectly well what he wanted though it was wise to let him broach the subject himself. He asked:

'How are you Minister? How is Madame Chantal? And Mademoiselle Georgina? And Master Daher?'

Chantal is my wife. Georgina is my daughter, who isn't even ten years old yet. And Daher is my son who isn't even six. I smiled and said:

'Fine. Everyone's fine. And how are you Albert? And Madame Nicole? And the children?'

'Thanks be to God, they're all fine.'

'And how's the hotel business?'

'Thanks to the noble endeavours of your good self, Minister, everything is perfect. The tourists are flooding in and the rooms are jam-packed.'

'That is gratifying news.'

'This tourist boom is the reason I'm here, Minister, to request a licence for a new hotel in Gandoura.'

'Every hotel that opens is an addition to the national economy and contributes to national development. You know my position on encouraging tourism.'

'The Minster's position is well-known and were it not for such a position the economy could not have extricated itself from its stifling crisis.'

'That is my job.'

'By the way, I've been talking to Mister Ilyas Shahtout and . . .'

I was aware of what had transpired between Mister Albert Zantout and Ilyas

Shahtout. Mister Albert Zantout had donated half a million dollars – gratefully received – to the Absolute Equality Party.

I interrupted the visitor:

'Listen to me Mister Albert. Government is government. The party, the party. In this office I am a government minister and party affairs do not concern me. What takes place between yourself and Mister Ilyas has nothing to do with me and I do not wish to know.'

'Understood, Minister, understood.'

'Submit your request, and you will have your licence. And to top it all, a kiss in recognition of your praiseworthy efforts in the development of tourism.'

'May God protect you, Minister, as a treasure to us and the national economy.'

'Thank you very much.'

The evening came, as did my rendezvous with Galnar. My friend Hi Baby was not lying when he said she was the most beautiful woman in all the countries of Arabistan. Perhaps this was the reason for her astonishing success. Her beauty throws her guests off-balance so they don't realize what they're saying. After every encounter she emerges victorious, and after every encounter the guest emerges vanquished. I will try to forget that I am talking to an incredibly beautiful woman. When looking at her, I will imagine that I am looking at His Excellency, the Speaker. Galnar began:

'Ladies and Gentleman! Our guest this evening is a curious collection of contradictions. A feudalist who heads a party called the Absolute Equality Party, a millionaire who leads the socialist movement, not just in his own country, but throughout Arabistan. His enemies will acknowledge his administrative effectiveness before his friends, and his friends will acknowledge before his enemies that the methods he uses are not always like Caesar's wife. In addition, our guest is a world champion racing car driver, or, more accurately, was a world champion racing car driver until he retired following an accident from which he miraculously escaped. He also has the largest stamp collection in the Middle East. And he has a collection of rare archaeological artefacts. With this extraordinary man, Mister Raymon Abu Shawka, Minister of Tourism and International Co-operation in Arabistan X, we begin our show tonight. Welcome, Minister.'

'Thank you, Mademoiselle Galnar. You are welcome in our capital city. I hope everything is to your satisfaction.'

'The tourist services are very good, if that's what you mean.'

I laughed and said:

'I will convey this testimony to the minister responsible.'

'I want to begin with a question which has become something of a ritual in view of the many times it's been asked. But, forgive me, Minister, if I say that I haven't yet heard a convincing answer. How can a feudalist lead a party which calls itself the Absolute Equality Party?'

'A feudalist?! Where is the feudalism?! Aren't you aware that the sum total of all the agricultural land I own is no more than 2,000 dunums. Is this called feudalism?'

'There are some who say . . .'

I interrupted her:

'I will say now, on the air, that if anyone can prove that I own more land than the amount I've just mentioned, they can have the difference. I'm saying that now, on the air.'

'I trust your sincerity. But you cannot deny that you belong to a feudal family.'

'Mademoiselle Galnar! The total surface area of our country is not even a quarter of the area covered by the feudal statelets that once existed in Europe.'

'All things are relative.'

'That's true. But I'm not a feudalist by any standard. Would you like to talk about the meaning and history of feudalism?'

'I have no doubt that you would win were we to enter a debate about feudalism. I will just ask one question: Do you deny that you belong to a once feudal family?'

I laughed and said:

'That's better. I'm not going to disassociate myself from my family or its history. You, for example, Mademoiselle Galnar, would you disassociate yourself from your grandfather who used to hang people?'

A blow to the heart! Below the belt! Galnar's lips trembled and she turned pale. There was silence. A silence I did everything not to break. Then Galnar regained her composure and said:

'Minister! I must congratulate you on your breadth of historical knowledge. My grandfather did, indeed, work for the prison service as a hangman but, contrary to what you said, he did not hang people. He hanged criminals and murderers who had been sentenced by the court. He was getting rid of the dregs of humanity. And I sometimes wish he was still alive to . . .'

Things were slipping dangerously out of control. I interrupted her:

'Well done Mademoiselle Galnar! No one should be embarrassed by his origins or his family. I, like you, am not embarrassed by my origins or my family. I'm sorry, what was the question?'

I knew perfectly well what the question was. I also knew that, from the shock, she had forgotten it. She said:

'We were talking about feudalism and whether feudalism was a relative concept. We were discussing the history of feudalism . . .'

'In fact, you asked me how a feudalist could become leader of the Absolute Equality Party.'

'Precisely, and I haven't heard an answer yet.'

'I think we agreed, a moment ago, that I wasn't a feudalist and that the question was irrelevant.'

'We agreed that you . . .'

'That I am not a feudalist.'

'But you belong to a family which was a feudal family.'

'Mademoiselle Galnar! Are you going to execute me?'

'I'm sorry?'

'We know that your grandfather used to hang people. Are you going to keep on hanging people just because your grandfather used to hang people?'

'This programme is not about my grandfather. And I have already explained to you, Minister, that my grandfather only hanged murderers and killers.'

'I think you get my drift. The fact that my family was once a feudal family does not mean that I, at this moment in time, am a feudalist.'

'Do you really mean to tell me that you believe in absolute equality among people?'

'Definitely.'

'And between your sect and all the other sects.'

'Everyone knows that I am sectarianism's greatest enemy.'

'But every member of your party is from your sect.'

'The party is open to all sects and most sects are represented in it.'

'Fine! So let's focus the discussion on your party. Do you believe in equality between you and the wretched member of your party who is subject to you and kisses your hand because you're his feudal overlord, just in the same way that your father was his father's feudal overlord?'

'Mademoiselle Galnar! No one in the party is subject to me or kisses my hand. Everyone is equal. Today I am the leader of the party. Tomorrow another member of the party will be leader, any other member.'

From the file in front of her, Galnar pulled out a picture and asked the camera to zoom in. In the photograph a man was clearly kissing my hand. The bitch! I said quickly:

'Aahh! That's Joseph Abu Shawka. He's one of my nephews. He's younger than me. The younger members of the family kiss the hands of the older members on special occasions. This has got nothing to do with equality.'

'I'm sorry, Minister! This is not one of your relatives. His name is not Joseph. He is a member of your party called Tunnous Qaysar and he is older than you by ten years.'

'Aahhh! Tunnous! Tunnous Qaysar! That man kisses the hand of everyone he meets.'

'Don't you think that a man who believed in absolute equality would stop people kissing his hand?'

'Mademoiselle Galnar! If I imposed on people what they should do or shouldn't do, I wouldn't be a believer in equality, I would be a dictator.'

'So, if a member of your party decided to kiss your feet . . .'

For the first time in the interview I was beginning to feel angry. I realized that if I gave in to the anger, it would grow and I would lose the battle with this deadly seductive tigress. I smiled and said:

'If someone was of a mind to kiss my feet, I would stop them. You must have other questions.'

'Sure. My second question has also become standard because of the many times it's been asked. How do you reconcile being a millionaire with being leader of a party which calls for socialism, a party which is probably the only one left in the whole Arabistani nation calling for socialism.'

'Mademoiselle Galnar! That is an honour we do not deserve. There are numerous socialist parties spread throughout the Arabistani nation.'

'Maybe. But there are no other Arabistani socialist parties which are members of a capitalist government, which are represented by MPs in a capitalist parliament and which lead the economy down a capitalist path.'

'Is this not real democracy? Is not coexisting with others and working with them the very culmination of democracy? Where's the objection in that?'

'The objection is a millionaire claiming to be a socialist. Permit me to say, Minister, that many people consider this political hypocrisy and contempt for people's intelligence.'

'I do not have contempt for people's intelligence, nor do I practice political hypocrisy. The socialism of the Absolute Equality Party is not incompatible with the market economy or individual enterprise. Our socialism is based on the state owning the natural resources and the basic industries, and these things alone. The remaining spheres of activity must be left, ultimately, to the private sector. Where's the contradiction? Is this not the situation in European countries governed by socialist parties?'

'However, in Europe, as you well very know Minister, there is a system of progressive taxation as a consequence of which the profits of the private sector go towards public services which the people as a whole benefit from. Here, however . . .'

I interrupted her:

'Well Done! Well done! As you've been doing your homework on this humble servant of yours, you will no doubt be aware that I am the leader of the one and only party that has been calling, for more than ten years, for the introduction of progressive taxes and the application of the tax laws on everyone, everyone without exception. You must know that the tax reform law that my party proposed is still frozen in the parliamentary committees.'

'I'm sorry, Minister! Do you know what people say about that law?'

'What do they say?'

'They say the law is "asleep" following an agreement between you and the Speaker and the leaders of the other blocs in parliament.'

'Mademoiselle Galnar! There is nothing dearer to me than my children. I swear on the life of my daughter Georgina and the life of my son Daher. I'm sorry! My wife! There is no one dearer to me than my wife. I swear on the life of my wife, Chantal, that . . .'

Galnar had fallen into the trap and had interrupted me before I had made the oath. The fact was that there was indeed an agreement to keep the law asleep. Galnar had saved me from lying when she said:

'I believe you Minister. I was just repeating what people were saying.'

'There are no customs dues on what people say.'

'Nor on the goods which your ministry imports, isn't that so?'

This bitch! I smiled and said:

'The Ministry of Tourism and International Co-operation does not deal in commerce. It neither exports nor imports. However, what the hotels import is, indeed, free of customs duties in accordance with the law on the encouragement of tourism which . . .'

'Which you, Minister, proposed to Parliament?'

'Yes. We have been able to build forty hotels in three years. Would it have been possible to build this vast number of hotels without the facilities provided by the state. And without these hotels would it have been possible for the number of tourists to increase from 20,000 three years ago to more than 1.5 million today?'

'You're saying that in your period of office the number of tourists has grown from 20,000 to 1.5 million?'

'In all humility, yes!'

'And that's why they call you the "Miracle Minister"?'

I laughed and said:

'This is the nickname that some newspapers have kindly given me. I don't believe in miracles. I believe in hard work, planning and what the figures say.'

'The problem, Minister, is that some people doubt the figures.'

'Mademoiselle Galnar! Some people don't believe the earth is round.'

'Perhaps. But according to my information, taken from official sources, from the immigration office of your own respected government, the statistics show that the number of tourists last year did not exceed 90,000.'

The whore, this murderer's granddaughter! That was below the belt! The bitch continued her attack:

'Who are we to believe, Minister? Should we believe you or your colleague, the head of the immigration office.'

I decided it was time to use my secret weapon. Galnar, of course, was not aware that the party's Special Operations Unit had arranged it at the main telephone exchange that only members of the party could phone in.

I smiled and said:

'Don't believe me and don't believe any other official.'

'What do you mean?'

'I mean you should ask the people. Why don't we ask them what they think, directly, on the air?'

'A good idea! The lines are buzzing and lots of people are on hold. We have a young lady, Fayrouz on the line. What would you like to ask the Minister?'

'Minister! Can you tell us how much financial aid the government has obtained in the last three years?'

'With pleasure. The government has obtained soft loans to the value of five billion dollars, grants of three billion dollars and commercial loans within the region of seven billion dollars.'

Galnar had a curious smile on her face and said:

'With us now, we have Melham on the line. Go ahead, Melham.'

'Minister! Can you give us some idea about recent investments in the tourist sector.'

I fielded all the questions. Brilliant question after brilliant question after brilliant question. And the answers were also brilliant. At the end of the programme, I felt some sympathy for Galnar, and a lot of desire. I had won the battle for the airwaves, would I win the battle for her bed where everyone else had failed, including, at the top of the list, my dear friend Hi Baby?!

Tuesday
The weekly cabinet meeting began with a pleasantry from the Prime Minister:

'Raymon! Yesterday's programme was excellent.'

'Thank you Prime Minister! Thanks to the successful strategy which you yourself drew up.'

The Prime Minister smiled and said:

'Best of all were the questions. Such spontaneous questions!'

The Telecommunications Minister broke in:

'Prime Minister! I was going to raise this matter. Something strange happened at the main telephone exchange . . .'

The Prime Minister interrupted him smiling:

'I think Raymon is popular in the country and this is in the interests of the government.'

The Telecommunications Minister came back:

'But the matter, Prime Minister, needs investigation. Someone had been messing around with . . .'

The Prime Minister interrupted him again:

'You are aware, Minister, that this matter is not on the agenda. Should you wish, I will come to some arrangement with you later about putting it on the agenda. For the moment, we have a lot on today's agenda.'

The Telecommunications Minister realized that the Prime Minister wanted the matter closed. And I realized that the Prime Minister would be asking me for something in return for leaving the matter closed. I would be hearing from him very soon. We spent the rest of the session on appointments. We appointed an ambassador from the Religious Rebirth Party. An ambassador from the National Legions Party. An ambassador from the Constitution and Liberation Party. Ambassadors! I preferred members of the Absolute Equality Party to work in our own country where they could take all the important decisions. The party's turn would come with the next appointments.

I returned to my office to find my old friend, Hi Baby, waiting for me. After a warm embrace and kisses on the cheeks, he said:

'Abu Daher! Brilliant interview! Especially the viewers' calls! How did you fix it?'

I smiled and said:

'People are intrinsically good, Hi Baby, and doing someone a favour will always pay off.'

'That's true Abu Al-Faqir and I've got several projects which are going to help the poor.'

I spent a few hours with Hi Baby. In the end we reached an agreement under which The Crimson Desert Bank would organize a new international loan and Hi Baby would be given licences for three Camelburger outlets. We decided we would resume our discussion of a shawarma canning project in the future. At the end of the meeting, Hi Baby said:

'Raymon! This morning I was with Ilyas . . .'

I was well aware that Hi Baby had made a donation that morning of a million dollars, which had been gratefully received, to the Absolute Equality Party. I interrupted him:

'Hi Baby! You're one of my dearest friends. But I can't mix work and friendship. I can't mix my work for the government and my work for the party. Ilyas is not a state official and what went on between you is of no interest to me one way or another.'

Hi Baby laughed and said nothing.

Tony, my very personal secretary, came in. He whispered in my ear and left. I asked Tina to get my wife on the phone. I began:

'My darling! Forgive me! Please forgive me! There's a huge delegation from

Japan. An important tourist delegation. I'll have to invite them to dinner. Huge investments from Japan. I forgot to tell you. I'm sorry. I should have told you. Pressure of work. I'll be a bit late. Kiss the children.'

I went with Hi Baby to the Party's apartment, which had a view of the sea. There we found two rising starlets: Dalida and Lolita. I kissed them and said:

'This is my friend. My dearest friend. Hi Baby! Lolita! Did you bring your dancing clothes?'

Wednesday
The first visitor was the prime minister's nephew. He had come to ask for a licence for a new hotel. He got his licence. Nobody could accuse the prime minister of being slow off the mark!

After the esteemed relative had gone, I was visited by a delegation from my beloved village of Kohl'ayoun to thank me for the hospital whose foundation stone had been laid the week before by the president of the republic. I explained to the delegation that everything I did was part of my duty to the whole country, from one end to the other, without discriminating between one region and another. At the end of the visit the delegation asked me to agree to a statue of me being erected in the village but I refused. The delegation insisted but I did not give in to the pressure. I told the delegation that all I wanted was the people's and my own contentment; as for statues, leave them to those who seek fame and glory.

After the Kohl'ayoun delegation had left I was visited by Mr Steward, regional director of Universe airlines. He asked for permission for his company to double the number of flights to the capital. I told him that I was extremely sympathetic to the request but the matter came within the purview of the Ministry of Transport. I promised I would do my utmost to convince the Transport Minister to agree. God only knows how much the minister would be asking. Most likely he would ask for a lot of shares in a number of hotels to be allocated to people specified by him. What would I get out of increasing the number of flights to the capital? Nothing! The only beneficiary would be the national economy. That was the difference between me and the other ministers. All of them were working for their own personal interests. It was only I who gave a thought for the interests of the country and its citizens.

After that came the deputy head of the legal administration of the World Bank. With him came a retinue of lawyers to discuss the agreement we wanted to sign with the bank under which the bank would provide part of the finance required for the Na'oura Dam. I summoned my legal team and we spent more than three hours in heated discussion until we were able to reach a semi-final agreement.

However, the morning schedule was a pure delight compared with the afternoon schedule: the weekly session of Parliament. A number of honourable members had already tabled questions relating to my department and today I was to reply to these questions. An honourable member began, asking:

'I would like to ask His Excellency, the Minister for Tourism and International Co-operation, the reason why his ministry continues to hold fifteen per cent of the shares in the International Casino despite His Excellency's repeated promises to place these shares in the public domain?'

The real reason was that surrendering these shares would automatically mean surrendering all the privileges I currently enjoyed at the Casino: free dinners and free gambling, even for my guests. Parliaments, however, were not there to discuss the real reasons for anything. I smiled and said:

'I am grateful to the honourable member for his worthy question. I would confirm to him that the ministry is preparing the final arrangements for placing the shares in the public domain.'

The reply did not convince the honourable member who then asked:

'When precisely will the shares be in the public domain?'

'As soon as certain legal problems have been finalized.'

'We are not aware of the existence of any legal problems. His Excellency the Minister has not previously spoken of such problems.'

'My apologies! I used the wrong word. The honourable member will forgive me. Unlike the honourable member, I am not well-versed in the law. I meant to say legal formalities. Honourable members will recall the rules that this venerable parliament has established for the regulation of privatizations. These rules relate specifically to the price of government shares, the number of shares which a single citizen may hold and the necessity for share issues to be equitable. As soon as these formalities have been finalized, the government shares will be in the public domain.'

'Is His Excellency the Minister able to state how long this will take?'

'A few weeks, at the most.'

The second question was, relatively more difficult than the first.

An honourable member rose and said:

'I would ask His Excellency the Minister to enlighten this parliament about rumours circulating to the effect that the ministry is granting members of His Excellency's sect special privileges, something which is in conflict with what His Excellency has repeated at every opportunity namely, that he is sectarianism's greatest enemy.'

I smiled very politely and said:

'Since my appointment I have only appointed two senior officials to the ministry: Hussein 'Abd Al-Nabi and 'Abd Al-Azziz Gaylani. I am not aware that either of them is a member of the sect of which I am a member.'

Parliament erupted in laughter. The speaker banged his gavel until calm was restored. The honourable member said:

'My question did not relate to appointments to the ministry. I was speaking about the government-run hotels. It is said that openings in these hotels are restricted to members of certain sects, to the exclusion of all others.'

'I should like to remind the honourable member that recruitment in the hotels is not the task of the ministry but falls under the responsibility of the hotels themselves. It is the hotels which announce the vacancies. It is the hotels that process the applicants. And it is the hotels that employ successful applicants. The ministry does not interfere in this process. Nevertheless, I would say to the honourable member that if there are specific violations then we at the ministry are more than prepared to look into them in conjunction with our colleagues at the Ministry of Labour. However, I can only take action when there is a specific complaint.'

The honourable member stood up and said:

'What I would like to say, in all honesty, to His Excellency the Minister, is that there is a specific religious minority whose members are not being employed in the hotels. And I believe that this matter requires clarification.'

I looked at the Speaker, feigned a certain hesitation and then said slowly:

'The point that the honourable member has made raises a sensitive issue, and it is an issue on which I am unable to comment. I cannot force citizens, who refuse to work in hotels because what goes on in them is against their conscience, to work in hotels and go against their beliefs . . .'

The Speaker interrupted me:

'His Excellency the Minister is right. This is a matter for the conscience of the individual citizen. The government has no right to force someone to work in a post and this parliament has no right to discuss the religious beliefs of citizens.'

I looked at the Speaker and said:

'I am grateful Mister Speaker. That is what I wished to say.'

The third question was harder than the two previous ones, though all things are relative, naturally. An honourable member rose and said:

'I have raised this matter a number of times before, more than ten times, and nothing has been done, the government has not taken any action. Why are agreements concluded by the Ministry of Tourism and International Co-operation only submitted to us after they have been signed by His Excellency the Minister? Why aren't they submitted to us before they are signed? What is the use in submitting an agreement to Parliament after the government is already bound by it?'

'The honourable member has raised this matter before and we, my colleagues and I, have answered it before. For many years there has been an agreement between the office of the Speaker and the office of the Prime Minister to the effect that agreements signed by the minister concerned are submitted for approval and that it is the absolute right of this parliament to amend any article thereof. In the event that this venerable parliament objects to an article we go to the other party and inform them that we are unable to be bound by that article and we ask them to amend the article so as to be in accordance with the wishes of Parliament. We in the government believe that this venerable parliament must have the first and last word on any international agreement.'

The honourable member rose and said:

'The problem, as His Excellency the Minister knows very well, is that these agreements are submitted to us in one fell swoop, in thousands of pages, and we are asked to give our consent in just a matter of days. How can the members of this parliament study lengthy and complex agreements in just a matter of days?'

I looked at the Speaker and said:

'It is the right of this venerable parliament to formulate the measures it deems necessary to scrutinize agreements and we will abide by the will of Parliament.'

The Speaker intervened:

'I am grateful to His Excellency the Minister. I am grateful to the honourable member. In fact, we are currently in contact with the office of the Prime Minister and the Constitutional Council to review all aspects of this subject. When we have arrived at an appropriate legal formula, that formula will be submitted to honourable members for their assent.'

The last question was from a member of the Absolute Equality Party bloc. The member asked:

'I would ask His Excellency the Minister to inform us of the most recent statistics relating to tourism.'

'It always gives me great pleasure to bring good news to honourable members. Last month saw a record increase in the number of tourists. In a single month, the number of tourists totalled 95,631. If we bear in mind that last month fell in the low season, we may permit ourselves to expect the number of tourists this year to reach record levels.'

I dined at home with Chantal, Georgina and Daher. After dinner I begged Chantal's leave, as I had promised to drop in on the party that Hi Baby was holding that night. Chantal, who knew Hi Baby and understood the importance of his investments, agreed after a moment's hesitation.

At the spacious penthouse in the luxury hotel owned by Hi Baby, the party was in full swing. Everyone was there: ministers and MPs, businessmen, journalists, and the stars. But, of the whole gathering, the only person I was interested in was Galnar, who was standing in a distant corner like a queen, surrounded by a crowd of admirers. She glanced at me and smiled. I gave her a bigger smile back. I went quietly onto the balcony overlooking the sea. I smoked as I watched the stars swimming among the waves. I needed some peace and quiet away from all the dignitaries and their titles and Hi Baby's crazy ideas.

After a few minutes I heard the swish of silk and became aware of a warm faint scent. Galnar spoke:

'Why are you standing here all on your own, Minister?'

With genuine pleasure, I said:

'Mademoiselle Galnar! Hello there! I was looking at the stars playing on the waves. When you have a job like mine, dealing with hundreds of people every day, being alone with nature is a rare pleasure.'

'And with stamps?'

'And with stamps.'

'Is it true your collection is worth more than fifteen million dollars?'

'That's what some experts have said. However, I'm not selling and I don't know their real value. With stamps, like oil paintings, you only know how much they're worth when you put them up for auction.'

'I'm not trying to do a re-run of the programme, but are you aware of what people say about this stamp collection of yours?'

'Mademoiselle Galnar! What they say about my stamp collection is the same as what they say about my collection of antiquities. They say I used my position to expropriate, I mean, steal, these stamps and antiquities from various old, practically forgotten, museums.'

'That's exactly what I'd heard.'

'In this country, in this very country of ours, for reasons which it would take too long to go into, we have more malicious and jealous people than anywhere else in the world. People only believe tales of bribery, corruption, extortion and decadence. For your information, the curios in my possession have been handed down in my, as you call it, feudal family, from generation to generation. I am more than willing to show you a photograph of my grandfather, taken before I was born, with him surrounded by most of these objets d'art. My father continued the hobby and added to the collection. And I, in turn, have added a few things.'

'And the stamps?'

'The value of the collection might appear fantastic, but stamps are a strange commodity. A stamp I buy today for a dollar could be worth $10,000 in ten years time. I had an ordinary stamp which I didn't attach much importance to. I was astonished to find that it was worth more than half a million dollars. One stamp! And why? Because there was a mistake in printing the date. Can you imagine?! A small printing mistake turns a one-cent stamp into a treasure worth half a million dollars. By the way, why didn't you ask me that on air?'

'Personal hobbies don't interest viewers, unless they're very odd.'

'Very odd?'

'Like breeding scorpions or poisonous spiders. I prefer the programme to focus on public affairs.'

'I must apologize for any embarrassment I caused you.'

'There's no need to apologize. You were playing the same game as me. But the phone calls are another matter.'

I feigned ignorance:

'Phone calls? What do you mean?'

Galnar lit a cigarette and slowly blew a succession of smoke rings into the air and said:

'See those rings? What do you think?'

'Beautiful. Perfectly round.'

'Exactly. And not by chance. Deliberately so.'

I laughed and said:

'Perhaps some younger members of the party . . .'

She interrupted:

'Anyway, the programme's over now. I have to admit, Minister . . .'

'Can't we dispense with the "Minister"?'

'I have to admit, Raymon Bey, that you won the battle, but you'll find out you lost the war.'

'What do you mean?'

'There's not a single viewer who doesn't know that trick with the telephones. A very crude trick. You proved in front of two million viewers that you won't shrink from using any means, even illegal ones. I assume spying on telephone calls is against the law in this democratic country.'

I sighed and said:

'Ok! Ok! I lost the battle. I lost the war. Maybe I'll go to prison. What I want now is a peace treaty, a comprehensive peace treaty between you and me. Is there any hope?'

'There are no personal problems between you and I.'

'True! True! However, I hope, merely hope, that we could become friends, or something like friends.'

'Something like friends?'

'I mean a relationship that could lead to friendship.'

'You can consider yourself, as of now, my friend.'

'Really?'

She smiled and said:

'On the life of my famous grandfather, the hangman.'

I mumbled:

'I apologize again. Sincerely apologize.'

'And I'm saying, again, there is no need to apologize.'

'If you truly consider me your friend, would it possible for this friend to do penance for his sins by inviting you to a private dinner.'

'In Kohl'ayoun?'

With my hand I pointed to a small, I mean very small, yacht with its lights shimmering on the sea a couple of kilometres off shore. I said:

'Do you see that boat . . .'

She interrupted:

'You mean yacht?'

'Ok! From a purely technical point of view you're correct. A boat which is longer than fifty feet can be called a yacht and that boat is sixty feet long.'

'Ok! What about it?'

'That is my boat. Or my yacht. I would be very pleased if you would dine with me on board before you go.'

'Alone?'

'If you have no objection.'

'I could swim to the yacht.'

I laughed and said:

'No! No! There'll be a boat at the jetty to take you. When shall I have the honour.'

'The only time is Sunday evening.'

'Sunday evening then. The boat will be waiting for you at the jetty at eight o'clock.'

'Can we make it nine o'clock?'

'Nine!'

'I just have one request.'

'It's not a request, it's an order.'

'Don't send a boat. I'll take my boat to your yacht.'

'Do you have a boat here?'

'My friend, inside, Hi Baby, has a number of boats moored at the hotel jetty. I'll borrow one of his.'

'Come by whatever means you want. By submarine if you want. I'll be waiting for you.'

'See you then.'

'Chantal immediately saw on my face the signs of pleasure which I had tried to conceal. She said:

'You look happy. What happened at the party?'

I hugged and kissed her and said:

'A new project my darling. A very important project.'

I wasn't lying to her. Was I lying to her?

Thursday

This was a day of conferences, symposia and meetings. This morning, on behalf of the President of the Republic, I opened the conference on the Reconstruction and Investment Phase which was attended by a large number of businessmen from all over the world. I think my speech was received with approval. I attended the morning session and the lunch given by the ministry at the hotel High Life in honour of the guests.

The afternoon I spent at the third symposium on tourism. Invitations to the first symposium were sent out as soon as I took over the ministry. It was such a success that I made it an annual event. The symposium included representatives of all the tourism companies operating in the country or having dealings with it. It discussed the problems faced by these companies, problems faced by tourists and the ways to solve them. What most people didn't know was that a number of the proposals I had presented to Parliament and which had become legislation for the promotion of tourism, had sprung from this symposium. I gave the opening speech and attended the meetings of some of the committees. I then returned to my office to deal with papers and visitors.

In the evening, Chantal accompanied me to The Cascades' Third Tourism and Culture Reunion. This was also one of my successful ideas. Despite the fact it had only been going for a short time, the Reunion had become famous throughout Arabistan and had come to rival the well-known Alhambra symposium. Successive cultural presentations were given and the evening ended with poems. My attention was caught by one poet in particular who was described by a connoisseur of such occasions as 'a leading exponent of modernism in contemporary poetry'. He had a somewhat strange name, Fulayfila or Fulfula. The poem he recited was also extremely strange:

> *I penetrate your navel*
> *Ecstadelirial in flagons of lust*
> *I burst out from your navel*
> *Enlechered by the smell of the earth*
> *With your nipple I stab the bladder of my gall*
> *Thrust . . . after thrust . . . after thrust*
> *A talloned rain penetrates*
> *Your navel*
> *I feel like an untameable Tartar stallion*
> *Ravishing your violet roses*

As soon as the poet had finished his poem, for no clear reason, I felt a sudden sexual urge. I turned to Chantal and saw that proverbial gleam in her eye. Afterwards, in bed, Chantal asked:

'What does "enlechered" mean?'
I said:
'I'll tell you when I've finished ravishing your violet roses.'
We laughed as we enlechered.

Friday
I spent the whole morning in Kohl'ayoun where I was greeted by the usual crowds and shouts of 'long live the Father of the Poor!' from all directions. There were pictures of me on every wall and the party's slogans hung from every window. An election atmosphere without the elections. I reminded Ilyas not to allow any photographs while the villagers came up to greet me. But, following the *Eyes of the World are Upon You* programme, Ilyas needed no reminding. A strange world! None of us, from now on, could let any of the villagers kiss his hand.

The monthly meeting of the party's political bureau met under my chairmanship. A number of positive decisions were taken. The treasurer, Paulus Massari, announced that the party's coffers were full of donations from supporters. The political bureau decided on a twenty-five per cent increase in allowances to families which were members of the sect, I mean needy families which supported the party. It was also decided to increase, by the same amount, allowances to members of the militia which was now called the Sports and Scouting Group. On my personal recommendation, the political bureau decided to increase salaries for those working in the Special Operations Unit and the Information and Monitoring Unit by fifty per cent. We then discussed the party's annual elections which would be held in two months time. We decided to submit to the party conference the same annual list of candidates, with me as conference chairman. Usually, the list of candidates was elected unopposed and I wasn't expecting any changes this year. However, Ilyas Shahtout asked to speak. He said:
'Minister! I have been informed . . .'
I interrupted him:
'Ilyas. I'm not at the ministry now.'
He corrected himself immediately:
'Mr Chairman! I have been informed that this year there will be another list of election candidates.'
I said in astonishment:
'I'm sorry?!'
'One member has put himself forward as a candidate for the leadership of the party together with a different list of candidates.'
'Who is he?'
'Rizq Al-Bandoura.'

Rizq Al-Bandoura?! This was the end of the world! The filthy peasant! Had getting a university degree gone to his head? Or getting a top job in the hotel? And where had this degree come from? Wasn't it my late father who had paid his tuition fees? And where had his job come from? Wasn't it me who had appointed him? Was this the result of being kind to people?

I turned to the members of the political bureau and said:

'This is delightful news. This is the best news I've heard in a long time. Our opponents are always criticizing us for getting elected without opposition. In vain have we repeated that this was the will of the massed ranks of the party. Now, as there is a competing list of candidates, no one can criticize us. Ilyas, please tell Rizq that we, the members of the political bureau and myself, give our blessing to the democratic move he has made and wish him every success.'

When I left the party headquarters, news of the increased allowances had already leaked out and I was even more warmly greeted. I was carried aloft on people's shoulders to my car and the cries of 'long live the Father of the Poor' were deafening. Before getting into my car I asked the head of the Special Operations Unit, Sa'id Abu Battha, to go on ahead of me to 'the Centre'. 'The Centre' was a secret villa in the suburbs of the capital which only he, four members of the Unit, and I knew about.

I found Sa'id waiting for me at 'the Centre'. Immediately I asked him:

'What's all this about Rizq Al-Bandoura?'

'It would seem, Minister, that someone is egging him on.'

'That's for sure. But how could he let himself be lead on by our enemies after all I've done for him?'

'Criminals are never grateful.'

'Don't you think we should warn him of the consequences of his actions?'

'Do you think I haven't?! I've warned him loads of times.'

'And the bastard won't back down?'

'He won't back down.'

'What are we going to do now?'

'Leave it to me.'

'What are you planning on doing?'

'Rizq has a clapped out Peugeot.'

'Ok?'

'He gets it serviced by Ifram Abu Al-Zawq. A member of the Unit.'

'Ok?'

'And it's now with Ifram for a full service.'

'Sa'id! Well done! Well done! Tell Ifram that Rizq Al-Bandoura is my protégé and that he's very special to me. Tell him to service his car very carefully. We don't want any accidents happening to the man. Tell him to be particularly careful with the breaks. Many accidents these days are caused by driving too fast and faulty brakes. There are bastards everywhere, Sa'id.'

'May God protect us from them, Minister.'

'Amen to that.'

Saturday

Before and after becoming a minister, before and after becoming leader of the party, before and after taking on all these chores, Saturday, from beginning to end, has always been a sacred day, devoted to the family, and the family alone.

As usual, we, Chantal, Georgina, Daher and myself, went to Plaza beach. We spent most of the time swimming and playing water sports. We had lunch at the chalet and only came back at dusk.

As usual, the evening was devoted to the wider family, the Abu Shawka clan and the Abu Shama'a (Chantal's) clan. Visitors came and went. Some stayed a few minutes, others stayed an hour. Some of them ate and drank, others did not eat or drink. Some of them played cards or backgammon and smoked a narghile, others did not play and did not smoke. However, all, without exception, came with requests, written or verbal. This evening there were more than sixty visitors. In other words, in the coming week, I would have to deal with at least sixty requests. Some of the requests were reasonable: those asking for simple material assistance would receive it in envelopes during the week. Some requests were difficult: jobs in hotels or tourism companies. Those qualified would get the job, the others would have to be apologized to. Some requests were unreasonable: an illiterate relative who wants to be an MP or a general manager. Those making unreasonable requests received no response from me but, usually, they would be back in a month or two with the same request.

Half my income, half my income and maybe more, goes to the clan. Sometimes I think I won't have anything left to leave the children. However, what am I to do with the demands of leadership? What is a man worth without a clan? Could I have got where I am had it not been for the clan? Could I maintain this position without the clan?

After the visitors had left, Chantal asked me with a smile:

'I've forgotten that strange word that poet used. Was it "enleckered"?'

A nod's as good as a wink. I laughed and said:

'I'll tell you in bed.'

No wonder this poet called himself Fulayfila. His poems were very spicy!

Sunday

I spent the morning, the whole morning, as usual at Kohl'ayoun inspecting the affairs of the village. I mean, the affairs of the party, I mean, naturally, the affairs of the constituents I represent in parliament. I visited a number of sick people.

I accepted numerous invitations to take tea. I had lunch at the home of Um Michelle, the widow of the late Dagher Abu Doulab who had been the chauffeur of my late father. The food was simple, agreeable and home-made. I whispered in Ilyas' ear for him to send her an envelope containing $2,000 the following day. I think my sobriquet 'Father of the Poor' will end up making me the poorest of the poor. Nevertheless, a man is worthless without his village and his villagers. And money is worthless if it is not spent on the needy in the village.

After lunch I returned to my office at party headquarters. I had a very private meeting with my very private secretary, Tony, to make sure the evening would go as I wanted. I asked Tony to order the food from the Winterland hotel and to make sure the food was light and delicious and that the dishes were made up of caviar and seafood. I asked him to get from the same hotel six bottles of Rothschild champagne. (Any hotel is pleased to be asked to supply such simple facilities from time to time.) I asked him to have the small launch ready to meet me at the jetty to take me to the yacht at eight o'clock. I asked him to arrange that the launch would take me to the yacht and return the captain and crew to the shore and to come back for me at one o'clock. Tony assured me everything would be to my 'taste'. Aaahh! Taste! – personified in Abu Al-Zawq! I wonder if there is any news of the car?

I had enormous difficulties in persuading Chantal to let me go out. (I usually spent Sunday evening at home.) I was forced to use my greatest weapon: a secret meeting with the president of the republic on which the fate of the government depended. Chantal could no longer face life without being called 'the wife of His Excellency the Minister' or even sometimes 'the Ministress' and I obtained the necessary permission.

At half past eight I was pacing, with increasing anxiety, up and down the deck of the small yacht drinking glass after glass of champagne. My friend Hi Baby had told me that I was wasting my time with Galnar. He said he had tried – using every trick in the book – to no avail. Even the magic of Dr Basir Al-'Aref had been no use. He said he was almost convinced she was either a lesbian or frigid. Personally, I thought Galnar was neither a lesbian nor frigid. I thought she was a real woman who needed a real man who could tame her in the same way a skilful rider could tame a wild horse. Such were the thoughts going through my head as I paced up and down the deck watching the stars dancing between the waves. My memory took me back to romantic days, romantic trysts, romantic love. To those bygone days before 'At your command, Bey!' and 'Straight away, Minister!' and rising starlets who took off their clothes before even saying 'Hello'. My rendezvous, this evening, was of a different order, like the romantic trysts of times gone by.

Galnar arrived on time. At nine o'clock precisely. She whispered something in the ear of the helmsman then elegantly climbed the accommodation ladder. She called out with spontaneity:

'It's a beautiful night! The yacht is beautiful. A beautiful small yacht!'

I showed her into the cabin but she preferred to stay outside on deck. We sat on two seats with a table laden with bottles of champagne between us. I filled a glass for her and she began to sip it very slowly. Suddenly, as if in a flash, I saw an astonishing similarity between her and Colette. I wonder if that is what had made me fall passionately in love with her from the outset? Aahh! Colette! The memories of youth. Wandering round the Latin quarter until the early hours. Restaurants by the river. Hot onion soup. The craziness of it all. Colette, whom I loved to the point of madness and who loved me to the point of madness. We would have got married had it not been for my father. He insisted I married Chantal. Chantal Shehab Abu Shama'a! A somewhat fiery name! To restore the unity of the sect through the union of its two main clans. So I had left Colette and married Chantal. Luckily for me Chantal was extremely beautiful with a cheerful disposition and very enlechering. The political alliance had become a successful marriage. The only problem with Chantal was getting out of her clutches. And even this difficulty had diminished once she became 'the wife of His Excellency, the Minister'. But Colette . . .

Suddenly Galnar said:

'You look as if you're miles away, Minister.'

I said:

'Didn't we agree to . . .'

She laughed and said:

'Ok! Raymon Bey! What's on your mind?'

I didn't want to share my thoughts with her. Instead, I studied her carefully. She was wearing a white cotton dress patterned with waves of blue circles. Her long hair was tied up in a small bun. She was wearing a pair of cheap earrings and a cheap necklace. How could a woman look so beautiful yet dress so simply? I said to her:

'May I speak frankly?'

'I thought we always did.'

'I was thinking how can a woman look so elegant when her clothes and jewellery can't be worth more than $300.'

Galnar gave a long musical laugh and said:

'Do you own boutiques?'

'No. But I visit them from time to time.'

'Your valuation is very accurate. The total is a little less than the sum you mentioned.'

'Did you buy them here?'

'I buy all my clothes in London. In the sales.'

'Aahh! London! Shopping's capital city!'

'Things other than shopping attract me to London.'

'Things of the heart?'

'You could say that. The same things which attract you to Paris. And Colette.'

I could not conceal my astonishment. I said:

'How? How did you know?'

She laughed again and said:

'Mind reading! I learnt it from our mutual friend, Doctor Basir Al-'Aref.'

This amazing woman! How did she know about Colette? And about Basir?

'You know Basir Al-'Aref?'

'I know him very well. He came on my programme once. It was one of the most successful. Which brings me to the real reason I'm here tonight.'

'I thought . . .'

'Don't worry. I'm going to have something to drink and eat. I'm not leaving just yet.'

'What is the real reason?'

'I would like to invite you to a private celebration. A celebration which is very important to me. More than you can imagine.'

'Your birthday?'

'It is a birthday, but of a different kind. In exactly three months, it will be the seventh anniversary of *The Eyes of the World Are Upon You*.'

'Congratulations in advance.'

'Thank you. I'm organizing a special celebration to mark the occasion. Very special. On an island.'

'An island?'

'A very small island. I'm going to invite a number of illustrious public figures who have appeared on the programme. Seven guests.'

I found myself repeating like an idiot:

'Seven guests?'

'You know most of them. You might know them all.'

'Who are they?'

'Let's start with our mutual friend, Doctor Basir Al-'Aref.'

'He'll be there?'

'He'll be there. He's accepted the invitation. With pleasure, so he claims. There will be another mutual friend, Hi Baby. I think you saw the third guest this week. He attended a tourist symposium . . .'

'The poet? Fulayfila?'

She laughed and said:

'The poet. But his name is Ken'an Filfil. The fourth guest you'll definitely know, Mass'oud As'ad.'

'That . . .'

She interrupted me immediately:

'All the public figures I've invited are controversial but they can all be seen from more than one perspective. The fifth guest is the unique Arabistani philosopher, Doctor Jamal Al-Din Marsi.'

'Never heard of him.'

'It doesn't matter. You'll enjoy meeting him. Philosopher Pasha, besides his extensive knowledge of philosophy, is a very charming man.'

'"Philosopher Pasha"?!'

'It's a pet name. Like "Father of the Poor".'

I don't know if, in the dim light, she saw the reaction on my face.

I said:

'Why aren't you drinking?'

'I am drinking, but I'm in no hurry. Are you in any hurry?'

'No! No!'

'I think you know the sixth guest. Doctor Anwar Mukhtar.'

'I know him very well. A curious psychologist. If someone goes to him to give up smoking he advises them to carry on smoking. If a patient sees him . . .'

'He has his own logic which he has explained in several books.'

'I started reading one of them but couldn't finish it.'

'You'll be able to get to know his theories from him directly. That leaves the seventh guest.'

'The seventh guest?!'

'My real reason for coming here tonight is to invite the seventh guest. You, Excellency!'

'Me?'

'You!'

'Seven men?!'

'And one woman!'

'But you've had hundreds of guests over the years. Why have you chosen these seven?'

'Promise me you'll come and I'll tell you the reason.'

'I'll think about it.'

'I want a definite promise! And I want it now!'

'Will the party last one day?'

'Seven days. And nights.'

'And why seven?'

'That's a question Doctor Basir Al-'Aref would enjoy answering. The number seven is full of mystery and magic. There are seven planets, seven colours in the spectrum, seven days in the week, seven notes in a musical scale, seven heavens, seven continents, seven . . .'

'Ok! Ok! I think I could do with a short seven-day break.'

'And you wont find anywhere more beautiful than this island to spend it.'

'Where is this island?'

'It's called Medusa. A Greek Island. It's not much bigger than this yacht. On the shore is a beautiful villa owned by our mutual friend, Raf'i Rif'at. He . . .'

I interrupted:

'Raf'i Rif'at? Will he be there?'

'No. He can't be there. Put he's put all the facilities at our disposal. We'll meet in Athens then we'll fly by helicopter to Medusa where we'll spend the week.'

'Seven men and one woman!'

'Does the idea scare you?'

'It excites me more than it scares me. So, tell me now how you chose your guests.'

'It's very simple. Each is the most illustrious in his field. The most illustrious men in the Arabistani nation. You, for example, are the most brilliant minister . . .'

I interrupted:

'Please! Please!'

She said:

'The modernist poet is the most popular poet for today's generation of readers and critics. And . . .'

'And Mass'oud As'ad?!'

'Ok! The Arabistani governments fear no journalist more than Mass'oud. Do you want me to give a review of the other guests?'

'I think I get the idea.'

'Should I consider your agreement final?'

'Of course. Provided nothing crops up. Can we talk about London?'

'You mean why London is significant for me?'

'Yes.'

'There's nothing novel about it. The same old story. A man who can love but can't marry.'

'Aahh! He was married?'

'Every attractive man is married, as every attractive woman has noticed.'

'So the story ended in separation?'

'Separation for ever.'

'What do you mean?'

'I mean there is no likelihood of any meeting. Unlike you and Colette.'

'I intended to marry Colette.'

'So why didn't you?'

'Duty.'

'You mean being leader of the clan.'

'Being leader didn't interest me. In fact my late father was preparing my elder brother to be leader. That didn't bother me. On the contrary, I wanted to be free and do what I wanted. Fate, however, intervened.'

'Your brother died.'

'He was killed in . . .'

'I know the circumstances. A tragedy! And you, despite yourself, became heir-apparent.'

'That's what happened.'

'And you decided being leader was more important than love. You left the woman who loved you to marry a woman you didn't know who had been chosen for you by your father.'

'That is what duty requires.'

'Duty?'

'Yes. Shall we dine?'

'You have a dining room on this small boat?!'

'It's a very small 'dining room'.'

'I'd rather stay here.'

I went in and returned with the various dishes. Galnar resumed her question:

'Duty? What duty?'

'Duty to the nation.'

'You mean to the clan?'

'Is there a difference?'

'What do you mean?'

'What is the nation? Is it this sea? The Azores are more beautiful than this shore by far. Is it those mountains? The mountains in Switzerland are more awe-inspiring. The nation is not a piece of land.'

'So what, then, is the nation?'

'The nation is a piece of bread, a roof over your head, a sense of belonging, warmth, a sense of dignity. Here, none of that can be realized except through the clan.'

'That is a glorification of sectarianism.'

'No! That is the foundation of democracy. In our situation, you only get stability either through tyrannical military rule or an equilibrium between the various sects. Personally, I prefer an imperfect democracy to a full-grown dictatorship.'

'And that's why you left Colette?'

'Why aren't you eating?'

Galnar took a small piece of bread and slowly chewed and swallowed it. She said:

'And that's why you left Colette?'

'That's why I sacrificed my love for Colette.'

'What about your marriage to Chantal? Was that another sacrifice?'

'It was my duty.'

'Did you know that Colette married a general and has two daughters by him?'

'Of course. We exchange greetings at social occasions and what have you. We write each other letters sometimes.'

'I think she still loves you.'

'After all these years?'

'After all these years.'

'How do you know that?'

'I've spoken to her.'

'You! You've spoken to Colette?'

'At length. I was preparing my interview with you.'

'And she told you she still loves me?'

'Not in so many words.'

'What did she say?'

'She said the time she had with you was the "golden moment" of her life.'

'The "golden moment"! That was one of her favourite expressions.'

'Did she have many such expressions?'

'I think she was created to be a poet. But she preferred to be a painter.'

'And she's become quite famous.'

'She would have been even more famous had she stuck to poetry. She could recite hundreds of poems. When she was talking about everyday things anyone listening to her would have thought she was composing a poem.'

'It seems you still love her?'

'Love?! That harsh luxury!'

'Was that one of her favourite expressions?'

'No. She did not consider love a luxury. But she realized that every man had to face his destiny.'

'Every man?!'

'I mean person. Every man and every woman. She knew that my destiny required me to take the position I did.'

'Destiny or duty?'

'Duty was my destiny.'

'Are you happy with your destiny now?'

I collected my thoughts.

I was surprised by the tears falling from my eyes. From where had these tears come? The champagne? From the stars swimming with the waves? From Galnar? Or from Colette.

Galnar said:

'You haven't answered . . . Are you happy with your destiny?'

'Naturally. Isn't that obvious? Can't you see how exciting and full my life is? Conferences, speeches, passing legislation, elections, hotels . . .'

'And parties and female artistes?'

'And the clan which kisses its leader's hand. And the immense wealth. And the beautiful wife. And the good-looking daughter. And the handsome son. Isn't that happiness?'

'A happiness which makes you cry?'

'Tears of joy.'

Suddenly, by some mysterious, magical means, the woman sitting before me was transfigured into Colette. I heard myself say:

'Colette! Colette! I still love you. I love you more than in the days we were together. Don't believe these illusions I'm living. It's all a big lie which . . .'

My deranged talk was interrupted by the sound of the launch approaching and weighing anchor off the accommodation ladder. Galnar stood up, smiled and said:

'It's midnight. Cinderella has to go otherwise the launch will be turned into a shark.'

I remained seated, unable to move, the tears flowing down my cheeks. I watched Galnar come over to me and place a kiss on my forehead, saying:

'See you soon, Mister Romantic Minister, on Medusa.'

Later, Chantal asked me:

'How was the meeting?'

'What meeting?'

She said, startled:

'The meeting you were at. With the president.'

I quickly made up for my lapse:

'Relax! Relax! The government will survive.'

'That's good news. I was worried the rumours were true. By the way, Sa'id Abu Battha has been on the phone several times and wants you to contact him. He says it's very urgent.'

I dialled and listened to Sa'id. Then I said slowly:

'What a loss! What a loss! So young! In the prime of youth! Listen Sa'id! I want the death notices to be published in the press in the name of the party. You organize an appropriate funeral. I will personally receive those expressing their condolences.'

Chantal asked:

'What's happened?'

'A member of the party. Died in a car accident.'

'Who was he?'

'Rizq Al-Bandoura. I don't think you knew him.'

'Do you really have to receive the condolences yourself?'

'Chantal! The party rests on a single pillar, and that pillar is called loyalty.'

The Island

That singular day is bound to come
When after the laments I listen long
Al-Mutanabbi

My seven exciting men. Their seven exciting weeks. Which man will be chosen for the great prize? The last night on Medusa. The Medusa which has been punished – and has punished. The Medusa which is now trying to take possession of me. But I refuse. I resist. I don't want my poetry to turn into deadly snakes. The Medusa which Al-Siyyab spoke of in *The Blind Whore*. Al-Siyyab was mad about Greek mythology. 'Greek' is a beautiful word, particularly in poetry. Aahh! Poetry! Should I choose our modernizing poet, that tempest of inspiration who has mephiterized Arab poetry, who is rescuing it from mummification and bovinification and nourishes it with new words which no one has ever heard before. New words! Why not? Are not the old words too confined for our new emotions? Don't we have to invent new words, completely new words, every day? No! Every hour! No! Every minute! Do we not every minute have new experiences which we cannot express with the words dug out of dictionaries. Or the language academies. The dictionaries were frozen ten centuries ago. The language academies were stillborn. Doesn't our poet deserve a night with me as a reward for the new words he has invented? Aahh! How I wish I could invent strange words to describe my strange states of mind and being. How frustrated – such a very ugly word! How frustrated I am when I find word after word incapable of describing what I feel. What are words? How can one word convey a thousand and one experiences? The early Arabs who invented hundreds of words for clouds, the camel and the sword understood the limited power of words. But we have just taken their words and added nothing to them. To be more precise, most of them we've suppressed. 'Hungry'! A very clear word. And when we want to explain it further we say 'very hungry' or 'slightly hungry'. How can the infinite states of hunger be classified under the word 'hungry'? And 'love'! Is one love like another? And lust? Is one person's experience of lust the same as another's? The poet who lives with his wife/the cow is at least trying – trying to come up with new words. They may be laughable or stupid, but he's saying what he feels. Isn't that poetry? To express new feelings with new words? Isn't this the single difference between poetry and prose? Prose is familiar words expressing familiar experiences. Isn't that what we mean when we say that something is 'prosaic'? Prose! In prose words mean the same as the meanings stored in the dictionaries. Love is love. Antar's love, Qays' love and Romeo's love. But Antar's love is not the same as Qays' or Romeo's. There should be a particular word for each particular love. And if one doesn't exist, we should invent one. Why the fear? Wasn't every word in the dictionaries invented? Why do we remain prisoners of the dictionaries we invented? Why should we remain until the end of the world a slave to the dictionary? Prisoners of those words which come only out of dictionaries. Poetry which you can source back, word by word, to a place in the dictionary. We may not approve of them today. We may laugh at them. But who knows what tomorrow will bring? And our poet steals poems from other people, from obscure western poets. And theft when it comes to poetry is the same as any other kind of theft. That's what the dictionary says. But what the dictionary says is clearly wrong. There's theft, and there's theft and there's theft. There's a difference between stealing milk from a baby and stealing a couple of verses from an obscure poet. The one is a deadly crime, the other cultural cross-pollination. How wonderful are the cross-pollinated cultures! The dialogue of cultures! The clash of cultures. Has there ever been a poet who didn't steal? Where are most of the crimes of theft perpetrated? In dark alleys? No! In well-known universities. Every masters thesis has been stolen from others. Obvious theft. Every doctoral thesis has been stolen form others. Latent theft. Concealed by a thousand footnotes. And a thousand bibliographical citations. And a thousand pages of drivel. I don't want to talk about the drivel at the moment. I want to talk about poetry. The story of my relationship with poetry is a very long one. It began when I was fourteen years old and wrote my first ever poem. I wrote it about one of my school friends. A girl. It wasn't a love poem. I don't know how to write them. Didn't I say that words have limited power. I wrote that I was happy when I saw her and sad when she wasn't there. And that I couldn't bear to see her smiling at another girl. That's all I said. And I gave her the poem. She never spoke to me again afterwards. Till this day to be precise. I'd only said what I felt. Isn't poetry an expression of one's feelings? But she got angry, ended our friendship and refused to speak to me. My second poem I wrote a year later, more or less. About a teacher this time. A fair-skinned teacher with long, black hair and brilliant white teeth. She was a teacher whose classes I eagerly looked forward to. I would listen to her attentively. At night I would dream she was my mother. Sometimes that she was my sister and sometimes that she was me. I wrote a poem in which I said: 'I wish you were me'. I only said what I'd seen in the dream. And I gave her the small piece of paper. No! What happened with the first poem didn't happen. Nothing happened at first. Then after two, three or four days she asked me to come to the common room when classes were over. I went and she asked me to sit down in front of her. I sat down. She began to talk about geography. Did I mention she was a geography teacher? She carried on talking until everyone else had gone. Then she stood up and locked the door. She came up to me. She said she'd liked the poem I'd written. And liked me. She began to kiss me. Then her kisses became more voracious. Then she began to touch me. The surprise left me paralysed. I let her do what she wanted. The sound of her voice became louder. She was groaning. Her hand groped me. I offered no resistance. Then the groans increased in volume. The old caretaker began knocking on the door. The geography teacher composed herself. Quickly rearranged her clothes and mine and opened the door. To the old caretaker she said: 'Aah! There you are, Hussein! You're just in time. Get a glass of water quickly. Galnar is having a fit of colic. Didn't you hear her groaning.?!' The good-natured caretaker went off. The geography teacher smiled. I drank the glass of water. I left the teachers' common room. I never saw the geography teacher again. I never went back to the school. I fled to another. And promised myself I'd never write another poem. And I haven't. Nevertheless, I haven't lost my interest in poetry. Or poets. Unconventional poetry. And unconventional poets. But I have lost my interest in conventional words understood in a conventional manner. My fellow pupil and the teacher had taught me the lesson. The pupil had thought I was writing her a love poem. The teacher had thought I was writing her a love poem. But I wasn't writing a love poem to either my fellow pupil or the teacher. I was trying to express a particular experience. An experience which didn't involve being kissed or being groped. Hi Baby thinks I'm a lesbian or frigid. But that's another issue which has nothing to do with my present issue which is poetry. My favourite poet, Ken'an, lives with his wife/the cow who hits him over the head with a saucepan full of okra. Nevertheless, he doesn't give in. He invents words. He steals poems. He adapts feelings. Intertextuality! But in addition to all that, he's written a whole collection of poems about me. A whole collection about me! Some of them are intelligible, but the majority aren't. It's still in manuscript form. Every poem in the collection is about me. Naturally, he didn't call it 'Galnar' for fear of his wife/the cow, his secretary/the cow and the critics/the cows. He called it *Nargal*. Ha! Ha! Ha! But would the cows realize that Nargal was Galnar? He said it wasn't going to be published until he'd achieved 'cartresis' – a word he'd made up from 'irresolution', 'carnality', 'intrepidity' and the 'seering' heat of passion. Will Ken'an be the man I choose? Will he achieve 'cartresis' on Medusa? And will the anthology be published which begins with the poem:

A woman made of fire
Lives among mountains of snow
Eating fruits halal
And climbing the forbidden tree

A woman made of men
She once killed
Whose noses she turned
Into a carcanet
To adorn her forehead

A somewhat frightening description. And the poem isn't talking about noses. It's talking about other parts of the body which a woman may not repeat. A woman made of men?! At least he didn't say a woman like a gazelle. Or a wild antelope. Or an oryx. Or a fish. A woman made of men! Am I a lesbian or frigid? That's not the question. The question is 'cartresis'. What about the others? What about the eclectic philosopher? Who has been attracted to me since I was a young student at college and who claimed on the air that he doesn't remember me – even though he's never forgotten me for a single moment. And has never given up trying. The sole Arabistani philosopher who has managed to do what the ancients couldn't – come up with an Arabistani philosophical perspective. Eclecticism! Does not this philosophical perspective express with astonishing accuracy the real situation of the Arabistani nation? A nation which chooses its cars from Japan, its maids from the Philippines, its guards from America, its executioners from Israel, its shoes from Italy and its tyrants from within. A nation that has turned eclecticism into a fine art. A nation that takes what it wants and leaves what it doesn't. A nation that takes mobile phones from the West but leaves research into cancer. A nation which takes from its own heritage the concept of slave girls but abandons jihad. A nation that takes the Yen from Japan but ignores Zen. A select nation. An eclectic nation whose spirit has been expressed by Philosopher Pasha in a way unlike any other Arabistani philosopher; its real, hidden spirit, which even the poets were unable to attain. Did not Roman philosophy, if the Romans had any philosophy, give expression to Roman presumption? Did not Greek philosophy give expression to the permanent struggle between caste and equality? Did not Christian philosophy give expression to the deep-rooted guilt complex in the minds of those who embraced the new religion and, with it, original sin? And what about Islamic philosophy? Aahh! Eclecticism again. The reconciliation between Reason and Tradition. Between Aristotle and Revelation. And what about the philosophy of the European Renaissance? Did not the Rationalists give expression to the volcano erupting in the face of centuries of myth? And did not the Intuitionists give expression to the fear of the new deity, science? And did not Existentialism announce the bankruptcy of former perspectives? And did not Pragmatism give expression to the deepest of America's passions: what is useless is worthless? And our philosopher, is he not worthy of being a pasha? Has he not given expression to the deepest inclinations of Arabistan? Selection. The easy option. An aversion to extremism. The virtue of taking a middle course between two extremes. Moderation in all things. A mid-course between fighting and peace. An eternal truce. A mid-way position between rectitude and decadence. Rectitude at home and decadence abroad. Rectitude in the open and decadence in secret. A mid-way position between the first and twenty-first century. The witchcraft of the first century and the computer games of the twenty-first. The eclectic nation and its eclectic philosopher who accepts a valuable gift only to give it to the registrar. Who registers a rich student and intends to keep him a student forever. Who insists that his daughter's husband wins the contract through a genuine competitive tender. Who is a member of a US-financed centre yet warns of fundamentalism in America. Philosopher Pasha! The intellectual who is loved by widows and virgins. Philosophical attraction. Philosophical charisma. Are not all philosophers sexually attractive? No! That's taking things too far! But at least some of them are. The unattractive Sartre had more relationships with women than Michael Jackson. A crude example! More relationships than Clarke Gable. Isn't it time for me to uncover the sexuality of philosophical charisma? There is little room for choice. Very little. One philosopher in a nation of 250 million would-be philosophers. An opportunity which might never return. With him on an island far way from his daughters and their husbands and his rich students. And Doctor Tuffaha Qut Al-Qulub and Ms Dalal Wasif. An opportunity to make a choice which might never be repeated: choosing the Philosopher. I have chosen you, the Philosopher of Eclecticism! Because I am attracted to your philosophy. Attracted to its sense of realism. But more than that, I have chosen you because of my love of exploration. Can sex be separated from the love of exploration? Is not the love of exploration the principle motive for sex in men? Curiosity. Discovering the unknown. What does a man talk about to his friends after each new woman? Her breasts. Her hips. Her stomach. A man doesn't talk about how happy he is or how happy the woman is. Or his pain or her pain. The whole thing is a question of discovery. New data to be added to the statistics. And what do his friends ask him: 'Is she a goer?' 'Does she cry out in bed?' 'Does she bite?' Data! And what about the woman? Doesn't the same principle apply? Why would a woman want to sleep with a famous film star? Isn't it because she wants to find out the difference between the star and her husband? The physical difference. What's he like with his clothes off? Can he last a long time? Data! Isn't the philosopher a male territory worthy of a woman's interest, this woman's interest? Does he follow his eclectic philosophy in bed? Does he choose just one part of his body and ignore the rest? Does he make philosophical statements during 'cartresis'? Does he cry out? As the geography teacher cried out? Aahh! An exciting experience. Phi-sexuality, i.e. philosophy/sexuality! But there's no need to hurry in making a decision. There's plenty of time till midnight when I join my seven men whom I have asked to come to the small bay and wait for me on the shore. I've told them I'll be coming at the witching hour. On the hour. And I will take one of them. Just one! To a place on the island unknown to anyone but me. And there I and he will spend the last night. There's no need to hurry. The blackmailing journalist is also an exciting man. He lives a more than exciting life. A hand grenade explodes in a briefcase which was supposed to contain a million dollars. An old witch kisses him viciously, in her own name and then on behalf of her daughter. The trade in information is a profitable business. Everywhere. The next big thing. Most press barons are billionaires. And those who own television stations. Nothing is more exciting than information. In the age of the market place. Marketable information. Princess Diana and her lover. The Duchess with her boyfriend who loves licking toes. The MP and his secretary. Information for sale! Does Mass'oud As'ad do anything apart from that? Collect information and sell it. Ok! Ok! I know what he does is blackmail. So what? Aren't we all, in one way or another, blackmailers but without using that filthy word or mentioning the filthy price? Doesn't every secret we hear about others turn us into blackmailers. Did not blackmail save me from being abused by my mother's husband? When I was eleven years old I had the body of an eighteen year old. He didn't stop abusing me until I photographed him with the maid. With a simple camera. I didn't say anything to him. But he didn't abuse me afterwards. He knew that any further attempt at abuse would mean the photograph reaching my mother who would never have believed if I'd told her that he'd been abusing me. But she couldn't have called the photograph a liar. The grey-haired bankrupt man with the fat ugly maid. I have no scruples about blackmail or blackmailers. Those who allow themselves to be blackmailed should not do things that lay themselves open to blackmail. A reasonable request. No one blackmails respectable people. No one blackmails a mosque Imam or a faithful housewife or a real estate agent who doesn't cheat people. Blackmailers choose their victims – or clients! – very carefully. And in many cases, the victims of blackmail are, or have been, blackmailers themselves. And if blackmail did not exist, life would have lost one of its most exciting aspects. An aspect which burns like spices. And arouses the appetite. And our friend Mass'oud As'ad could excite the appetite of any woman. A moving treasure trove of information! Wouldn't it be exciting to transform a dealer in information into a piece of data? Wouldn't it be exciting to blackmail the blackmailer? If he couldn't perform. Or didn't come up to expectations. Listen Mass'oud! Half a million dollars or I tell everyone you couldn't do anything or finished before I could get my clothes off or were below the international average. A dangerous game when you play with a veteran blackmailer who could turn the tables on you. Sleep with me twice, three times, four times or else. Or else I'll tell people that the breasts with which you entice everyone are full of silicone, that your thighs are covered in spots or that the well is bottomless.

When it comes to blackmail, it doesn't matter if the information is true or false. What is important is that people believe it. Would not this be an exciting adventure? To sleep with a blackmailer then blackmail him. Or to wait until he blackmails me in the *Voice of Truth*. An adventure no less exciting than sleeping with the very exciting psychologist who is challenging Freud in his own cultural backyard. And has written a book on Freud called *The Voodoo Doctor* which sells in millions in various languages in the capitals of Europe. The psychologist I visited several times when I was in London during a tempestuous love affair with that person. The psychiatrist tried to convince me in the same way he tried to convince Bustan. By using what I knew already. And what Bustan knew. He's taking advantage of you and has no intention of marrying you. He is in fact married. Stating the obvious! I knew, Doctor, that he was married. And I knew, Doctor, that he wasn't going to marry me. And I know, Doctor, that I'm not a lesbian or frigid. And I'm not suffering, Doctor, from any conflict between the old mores and modern ways of behaving. Do you know the reason? The reason is I grew up without mores or values. I grew up morally neutral. Do you know the reason? The reason is my father abused me when I was five years old. I told my mother. She refused to believe me and beat me. And he beat me. My father used to hit me every day before he abused me, while he abused me and after he abused me. He would hit my mother everyday after sleeping with her. I told you I grew up without any values. My problem was not caused by a struggle between values and ways of behaving. My problem was love. What I wanted, Doctor, was a cure for love but you were trying to cure me of the old values. And when I tried to explain things to you, you refused to listen. You said you didn't believe in Freud's myths. Or in childhood stories. But my relationship with that person had nothing to do with Freud's myths or childhood stories. I would melt when he touched me. I would burn when he kissed me. I would fly in the air when he spoke to me, though he only rarely talked to me. That person was engrossed in his own private affairs, his own world and human rights. And his other women. I knew all about his other women. Is it possible for a woman to meet that person and not fall in love with him? That person was the most exciting man I've ever known. But I do not, Doctor, wish to be unfair to you. You too, Doctor, are not unexciting. Maybe you deserve the star prize in reward for your unconventional ideas, your unconventional treatment and your unconventional sleeping with your patients. We shall see. There's no need to hurry. More speed, less haste. The last night may be the lot of another man. The spiritualist astrologer who has used every incantation he knows to win me but without success. Who has used all his magneto-hypnotic tricks, but to no avail. Who has never given up hope over the years. And who is now trying to persuade me by means of his new friend, Atawit! – the rose-skinned young slave, the genie! I still remember the spell. What if I began to recite it? What if he didn't come? Wouldn't I be stupid to believe the nonsense of a charlatan who claimed to be a doctor? And what if he did come? What would I do with a handsome rose-skinned slave? Aahh! I'd talk to him. I'd ask him to help me choose one of my seven men. No doubt he has sources of information different from more orthodox ones. At any rate he could help solve the Aids riddle. Has one of my seven men been infected? And what if the rose-skinned slave wants me for himself? Wouldn't it be exciting for a woman to sleep with a genie? As Niran did? No! The astrologer is more exciting than the rose-skinned slave. The astrologer is a worker of miracles and can defeat the Brazilian team. Psycho-spiritualist weapons! Wouldn't sleeping with this man be the adventure of a lifetime? Who knows what could happen? Or not happen! The bed might fly up into the air with us. Contact might be made with the spirit world. The rose-skinned slave might join in the adventure. The spiritualist astrologer who, in his desire for me, forgot the advice of his lord, the greatest of the spiritualists, and travelled on board a private plane by which he came to the island. Or maybe a helicopter, from the spiritualist point of view, isn't considered a private plane? But what about Hi Baby? Doesn't he deserve a moment's consideration? The globalization man. The man of the hour. The man of the future. The man who knows how to deal with the mechanisms of the market, and legal supervisory bodies. And with Japanese industrialists. And western women. The man/the computer. The man who has sent me more than a million dollars worth of gifts. A million! And I sent them all back to him. He thinks I'm a lesbian or frigid. Doesn't such lavish generosity deserve a single night? The Arabistani who has exacted revenge on behalf of all Arabistanis. He sold the Americans contaminated meat claiming that it was camel meat. Before that he'd sold them something called Souvenirs of the Sahara. After making millions, it emerged that Souvenirs of the Sahara was just onager dung dyed with a shiny plastic substance. He won all the lawsuits against him because he hadn't been lying. The law doesn't protect suckers. The Arabistani who seduced a Jewish woman (most likely a Zionist) on board an aeroplane and then handed her over to another Arabistani friend. The Arabistani who enslaves Jewesses. The father who employs three maids with doctorates to look after his son. The man who has canned everything that can be put in cans: locusts, frogs, you name it. The man who dishes out envelopes stuffed with dollars wherever he goes. Who earns millions even in the poorest countries. Who desires me in a way which none of his companions does. Who has tried in a way which none of his companions has tried. He has tried everything he can think of. Both legal and illegal, scientific and magical. The man who was warned by the guru about me but paid no heed to the warning. Does not this passionate admirer deserve the great prize? The extraordinary man who was suckled by a hyena and who was saved from a wolf by the teeth of a camel. The man of the crimson desert and the Crimson Desert Bank. The pioneer of Islamic investments. A friend to all, from the Atlantic to the Caspian. The man who loved his father and named a centre for the treatment of haemorrhoids after him. And loved his son and turned him into a poet. And loved his wife and gave her her own life. Will the last night fall to the lot of the businessman? Why not? But one moment, Galnar! Have you forgotten the other businessman? The famous and important minister. The husband of Chantal. What an exciting name! But she prefers to be called 'wife of His Excellency, the Minister'. This would make me, were I to grant him the night, the lover of the husband of the wife of His Excellency the Minister. A complex arrangement! The owner of a yacht who calls it a boat. The Miracle Minister. But I don't find ministries exciting. Nothing is more boring than sleeping with ministers. Particularly the minister who agreed to do the programme whose seventh anniversary we're celebrating here. What excites me about Abu Shawka is something else. Something completely different – his capacity for killing. The cosy kill. Brakes which refuse to work just at the right moment. The civilized kill. Just like I killed my father. My father who had abused me when I was five years old. And violated my virginity when I was ten. An early developer! Am I a lesbian or frigid?! No! I didn't kill my father. The gas killed him. The gas I'd allowed to leak out of the gas canister. The gas which exploded in his face when he went into the kitchen drunk and struck a match to make coffee. The kitchen blew up. The sound of the kitchen exploding woke me and my mother up. We saw the flames and fled from the house. We went onto the street. On the pavement I asked her: 'Where's my father?' She gave me a look which made me realize that she knew that I knew where my father was. And just like I killed that person in London. Under the cover of darkness – a beautiful expression! – at least when it was first coined. Before it became hackneyed. I killed him for love. Or I wonder if he killed himself. The last night. The night of farewell. He couldn't see me. His life, his priorities, human rights, his wife, his other women. The usual boring stories. But then he could see me. In the flat overlooking Harrods. The last time. I made his desire come true. We stayed awake till the early hours. I don't think I'm a lesbian or frigid. Then he had a heart attack. These things sometimes happen. A sex-induced heart attack. Perspiration exploded from his face which suddenly turned yellow. He began to gasp for breath. He pointed to the telephone. An ambulance! Naturally! I ignored his gesticulations. I dressed slowly as it became increasingly harder for him to breathe. Then I walked over to him and kissed him on his forehead which was covered in perspiration. He looked so gaunt! I smiled and left the apartment. A couple of days later I read about his death in the paper. No details. A martyr to love! Killed by his lover! Under the cover of darkness in London. Do I have the right to object to murder when I've enjoyed doing it twice? And our friend the leader only acts in accordance with the logic of the male. Don't male animals kill to defend their right to have the final word with regard to their territory? And their females? The leader is only protecting his territory and his females from another potential leader. And what he does he does in a civilized manner. He handles the funeral expenses and he himself receives those offering condolences. All killers are exciting sexually, both male and female. The evidence is in my grandfather's memoirs. The Hangman! He wasn't very good at writing but he dictated his memoirs to a journalist who wrote them down in a wonderful style. The journalist, however, died before finishing the book. And my grandfather died before finding another journalist. The manuscript is in my possession: *Memoirs of a Hangman*! the memoirs aren't important. What is important are the exciting sexual confessions which my grandfather would hear from those he hanged, including the women (of whom there were three!). Before they were hanged, naturally. The relationship between killing and sex is definite. Even deadly animals are sexually exciting. Unlike domesticated animals. The viper. Since the dawn of time the snake has been a sexual symbol and will remain a sexual symbol forever. And why? Because it kills. It thrusts its lethal member into the body. And creates the ultimate tremor. Who has ever seen a woman yearning for a sheep or a rabbit? I yearn violently for a tiger. If there were a tiger on the island, it would have the last night. But there are no tigers on the island. There are only seven men. A poet who steals other people's poems. A philosopher who attacks the philosophy of others. A journalist who blackmails people. A psychiatrist who is an addict yet treats addicts. A charlatan who dreams of a rose-skinned slave, a genie. A businessman who made millions selling rotten meat. And a leader who murders a rival and goes to his funeral. I have to choose one of these. The élite of the Arabistani nation! And now Medusa is taking possession of me and I don't resist. And now my grandfather is taking possession of me and I don't resist. Medusa cries out: 'I have condemned your seven men to death'. And my grandfather cries out: 'On the charge of betraying and degrading women'. And Medusa cries out: 'And on the charge of being corrupt and spreading corruption'. And my grandfather cries out: 'And on the charge of stealing and plundering'. And Medusa cries out: 'And on the charge of murder'. The world spins before me. I think of the rose-skinned slave. I begin the incantation: 'I call upon you . . .'.

I close my eyes. Then I open my eyes. I do not see Medusa. I do not see my grandfather. I see a handsome, rose-skinned slave smiling and saying:

'Hello! Galnar! I am Atawit! Close that diary. Let's talk about your seven men.'[1]

---

1. Galnar's diary ends here.

Athens

Death is but a nimble thief
Who with neither hand assails
Nor by foot makes his getaway
Al-Mutanabbi

The Coroner's Report stated that the seven men had died by drowning. Blood tests revealed that they had consumed large amounts of drugs and alcohol . . .

As for the woman found naked on the shore, the Coroner has as yet not determined the cause of death. No traces of drugs or alcohol were found in her blood. There were no signs of physical assault. In addition, the autopsy revealed she was a virgin . . .

From an Athens police report.